THE NEW UNDERWORLD ORDER

Don Italo, the aging godfather, but still cunning enough to mesh new tricks of terror with time-honored means of murder . . . *Charlie Richards*, the imitation WASP who rose to the top of corporate America but could not rip away from his family roots . . . *Stefi Ricci*, the Mafia princess who was as tough and sex-hungry as any man who tried to tame her . . . *Vince Ricci*, the contender for the top who made drugs and passion his keys to the kingdom . . . *Winfield Richards*, Charlie's beautiful daughter, a brilliant lawyer who proved the most resourceful foe the godfather ever tried to destroy . . . *Kerry and Kevin Ricci*, the twin brothers as different as night and day, good and evil . . . and shadowing them all, *Shan Lao*, out to extend the rising power of the East over the underworld of the West.

All came together in a war where all was fair and no prisoners were taken. . . .

MAFIA WARS

"A riveting blockbuster!"—*Lifestyle*

"If historians of the 21st century want to know what our era was really like, they must consult the novels of Leslie Waller."
—*The Los Angeles Times*

MAFIA WARS

Leslie Waller

AN ONYX BOOK

ONYX
Published by the Penguin Group
Penguin Books U.S.A Inc., 375 Hudson Street,
New York, New York 10014, U.S.A.
Penguin Books Ltd, 27 Wrights Lane,
London W8 5TZ, England
Penguin Books Australia Ltd, Ringwood,
Victoria, Australia
Penguin Books Canada Ltd, 10 Alcorn Avenue,
Toronto, Ontario, Canada M4V 3B2
Penguin Books (N.Z.) Ltd, 182-190 Wairau Road,
Auckland 10, New Zealand

Penguin Books Ltd, Registered Offices:
Harmondsworth, Middlesex, England

First published in the United States by Onyx, an imprint of New American Library,
a division of Penguin Books U.S.A Inc. Published in Great Britain in hardcover by
William Heinemann Ltd., and in paperback by Mandarin Paperbacks.

First Onyx Printing, April, 1993
10 9 8 7 6 5 4 3 2 1

 REGISTERED TRADEMARK—MARCA REGISTRADA

Printed in the United States of America

PUBLISHER'S NOTE
This is a work of fiction. Names, characters, places, and incidents either are the
product of the author's imagination or are used fictitiously, and any resemblance to
actual persons, living or dead, events, or locales is entirely coincidental.

For Pat, again

Novels are the bearers of news,
the news you won't read in newspapers.
If writers don't say it,
then it won't be said.

—Carlos Fuentes

June

One

Fear came at last. On Saturday.

In an ideal world, Charley knew, life would be without fear. He knew his life had been ideal; real, sweaty fear had never exposed its obscene self. It visited those who cringed without protection. But so cushioned was his position of privilege that he wasn't prepared for Saturday.

On this sunny June morning, from the twin towers of the World Trade Center, more than one hundred stories above Wall Street, one could see planes taking off from both La Guardia and JFK airports. The slim high-rise nearby, which ascends thirty more stories, is Richland Tower. From it only one man could look out. He was Charley Richards. Today he felt he could see . . . everywhere.

How could fear come here, to the top of the universe? He had worked hard to stand here alone. The privilege of his family had helped, a family that balked at nothing in its surge toward power. But the ideal life he enjoyed was only partly due to family. Mostly, Charley felt, he had earned his privilege by hard work. Normally a quiet, scholarly sort of guy, he had successfully impersonated the highest success America grants its pushiest sons.

That was how this day began, King of the Hill patting his own back. As he shaved and dressed the only rough among the smooth was that this lofty apartment/office, the envy of all, was chilly. It hadn't been meant for living, this aerie, but since he'd walked out on his wife he had called it home.

He inspected himself in the a mirror. Far, far below, a siren moaned. He had gotten so used to his lover, April Garnet, inspecting him, brushing the curve of his dark blond hair, that he paused, waiting for her touch.

It was a new vision of himself that Garnet had shown him. For Charley its promise was dazzling, nothing less than freedom from his family. Last night he had made his first moves toward loosing those bonds.

A temporary move; today belonged to the family: a morning in Connecticut, a noon wedding reception back here in the Tower. He had longed to invite Garnet, but, as of last night, she had become controversial.

"Treacherous filth she's put in your head," was the mildest of Zio Italo's reactions when Charley had hinted something of his new ideas. He was still smarting from the old man's anger.

Never mind. Once the plan was spelled out, Zio would see things Charley's quiet, well-organized way. It only required guts on Charley's part to keep pressing hard. It only required an almost fanatical urge to begin life without his lifelong family connection, his link to the Ricci clan.

Except for the blood, of course. The blood would always be Ricci.

Charley Richards sighed unhappily. The urge for freedom lived in his head. Garnet had planted it there, but it hadn't sent roots to his gut. He still enjoyed the privileged life too much to cut himself free.

Today, Saturday, had been the only time the Connecticut senator could meet with the board of Jet-Tech International, which had recently snared a Department of Defense missile contract with refit capability. It was puny as these great scams go, only $1.1 billion, but all of New London could smell the faked overruns.

As chief financial officer of J-TI, Charley Richards had to show up, just as the senator did, to claim credit. The newspaper had spelled his name Richland, a forgivable mistake since Richland Holdings was the major stockholder in J-TI.

The express elevator plummeted him to Richland Tower's basement garage. His chauffeur, Pino, gently guided the long Cadillac through a deserted financial district and down Coenties Slip. Pino was Charley's age, late forties, and a second cousin. The pocket park at South Street sparkled pale emerald in the sun. Across South Street, at the heliport, Charley could see the small Vertol, rotors whirling.

A Nissan pickup, doing at least sixty miles an hour, roared down on them along South Street. It slammed head-on into the driver's seat of the limo. A yard to the left of Charley's head.

The heavy limo lurched sideways in a spray of glass. Charley was thrown violently. He could see the Nissan, its front reinforced by welded I-beams, reverse and roar southwards again, steam howling from a ruptured radiator.

"Pino! You OK?"

Pino said nothing. Shattered safety glass had covered him with a dew of diamonds rapidly turning ruby as Ricci blood pumped from his neck.

Charley blacked out. It was a strange state, not unpleasant, in which he could almost sense what was happening around him even though his eyes were shut. Sirens howled. Paramedics bundled Pino onto a canvas carrier and hauled him away. Sirens whooped. Charley opened his eyes reluctantly, still enjoying the freedom of being unconscious, not yet ready to take on reality again.

Someone put a paper cup of coffee in his hands. A fine tremor made ripples in the dark liquid. He sipped and thought and sipped.

The Nissan pickup had delivered a message to Charley Richards. It hadn't been meant as a take-out; otherwise the pickup driver would have come shooting. This was what came to him away from his eagle's nest.

For years now, ever since he'd built Richland Tower and occupied its pinnacle, Charley had lived a sharply delineated them-and-us life. Them below, toiling nobodies; us above, masters of life.

Even now, in shocked confusion, he still was privileged. The heliport people were terribly helpful. Richland Holdings was one of their largest corporate clients. They insisted on having a nurse check Charley for bruises and cuts. "Caddy limos," she said helpfully, "are truly super-padded." She produced a tremendous do-anything-you-want-with-me smile as she stroked his hand.

Charley's mind whirled, thinking of Pino, of the pickup truck, of being only a yard back of the impact point. The message: Richards may live 130 stories in the air; here on earth he's worm-food. Who had contracted the hit? What had the orders been? Show the bastard that he can live and work in an eagle's nest but we can touch him with the finger of death any time we want.

Charley placed a call to his young cousin, Kerry Ricci, to make sure Pino was looked after and to try to trace the pickup.

"If the Nissan escaped through the Brooklyn Battery Tunnel," Kerry mused, "they could be breaking it up and redistributing the parts by now."

During the New London ceremonies Charley felt disembodied, woozy, not really here. He kept asking himself more questions about the collision. But still he felt no fear. What he had begun to feel was anger. Someone thought he'd grown too big? Someone wanted to remind him all men are antipasto for maggots? Would his life always be lived among people whose idea of reasoned communication was a car crash?

On the helicopter flight back, he finally succumbed to shock. He dozed, despite the Vertol's fearsome noise. Perhaps taking Zio Italo's abuse last night, and the hit-and-run this morning, spotlighted his uncle more acridly.

It was an old dream. He and his uncle sat at a restaurant table, Italo patting the deep dish before him with a napkin that changed from white to a sanguine red like lasagna drenched in too much sauce. A dream-siren moaned. Zio smiled that sharp-toothed, splintered smile of his. "Ecco Il Professore. Beve, mangia," he would croak.

The green lasagna was what on the street are called Bens, $100 bills showing Franklin's face. "Beve, mangia," he repeated, the priest's offer of wine and host for the blood and body of Jesus Christ. The money tasted salt-blood hot. Charley gagged and began to vomit mangled Bens.

All his life his family had force-fed him such meals, the scholar-genius who legitimized their cash flow. He was the Harvard MBA who boosted Richland Holdings into the top ten corporations. That was when Italo had tagged him Il Professore.

But it only took one question from the woman he loved to undo everything. Garnet, in a gentle but firm voice: "Is this how you want to spend the rest of your life, raping the world to launder Zio Italo's cash?" The subtext: any moron with that much cash could produce the same results. That made the world, which thought Charley a genius, dead wrong. That made Il Professore a fake, sailing under false colors. He stood exposed as an ordinary guy with horseshoes up his ass.

At this point of the nightmare, never before, only at this stage of the humiliation, he would lurch wide awake, horrified at the act of abject submission demanded by Zio Italo. Awake, Charley felt ashamed that such a crude mirror could so perfectly reflect the ugly truth of his diminished life.

Remembering the dream as he stood high atop Richland Tower again, Charley saw he had been too tentative, too polite last night with his uncle. He should have laid his plans on the table: "Take 'em or leave 'em, I'm committed to 'em."

He telephoned the hospital where they had taken Pino. He was having trouble with his breathing. There didn't seem to be enough oxygen in this rarified atmosphere, 130 stories above the excreta of Manhattan where, even now, the sounds of two real sirens criss-crossed like conflicting hounds of doom.

"Pino," he kept repeating. "Pino Ricci. They brought him there this morning."

Breathless, he phoned Kerry, then remembered Kerry would be at St. Pat's, for the wedding. Charley started to call Garnet. He realized that the turbulence inside him had a name. A new siren spoke on the streets below, whooping like a loon. The way his lungs struggled had a name. He mustn't share it with her.

It was called fear.

His hand, relinquishing the telephone, had begun to shake. Not the fine tremor of this morning, produced by shock, but a broad, brazen vibration which made the phone rattle as it was replaced. He had never before felt fear but he had seen it in others. Fear was how you felt when someone came within one yard of killing you. Someone whose specific message was only half-delivered.

The full take-out is always specific; it's the ultimate way of saying, "Stop what you're doing, permanently." But an attack meant to frighten was always in two parts. Fear came first. Then came the specific command.

The wedding reception was scheduled to begin here at noon, after the cavalcade of Rollses, Daimlers and Caddies snaked fifty blocks south, through the tranquilized streets of Saturday from St. Patrick's Cathedral where Cardinal Foley had said the Nuptial Mass.

Charley had only minutes to change clothes. But first his hands had to stop shaking. Shameful to think he would have to bother Zio with this hit-and-run thing but only Zio had the proper mentality to read the undelivered text.

Only last night they'd discussed Charley's still unformed idea of separating legitimate Richland financial operations from the rest of the family. Did that trigger a death threat? What kind of man valued profit-power so highly he regarded death as a routine bargaining chip?

Charley gazed west across the Hudson river, through air so clear he could make out the cruel, ragged teeth of the Ramapo and Catskill ranges sixty miles away. They reminded him of Zio Italo's unforgiving mouth and bite.

How could he ever explain this to Garnet, this satanic side of his family, where blood meant nothing except as something to spill? Dear Garnet, intent on rescuing Charley, as he was determined to rescue her.

Charley pictured his uncle, leaving his little fortress down on Dominick Street in Greenwich Village, the storefront with the blacked-out windows and the sign: San Gennaro Social Club. No limos for Zio Italo. No sirens. Three bodyguards and an old old Buick, with a small guard car driving a few yards ahead. A don of the old school, no headlines, no expensive entourage. But one glance from those dark eyes and you saw the essential seriousness of his life. Only such a man could be given the entrails of the hit-and-run and make of their bloody swirls a prophecy.

To get this high-priest's reading of the omens, Charley knew, he had only to swallow Zio Italo's blood-soaked Bens, as he had for twenty years, and continue raping the world. An easy life, privileged, and, oh, what a view!

Above Charley a small Lynx helicopter skittered in circles, keeping Richland Tower under surveillance. Charley watched the faces of the two men in the Lynx. Hired help. A blood relative should have been keeping an eye on things. But every ranking blood relative was a guest at the reception.

Re-dressed, Charley examined himself. He hadn't yet

turned fifty, looked thirty-five, still had all his hair and his slim figure. Still didn't need spectacles, so resented the Il Professore tag. Still had that blue-eyed, blond Wasp look that had never matched his baptismal name, Carlo Antonio Ricci.

But ten centuries back, before raping England, the Normans had raped their way through Sicily and Calabria, leaving a lot of blue-eyed bastards. Both his daughters had the same look. No question, the Richards name he had adopted at Harvard made a better match for his "Norman" look. Deceptive. But so was Richland Holdings itself.

"Deception is no sin," he had explained when his cousin, Kerry, had started on Richland's executive training program. "It's the duty of every investor to inform himself. That's the first law. Hell, it's the only law."

"Uncle Charley," Kerry had intoned, tongue firmly in cheek, "it's more than a law. It's an article of the capitalist faith."

But, dammit, deception *was* a sin. As Garnet had pointed out: if you used the illicit cash flow of the Riccis, what dolt couldn't assemble a mighty empire?

Charley envisioned a separation of the clan. Then he would be able to prove how clever he actually was, divorced from Zio's cash. Then he could channel massive support into the environment work Garnet did. For the first time he wouldn't be taking, always taking, from "them." For the first time he'd be giving something back to the world.

To give back what he had stolen for "us"? Family would call it unthinkable. Funny, what they considered "thinkable." When Charley had moved out on his socialite wife, who had been cuckolding him, a violent Sicilian murder was very thinkable. A politely icy separation was unthinkable.

Overhead, the Lynx bobbed up and down in thermals until it succeeded in attracting Charley's attention again. The way it jumped and bucked like a hummingbird in Manhattan's updraughts made the helicopter a liability among the dagger-like spires. And what a noisy intrusion on the wedding reception.

Resplendent in gray morning coat, high collar, white tie and striped pants, Charley strode past long tables filled with hor d'oeuvres, past four bars. He let himself into a large room locked out of sight of the prospective guests.

It was cool in here. His eyes adjusted in the gloom to banks of computer terminals and data-storage cabinets. Charley snapped on a small transceiver base station. "Tower to Lynx One. Canceling copter coverage. Do you read me?"

Through a triple-glazed window Charley watched the tiny aircraft tilt sideways and disappear to the west. "Yes, sir. Canceling copter."

As Charley shut down the transceiver he heard the door close behind him. He whirled and looked into the olive-dark eyes of his Uncle Italo, his father's brother, one of the original four Ricci boys, the only one who had never married because he had arrogated to himself leadership of the clan.

Italo stood a head shorter than his nephew. He watched him from deep-set eye sockets in a narrow face under a short tonsure that could have belonged to a medieval abbot of particularly ascetic tastes, perhaps something of a mystic. The morning coat and white tie did nothing to dispel Italo's antique air.

"No copter? Your brain needs an enema."

Hot words almost escaped Charley. This intrusive old—! "Every second he looked like he was going to crash."

The old man thought, then nodded as if affirming the literal transubstantiation of Christ into wine and bread. "I wouldn't want that."

"Nor would the bride." Charley watched him closely and decided a bit of a joke would help matters. "I can see you now, heading up a Spanish Inquisition. What stronzo ordered this crash? Eh?"

Italo's smile was a splinter of glass. "To the stake!" he snapped, his kind of joke. Through the triple-glazed window clouds began to build up over New Jersey's ragged teeth. "This view, Charley. Meravigliosa. Worth every penny."

His uncle's effect was always daunting, even without last night's abuse. The two of them, dressed in attire that mimicked turn-of-the-century garb, stood amid the muted chuckle of computers that took in data and gave it out. It might be midday in Manhattan but it was evening in

London and Basel, morning in Sydney and still Friday in Hong Kong and Singapore. In any part of the globe one of Richland Securities' two hundred offices might be querying the master database.

A light blinked on the transceiver and Charley said: "Tower here."

"Enzo at street level. The limos are starting to arrive." Charley escorted his uncle out of the databank, locking the doors behind them.

"Champagne," he told a bartender who filled the two tall flute glasses. Charley lifted his glass. "Zio," he said with intense seriousness, "once you have thought it through, you'll see why our future must be as I suggested last night. You may hate it. Now. But you're wise enough to change." A faraway siren hooted.

Italo's dark eyes snapped. He lifted his glass. "Cincin."

Fear seemed to drain away. Charley took a long, full breath and the air was sweet. The Norman crusader on his way to the Holy Land had asked a blessing from his abbot, the one who sent heretics to the stake to burn. Zio hadn't given that blessing, yet. But neither had he called down an auto-da-fé of revenge.

Perhaps Zio had other worries, other threats. A man who regularly, even casually, dealt in violence, in beatings, blackmail and death, might be in danger on half a dozen fronts.

Behind them a waiter coughed discreetly. He handed Zio a small portable radiophone. "Si?" Listening, Italo's hard face sharpened to dagger points. "Too bad." He frowned. "And the other man?" He nodded. "Ben fatto, cugino. Arrivederci." He handed the telephone to the waiter, who took it away. Zio Italo's hooded glance raked past Charley twice, then focused on his eyes. He made a sad face: "Pino, dead on arrival."

The two men stared deep into each other's eyes, as if paying their dead cousin a final farewell. Information tried to trade back and forth between them, extrasensory messages not always delivered, not always understood. Who? Charley's unspoken question. Who wanted to teach him he had risen too far?

Stone, Zio's answer, the stone-blind stare of the powerful coldly regarding the not-yet-dead. Charley felt a wave of rage mount inside him like bile. This man, this uncle, this confederate, this co-conspirator. Was he above contracting a hit-and-run on his own dear nephew to trim his wings?

"And the other man?" Charley knew he was out of order. One never confronted Zio Italo that boldly. To hell with that. Wildly Charley persisted, repeating Zio's second question.

"Professore, what other man?" Zio asked. He lifted his untasted champagne. So did Charley.

With no more sound than a contact lens would make falling to the carpet, a steel-jacketed slug passed silently through both glasses, sending shards of glass and foamy wine in all directions.

"Hit the deck!"

The bullet slammed into a steel pillar holding up the terrace sunroof. As the projectile flattened itself against the pole, the upright twisted several degrees out of line like a smashed knee. "Down, Zio, down!"

Charley and the older man dropped to the floor. The Lynx helicopter bobbed sideways and disappeared at high speed, redlining it. "My God, Charley!"

Charley pulled Zio Italo up out of the puddle of champagne. The air had grown thin and unbreathable. Guests appeared now. Two sirens howled below. The fear had returned. He patted the old man dry and escorted him to the arriving guests.

Near tragedy; now the comedy began, the two men standing side by side, shaking hands, bobbing and weaving, punching shoulders, hugging, miming family love, pecking cheeks, patting faces, punching paunches.

Charley watched himself, dressed like a seal performing for stinking bits of fish. Did all these ignorant people see through him? Genius? Just another ignoramous who had conned everybody into believing that luck was skill. A seal in a thousand-dollar suit, slapping his fins and playing "God Bless America" on a row of tin horns.

For the first time, as he touched people, a choked feeling of disgust made him almost physically ill. He trembled with the shame of it, gasping for air. The faint aroma of performing seals. To consort with these murderers, these extortionists, these cheats, these scheming sociopaths, these . . . these blood relatives.

Fresh sirens moaned and yelped, forcing themselves into his ears. New York was like that, some days. With a brilliant faked smile, he ordered someone to tighten security downstairs. It was obvious now, wasn't it? This morning his own dear uncle had delivered a message. To him. Pino had died to emphasize it. This afternoon, someone had delivered a message to his uncle. Did it matter who? He was shaking.

Some days in New York, the sirens never stopped.

In the distance, over New Jersey, a tall leaden thundercloud had begun to build height and opacity. Charley shuddered and couldn't stop the tremor. The stormhead seemed to be moving east at high speed. In a moment, as casually as his life had almost been taken, the storm would blot out the sun.

Two

It was an ordinary, beat-up New York Checker cab, not a limousine. Bunny Richards had hailed it at the shuttle end of La Guardia Airport, where flights arrived from Boston.

Nikki Reflet carried her shoulder bag and his. They had met at school earlier in the year and become lovers, but had kept it a secret. Now they were going public with it. Somewhere between La Guardia and Richland Tower, they would both have to change to formal attire.

Although Nikki was tall for a Eurasian, just under six feet, Bunny was his height. She got it from her father, Charley, and her elegantly elongated mother, Missy. The only taller member of her family was her older sister, Winfield, who was just over six feet and formidable.

"Driver," Nikki called in his French-accented voice, "plis turn your mirroir away. We need privacy." Educated in Britain, his speech was a mélange; nid for need and privacy pronounced privy-see.

"You needit, you goddit," the driver grunted.

Nikki had stripped to his briefs and was busy replacing tennis socks with pale black dress ones that went with

patent-leather dancing slippers. At this close range, or
any other for that matter, Bunny found it impossible to
keep her eyes off his body. To her he looked entirely
French.

At eighteen, Bunny hadn't seen that many naked
Frenchmen, but she had met Nikki's mother, Nicole, who
had the same fine-grained ivory tone of skin and broad
shoulders, the same long fingers and arms, the very narrow waist and legs whose length was in their tapering
calves.

His father, who was evidently an Asian by the slight
added fold of skin over Nikki's black, black eyes, was
never spoken of. Not even in the third person. Probably
Nikki was illegitimate. But one thing was abundantly
clear: his father was incredibly rich.

As she slipped out of her track suit, Bunny lay back
seductively on the cracked leatherette seat. The very
closeness of the cab's rear seat elevated every movement
to more erotic levels. She fondled one of her breasts.
"Let's play horsie, mm?"

Trying to incite in him a reaction that matched her own
she did a quick pantomime centerfold pose, fingers
clutching her muff inside the sheer peach G-string un-
derpants as if masturbating.

"*Ne touche pas,*" Nikki muttered, struggling with his
trousers.

He exuded a scent of expensive soap. Bunny knew she
smelled of sex from this morning and last night. She
would import this hymeneal aroma to the wedding reception. Fittingly enough.

Outside a police car, siren blaring, roared past. She
glanced out of the cab window at the traffic racketing
toward Manhattan along the crowded Long Island Ex-
pressway. A sudden slowdown brought her face to face
with a truck driver whose higher elevation, above the
cab, gave him full frontal views. He moaned loudly for
her benefit and licked his lips.

Bunny rolled sideways and began burrowing in her escort's trousers, pulling them down to his knees and yanking his briefs to the same level.

"For Chrassake, Bun!"

"Just giving the truck driver a show. They're all gay."
Grinning, Nikki pulled himself back together again.

''Will you get decent?'' he demanded. ''They won't let us through the Midtown Tunnel this way.''

''Shewuh they will,'' the cabby informed them. ''I'll tell'm you're nudists.''

''He's my horsie,'' Bunny announced.

The driver shook his head firmly. ''Stick to nudist is my advice.''

The Daimler limo was leased to Richland Securities and checked out to Farrington Ansbach Reid, first vice president. Andy was neither a Ricci nor a Richards but his need to attend this wedding was obvious, if only to escort Missy, his boss's estranged wife, and Winfield, her older daughter.

Sitting on a jump seat facing backward, he gave both women his lovely smile, speaking of true camaraderie, top genes and outstanding dental care. Said the smile: we are one; it's even possible we use the same dentist.

''You two look,'' he told Missy, ''like sisters.''

The lamentable unreality of this seemed to go unnoticed for a moment until Winfield, returning the smile with even better dentition, remarked dryly, ''I'm the older one.''

In every line of work there are always the real and the fake. Nowhere is this truer than in investment, merchant banking and venture capital, in which Richland Securities engaged as part of the larger Richland Holdings. Someone with impeccable social connections, like Andy Reid, would always find a top job in financial work. Never mind that, even on a good day, Andy didn't know a short sale from a convertible debenture and never would. He had other attributes. People of the same social class found it far easier to deal with each other, on a handshake basis, than with bright strangers like Charley Richards, whom no one could forget was related, despite that Wasp exterior, to one of the nation's leading families of organized crime.

It suited Charley, therefore, to use a brainless beefcake like Andy as a Richland front man. When he found out that Andy was also having an affair with Missy, Charley's blood came to a quick Sicilian boil. But of the whole family, after Winfield, Charley had the best built-in refrigeration.

He had only met Garnet this past year, since he moved away from Missy. But if he hadn't been living alone when he met Garnet he would have died of longing.

Permanently shedding Missy would have been ruinously expensive; a mysterious anstalt in Liechtenstein was never mentioned by her Boston lawyers, nor was divorce. All Missy asked was astronomical maintenance. Under New York State law, such a separation paved the way for a no-fault divorce but fell short of sorting out the anstalt. All Charley asked was to keep Missy occupied and the anstalt unquestioned. For this, alone, Andy Reid was worth every penny he got.

He had been a coke-head for some years—one of the foundation stones of his widespread popularity—and had brought Missy to the point of dependency on the one drug that makes one feel not merely good but also terribly righteous about whatever dirty things one does in private.

It made for a powerful bond between them. He was smiling for her alone as the Daimler crossed 14th Street, heading south on Broadway through a Greenwich Village that had started to darken as storm clouds swept in from the west.

"There goes our day," Winfield murmured.

She had just graduated from Harvard Law and was awaiting the results of her bar exams. Meanwhile, this tall, handsome young woman had taken a job with a feminist law firm. She knew precisely the state of affairs between her mother and Andy Reid, having politely refused a snort on many occasions.

In Winfield's rather too orderly mind, her mother and her sister, Bunny, whatever their other dependencies, were penis junkies. At eighteen, Bunny could be excused. At forty-five, her mother was a basket case.

Although both women in the limo had discreetly applied perfume, the automobile's atmosphere was laden with Andy's aftershave lotion, a ballsy mix of hay and vanilla that had begun to cloy. Winfield surveyed her mother and Andy for signs of needed repair, but both of them, she reflected, belonged to a class which, once dressed, continues to look well-kempt through thick and thin. It was probably a racial characteristic, she thought, which Bunny also had but she didn't. I'm more the messed-up Mediterranean type, she thought.

Almost at the pointed foot of Manhattan Island now, the Daimler stopped short of Battery Park and swerved right along Cedar Street toward the Tower. Even a block away, Winfield saw, the streets were choked with limos.

"What's the delay?" Missy demanded in her New England voice, its consonants very crisp, its vowels almost British.

"They seem to be searching cars," Winfield said.

"Deah Gard! This is what comes of letting the maafiar stage an uppah-clahrs wedding. Anything more complex than a bahbecure is beyond theah tiny minds."

Andy snickered. He and Missy boasted a third string to their relationship, Winfield saw. They were lovers and co-junkies, but that wasn't enough. They also shared a strong distaste for the Sicilian side, the part that made both their lives possible. One might even call it a hatred, to judge by the look of disdain on her mother's elegantly handsome face, a kind of elongated Katharine Hepburn look, all cheekbones and jaw.

Hoping to clear the vanilla-extract stench of Andy's scent, Winfield opened the nearest window. "Mother," she murmured, "you seem determined to forget that I'm half-Ginzo."

"Not you, darling," Missy's smile was vague but not friendly. "You're one hundred percent ice."

Andy's smile was much more sincere. He'd mastered the trick a long time ago. "I do love those Italian ices. So delicious. Non-fattening. Yum."

Missy's pretty mouth moved twice, forming words she was still enough in control to suppress. Then, with a shocking burst of intensity, "Keep away from my daughter, Andy. You hear me?"

In the distance, big men in headwaiter suits stopped each limo and held brief conversations with the passengers before letting the cars progress. To her mother this signaled typical mafia awkwardness but Winfield knew better.

She could sense, almost as if she'd been told, that there had been an incident. It was rare for the family to convene this way. If they did it was most often at her Aunt

Stefi's seaside home on Long Island Sound, where incidents could be controlled.

Something had happened. She could feel it in the skin across her shoulders. Nothing less than a hostile incident could have caused her father to turn Uncle Italo's goons loose on heightened surveillance.

Poor Father. Italo called him a co-equal, responsible for managing the largest and most profitable side of the family empire, its legitimate companies. But Charley Richards, who had never been cited for even a parking violation, was not the Ricci who commanded the fighting troops.

She, who felt her Sicilian genes so keenly, understood that in her own full-blooded father the flame flickered low. Decades of looking, talking, working, and thinking like a member of the East Coast Episcopacy had thoroughly deracinated him. She was poignantly aware of the word's meanings: to shed the characteristics of one's racial inheritance and, in a second definition, to be uprooted without finding another soil in which to re-root.

It was ironic that her father was being re-rooted by a woman whose people had been the object of a nearly successful campaign of genocide. As Winfield recalled, Garnet was half Hopi.

Poor Dad. Still smarting, after all these years, under that derisive nickname Italo had given him. Being Il Professore was not a compliment. Nor did it signify heightened erudition or intelligence. But among the meanings Italo meant for it were concepts of stuffiness, bloodlessness, outsiderness and a certain air of being a paid flunkey. It was a racial hangover, this jeering nickname, from a century when the Riccis had been princes of Sicily. They never had, of course, but Italo carried himself like one who had relinquished titles. In such noble families Il Professore was the itinerant who taught the daughters to tinkle at the pianoforte. The defrocked priest on a sad mule who taught the sons their alphabet. Certainly not someone to whom the command of troops might be entrusted.

And now something had happened to bring the troops out into the open. She started to voice this insight aloud but remembered that neither her mother nor her mother's pet stud had a need to know. In fact, if the two of them could be counted as enemies, there was every need to keep them in ignorance.

As she stared ahead, unhappy with such thoughts, Winfield saw a short, tight arc of lightning crack almost sideways into the gleaming copper tip of Richland Tower. A gigantic thunderclap exploded along the canyons of the Wall Street area. A brassy, burned smell filtered through to her nostrils.

Rain poured down in sudden streams, thudding on the roof of the Daimler like kettledrums. In an instant New York City seemed to cool off. The simmering violence, heralded by police and fire sirens, seemed suddenly quenched. Awed by this burst of naked power, Winfield closed her window, sat back and closed her eyes. Poor Dad.

Three

"Fuck the world," Vince Ricci said.

His Rolls inched slowly forward along Cedar Street, one of a mob of limos being stopped and questioned in the rain. Although it was his own niece whom Vince was marrying off today, he had been against this public display of family clout. But his cousin Charley had always been able to con Zio Italo with his blond, blue-eyed charm.

"I want to shout to the world we're just like everybody else, Vince."

"Fuck the world," Vince had responded. "I don't want cops mousing around for handouts and Feebies shooting videos and, who knows, some outside mob taking pot shots. I like a private life, Charley, and you do, too."

Vince, who was only an inch shorter than Charley, had the other kind of Sicilian good looks; olive-skinned, night-black hair, eyes even darker and faint Arabic blush-colored cheekbones like horizontal knife blades. His big eyes, formidable to stare into head-on, seemed to nest in eye shadow.

He had a tango dancer's body, his long torso slim through the hips. And he moved like a dancer, purposefully, pointing his feet forward, heel before toe, all in all an elegant outcome of such tangled bloodlines. His tight black curls were kept exactly an inch long by almost daily barbering.

The arguments for and against a public wedding had been carried on in the rear of the San Gennaro on Dominick Street. Ever since he'd been a kid, Vince recalled, Charley had been full of this establishment bullshit. Fine, as strategy. But Charley had overshot his goals and was now operating, Vince felt, against the entire grain of the 1990s, as if any businessman, Wasp or not, could ever keep profits separated from crime.

If these last decades had taught the world anything, Vince mused, it was that nice guys finished last and the only game was winning. Charley, perversely, was running against the full flow of world power while his half-breed chick pissed ecology in his ear.

Recalling that argument as his Rolls edged west through the downpour toward where the guests arrived limo by limo, shielded by umbrellas, Vince made a face, as if French-kissing a girl who was a heavy smoker.

His first wife had been one but that wasn't why she lay in the family plot. His second wife, Lenore, seated beside him now in a nifty garden-party dress and cartwheel hat, knew better than to smoke.

Inviting a new woman to share his bed, Vince would stipulate his conditions: anything kinky but no smoking. Vince was very neat, fussy about his clothes and what he put in his mouth. Like a cat, he would spurn any taste he disliked.

Vince sniggered. Lenore glanced at him. "Charley's got a thing about how the world sees us," Vince told her. "For him it's important, Il Professore." His laugh was a short bark. "They taught him a lesson this morning, though." A somber chuckle. "Poor Pino took the strain for Mr. Clean."

A petite brunette with big, dark eyes in a pale, frail face, Lenore was twenty years younger than Vince. She had chosen an ecru dress with eyelets, a broad-brimmed floppy hat and high-heeled pumps of the same material. "I told Charley, 'fuck the world.'" Vince smiled in his sinister way. "I don't want the world to know us. Fear us, OK. Fear and respect."

"To you it's the same word, huh, Vince?"

He glanced at her. "Put the shivs away, Lenore. This is supposed to be a gala occasion."

"Some nice Italian girl getting married?" Lenore asked with mock innocence. "A life sentence: three meals a day and a dozen bambini. What could be more joyous? Another slave to love."

"What would you know about bambini?" Vince's voice had such a deadly undertone to it that Lenore shivered.

Lenore knew she'd been out of her mind to marry Vince Ricci. He was lethally attractive and quite high up in family matters. But her brothers, who ran the Cianflone family's holdings in Montauk, had warned her Vince had personally iced his first wife when she couldn't have children. Now, after a year of steady trying, Lenore had yet to miss a period.

Vince had a way of reminding her almost nightly of the fate of her predecessor. He didn't admit what had happened. He only indicated that it could happen again. If he'd been ugly or openly vicious the world would have sympathized with Lenore. But the world didn't see Vince from her viewpoint. Women adored him. Even Stefi Ricci, who was normally the most level-headed of the family—so smart about men that she'd never married but still had produced big, handsome twin sons—even Stefi thought Lenore was being "picky" about Vince.

But there was an undertone to him that made the skin at the back of her neck creep with fear. People who owed him money knew it. Women he was getting rid of after a night or a week knew it. Employees caught cheating knew it. The undertone was a vibration the ear could barely hear, a kind of hiss, never quite absent, never quite there. It kept Lenore close to panic, not far from a breakdown. Vince had chosen the neighborhood himself.

That he hadn't ended up in his father's boots, doing the Riccis' termination work, was a tribute to Vince's intelligence. His father had been an expert with the ice-pick. After a lifetime of contract killing he had ended up in the trunk of an Olds 88 on the Belt Parkway near JFK Airport with an icepick in each eye.

Vince had opted for a softer venue. He ran Ricci Entertainments, Inc. which operated casinos and resorts in Atlantic City, the Caribbean, Mediterranean and far eastern entrepôts of sex like Macao. Besides producing a cash flow that was the envy of the world, it gave him access to rich widows, dissatisfied wives, world-class entertainers and other suitable vessels for the spilled Ricci seed.

Thinking about his women, Lenore realized that most of the time she got the last spurt. A little token barley-water. No wonder the gametes would be weak. Dr. Eiler, her good-looking young gynecologist, had given her all sorts of medical pamphlets to read. If she didn't get pregnant, it wouldn't be the doctor's fault.

But if she didn't, she was dead.

The FBI often participated in Saturday seminars like this. They were run in the park-like headquarters—leafy trees and bushes—of the international accounting firm of Lutjens, Van Kurve and Armatrading just over the Tappan Zee Bridge. The fact that it's owned by Richland Holdings is unknown.

Unknown, certainly, to Lutjens clients. If they found out that their confidential tax consultant was owned by the owners of their biggest rivals, companies would fear for their carefully kept secrets.

The FBI's seminar was "How to Fight Mafia Infiltration." Charley Richards had sent Kerry to the morning session only because he had to return to town for the wedding reception. The FBI had sent Agent Noah "Nose" Cohen.

Nose was a tall, thin, cowboyish fellow whose nose was not large. But he had come into the Bureau during the first burst of space exploration when nose cones made headlines. After years of insults, practical jokes and merciless isolation, he had been accepted, not as an agent, but as a jester.

"My speech," he began, "is entitled 'How You Can Tell You've Been Targeted.' And here's my speech: 'You can't.' "

If this didn't get a laugh, Nose would walk off the podium as if his speech had ended. This morning, thanks to Kerry's start-off laugh, Cohen got the response he wanted. He held up one hand and counted off fingers.

"One, is there really a mafia? Two, why should it concern you? Three, you don't gamble or snort coke or play around with hookers so forget the mafia. Four, your company never needs strikebreakers, help with licenses, off-the-book loans, transportation, rationed materials, political clout, hazardous waste disposal or confidential data about competitors, so, five, go away, Cohen, and get lost."

He waited for his second laugh. Kerry took notes on his Thinkman, a small hand-held computer like a jotting pad. In what agents referred to as Stone Age, before the death of J. Edgar Hoover, the FBI never concerned itself with organized crime. But now it needed to educate all those self-deluding folks who couldn't see how organized crime touched them.

". . . You can all figure out how mafia price-fixing and control of labor affects you," Cohen was saying, "but let's talk tax evasion."

The audience shifted uneasily in its seats. "None of your companies cheat," Cohen continued. "You're the good guys. Let's call you Company A. Company A hires accountants and lawyers to cut its payout to a minimum, legally. Bravo, Company A. But Company B cheats its head off, concealing taxable assets and income, filtering corporate results through dummy entities and offshore trusts. Company B drives Company A to the wall and buys it out. Now tell me the mafia doesn't touch your lives."

Cohen paused and produced a wry Gary Cooper grimace. "Last time I looked we paid something under half a trillion dollars a year income tax. The average payment by a private person is three or four thousand. Not bad?" This time he paused longer to let the figures sink in. "But if we got the mafia to pay its commercial and personal taxes, per-person taxes would drop by a third. In short, you good guys pay what I call . . . the mafia tax."

Kerry held up his hand. "Sir, that half a trillion dollars only services government debt. It doesn't go to improve interstate highways or buy you FBI guys computers. Now, t—"

But the rest of Kerry's words were never heard. People

began shouting angry questions about debt. Later, debriefing himself to his boss, J. Laverne Suggs, Nose Cohen had to admit the seminar had dissolved in recrimination.

"And the smartass kid?"

"He blew before lunch," Nose said. "But they imaged him off the conference videotape. They're sending me five blowups and a full ID. He's all but nailed."

"And that," his boss smiled broadly, "is what *his* taxes buy."

It isn't easy changing flight plans in the high-density air traffic above New York City. But the return flight plan for the Lynx helicopter had always been a false one. The real plan was to touch down in farthest Long Island where a STOL-craft would be waiting to take both the pilot and the marksman directly south, over water, to a friendly base on Grand Bahama Island off West Palm Beach.

A clever plan. The marksman, who prided himself on his own intelligence, could not find a single flaw. They grounded the tiny helicopter and pushed it under some sheltering maples. Then they scanned the horizon for the rescue plane, a Mooney with extra fuel tanks for overwater flight.

The marksman was still quietly cursing Manhattan's unsettled updrafts, which had stolen from him the shot of the century. God, so close! But he'd insisted on advance payment in full, whatever happened. That was being really clever.

As he smiled slightly, the clever marksman heard the incoming Mooney cut its engines, circle upwind and land. He swung his small knapsack on board. All it contained was a shaving kit and fifty thousand in hundred-dollar bills. The pilot carried his payoff in a briefcase which he also pushed on board ahead of him.

As the marksman and the copter pilot climbed up into the plane, the pilot of the Mooney glanced at them through Ray-Bans so dark they looked black. He then emptied half a thirteen-shot .9 Browning magazine into the marksman and the other half into the helicopter pilot. Instead of opening up a series of messy holes, the result was one big aperture the size of a squashed and dripping overripe peach.

He hadn't switched off the engine so the shots were neatly camouflaged. Shaking loose the clever marksman's death grip on the open canopy of the Mooney, its pilot slammed it shut and taxied into a quick takeoff.

There is a point where those inside a conspiracy become inconvenient witnesses. If the marksman had been successful there would have been celebrations in several parts of the world that night. But it was never planned that he be a guest at any of these revels.

As it was the rejoicing had to be postponed but there were surely no loose ends that needed tidying. The only person who needed to worry now, in his dark Ray-Bans, was the pilot of the Mooney.

Four

No question about it, the "incident" had shaken Zio Italo. Always physically frail, he was beginning now in his seventies to lose mental flexibility. "My God, Charley. My God," he kept repeating under his breath in the moments after the shot. "What is this world coming to?"

"High-tech take-outs," Charley responded grimly.

"We're surrounded by barbarians," Italo whispered. "Our world is coming to an end. The rest will be chaos." Then the guests, and the rain, had arrived.

Once the downpour ended and the reception moved out onto the terrace Italo had made his ceremonial withdrawal. In the privacy of Charley's apartment/office, lodged at the very top of the tower, above the terrace where lightning often struck the copper cupola, Italo sat in an upholstered armchair.

There was no view like this in the whole world and Charley had it. And who had bought him the view? Whose seed money had financed all his operations, covered his cash-flow needs? Italo hardly noticed the merrymaking below, his eyes unfocused, as he inspected the threatened death of his world.

The Edwardian finery of his morning coat and white tie looked bizarre in the merciless light that surrounded

him 130 stories above Manhattan. The air, washed clean
by the storm, turned the south and west windows into a
kind of floodlamp that picked out every impurity, every
speck, every flaw.

Not fear, he assured himself. Fear he had seen on
Charley's face, where it goddamn well belonged. What
Italo felt now was rage at how vulnerable he had been
up here in Il Professore's top-of-the-world aerie.

Italo had often wondered if his low-key, low-profile
base on Dominick Street was safe for him, so close to
the rot and stench of life on the streets. He told himself
now, with the implacable insight he reserved for his own
life, that when they came for you, being 130 stories in
the air didn't help. It was like being married as a buffer
against life. Sicilian men saw it that way, a woman to
cook your meals and warm your bed and give you heirs.
What illusions!

Marriage was as treacherous as sitting 130 stories in
the sky. Not that he didn't envy Charley this view. You
could convince yourself this was the entire world, a view
reserved for aviators and gods.

Italo had always had an affinity for the sky. His father
had named him for Mussolini's handsome, dashing aviator, General Italo Balbo, who had bravely poison-gassed
thousands of spear-carrying Ethiopian tribesmen from the
air. In the 1930s Balbo had led a squadron of speedy
Savoia-Marchetti seaplanes on an American visit that
placed the might of the fascist state at the forefront of
the world, long before that impostor, Hitler, stole its good
name.

Feeling his age in every joint, Italo rose creakily to his
feet now and paced toward the east windows. Below him,
on the terrace, he could hear an accordionist playing the
theme from the *Godfather* movie, a Neapolitan-styled
tune full of dark longing and heartache. What did fools
know?

From time to time, one of them would look up and,
seeing Zio, wave. Italo had spent a lifetime cultivating
his ''Uncle'' image. But family feeling didn't exist in his
heart. Feeling of any kind had no place there. Those
outside the mafia could never understand this side of the
mafia soul. Now even the family was forgetting, so soft
had life been for them in this generation.

Few of them knew, firsthand, what true mafia strength was based on: a total absence of human feeling that allowed any cruelty, any lie, any sin to protect and expand power. As the Pope was Christ's vicar on earth, men like Italo were earthly managers of the power that kept the universe operating.

The Sicilian peasant said: potere é potere. Only a Sicilian understood that this was no oafish redundancy. Power was everything; the rest nothing. God was a doll on a cross, his priests corruptible beggars.

But they paid a price. At Italo's heart lay this secret that he alone, and perhaps people of Vince's age, understood: that when you assumed leadership you abjured mercy. You neither gave it . . . nor got it.

Italo had expected Charley's demands, ever since his spies had told him of the liaison with this new philanthropic person called Dr. April Garnet. His own Charley, the son he'd never had. How sharp a wound it was!

Italo had expected this for years as he watched Charley join the right clubs, marry into a right family, get the big awards and grow further from his heritage. There had been a time when he'd even contemplated changing his religion, but Italo had come down heavily against it and Charley was still what every Sicilian male claimed to be, a non-church-going Catholic. Sicilian women went to church; males considered it a racket to be treated with respect.

I made him, Italo mused. I turned Il Professore toward his destiny. Could I see that his fate was a woman named Garnet? And that, for her, he will now betray me?

There is a time, as every good Sicilian knows, to ignite into a fury so incandescent as to destroy all before it. Now was not such a time. The challenges of keeping order demanded a heart of steel. That was what some Duce, like Italo Ricci, needed to bring order out of chaos. Once fractured, Italo feared, order crumbled back into chaos. And it was chaos the world most dreaded.

There was no one else in the family to help him with this lethal puzzle. Il Professore's brain would have been welcome but he had become useless under another's influence. After Charley no man stood next. It was Italo's niece, Stefi, whose brain was Charley's equal. And a grand-niece, Winfield, who was the true inheritor of Italo's cold-blooded intellectual power. But the work of women was giving life. The business of death was exclusively a male concern.

His great, dark-green/brown eyes, hooded in their deep sockets, suddenly opened wide. The concentrated power of their glance, over the commanding curve of his sword-like nose, had an almost physical weight. One of the dangers of concentrated power, he reminded himself, was too single a viewpoint.

The hit-and-run had targeted Charley. As for the helicopter attack, who could guess its real target? Charley had to be persuaded the same hand had paid for both, the hand of some faceless common enemy. Italo's icy grin slashed sideways.

"Why must they play mafia music at mafia parties?" Bunny Richards asked her sister. The two tall, slender blondes, with Nikki Reflet, made a rather glamorous grouping at the corner of the terrace that faced east, toward the airports, the Atlantic Ocean and, eventually, Europe.

"Music has no provenance," Nikki countered. "I'm doing an essay on it for my summer school Crit. Lit. Music's only notes."

"Nuts?"

"You have to excuse Bunny," Winfield explained. "She still thinks a foreign accent is something to make jokes about. Especially sexual ones."

Winfield moved off across the eastern parapet of the terrace to where a woman stood chatting with one of her twin sons. Stefanie was a cousin, not Winfield's aunt, but she had always played the aunt's role with the Richards girls, being closer in age to their father, Charley.

After ritual kissing, Winfield stood back. "Kevin?" she asked of the young man about her own age. His pale brown hair had been chopped into a kind of tall crew cut above grayish eyes and an unformed face. He and his twin brother had gone to the same private high school as Winfield. Even then she couldn't tell them apart. Now he clutched a large blue-and-white golf umbrella he had been holding over his mother's head.

"Kevin, the villain," he corrected her, "is off somewhere abroad. I'm Kerry, the financial drudge."

"My father's right hand."

"As a result of which, I spent the morning getting lectured by the FBI. What a waste of a Saturday."

"Kev and Ker," their mother murmured, as if counting assets. She smiled at Winfield. Stefi had a long neck and close-cropped brunette hair. Her strong-jawed, handsome face hadn't been passed along to her twins. Her compact body with its ample breasts had remained small-waisted through the years. She had to be Missy Richards' age but seemed much closer to her sons. Nobody knew who their father was, Winfield reminded herself. It was a mystery that seemed to keep her looking very young.

"And you, Winfield?" Stefi went on. "Has anybody ever in your whole life called you Winnie or Win or Whatever?"

The accordionist, strolling now from group to group, had wandered as well into the sentimental throbbing of "Come Back to Sorrento," with its plaintive alternation between major and minor.

In the southwest corner of the terrace a man dressed in a foolishly with-it costume of fringes, boots and a ponytail, began to caterwaul the lyrics in Italian. He was Cousin Tony, who fancied himself a producer of rock music for Ricci Entertainments, Inc.

Winfield shrugged. "Missy never called me anything else because it's her family name. And Dad . . ."

"Il Professore," Stefi continued, "rarely breaks new ground."

"He did insist on Missy being here today. The bride has always liked her."

Stefi's face went deadpan. "Not easy, liking Missy."

"Inviting her is part of Dad's image," Winfield explained. "No normal Sicilian would dream of such a thing. But it's quite common on the Northeast Wasp Circuit. People separate, divorce and marry someone else from their set. It's an extended family, based on remembering to send bread-and-butter notes."

"No hatred? No sorrow? No need for revenge?"

The younger woman turned more directly to her, but something in Stefi's glance stopped her, almost like a hand placed over her mouth. It was hell, Winfield thought, to have Sicilian blood in veins you were trying to keep properly refrigerated.

Stefi took the umbrella from Kerry. "Find your girl and dance with her."

"Vince is putting the moves on her."

"That's what I said, go dance with her, stupidog-gine." Stefi gave Winfield a how-dumb-can-men-be look as her son left them. Kerry had become handsome and something of a stuffed shirt, Winfield noted. The missing black sheep, Kevin, seemed more glamorous as he disappeared into the clandestine side of the family.

There was something familiar about Kerry's face. The long lashes he got from his mother. But the small, almost pug nose he got from his unnamed father, together with that firm, discreet mouth. She looked at her sister across the floor. Bunny's nose was small, cute, almost pug. Winfield's stare returned to Stefi. She and Charley had always been close friends. No one made a mystery of that. The twins were Winfield's age. It could be that long before his marriage, and surely after it, Charley Richards and his cousin, Stefi, had been lovers. In which case, any cousinly dalliance with Kerry was ill-advised.

Suddenly, Winfield realized that her mind was being read. Italo-like, she quickly threw in a diversion. "Did we have some sort of incident before the reception began? All those heavies downstairs checking the limos?"

Stefi produced that southern Italian shrug which denies all knowledge of everything on the planet earth. She stepped sideways long enough for Winfield to see that she had been standing before a canopy upright cruelly dented as if by a sledgehammer blow and looking like a fractured leg.

Stefi's luscious mouth had relaxed into a teasing smile. "Winfield," she said, making fun of someone who bore no nickname whatsoever. "Winfield. My favorite niece." She gave her a hug and a big, hard kiss on both cheeks. To Winfield, it spoke volumes.

"You're looking well," Charley told his wife in a tone that could have served to tell her she looked dreadful.

"And you," Missy said, completing the circle of insincerity described by Winfield. Then, brightly: "You wops are real party animals."

"Great seeing you again," Charley said, moving off so quickly his estranged wife had continued insulting him, not realizing he was gone. Charley ended up at one of the bars with his oldest daughter.

"Only a lunatic," Winfield murmured, "would have invited Mom today. You really overdo this Wasp imitation."

"It's my only chance to monitor her downfall."

Father and daughter eyed each other from the same level, about six feet, which put them well over the heads of most guests. "A line after lunch and a couple more to brighten up the evening," Winfield said very quietly. "Just about the same intake as last year. If I promise you regular reports, will you stop feeling you have to check up on her personally? I can see what it does to you."

"Yes, well." He lifted his champagne glass to her. "Here's to you, kid. I do appreciate your help."

She clinked with him. "How was your Connecticut thing this morning?"

He made a face. "You know what thieves those procurement admirals are."

"Only to a Galahad like you."

"I'm the pipeline that conveys Italo's cash flow into Pentagon pockets."

She took a long time answering, her pale green-blue eyes growing muddy with thought. "You have really changed. It's Garnet, isn't it?"

"As a matter of fact, yes." He paused. "What's that song? 'Just in Time'? We found each other just in time to establish a . . . a mutual rescue mission. You're practically the only person in the whole world I could admit that to. Is that a sad state of affairs or isn't it?"

"Who told you you needed rescuing?"

"Garnet. Not in so many words. But I'm a quick study."

This time Winfield took even longer to speak. "I don't know another soul like you," she said. "All my friends are hustlers. We have to be. In the final decade of the century, we hustle just to keep from being buried alive."

"Is that why you joined a non-profit feminist law firm?"

She grinned. "I can afford to. I have a rich father. Anyway, my boss didn't plan it to be non-profit. She's stainless steel, like you. The only difference is that you're the Professore who shows a profit.''

At the word he almost flinched but managed to return her grin. ''Winfield, I'm no brain and you know it.''

''Don't confuse me. My mind's made up.'' When she paused again Charley could almost feel her mind spinning through its endless microchips searching for answers as her eyes scraped information from his face. He had been standing up to this ruthless inspection all her life. It no longer intimidated him the way it had when she was three or four years old and asking a question a second.

She nodded firmly. ''You're heading for a second separation, aren't you? Now that you have the knack of it, you want to be free of all those illegal Riccis, don't you? April Garnet has you believing, in this dying decade of a dying century, that you can show a profit and remain a Galahad.''

''A Parsifal. She took me to hear it last week. My God, what an endless bore. And no swan.'' Both of them began laughing.

''An honest man,'' she said at last. ''Don't you read the papers? Nobody's honest. Politicians lie. Athletes cheat. Businessmen steal. Cops frame innocents. And everybody cooks his income tax.'' She touched his arm. ''Be careful. Please?''

He kissed her cheek. ''From the mouths of babes,'' he said and continued circulating around the room.

That was why he didn't see her eyes well up suddenly, nor see her try to touch her lids with a handkerchief. Winfield Richards had little experience with tears; she ran into the ladies room and stood over a basin, a big girl crying like a baby.

When her sister Bunny found her there, she wouldn't explain the tears. ''No idea,'' she lied brusquely. ''Weddings do that to people, don't they?''

Bunny's glance locked with hers. ''So do funerals.''

Five

His heart was pounding for no reason at all. Unless you counted Singapore's thick humidity. But he was no longer down on the streets, being sautéd like dim sum, he was up in the sky, wrapped in quick-freeze air conditioning. Like Cousin Charley at the top of Richland Tower.

Kevin gazed down and thought: from the air at night, with its offices still lighted, the clean-swept high-rise jungle of Singapore resembled lower Manhattan or any other place where making money is the sole reason for being.

Kevin Ricci craved Charley's view more than anything else in life. Even though he worked for Zio Italo, the man he most wanted to replace was the tall, blond, good-looking Il Professore. He envied not just his view but the entire Charley, his style, his dress sense, his ability to keep his fingers clean no matter what he touched. Hell, his sheer nerve in being the first Ricci to move out on his cheating wife. His un-Ricciness. Hopeless dream. His brother Kerry, something of a Professore in his own right, might some day succeed Charley, but never Good Old Kev. Kev the villain. Kev the pinza Zio Italo used to touch anything dirty and liable to infect, anything dangerous.

He had been warned not to dawdle. This was only an information grab, nothing serious, nobody hurt, but embarrassing if discovered. Still, he had to pause at this brilliant, humid emptiness and fantasize that its counterpart view, overlooking Wall Street, would some day be his. He could feel his blood pulsing in his ears.

Most of Singapore was asleep. A skeleton staff serviced the Daiwa Building, into which Kevin had broken. The structure reminded him of Richland Tower because it was the tallest of any nearby. But the comparison was misleading. Cousin Charley's operations actually filled most of Richland Tower. Daiwa was one of Japan's Big Four brokerage houses, along with Nikko, Nomura and Yamaichi. These, and many smaller firms, tenanted the

Daiwa Building. Their diversity made internal security hard to maintain. Which served Kevin's purpose perfectly.

An hour or two before, as he had begun to case the job, he noticed first that Singapore's mist-shrouded streets were as thick with cops as a dog with fleas. The pigs were empowered to arrest or fine you for almost anything from littering to not flushing a public toilet. He had therefore concealed himself in a loading bay of the Daiwa Building, sweating as he waited for the last employee out to lock him in. It was at that point that the adrenaline began to flow.

At first the waiting in shadows was bearable. Then, as he slipped back through cooler basement corridors, pausing at each intersection to listen for sounds and look for detection devices, the tension began to mount. Like most burglars, Kevin depended on victim carelessness. It would have been much harder, for example, to break into Daiwa's main office in Tokyo. Not even worth considering, since he couldn't read Japanese. Here he had a less secure office to burgle in a former Crown Colony where records were kept in English even though most Singaporeans were Chinese. A guard in uniform sat at a gigantic desk console of TV monitors. Here the air conditioning began in earnest. Since Kevin had seen no cameras in the basement halls, he assumed they were all for the sixty business floors of the building.

The elevator in one shaft blinked into life. Someone near the top floor was coming down. Two young Chinese men in business suits, hauling overloaded briefcases, signed out, showed passes bearing their photographs, and left.

Once upstairs in the Daiwa computer area, Kevin would know his way around. His mentor in these matters was one Zio Italo had kept on the payroll for nearly a decade, a Malaysian who served as one of Singapore's more trusted computer security consultants—for Daiwa and a dozen other leading companies.

"Here are the access codes," he had said at dinner that night, slipping Kevin a small card. "It's a normal third-generation NEC-IBM configuration on MS-DOS. You can easily download into your Thinkman. Daiwa operates a strictly chronological database. You only have to access October of 1987.''

Helpful as this had been, it hadn't prepared Kevin for the tension. His clothes were damp with perspiration. He had watched the lobby guard watching his bank of TV monitors. The one on the far right was grinding out an old John Wayne movie. Now Kevin returned to the basement and summoned the elevator.

He emerged on the fifty-ninth floor, reaching into his back pocket for a small case resembling one for a pair of spectacles. He tiptoed along the corridor to the door his mentor had described. He knocked loudly. He had been promised only one man on duty. The door lock clicked and a short Chinese lad in his early twenties appeared.

Kevin snapped open the case. A sharp smell permeated the air. He shoved the chloroformed cotton wad against the lad's mouth and nose and clamped down hard, trying not to breathe himself.

He hustled the Chinese into a storage room, gave him a 10 cc. Tuinal injection from a plastic hypodermic and locked the closet from the outside. He took a long, steadying breath now but it didn't help.

Then the upgraded air conditioning hit him. The rooms were ten degrees cooler than the corridors. Banks of computers, all generating small amounts of heat, had to be kept fresh as eggs.

Standing at a window and staring down on Singapore, Kevin sought an inner calm. He had been doing what he knew best, breaking and entering. The next part required his brother, Kerry.

Kevin grinned crookedly. They had fun, the two of them, playing Good-Guy-Bad-Guy. But it was woven into the fabric of the family that some Riccis had to be one and some the other.

A great game. This little mission tonight told him what a farce it was. Charley Richards had picked up a rumor long before Christmas of last year that the worldwide market crash of October '87, had been generated in Tokyo by the Big Four. Accidentally? Charley had to know and he turned to the one person who could find out for him, Zio Italo.

Kevin glanced down at his hands encased in surgical-weight rubber gloves. Doing Kerry's office work would drive him nuts. But there were moments, such as this, when clandestine work scared him shitless. Too much depended on him.

What if he couldn't access what Il Professore wanted and the mission bombed? Kevin's mouth had dried to the consistency of desert sand. His failure would confirm Charley's view of him as a thug, and a dumb one at that. It would also hurt Kerry's chances, being the twin of such an incompetent.

He glanced at his watch. A quarter past midnight. He had a bit less than six hours. From his other hip pocket he removed a second black case not much larger than a king-size cigarette packet. It bore the logo: Thinkman.

Think, man, he commanded himself. Think of succeeding Cousin Charley one day. Think of toppling him from his tower and having that view all to yourself. Instead of being the dumb brute twin brother, only good enough to touch filth, to ice somebody who was in the way, instead you'd be the boss. Ha!

With a sudden grin of pain, he realized he was having the time of his life.

Six

Wedding guests were leaving now. The sun, with no taller building to intervene, still cast horizontal yellow rays on the Tower terrace and would continue to do so long after the streets below were in twilight.

Vince Ricci had made a pass at a nice girl Kerry had invited. He had been told off by everybody and was now sulking on the south terrace. Women rarely said no to Vince. Neither would this one, if it hadn't been for the smother of a family he carried on his back.

His brother-in-law Al, who worked for Vince as pit boss and manager in Atlantic City, had visited him back here to see if he was drinking. Vince was far too fastidious for indiscriminate boozing. But every now and then being denied something he knew was his could start him on an all-night binge.

His cousin Pam, married to the rock music producer, now approached him. "Just pray *he* didn't get wind of it," she said, indicating with her thumb Zio Italo, upstairs, a Deity of terrifying nearness. Vince's nose wrinkled with derision. He swung open a door to one of the inner offices and walked inside hoping Pam wouldn't follow. She did.

The notion that any Sicilian male would discipline a nephew for an active sex life was ludicrous. Grinning, Vince reached for her to give her a pinch where it would do the most good. She stepped clear.

"Such active fingers," Pam said.

"Other parts of me are even more active." Vince let the grin die out. He ran fingers through his short black curls. "Who elected you my keeper, Pam?"

"You need one just to keep what's yours inside your pants." Her voice was very low, like a bass viol. It stirred something inside him, if only by sheer vibration. He understood she got nothing sexual out of her marriage to Tony, a self-absorbed flyweight. Pam had been circling Vince for years, wondering how to set up an affair without getting run over in general traffic.

"You know something, Vince? You're an animal."

His heavy eyelids lowered. "Is that the best you can do by way of a compliment?"

"The way you treat Lenore, it's inhuman."

Pam mimed outrage very convincingly, her deep voice like a long, drawn-out cello note. But Vince had the idea what angered her was that he wouldn't come on to her and she didn't know how to get him started.

Of all the Riccis she was the one with artistic talent. She had begun by designing the album and tape cassette covers for her husband's recording label. Now she was managing his groups, designing their clothes, writing the songs.

He watched her work up to another assault. Normally, like most of his family, she bored him. Angry, she was marginally more interesting. Hard up, she might even be bearable. Teasing her unmercifully would be a real pleasure.

"Vince, what makes you so sure the reason you don't have kids isn't you? Not either of your wives. You."

What saved Pam was that the slap, aimed at her face, only landed on her shoulder. It nevertheless sent her reeling into the wall. She recovered quickly and her look of hatred finally drew Vince's silent approval. She did have some spirit after all. "That's it, Vince! Brutto animale! Che vergogna!"

Pam slammed the door on her way out. As if triggered by this, the phone at Vince's elbow began to ring. He frowned, trying to make the two phenomena match. Finally, deciding it was beyond him, he picked up the phone.

"Who's this?" a man demanded.

"Vince."

"Vinnie, it's Renzo Cianflone, out in Montauk."

"Renzo who?" Vince asked his own brother-in-law, Lenore's eldest brother.

"Cut the comedy. Zio Italo ast us what we could dig up. I guess he ast everybody. Tell him we made the two near Peconic Bay, copter and all."

Vince frowned. "Zio must talk to them."

"Not possible, Vinnie. Somebody got to 'em first."

"Says what?"

"Double take-out. Nobody's ever gonna tell nobody nothing."

Triple, Vince thought, if you included poor Pino.

As in so many developing lands, the business establishment of South Korea is also the government. So it was no more than just that the tour of this new electronics plant included everyone from the President to those heads of leading banks and brokerage houses who were not at the moment in jail.

Shan Lao, guest of highest honor, took it in his usual low-key manner. After all, he had put half of them in office. He was a short, slim, neatly turned-out man whose head was possibly too big for his body and whose eyes, certainly, seemed so huge that they devoured everything in sight.

The new plant had already been in operation a year, turning out unbranded television receivers, video recorders, computers and other equipment. But this walk-through was Korea's first acknowledgment that the source of these hundreds of thousands of high-tech products being dumped in the markets of the West at cost or below-cost retail prices, was actually Korean.

Until now one could search these refrigerators or computers from top to bottom and find no country of origin tag. This enabled a number of well-known manufacturers in Taiwan, Tokyo and Singapore to place their brand logos on the products and up the wholesale price by sixty-six percent. No company hesitated to do so since the quality of the products was good. Anything Shan produced had built-in acceptability based on draconian quality control.

At the very end of the ceremony, in the ornamental garden of flowers, ponds and sculpture, Shan and top government officials stood to attention as a battalion of infantry marched past, flags streaming. All eyes were on Shan, a recluse from all the industrial and financial hubbub his immense power had created. A very faint frown crossed his smooth forehead and, for a moment, those nearby thought they detected displeasure.

But the frown had been occasioned by Shan wondering whether his own people had arranged for a smooth departure in precisely one half-hour. His aide-de-camp on this mission was a young Chinese Shan had "bought" as a schoolboy and sent to college. Choy was his name, and New York was normally his working area. Choy's English was so good—he had learned it from Irish Jesuits—and his intelligence so high that he was frequently drafted for extra duty.

Today was a good example, where the timing had to be as precise as possible. Shan was due in Jakarta that afternoon to inaugurate a large petroleum refinery adjunct devoted to producing industrial plastics for the new radar-proof U.S. bombers.

He forced the frown away. For Shan's staff to fail him was impossible. For Choy to fail him was not even to be considered. As the last flag passed, he turned to the President and bowed ceremonially, hands clasped together. When the others on the dais looked for him a few minutes later, Shan Lao was nowhere to be found.

He had vanished, thanks to Choy, leaving an almost palpable aura of power simmering behind him.

* * *

''Why must they play mafia music at mafia weddings?'
the young girl asked.''

Nikki Reflet wrote this in his spiral notebook, followed
by: ''Does music have any provenance at all? Does existence? When Debussy calls a suite 'La Mer' does that
give the music salt, swells and tides?''

In the bedroom Missy Richards had assigned to him
for his overnight stay a small light burned faintly. Nikki
felt privileged. Bunny's family knew so little about him.

He was sailing under false colors, but those had been
his orders. In the West he and his mother used her maiden
name, Reflet. In the East he had a strong provenance:
Nik Shan, only child of Shan Lao.

''Any more than Brecht,'' he scribbled now, ''writing
a Marxist poem, could call upon Weill for a Marxist
tune.''

Few roads were open to Nik Shan. His father had yet
to invite him to follow in his footsteps. So he had found
something at which he didn't seem totally incompetent:
journalism. His summer work for Crit. Lit. would be
essays, ''Letters to My Father.'' Shan Lao had no gift
for parenthood, Nicole had explained, but he loved his
son. Evidence of this was crushingly slim. Hence: ''Letters to My Father.''

Without warning the door to Nik's room eased silently
open and Bunny, tall and nude in high-heeled strap san-
dals, slipped inside. She closed the door and posed
against it, thrusting out her breasts as if straining to get
free of the doorknob.

''Here, horsie,'' she whispered.

Seven

Almost the last to leave the Tower was Charley Richards.
Considering the anger Zio Italo had kindled in him,
Charley's control had been masterful. They hadn't run
out of booze or ice. There had been umbrellas standing
by. Nobody had started a fight. A third take-out had not

erupted. His cousin Pam had come on to half the males. And tomorrow was Sunday.

He'd had only two tense scenes. The first had come when greeting guests and finding himself repelled to the point of nausea. Like all self-loathing, it passed. Temporarily or forever, only the success of his separation from Italo would tell. The other bad scene had been with Vince.

"That Kerry," he'd complained. "He's another stainless-steel Professore, like you. You'd think I was a child molester."

Charley's grin, by now so overworked as to be fake, tried to soften his response: "If you thought you could get away with it, you would."

"Hey, cornuto, you're no monk."

"I'm no Bluebeard, either."

Vince's dark, Arabic complexion flushed hotly. "Watch it, Charley. You clowns on the legal side of life, watch what you say to the rest of us." His utterly black eyes seemed to bore coldly into Charley's pale ones. "And don't tell me you wouldn't be better off with that junkie wife six feet under."

Charley's mouth went flat. "Vince, with all your skim, your junk, your hookers, your rackets, your bought cops, your vigorish, your scams, with everything going full blast, Richland Holdings still out-nets you. And we pay taxes." He strode off, too angry to say any more.

Remembering the scene, Charley's cheeks grew warm again. He tried sighing the tension away. For the first time since the day of violence had delivered its messages, Charley tried to relax. He stood on the terrace's northwest corner, watching the die-hard remnants of a sensational sunset over the Ramapos, a vivid contusion of hot, dark reds and gauzy mauves that no one else in Manhattan could see because, poor fools, they weren't high enough.

As an exercise in public relations, the day had been a success. From the Nuptial Mass at St. Pat's to the top-of-the-world reception, with limousines slipping through the arteries and veins of Manhattan like corpuscles of power, today had been a watershed statement. A proper prelude to Charley's splitting the clan in two. Gaze upon this picture and upon this. No longer two sides of one coin, but separate emblems. And to think, only a year ago he'd never even heard of Dr. April Garnet.

He'd been flipping through the annual report of a Richland Bank and Trust Co., NA, and come upon a photo of a forest newly planted in oil-spill-ruined Alaska by Richland Oil. Three or four bank people, looking cold in fur hats and parkas, were posed in front of baby pines meant to atone for pigging up a wilderness. Beside them stood this slim woman with a tousled mop of coarse prematurely white hair, cut in a short bob, ear-length, with bangs like a medieval squire's. She looked so familiar, with her short torso and long legs, her wide cheekbones and aquiline nose. But the caption underneath had identified her as Dr. April Garnet, Acting Manager, Richland Philanthropies.

Never having heard of her, of course, within twenty-four hours Charley had a memo from her. Invited to his office, she turned out to be in her late thirties, but something about her sun-bronzed face, set off by the intimidating white thatch of hair, gave her an elfin youthfulness. Where had he seen that face before? In his youth?

Three Richland companies, she reported, including an oil-reserve firm in western Pennsylvania, had been caught polluting the environment so openly that even replanting Alaska and funneling cash to ecological causes could not prevent bad publicity from breaking soon.

"The problem is that we're only giving lip-service, Mr. Richards."

"Ours is a nation of voters trained to believe lip-service."

An astonished laugh from her. Then, "What an indictment of our educational system."

"Know-nothings teaching know-nothings more nothings."

"Is this a bad day for me to bring this up?"

It had been that outburst of his that unleashed her from her formal pose as an employee. Within minutes they were talking directly, as if friends of long standing. Where *had* he seen her before? Dreams?

"This is usually the make-or-break point for me," she admitted in that first conversation. "Since I left the faculty at Columbia, I have reached this crunch with two previous employers and I've had to resign. They were interested only in lip-service.''

"Ah, you're a professor, too," he said, almost under his breath.

"I was."

"A good one?"

"I kept correcting people's grammar and logic even though I was only supposed to teach environmental sciences.'' Her face lost its animation. ''I could hardly believe it, graduate students who hadn't mastered sixth-grade English.''

"You and I," he said slowly, "are going to get along, Dr. Garnet.'' Her warm-brown eyes fixed his in such a way that he found it impossible to look away. Nor did he want to. He heard himself asking, ''Do you have Sicilian blood, Dr. Garnet?''

"Hopi father, Irish mother."

Remembering that moment, Charley thought now of how much he had missed having her at the reception. But it wouldn't have done to invite her. As much as he wanted to be with her all the time, today had to be dedicated to family, especially since Italo had begun bad-naming her.

If only Zio Italo had seen her in action, just last week. One of the Metropolitan Museum's huge, airy courtyards had been given over to an exhibit of rain forest ecology among Indian tribes along the Amazon. "Lecturer: Dr. April Garnet, Richland Bank and Trust Co., NA,'' a small placard read.

Over the public address system the breathy flute notes of South American native music piped, those hoarse whistling tones speaking of immense lungpower in high places. ''. . . Actually a broad, vertical belt, ranging southward from the tundra of the Inuits and Aleuts of Alaska and Canada into the high Incan culture . . .'' Garnet's voice was husky with fatigue. She had made these remarks five times to five audiences. But her bright face never lost its excitement. ''In this great crescent we find the same exploitation of resources that impoverishes and kills off first the local tribes, then the ecology of local nations and, finally, the planet itself through oxygen depletion. Why do we assume oxygen comes out of nowhere?''

La Professoressa.

He had let her voice drench him in his own feelings for her. Now he watched the audience, glances fixed on this extraordinary woman, her face a beacon. The sun swept in sideways from behind her slim body, igniting her white cap of hair into a nimbus, as if the rays were generated within her.

The flutes panted and rasped, speaking of great primitive joy. He loved her body, her thoughts, every part of her. He had had a narrow escape. This woman, with the light shining out of her, gave him an almost mystical feeling that she had been sent by a power in which he had never believed.

Zio Italo had no such faith. Worse, he knew the deity Italo served. Even so, Charley felt himself relaxing into optimism. When he listened to Garnet.

"There is no us and them," she had told him once. "We are all us, every animal and plant and rock. Each is one. All are one. It's not hard to conceive, Charley. They call you a genius."

"I'm as dumb as everybody else. Only Italo's smart."

"Even Italo is us. It suits you to think of him as the brilliant enemy. If you think of him as a victim—" Charley could almost see the steel-jacketed slug explode the two glasses of champagne.

A metallic rapping sounded overhead.

He saw the old man's hawk-profile at one of the windows, tapping the bulletproof glass with a coin. The vision blended instantly into the diabolic dream image, Italo sponging blood off piles of Bens. Garnet was right: he couldn't see the old man any longer except in his nightmare role.

The idea that his uncle, too, was a victim failed to convince Charley. If he wanted to make the old man swallow his greed and say yes to the split, Charley had to be firm, implacable, angry enough to ram it through to success.

Charley let himself into the cooled computer room and took a spiral staircase up to his own apartment/office. Italo was waiting for him with two tulip glasses. "We never did have our champagne."

Charley listened to the conciliatory tone. OK, so the man who had bought Pino's death was now as scared as he was. Perhaps that would stop him from firing on his own troops.

"Some spoilsport took care of that first drink."

Italo, who could rarely express himself in any way but hot directness, appreciated Charley's more laid-back style. The old man poured the glasses halfway. Charley accepted his and they touched with a small click. "Cin-cin," Zio Italo said.

The champagne was flat. Italo had probably saved a half-opened bottle and it had lost its fizz. He was full of such peasant economies. Still, it went down cold and prickly. Charley finished half of his in one swallow. He could feel his heart beating faster.

"Zio," he said, "about our talk last night."

Italo instantly switched subjects. "That copter crew? Double take-out near Montauk. We'll never know who paid. I guess they also bought Pino's death." A grin seemed to saw his narrow face in half as he switched again. "Remember that rumor you picked up about the Japs?"

"I mentioned it six months ago."

"Some things take a while," Italo told him. "Tonight a scrambler call from Singapore reached me here in your office. The rumor was on the button. The Big Four in Tokyo led off that market scam back in '87. But a fifth guy dreamed it up, some mystery financial genius. Not a Jap. A Chink."

"He nearly wiped out half the world."

"It was an experiment. The idea that one slant-eyed slope could bring down all the securities markets appealed to his mind."

"Is he still loose?"

"Operates between Taiwan and Tokyo. Very in with the mainland Chinks. And get this: he brokers all the top Golden Triangle shit Vince and his boys distribute. He calls himself Shan Lao."

Charley glanced at his watch. Ten o'clock. He felt his mouth tighten with determination. Fear? Hell, no. Anger.

"You gotta date with Pocahontas? Buon viaggio."

"I'm not going anywhere, caro Zio, till we talk." Charley heard himself say it without a tremor. Without a sign of fear.

''It sort of makes me wonder,'' Italo began his third attempt to detour him, ''was I the target of that copter hit? Or was it you?''

''Zio, sit down.'' Charley watched the old man slowly sink into a glove-leather chair. One of his hands made a dabbing gesture, feeling for support. Dabbing off the blood. Charley felt heartened by the movement's feebleness. He had thought of starting by forgiving his uncle for the death of Pino, but saw that he didn't need that much leverage.

''With your money, Zio, I have made Richland immense. Our construction and transport and electronics, our supermarket chains, our stake in the entertainment field. All are highly profitable. I want to give it back to you.''

''Thanks for nothing.''

''I want to keep our financial operations, brokering, banking. This is what I know best, Zio. The rest any competent manager will run for you better than I can. In return for your cash flow over the last quarter of a century, you will now get the lion's share. In return for my sweat and smarts, I will get the rest.''

He stuck out his hand. It jutted steady as a rock. ''Deal?''

''Are you crazy? I turned you down last night. This is just more shit dreamed up by that redskin of yours.''

Brutal words pressed forward, urgently demanding to be said. The anger in Charley had reached such a point, however, that he was afraid to use anything but the fake voice of sweet reason.

''Zio, the truth: it comes from me, me, only me.'' His uncle sat forward, cupping his ear. ''I'm sick at heart. Blood money does that, dues paid by ruined people.''

Italo winced but listened on, straining to hear the soft, deadly words. ''I can't lie to you, Zio, I want a fresh start to pay back what I owe the world. I'm making a fair offer: split off Richland's financial. I go my way. You go yours. And God bless you.''

Dominick Street is two blocks near the Holland Tunnel in the West Village. Nothing fancy. Nobody shoots TV commercials on Dominick. If they applied for a permit, the San Gennaro Social Club would see they didn't get it.

Italo sat alone at his immense oak rolltop desk in the back room. Nearby church bells struck twelve times. A long day, this one. In the club's anteroom, two young cousins were playing klabiasch, waiting to safeguard Italo's trip home and to bed. But the last thing on his mind was sleep.

What occupied his thoughts was a refrain like an evil mantra: *A curse on the woman. May she rot in hell and release the soul of Charley.*

Only today Italo and his nephew might have gone to their Maker. As hard as such a fate would be, it was preferable. Better two leaders died than to let the entire family be wiped out.

Such ignorance, such arrogance! Blood money? What else had sent him to Harvard for eight years? What else had financed every venture Il Professore started? What else had built that 130-story view of his?

Goddamn America! Three thousand miles of illusions, tricks, lies that Americans told themselves about themselves. Double lives! Poses!

What an evil moment when Charley had fallen under that spell. He believed the whole thing. He bought the self-delusion that this nation had grown great on hard work and spotless honesty: that he "owed" it something, some garbage about clean air and water; that now he would cut his own throat to prove it.

Italo rubbed slowly at his aching heart. Potere é potere, he almost groaned aloud. Ahh. The power of power was everything. Nothing else existed. He straightened in his chair and his face went blank. There was only one thing to do. Blood, Charley had said. All right; blood it was.

July

Eight

Sunday morning, eight a.m., the security guard in the basement garage of Richland Tower flashed a snappy salute as he recognized the passenger in the tiny white 205 Peugeot 1.9 GTI. "Morning, Mr. Richards, sir."

Charley nodded politely but, since this wasn't an armed forces installation, didn't return the salute. He and Kerry took the non-stop elevator 129 floors straight up. Charley could feel something click in his ears. He swallowed twice.

He sat at one monitor screen and Kerry sat across from him. "Access File 037. The first password is Grandissimo. The second—" he examined his calendar watch, "—is Grievous."

His screen lit up. After a moment words and figures began to scroll. "Slower," Charley yelped. He kept working the copy-and-paste software, abstracting the name and financial status of each corporation.

The memories here! Kerry hadn't even been born when Charley had founded Mid-Atlantic Cement and Aggregate, Inc. Today MACA netted just under seventy million in profit after taxes.

Continental Artists had been a sleazo talent agency when Charley had bought it, fired the management and started fresh just about the time Bunny was born. Today it represented the top film/TV stars and directors and produced a third of the networks' evening offerings.

Jet-Tech International had been a sick electronics giant when Charley had started buying in. Winfield had just started secondary school by winning a place on the basketball squad. J-TI was now a main Pentagon supplier, and, through a Far East subsidiary, a major importer of the new-generation Cray-speed computers.

FoodUsa had been his father, Gaetano's, chain of cheese stores. On Sundays Charley used to leave their nanny at home and take the girls to pick out their brunch, usually Milanese mortadella and mascarpone. FoodUsa was now two hundred mall supermarkets in five states, plus a warehousing and generic-brand facility that serviced a dozen other chains as well.

Down memory lane he copied and pasted until he had all seventeen non-financial corporations controlled by Richland Holdings. They represented twenty years of effort and time, uncounted night work, high hopes and hard slog. All of them were booming, a fit gift to Zio Italo. In return he would take Richland Securities, Richland Bank and Trust, NA, Richsurance Services, and Lutjens, Van Kurve and Armatrading. Behind him a laser printer sprang to life. "Now can I see?" Kerry asked. Charley nodded and the younger man stepped to the printer.

"So what's top secret about this?" he asked at last.

"To you, nothing. To the IRS, plenty." Charley glanced at his watch. "Eight-thirty. Can I be at La Guardia at nine?"

"Trust me. Those 1.9's are overpowered little bastards."

"In one piece. The Tulsa fat cats will expect me to look as sleek as they do." While Kerry puzzled over the list, Charley wiped everything from his data disk and then changed the access passwords.

It wasn't that he didn't trust Kerry. It was simply that, after all these years, it had become second nature to him not to endow others with information they could be forced to reveal.

Garnet had warned him that such habits were bad for him. "You have to trust people. You trust me. Why not others?"

"I trust Winfield. Two's enough."

"I don't believe it," Buzz Eiler said. "You mean there's such a creature as a mafia doctor?"

On Sunday God rested. So do most gynecologists, even those who consider themselves supreme beings. Buzz Eiler rarely deified himself but most of his patients did. He was, after all, the inventor of the Eiler Section.

Old money patronized old gynecologists. Young women tended to choose female doctors. But the stratum just below old money, wives of producers, lady advertising executives, TV personalities, brokers, best-seller writers, these were Eiler worshippers. Thanks to them, he was Gyno Flavor of the Year.

Benjamin J. Eiler, still in his thirties, was small, with a nice smile under messed-up sandy hair and pale green eyes. His broad cheeks had a rounded, flushed quality like the kewpies who used to advertise Campbell Soups.

When his wife, Eileen, first met him in college she saw him as a teddy for her bed. "Benjy Bear" was what she called him then, fifteen years ago. "Buzz" came from coxing the rowing eight. He would urge oarsmen with a throaty rasp.

Their apartment towered over 53rd Street near the Museum of Modern Art. Buzz had opened up the living room so that now, in July, they could move back and forth to their southfacing terrace. The rear wall bore two crossed sculls and Buzz's rowing sweater. The other walls displayed caustic Daumier etchings of French lawyers and judges of an earlier century, arguing mightily. None of doctors.

Eileen Hegarty was the attorney to whom these Daumiers related. She had her own firm, one female partner and one junior, just hired, called Winfield Richards. This was not her only connection with the Ricci family, but Eileen wasn't yet aware of it. Last Friday she had agreed to defend a prostitute accused of jeopardizing a john's life and ruining his career by giving him AIDS. At the moment the charge was reckless endangerment.

The case appealed to Eileen's feminist beliefs. These grew much stronger when she learned that her client had thought herself healthy. Her employer had provided weekly medical exams. The doctor had pronounced her and the other hookers clean and fit.

"I have his name." Eileen's thin nose wrinkled. "Salvatore Battipaglia, M.D."

"And that's his *job*?" Buzz persisted. "Checking out syndicate pussy?"

"That," Eileen said with mock dignity, "is what they pay him to do, once a week. But he obviously doesn't."

She lay back in her bright red bikini on a white wicker chaise longue and stared southeast toward the Chrysler Building. Barely five feet high and less than a hundred pounds, she had had a lifelong battle convincing judges, juries and opposing attorneys that she was a force to reckon with.

But in the heavily charged, highly dramatic field of litigation, she had finally won respect. It may have been her precise, firm face with its brunette complexion. It had the clean edges and corners of a medallion, freshly incised. A no-nonsense face, and pretty.

Picking up her Sunday *Times* she continued reading in the weekly roundup section a summary of opinion on a recent Supreme Court decision. They had used an old photo of her but at least they'd gotten her quote correct.

"Eileen Hegarty, Hegarty & Krebs: If ever the dead hand of a disgraced president could be divined in the non-logic of this court, a majority of which he appointed, it is there to be seen in this baffling decision which will cost the nation untold trouble for decades to come."

Then, like a lot of *Times* readers, her eyes kept sweeping rapidly from left to right while her mind roamed elsewhere. One of the reasons she had hired Winfield Richards was that she was a tall girl with obvious mental capability. She had seen Winfield's records from Harvard. But it was the picture of what the two of them would look like at the defense table that most appealed to Eileen.

One of the things she shared with Buzz was an ego-weakness toward showmanship. In a trial lawyer this is no bad thing. The picture of her and her new junior, the long and the short of it, struck Eileen as a winning combination. Yes, a gimmick. But, then, she reflected, so was the Eiler Section.

Buzz Eiler's immense reputation, at such an early age, was based on this. It brought hope to women who previously would have had to settle for adopting children. The Eiler Section had been devised for those with ectopic cysts or tumors which—in the brutal jargon of the day— "required" hysterectomies. In fact, as Buzz had once explained to Eileen, it was always possible to try removing those obstructions and let nature take its course, ova moving down the Fallopian tubes toward fertilization and implant.

But most gynecologists considered it far too dangerous and difficult for them to try. Malpractice lawsuits loomed. Because doctors were too maladroit, or lazy, or underinsured, women had to lose their whole reproductive apparatus. Science having progressed into ultra-sound and other imaging techniques, Buzz hoped he might excise growths and repair their sites because he could "see" what he was doing. Thus the Eiler Section, not so much an operation as a way of performing it successfully.

It took him five years and twenty-five brave volunteers before he could claim success. Since that time the Eiler Sections he and others had performed were responsible, on the East Coast alone, for the births of several hundred healthy infants who might otherwise never have been conceived.

It was no wonder, Eileen thought as she watched him working the Sunday crossword puzzle, that women idolized him. He could feel her glance. He looked up and smiled. "The hooker's champion," he said, raising an invisible glass to her.

She smiled. "I have an angle. The employer is a mafioso who insisted on regular medical checkups. There's a guarantee implicit there. And if he condoned fake medical exams, he's as guilty as my client of reckless endangerment. Or operating dangerous instrumentalities."

"Wow! Lead me to them!"

The portable telephone at her feet rasped its dry cricket chirp. "Dr. Eiler," Buzz snapped, "has died and gone to the Great Thighs in the Skies."

Eileen switched on the telephone and merely said, "Hullo."

"This is a terrible time to call," a woman began hurriedly, her voice unsteady. "Is the doctor there? It's an emergency."

Eileen held the telephone high over her head, as if submitting evidence. "Surprise! Yet another Sunday emergency." Then, "May I have your name, please?"

"Mrs. Ricci. It's a matter of—" Her voice shut down. "Hullo? Mrs. Ricci?"

Buzz made a face and reached for the phone. "This is Dr. Eiler." Then, "You'd better come in tomorrow. First thing. The usual, Mrs. Ricci. Lie down. Shower, no bath. You know." He listened again. "That's all right. Happy to see you."

He switched off the telephone and laid it down. "I'd swear her hubby's low on sperm. She doesn't dare ask him to take a test. Now she's a week overdue and anxious as a waltzing mouse. A frail little monster, like you.''

Eileen frowned. They'd never planned having children. Neither of their careers would allow for it, especially hers. Still, some day, before she hit forty, they would have to make a final decision.

"And meanwhile," Buzz went on, "she's afraid for her life. It seems the first wife—"

"Benjy!" Eileen's scream cut in, "Mrs. *Ricci*? Mrs. Vincent *Ricci*?"

"She calls him Vince."

"The capo who heads up Ricci Entertainments, Inc?"

When he shrugged in response, Eileen stared hard at him. "You're in luck, Doctor. I'll drive you to your office tomorrow morning. In return for which . . ." She wiggled her eyebrows suggestively.

"An intro to Mrs. Vince Ricci?"

"How'd you guess?"

Nine

Now that she had her first job, Winfield reflected, it was time to find her own pad. Despite what she'd told her father, she was tired of keeping an eye on a mother who left around the Park Avenue duplex liberal traces of Andy Reid.

"You're packing?" Missy asked. On a Sunday it was rare for her to be up this early. She stood in the doorway of Winfield's room, wearing a pale summer dressing gown of delicately flowered butter-yellow organdie, all ruffles and lace. "You're not moving out?" Her voice echoed with tragedy.

Her daughter listened to the cloying tone of mock regret that suggested, simultaneously, how sorry Missy would be to see her go and also how glad. "Darling, you needn't move away. This has always been your home."

Her daughter snapped shut the large suitcase. She sat down on the edge of her bed and stared at Missy. The word "mafia," of Arabic origin, signified a certain sinister bravura. A mafia horse had fire and temper and, moreover, was dangerous to ride. She remembered what a truly "mafia" young woman her mother had been, hard-drinking, gorgeous, laughing uproariously, opinionated, spoiled rotten in a way that men blindly adored.

Missy, now starring as "Mother," mouthed all the sugary clichés of old tearjerk movies from the era of *Stella Dallas* and *Imitation of Life*.

"Just packing away some winter stuff, Mother. You'll be the first to know when I find a place I can afford."

"Your father should provide a rent allowance." In short: don't leave home but here's who can give you the money for it. This was too silly even to acknowledge. Winfield got to her feet and found that she had to push her way past her mother to get out of the room.

Missy seized her by the shoulders. "It's no use calling you my little baby, is it?" she asked in that same fake voice.

"Not at my height, no." Winfield decided to jolly her out of this fit of fake sentimentality. She gave her mother a quick, fierce hug to squeeze her breathless for the moment, pecked her cheek and disappeared down the hall to the room Charley had used as an office when he lived there.

It contained the only communications terminals Winfield trusted; a Richland technician swept them clean once a week. It was much too early in the morning, ten o'clock, for Bunny to be awake. But there was a fax office in Boston that hand delivered even on Sunday. Winfield scribbled a quick note: "Bun, call me at my office without fail tomorrow (Monday) morning. W.R."

She switched on the machine and transmitted. That done, she tore up her original message and pocketed the scraps of paper. Then she opened the back of the machine where a duplicate copy of everything it had sent was stored.

That was how she found the copy of an essay Nikki Reflet had faxed a month ago: "Letter to my Father." Together with his father's real name.

The most important high-tech requirement of new TV satellite and cable networks was not electronic but political. To put together a steady supply of programming was simple enough with Richland's ownership of video production houses and several thousand old Hollywood films.

But it also required access to a satellite. For this political clout was primary. And that was why, here in Tulsa, on the grounds of the Mohawk Park Zoo, quite close to Tulsa International Airport, sat as unlikely a collection of old pols as Charley Richards remembered seeing on a muggy Sunday afternoon.

The rogue's gallery, he noted, began with the United States Secretary of Commerce. Behind him sat a man reputed to be the head of a very large Hollywood studio, but they came and went so fast that Charley couldn't be absolutely sure of it. Next came a gaggle of congressmen and two senators.

Charley glanced around again as he rose to the podium microphones. He should have felt potent, sprinkled with the same celeb-dust that sparkled on the shoulders of the others. Instead, as when he touched his own beloved Zio Italo, he felt unclean. Hold it. Hold it.

He almost stepped back from the microphones, so powerful was this feeling of disgust. But Zio was a criminal; he had bought decades of murders, cheated, suborned, perverted; he had planted rot at the heart of the system like a tapeworm which first poisons its host, then devours it from within. These well-fed celebs were only stooges. The odor of corruption might hover like a ripe mist above their heads. Garnet had shown him that. But their intent had never been criminal, had it? All they had wanted was to live well.

Charley took a breath and swallowed hard. "Mr. Secretary," he began, "senators, honored guests, you're looking at the latest state-of-the-art satellite home-base. It cost a billion dollars. I give you my solemn promise it will never transmit a single episode of *I Love Lucy*."

Seven minutes later, amid applause, Charley ducked out to catch the three o'clock to La Guardia. By five he had transferred to a small seaplane at the Marine Air Terminal. By six o'clock he was at Stefi's home on the Sound, the amphibian bobbing about in the water, moored to Stefi's dock, the pilot fast asleep. The sky to the east was growing indigo.

A corner of Charley's mind remained in Tulsa. What did they think, those polished fat cats, when they saw

Charley Richards in action? Smooth construct of the fertile brain of Zio Italo Ricci? Clever clone of a Wasp financial honcho? What did he care what they thought? He had needed their clout; he had bought their clout; the job was completed. End.

"Stop thinking," his cousin Stefi murmured, sipping espresso. She had been gardening and hadn't bothered to re-dress. Watching her, Charley realized he had neglected to tell Garnet that he trusted a third person after Winfield and her. It was Stefi. No men on his list of confidants, but being frank and open with three people should count for something.

"I'm going up against Zio full blast," Charley told her. "Those two hit-and-runs? I have to put them aside if I want to hold onto my nerve for a showdown."

"Do you have to do it so coldly?"

"A separation is always in cold blood."

"Garnet has no idea what she's asking you to do."

"This is my idea, Stef, not Garnet's."

She said nothing, her way of doubting his statement. Then, "Charley, let me speak plainly: Pino died for you. Next time, you will die for you. I'd let the whole thing with Zio drop."

"Twenty years of work," he pointed out. "Buying small, building big. Eighteen-hour workdays. My youth created that list of corporations. The girls' childhood went, to help me. My marriage burned up along the way. That's a lot of dues. Now I make it all a gift to Zio. And all I ask in return is that he leave my middle years in peace."

"That's not possible."

"I'm handing it to him on a silver platter. But life is a two-way street, Stef." His voice had risen almost to a shout. *"He also owes me!"*

She was silent and when she spoke there was a hoarse, haunted quality to her voice. "Charley, I have more reason to hate my own kin than you. You were always the white hope. I was always the next thing to a leper." She stopped for a moment. "Charley, I love you. You know? I love the way you look. I love your mind. I have always loved fucking Il Professore. You're special in my life, no matter who you're shacked up with. But that doesn't mean I'm with you on this."

"I don't understand."

She slumped a bit in her chair. "Do you think I understand how I can hate my family but never oppose it? I'm like every other Sicilian broad under the sun, too conventional ever to be a free agent." She shifted restlessly. "Winfield. She'll back you. Your new woman, she'll back you. If I'd married you, sure, I'd be yours all the way. If you were right, even now, I would give my life for you, Charley, for you and for the boys. You three . . . you could wipe your feet on me. But on this you're wrong." She took a deep, unsteady breath and her long neck seemed to rear back like a swan's. "Why can't Il Professore see that splitting the family businesses makes us weak? Holding them together keeps us strong. Why are you only thinking of yourself, Charley? Why are you throwing the whole family to the wolves just to please yourself?"

He knelt before her and hugged her knees. "Stef, what we own is a highly profitable empire of destruction, just like every other big holding company. Our businesses can't help being dangerous to the well-being of everything and everybody. You remember what my Dad, Zio Gaetano, used to tell you when you were a girl? 'Never look in back of a restaurant or a grocery store, or you'll never want to patronize them again.' "

She laughed. "Good advice."

"Stef, every business is like that, even the financial ones I want to hold onto. Every business cuts corners, cheats, lies, hides secret scandals."

"And since Garnet, you're burning to get away from all that."

He nodded.

She leaned forward until their lips almost touched. "Then God help you, Charley." She kissed him softly at first, then fully. "God help you."

On the flight back to town he had the dream again. His uncle sat at his oak rolltop carefully sponging blood from bound packs of hundred-dollar Bens. Italo's Bens oozed blood. His white handkerchief turned scarlet.

"Beve. Mangia."

Just south of the 59th Street Bridge, on the Manhattan side of the East River, sits an enclave of homes. Garnet had been house-sitting one for a rich friend who coddled his conscience by letting Green types use the over-large place. The seaplane moored at the helicopter pad north of the bridge and Charley walked down Sutton Place to her house.

"No," she had once admitted to him, "you're right. I don't want to own a piece of Manhattan. Anymore than I want to be your philanthropy officer for the rest of my days. I've never lasted more than a few years in any job or nest. It's not my Hopi blood that's nomadic. It's the part of me from County Clare."

Tonight the two-story house looked dark, untenanted. Charley let himself in with a key. It was nearly midnight. He'd been living on and off planes since nine this morning. The glamorous life of the haute bourgeoisie.

He made himself a Bushmills and ice and slipped off his shoes. He hadn't put on the lights. This way he could watch the river traffic, great barges, small sailboats, cruising past. Transiency invaded his soul. He wanted to be as lightly tied down as she was. He wanted them both free to cast off, raise sail and fly.

They were two halves of the same person, feeling alike about the nation around them, feeling that the key to it was a proper education, the kind American children hadn't had since the Second World War. But hers was the half with the razor's edge.

He wasn't sure she realized the kind of punishment a cutting edge was supposed to take. She'd booked herself for lectures to sixth-graders, ready for junior high school, who could barely read, couldn't write, nor multiply, nor divide. Twelve-year-olds who loathed schools and teachers and couldn't wait to break away into the drug-enhanced brightness of the real world of shopping and round-the-clock TV.

She'd been married once. That life, Charley understood now, was the one in which she had become familiar to him fifteen years before. That husband, as she explained it, had fitted a rather mystical need of hers, the other half of her life-mold, half Irish, half Zuni, with the tribal name of Runs White Antelope and the city handle of Gerry Mulcahy.

A fashion photographer, he'd made her a number one model for three years. Everyone, Charley included, knew her face. Her coal-black mop-top, her cavernous cheeks and her great, elfin grin became part of everyone's memory. And then, one night, Gerry had OD'd in their bed.

She'd gone west to forget and pick up college degrees. But even as Dr. Garnet she still preferred moving on to staying put. "I've always lived a Raggedy-Ann sort of life," she had told him.

Like anyone who had peaked early, she had tasted the pleasure of being paid serious attention. It was a drug not easily given up. She yearned to bring herself back up again to something more stable than modeling. With Charley's help, she could do it. And with her help, he could change his life, too.

The chandelier went on suddenly, a blaze of white-hot gems. "I thought you were a burglar. Didn't your cousin invite you to stay over?"

"Gave me a kiss, told me God help me and sent me home to you."

He grinned at her. Only on a passing yacht could anyone else have seen her bronzed naked body. Like some black-haired people, the blue-black kind, she was prematurely white only on top. Her pubic hair glittered in the chandelier's fractured beams like the wet fur of some Arctic seal, rich, thick, sable-black. She moved in on him. Holding his head in both hands she rubbed herself against his face.

In the morning they woke late. Her bedroom looked east into the rising sun across the river. They had thrown off the sheet. Monday had dawned hot and humid but neither of them had wanted to leave the bed to switch on the air conditioning. They lay side by side on their backs, legs entwined, sleepily staring up at the ceiling, with its pale rose matchboard sheathing.

"Did your cousin really say 'God help you?' "

"She tried to get me to give up the crusade."

"How . . . um . . ." She laughed nervously. "How hard did she try?"

"Stefi and I don't do that anymore." He was silent a while. "She's the third person in this world I trust. So, you see, I do open up. I'm not the strong, silent type."

"Three women." She frowned. "That ought to be enough. I have anti-feminist friends who would say it's two more than enough."

She massaged the bristly blond hairs on his chest, inflaming his nipples. There was nothing she did to him that didn't arouse. He supposed if she read him the weather report it would give him an erection. "If you had a phone I could call my office and tell them I'm still in Tulsa. Or Ouagadougou."

She nodded solemnly, her short white hair swirling outward like a ballerina's tutu from the center point of her skull. "And then I could coax that one last orgasm out of you and get the milkman to go for the undertaker?"

He started chuckling. "Dangerous to know you, eh?"

She made a deprecatory face. Her elf's eyes warped sideways. "I'm not so bad. I kind of pace you so there's always one drop left. I hate funerals," she added, crawling over him to get off the bed.

He twisted sideways and bit her small, rounded buttock. "It'd be nice to start my new life by picking up the phone and saying, 'Garnet, can I stay with you all of next week?' That tiny apartment on the 130th floor is like a tomb when the north wind blows. All of next month? Next year?"

A telephone began to ring. Charley reached under the bed for his portable radiophone and switched it on: "Richards here."

"Dad?"

Charley's eyes went up in his head. "Good morning, Winfield."

Ten

All during dinner at his Hong Kong club Mace thought of the two girls at Fat Luck's, of their chunky yellow bodies and of how deeply Shan Lao would loathe him if he ever learned what a disgraceful person he was.

In the past, when Americans disgraced themselves, they went west to California. British black sheep headed east to Hong Kong. Lord Hugo Waismith Mace had had to leave London's square mile, its financial district, rather hurriedly in the 1960s; Hong Kong was now his home base.

Tonight he left his British club after no more than two pink gins. His heart beat faster with anticipation.

A rickshaw stopped at his summons. Lord Mace was still trim, for a fifty-year-old who drinks a lot; and his weight was no test for a rickshaw puller. It was Lord Mace's belief that he must travel this way, rather than in his gunmetal-gray "R" Bentley, which let his chauffeur know that he was frequenting an opium den. The chauffeur, being in the pay of Lord Mace's boss, would instantly bear back to his employer the news that Lord Mace was at it again. Shan Lao loathed any addiction.

There were people who wondered why a major industrialist employed a wastrel like Lord Mace. Shan's reasons were like Charley Richard's reasons for employing Andy Reid. Lord Mace represented the image Shan wanted in the West for his enterprises, a white Brit who could straddle legal and illegal.

Only in the West did anyone insist on a distinction. In the East the same financier-industrialist manufactured TV sets and Number Four White Injectible. He could sell anything, risk-free. His protection was at the highest ministerial levels. Hypocrisy is a Western hang-up. Here everything was on the table.

At Fat Luck's, the two girls sat solid and naked in the small room off the foyer, smoking Marlboros. These "girls" were in their forties, clean, plain women who had been servicing Lord Mace for almost as long as he'd been in Hong Kong.

They understood the ritual that affluent opium smokers follow. It is a profane liturgy that goes back many centuries. Lord Mace preferred them to the cheaper boys because boys were too bony, not very clean and fidgeted.

The chubbier of the two women removed Lord Mace's clothing. The other prepared a fat pill of opium gum on the point of a jade-handled hat pin. She tucked the pill, the size of a hazel nut, into the bowl of a porcelain pipe. She turned it sideways to let the alcohol lamp's blue flame enter as she sucked and inhaled. The opium began to liquify and sizzle up a thin, pungent smoke.

Then Lord Mace curled naked in a fetal position with a woman fitted into him on either side, very tightly, their soft flesh enveloping him, an all-meat sandwich. He inhaled smoke from the pipe. He sighed happily. He inhaled more.

There would be dreams. There would be apparitions. Lord Mace nearly killed the chubbier woman two years ago in a rare opium dream. Fat Luck had had to empty a bucket of water over him to get him to release her neck from between his interlocked fingers. It cost Lord Mace double for the night. But, mainly, there would be peace, the sleep of the gods, cradled within soft female thighs, fleshy bellies, swelling breasts. The women had no other function but to be warm meat.

The heavily bolted door had a peephole. It flickered. Standing outside, Fat Luck looked in on the threesome. So many of his younger customers would choose the instant rush of heroin. They would expect the woman to service them sexually. Only an old China hand truly understood opium.

With a plump brush, Fat Luck painted a vertical line of characters in dense black ink on a scrap of paper, as his ancestors had done for many centuries. When it dried he folded and sealed it shut with four modern wire staples. He summoned a nephew and told him where to deliver the note.

The boy wheeled off on his bicycle without need of further instruction. In Hong Kong, as in Taipei, Seoul, Tokyo, Bangkok, and Singapore, everyone knew where to find the house of Shan Lao. He was always at home to Asians there and in mainland China, where he was deeply involved in private enterprises.

But European and American entrepreneurs dealt with Lord Mace. Shan's French wife, Nicole, also met Occidentals socially, as did young Mr. Choy, currently in New York. Of the three only Mace needed watching. His opium nights didn't bother Shan, but his carelessness did.

A month ago, from Manhattan, Nik had faxed a letter to his father directed to Lord Mace's office. It had sat, perhaps lying in the open, until the Englishman had remembered it only yesterday.

The hour was late, but Shan got up from the desk and went to his wall safe. He withdrew the single-spaced sheet of fax paper and brought it back to his large, intricately carved teak desk. Then he sat down and re-read it.

Dear Father,

"Why must they play mafia music at mafia weddings?" the young girl asked.

An artless question and, moreover, one that begs an even more artless follow-up: does music have any provenance at all? Does existence?

When Debussy called a suite "La Mer" did that suddenly give his music waves and tides? Could Brecht, writing a Marxist poem, call upon Weill for a Marxist tune?

In the same way, the mendacity and corruption of life have no innate meaning, other than what we give them. Yet people are endlessly surprised and affronted by both, as they are by music.

The working formula for Planet Earth is: *approximately one thief to every thousand fools*. If this seems unduly gloomy, think of the somber Italian folk saying, il mondo é ladro, the world is a thief.

Can it be that mendacity and corruption, which carry no inner message, are telling us that neither does life? Yet we know the thief-to-fool ratio cries out for it. We call this meaning the Great-Fool Theory.

It holds that no matter how useless or flawed something may be, there is always a Greater Fool out there who is ready to say: "Yo! That's for me! I must have that man for president! I must have Vitasmell, the new deodorant orange juice! I must have a forty-eight-inch TV with Chromozotic Afterzoom. Here is my credit card. Debit me while I roll over on my back, all four paws in the air, and let you scratch my belly to hypnotize me into buying another useless product."

But one has a choice. One can fight the meaningless tooth and nail, one hell of an unsettled life filled with anger and frustration. Or one can lie down and roll over, all four paws in the air and listen to the pretty music.

Shan Lao went to the window overlooking the bay. He was smiling, as he always did at Nik's acrid humor. Vitasmell, the deodorant orange juice! It was a smile his son had never seen.

He reminded himself to have his New York City man, Mr. Choy, find out from what Manhattan terminal this largely incoherent and amateurish message had been sent.

It signaled the end of Nik's adolescence, a flag, waving confusedly for attention. It was a warning that the boy had picked up a complete set of Westernized, cynical, liberal, relativist beliefs. It posed an either/or decision: either keep him in the West forever or bring him back now, while still pliable, and mold him in his father's image.

But that meant making him privy to *everything*.

For example: tomorrow Shan was off to visit his automobile factory near Yokohama. Beginning with motorcycles, the firm now produced a reliable, inexpensive family compact that sold half a million units a year. Nik would love all that. It fitted his young mind, stuffed with do-good thinking. But what would he make of Shan's Burmese operation? What would he make of the very successful Shan developments in the Philippines? With his Westernized view of life and the lip-service paid to carefully drawn hairline demarcations between what was allowed and what wasn't, what would Nik make of the modern East's tangled ethics?

Shan's smile was bitter. Let his woolly-headed essayist son try to fathom the difference, let us say, between a private killing of passion or greed and a public one, the so-called "license to kill" issued routinely to police, soldiers and secret agents by sovereign states the world over, or global orders of assassination often used by nations locked in holy wars.

What frightened Shan Lao was that his only child would not understand and accept what the lowest rickshaw puller knew: in the East, everything is allowed. Everything.

Eleven

Down Third Avenue from 72nd Street, where Dr. Eiler's office was located, a small coffee shop stood nearly deserted at ten in the morning, baking in a July sun that was already softening the asphalt streets.

Neither Eileen nor Lenore Ricci had had breakfast. They sat at the counter and listened to the blare of canned music from loudspeakers overhead. "I'm really sorry,"

Eileen was saying. "I know how it is," she went on in a louder voice, "when you're sure you're pregnant and it turns out you're only a week late."

Lenore's huge eyes stared into hers as she sipped coffee. "You're trying, too? I would've thought . . ." Outside, on Third Avenue, an eighteen-wheel semi moaned past in a roar of diesel. Lenore floundered for a moment but a rather strong affinity had already built up between them. "I would've thought, you being Dr. Eiler's wife . . . right?"

"That he could wave his magic wand and knock me up?" Eileen translated. "When we were first married, before I finished law school, we had a lot of scares. You know: you want a kid but not now." She paused. "Now, it's a question of will we ever. But your problem's different."

"My problem is life or death. Mine."

Overhead, the loudspeakers shifted to a noisier song, mostly yelps over bass thumps. The two women could watch themselves in the back mirror, against which were stacked unsqueezed oranges and bags of bagels and corn muffins.

Eileen saw the physical similarity. They were both petite and dark. But Lenore was beautiful in the romantic style, with those immense, vulnerable eyes, that thick mass of tangled tresses and plaintive, haunted look. She had the air of a heroine in an 1890s melodrama roped to a railroad track.

"I just can't believe a man would want a child so badly he'd threaten your life." The moment she said it, Eileen realized she had either gone too far or so over the top they'd be friends for life.

"I can't believe I'm discussing this out loud with another person," Lenore said mournfully. "But it's true. My brothers tell me it's true. Vince has left me in no doubt, Mrs. Eiler. If I—"

"It's Eileen. Can I call you Lenore?"

"Eileen's an Irish name, right?"

"Eileen Hegarty. Is that enough of a Mick moniker for you?"

Lenore's eyes narrowed slightly in thought. "Wait a second. Just yesterday in the *Times*. Right? The weekly roundup. Am I right? You're famous?"

"Do you always read the Sunday *Times*?"

Lenore's ivory skin darkened in a blush. "Only the magazine and the entertainment section and that roundup of the week section." The animation faded from her face. "Eileen, he's insane on this subject. He's twenty years older than me, right? He figures it's now or never for him."

"And my old man says you're fertile. So that leaves only one thing."

Lenore's head was shaking from side to side before Eileen finished. "If I ask Vince to jerk off for some doctor he'll bust my jaw."

"He's struck you before?"

Lenore's lush mouth tightened. Her full lips pressed together. She said nothing but her eyes transmitted the message. Silently, she sipped her coffee. "So," Eileen went on, "how much leeway do you figure you have?"

Lenore patted her lips with a paper napkin. "I figure if I'm not pregnant by Christmas that's it. Curtains."

"It's the easiest thing in the world to get an injunction and police protection. I could have you in protective custody by this evening."

Once again Lenore's head was denying this as it was being said. "You don't understand what I come from, Eileen. If I went to the cops my own family, my own brothers, wouldn't protect me. We don't bring anything to the cops. Ever."

"You just let them hustle you off to the boneyard, is that it?"

Lenore chewed her muffin for a moment to delay an answer. Then, after another sip of coffee: "We're in two worlds, Eileen. You're in the legal world, right? I'm in the other one."

"Lenore, what if I told you they are one and the same world?"

Lenore shrugged. "It still wouldn't help me."

"What if I told you I just took on the biggest case of my career and it's involved with a company called Ricci Entertainments, Inc."

A shocked silence fell over the coffee shop. It lasted several seconds before being broken first by a loud hissing from the three-tank coffee maker. Then a city bus moved by outside in a blast of engine rattle.

Lenore's perfectly smooth forehead furrowed very slightly between her great, dark eyes. "You're suing Vince?"

"It's more complicated than that. But nobody's above the law," Eileen told her. "Everybody's answerable. Even a husband who threatens his wife."

"You're going to bring Vincent J. Ricci into court?"

"If I can."

A tremendous grin lit up Lenore's face. "My God, Eileen, I believe you! But how's that going to help me?"

Eileen's hand covered Lenore's. "Maybe we could help each other."

The grin got broader. "You mean I could help you send Vince to the slams? With all his clout? How?"

Eileen squeezed her hand. "That's the least he deserves for not giving us a sperm sample."

Outside the coffee shop one taxi stopped for a fare. A second, following too closely, banged bumpers with it. The two cabbies got out onto the melting asphalt and began screaming at each other.

The philanthropic section of Richland Bank and Trust Co., NA, was not housed in the sleek spindle of Richland Tower. It occupied two rooms of a modest Richland branch below 34th Street, once a tatty imports area but, with the arrival of New York's publishing industry, filled with publishing's prime need, chic restaurants.

Formed by buying out smaller banks with stupid managements, Richland was at first all but unknown in a city of major banks. Its public relations officer had suggested the bank give to worthy causes and handle the accounts of such institutions on a no-charge, high-interest, preferred-customer basis. And publicize this policy.

Within a few years Richland was positioned as a "caring" entity, so much so that a philanthropy manager had had to be hired. The "acting" prefix to her title prepared April Garnet's exit if the job didn't work out. In her experience, it rarely did. Profit always won over philanthropy.

That had been before meeting Charley, which she considered her great good fortune. She knew she had an intimidating facade for the average office, far too exotic with her leprechaun face. And almost past the child-bearing nubility that attracted older men to fresh bodies with tender brains.

She had the kind of beauty that works best addressing an audience or camera. Up close, most men faltered and fled. Charley had not, nor would he. In his understated way he was also an exotic. His bloodlines spoke of faraway places and banked fires of interest in matters that surprised her.

Successful men in their middle years often talked about changing their lives. The rich man who had loaned her his house on the river was an example. But only Charley had that eccentric Sicilian streak.

"It'll take decades," he warned her, waving his arms. "The electorate is so ignorant it doesn't know how little it knows. Then it goes to the polls and . . . You see what kind of presidents it elects."

"But that means starting with the youngest students," she pointed out. "It's too expensive, Charley. The voters know that teaching children is a bottom-level activity. The teachers know it when they look at their pay checks."

"Nevertheless . . ."

She began testing his commitment to change the only way she knew. His MACA construction firm, with gravel and cement plants scattered all over the land, was a prime polluter. She got him to fit smokestacks with filtration units. By then they had become lovers but not yet close friends.

He was good to look at and intelligent without flaunting it. Also he liked women, that was obvious. In Manhattan these three attributes tended to isolate him on a pedestal with a very small peer group. He was sexually adventurous, Garnet had found, as much as she was. This spoke of good early training, undoubtedly at the hands of his cousin, Stefi.

From being an interesting date, he had escalated into her one and only love. It had happened almost without her knowing it, certainly without her willing it. One and only loves were dangerous. They could tear out your heart. Since her husband Gerry she had avoided them. But Charley seemed here to stay.

For her second try at greening Charley Richards, she pinpointed a Richland oil company in Western Pennsyl-

vania. It held leases on wells long capped because they
withdrew crude at prices too high for profit. Now the
price of oil was rising. But these wells were in a national
park devoted to hiking, fishing and admiring nature. Reopening them would deface and destroy this far more
important resource, beauty.

"Leave them closed," she pleaded.

"Garnet," Charley had explained. He always used her
last name after she confessed she had tacked on the April
when she had been a fashion model. Had she been a full-
blooded Hopi, her tribal name would have been Garnet
Two Snows. "Garnet, I'm not in love with the oil business. I'd like some other oil company to buy those leases.
They'll only do it if the wells are pumping. How else can
we prove they're not dry?"

"Are they?"

"Only one way to find out."

"Catch-22?"

Some she won. Some she lost. Between them a great
give-and-take began.

When she said she'd led a Raggedy-Ann life she was
recalling tragedies of love and other betrayals. She felt
she was capable of greater things than being flopped about
by fate. Having once flashed to the top, she hoped to rise
again, more patiently. She knew she could sway people.
The reason they paid serious attention to her was perhaps
only a trick of her looks or her voice. But she had that
kind of larger-than-human dimension that people turn to
for leadership as flowers wheel about seeking the sun.

And so did Charley. He was big enough for her. Together they could both get what they wanted.

As much as their physical attraction for each other, this
matching of goals defined their romance. Like most people past their extreme youth, a practical strain ran through
their relationship. It was passionate but rose above passion. It was almost doggedly romantic.

Il Professore. She loved him for that streak of scholar's
impracticality. She felt sure his uncle didn't. But the Professor had so abundantly enriched the old man that, no
matter how powerful, the uncle couldn't stand in the way
of their happiness. Each year his age reduced the span of
the time at his control.

Not that Charley had all the time in the world. But if

he slowed the pace of his attack, he could trickle his way to victory. And if his uncle, suddenly alarmed, began to fight back, surely his own human feelings would stop him. His better nature would soften his heart. Humans did that.

Surely Zio Italo had a human heart.

Twelve

There is a certain profile that airport security and customs guards watch for. The suspect—it doesn't matter of what crime—is young, wears athletic footgear, a T-shirt, a backpack, messy hair and dark glasses.

This was not, however, why Customs and Excise inspectors hauled Kevin Ricci out of the "Nothing to Declare" passage after Cathay Pacific had taken him without incident from Singapore to London's Heathrow Airport. The obvious reason they stopped Kevin was that, having no check-in luggage, he was the first passenger through. It is necessary, at Customs and Excise, to have one horrible example, belongings scattered, to show the other passengers. The fact that Kevin filled the profile for smuggler-terrorist-junkie-troublemaker was, in Customs and Excise's view, gravy.

He was carrying three microprocessor-databanks each the size of a pocket notebook, trademarked Thinkman and manufactured in South Korea, two meant as gifts for his Aunt Isabel's boys. All were instantly confiscated by Customs and Excise, which arrogates the authority to do anything, including search anal, glottal and vaginal passages, although not always simultaneously.

It took them a while to realize that they couldn't access his Thinkmen without a coded password. After peevishly messing them up with magnetic radiation, these were reluctantly returned to Kevin with a warning.

"And welcome to Britain," he called as he left.

Aunt Isabel was his mother's kid sister, married to Jack Winfield, brother-in-law to Charley of the magnificent view for which Kevin would gladly kill. If Il Professore's

estranged wife, Missy, showed a mid-life addiction to
cocaine, Jack had early blossomed as a scapegrace drop-
out, thanks to a family weakness for alcohol.

Now a member of Alcoholics Anonymous, he had been
taught the rudiments of finance by Charley and sent to
head up the important Richland Securities office in London. He did well, especially after he learned to call an
elevator a lift and a roast a joint. Isabel had been a pillar
of strength, producing two sons christened Rupert and
Peregrine.

While Jack was busy in the City being a Brit money-
wallah, Isabel swanned about in Laura Ashley prints to
her ankles, green Wellington boots and, in town or out,
a sleeveless Barbour quilt-jacket of which it could be said
that water was not the only thing it repelled.

It all tickled her nephew Kevin, although he did hate
to hear little Rupert and Peregrine refer to their Coke as
Cake. The boys, of course, would say it any way he
wanted as long as they could play with his Thinkman.
When he produced their two, joy went positively nuclear
in noise level.

"Kev, you shouldn't," Isable chided him. "They must
have cost the earth."

He remembered when Iz used to say "cost an arm and
a leg." He hadn't visited her in several months, during
which time her British accent had accelerated into hy-
perdrive.

In Jack's den, Kevin found a modem and linked up his
Thinkman. Then he dialed a New York City number that
rang only on Zio Italo's big oak rolltop desk at the San
Gennaro on Dominick Street.

"Buon giorno, Zio."

Italo's voice sounded frail. It was dinner time in Britain but in Manhattan he was taking a short nap after an
organic lunch of one Granny Smith apple, with skin,
scrubbed by himself with a brush and suds, plus two
small oakcakes. Frugal as the meal was, it required a
nap afterward.

Needing to rest was something new for the once fast-
thinking, once energetic old man. He was sure nobody
in the family was yet aware of his failing powers. He was
wrong.

"Charley?" Italo asked, clearing his throat several times. "Charley, when'll you be here?"

"It's Kev, from London."

"Of course it is. How's the boy?"

"Still a moving target. Listen, Zio, some Customs clowns were messing with my Thinkman. I want to dump down your line and let your computerheads figure out what they did or didn't do and what they got, if anything. Capeesh?"

"D'accordo." Kevin could hear a click. "Go ahead, Kev."

He started high-speed downloading of his Thinkman, via modem. When finished, he spoke again. "Zio, maybe these clowns had a contract on me."

"Was this the stuff you phoned me about from Singapore?"

"All the nuts and bolts of how he pulled it off."

"Where is it written a Customs snoop can't be bought? Whadya think they got from your Thinkman?"

"Fagioli. They didn't have access passwords. But you never know."

There was hesitation at Italo's end. Then "Listen, giovinotto, the reason I thought you were Charley . . ." His voice trailed off. Three thousand miles away Kevin reacted with surprise at the mighty Zio Italo feeling he had to justify his behavior. ". . . Is that he's due here now for a big sitdown. That's why I— Give my love to Isabel, OK? Tell her to find you one of those cute British girlies."

"Zio, this is Kev, not Vince."

How one feels the day after an opium night is never predictable. In Lord Mace's instance, how he felt was also conditioned by the fact that he had received a number one dressing down from Shan Lao. It didn't make sense. Shan rarely raised his voice above a librarian's murmur. Here he was, eyes bulging, giving Mace hell for delaying by a week or two some silly scribble his son had sent him.

"I understand," Mace said in a voice as humble as a British lord being told off by a slant-eyed upstart can sound. "It won't happen again, Shan."

"What makes me raise my voice, Hugo, is not simply

your unconscionable delay with Nik's communication.''

Shan was seated at a magnificent carved teak desk in his Victoria Park house. Behind him stood several packed bags. As usual he was off to another home. He seemed to roam the Far East like a typhoon. "What excites my apprehension," he continued with fearful slowness, "is the provenance of this facsimile transmission.''

Lord Mace winced at the polysyllabicity. Try, where the fax came from, he suggested silently. "Its originating point?" he asked out loud.

"A machine in the Park Avenue duplex of Charles Richards' wife.''

"Dear me." The Englishman put on a suitably shocked face.

"We knew Nik was seeing the younger daughter, Elizabeth?''

"Called Bunny.''

"But we had no idea he had been a guest of the mother. Baxter Choy confirms this from New York. My wife adds that my son accompanied the daughter down from Boston as a guest at a Ricci wedding. Do you fathom my meaning?''

"You mean the . . . ?" Lord Mace let his voice trail off. One of the documented aftereffects of an opium night is severe memory dysfunction. He had no idea what had gotten up Shan's nose. By now the fear was thick enough to choke a man.

"I mean the helicopter episode.''

Now both men fell silent, Shan examining a sheaf of letters, annotating some, signing others, Lord Mace trying to remember what in Hell's own name the helicopter episode could be. Then he remembered. He winced.

"Christ," he croaked. "Oh, Christ.''

"My son was apparently there in the center of things, an unconscionable risk. Suppose, for one horrid moment, that we had called for a grenade launcher rather than a marksman's rifle? If you think I spoke too plainly to you this morning, consider what I had to tell Choy.''

"But still," the Englishman replied, trying to ease the fear, "he must have handled himself splendidly, young Nik. I mean it is no bad thing to have such a trusted agent right in the bloody center of things, is it now?''

Shan looked up from his teak desk. The effect of contact lenses on his great black irises and pupils overpowered the rest of his eye conformation, as if the black centers had swollen enormously. "You think that wise?" Shan asked in a voice so devoid of humanity that Lord Mace couldn't tell if he thought the idea good or bad. "You consider the risk justified?"

"I think it bears thinking about," Mace temporized lamely.

"I think thinking is not your long suit, Hugo." Shan's chirrup held no mirth at all. "Let me do that part of it. Next." He frowned at a list on his desk. "We had to cause to deprogram some data at Heathrow, contained in one of our Thinkman databanks, the ones we make in Korea. You recall the problem? It concerns that break-in at the Singapore offices of Daiwa."

This time the Englishman's memory functioned perfectly. "They got the details of that 1987 market crash."

"If they feel the need to know precisely what happened, it may mean they suspect what I have in mind for them."

Shan got to his feet. He clapped his hands twice. In a world of electronic communication it still pleased him to summon his employees in such an archaic manner. Two men entered so quickly they had to have been waiting just outside the door. Shan indicated the packed bags and they removed them instantly. He was on his way to Burma next, a rough trip into the interior to visit one of his most lucrative investments. In addition to outdoor clothing, he had packed fine-mesh insect netting. He would be among violent, brutish men, all of whom feared him but feared their local warlord even more. It was an unusual position for Shan, to command respectful fear yet stand a step below supreme authority. One of his objectives on this trip was to determine if he should let this condition continue. Or correct it.

"Of one thing we must be very careful," Shan told his British employee. He paused for a long time to emphasize his words. "We cannot alarm the Richland people prematurely. Choy, who is on the scene, understands this quite well. Having an agent at the Richland center is perfectly acceptable. But when his surname is Shan, we raise risks more murderous than even the helicopter scheme."

He was gone. Lord Mace blinked and shook his head. Shan had been here, bigger than life, using up all the space and oxygen as was his wont, and now he had vanished, leaving an aura of fear. But the shakes had begun inside the Englishman. They would take quite a few pink gins to calm.

Damn opium.

Thirteen

Problems had developed with a chain of TV stations being bought on the West Coast; the time difference had messed up Charley's schedule. This morning, a day later, he sat in the back room of the San Gennaro Club on Dominick Street. He tried to look masterful. But in the pale light from high dusty windows, the room seemed dominated not by Italo so much as his huge oak desk. Seeing it reminded Charley that such a monstrous piece of furniture not only starred in his nightmare but also in the play, *The Front Page*, where it was big enough to hide a man. Instead of a fugitive from justice, this one held rows of pigeonholes and the monitor screen for a PC with a keyboard but no printer.

"Caro Zio," Charley placed a printed list in Italo's hand. "In dollars, your half is worth double my half. But it's only right we split that way."

Garnet had warned him not to do it this way. The list would look too intimidating, too aggressive. She had suggested a piecemeal thing, one or two companies and then a moratorium until Italo's fears receded.

Charley could hear the sheet of paper rattle dryly as his uncle's hand quivered beneath it. Dabbing at the blood. "Why, Charley? Tell me why? First do that."

"Off the top of my head, as I told you, like all legitimate businesses, ours have cut corners. They can no longer masquerade as being totally clean."

Italo made a noise, half grunt, half disgusted belch. "Make sense."

"Take food handling, the safety of meat and poultry

and dairy products. When health inspectors swoop, they're like any jungle predator, they go for the weakest. I want FoodUsa to look impregnable. Attack some other company. Don't mess with Ricci power. Understand?''

"That can't be your only argument. It stinks."

"The whole question of going public. Each of these legit companies is privately owned, tracking back to our *anstalt* in Liechtenstein. Each will come under major merger buy-out offers. Before that happens, I want our—your—identity of interest to disappear in a series of public stock issues while you retain control through a majority interest bought in street names.''

He paused and watched his uncle's hooded glance, bright with malice. Maybe Garnet's way could help. "Zio, we don't take out a full page ad in the *Wall Street Journal*. This will be done informally, piecemeal. To our own people it'll look like what it is: Charley wants to concentrate on financial, so he's turning over the rest. That's the truth of it.''

This time the older man's silence seemed to grow until it filled the room. "The truth of it," he echoed suddenly, his eyes zeroing in on Charley. The hand that held the printed list suddenly clutched it so violently that the paper creased in a dozen angry folds like a washrag used to sponge blood from packets of $100 bills. "The truth," the old man told him, "is you're so used to imitating a tennis-playing nutless Wasp flyweight you can't wait to kick your family in the balls and start throwing away money because some half-breed *putana* mouths off your dick.''

Outside on Dominick Street a heavy truck went by with a derisive grinding of gears and a farting blast of airbrakes. Charley could feel the same stress building inside him, but he spoke quietly. "Zio, I have served the family for more than tw—''

"Served?" Italo's voice made the word into a lance, hissing in flight. "You served us? You're an employee? A clerk? What the fuck is a family, Charley, is it some corporation you work for and then move on?''

"You know damned well I—''

"I know you lust for respectability." Remembering the relatives in the front room playing cards, he lowered his voice almost to a whisper. But it began to rise again anyway. "I have watched you over the years, Professore mio. I have seen the virus catch hold of you. Your Wasp wife infected you. Now this Indian has finished you off. You're burning up with it. You buy the whole lie. All the hypocrisies on which this country is built."

"Zio, look here, you—"

"You look. This country was founded on theft and massacre and slavery. Like all countries. Niggers and Redskins like her were the first. Now a few kikes and goombahs and Mick donkeys have a little control. Now and then they let us send somebody to the Supreme Court or the White House. They let us run a few cities, a few corporations. Window dressing!" He drew a deep, trembling breath. "Tell me something, you dumb guinea bastard: Lee Iacocca hijacked an established name, Chrysler. Could you have put together Richland Holdings if you hadn't borrowed a nice white, Anglo-Saxon Protestant name like Richards?"

By lunch time the tension had only tightened. The West Coast TV stations were under FCC investigation. It wasn't Richland Securities giving Charley trouble. What wore him down were Richland Holdings' other businesses, from TV stations to employment agencies. His head felt like a bale of cotton whose tight steel bands had been removed. Wisps of Charley streamed in the breeze.

Into his phone he said, "Counsellor, how's your calendar today for lunch?"

"Dad?" Winfield asked.

Whatever the weather, Winfield thought as she walked toward Central Park, they would meet at the corner of 60th Street and Fifth Avenue. Today they would have their choice of snack carts, from kielbasa and salsiccie picante to Nathan's all-beef hot dogs and other pseudophallic eats.

A boy called Alec at Cambridge had tediously explained to her that she was abnormally father fixated, that she had clearly had sexual relations with Charley but was suppressing the memory, that she was a big girl and needed weaning away from the paternal penis. To his. When he had finally run down, Winfield recalled now, she had pushed Alec into the Charles River. He'd nearly died of hypothermia. As a result of such treatment he kept calling her from Nebraska, suggesting he come east for a visit. "And a swim in the Hudson," Winfield responded, hanging up.

She got to the rendezvous corner a bit early and stood there watching people. Once in a while an older man came past with a younger woman. She found herself wondering if Alec had been right.

Her recall went back to her second year of life. It was now held in check by an IQ well beyond 150. She recalled kisses and hugs; nothing else. Bunny might remember, but asking Bunny was like sticking your head through a target and handing a loaded gun to the next stranger.

She could see him before he caught sight of her. He looked rundown, shoulders slumped. He bore two cans of Diet Coke and two souvlakis in pittas, shedding strips of lettuce as he walked.

"Straighten up!" she called. "Look good!"

He scowled. "The story of my life."

They found a bench near a balloon man, busy filling bright spheres with helium. "Any day that begins with being abused by Zio Italo . . ." Charley muttered.

"He doesn't want a separation?"

"I gave him a load of financial bullshit," her father confessed. "I know he didn't believe a word of it. But I've already told him my real reasons."

"Real reasons?" Winfield removed a shredded raw onion from her souvlaki and flung it in a nearby waste container. "He'd never buy them. It would never occur to him that the nice, clean-cut Professore in whom he's invested a lot of money could get nauseated by the whole thing."

"Did I tell you I gave another lecture? At NYU?"

"What horrible deficiencies did you uncover in your students?"

"Nobody knew what the equator was, or where it was. None of them knew what the Common Market was. Or the solar system. Or syphilis. Or Lillian Gish."

"What a thrill for you. Verifies your darkest suspicions."

"Lay off, Winfield. It's enough to be fighting off Zio. I've been the tightrope that leads from Ricci blood money to Richland legitimacy. Now I want off the wire, easy landing, and I'm willing to pay for it. My God, am I willing.''

''But Zio has no idea what you mean by blood money.''

Charley shook his head. He had yet to bite into his souvlaki. ''It's like asking a fish to describe water.'' He chuckled so mournfully that a tall man and a short man, passing by with hot dogs, looked curiously at him. ''It's so damned unfair, Winfield. I was urged all my life to come on like a Wasp parfit knight. Everything, my education, my marriage. Even my kids. Any time I could spend with you two was eaten up by business, business.'' He stopped and started again. ''Now he abuses me for behaving like what I became. What I *am*.''

''We had you on Sundays,'' Winfield said. ''It's what they call quality time. I remember visiting Grandpa's deli. Stop looking so glum. Straighten up. Zio isn't invincible.''

''No?'' He thought for a moment of telling her why Cousin Pino had died. But it would only frighten her. ''Just a nice cuddly little old nono, huh?''

She smiled crookedly. Her voice remained quite cool. ''The kind who has chauffeurs knocked off to teach nephews a lesson.''

''You m—?''

''Except there are some nephews who have already bought their own clip-on Parsifal halo. Listen, I'm on your side. I'm rooting for you. If you have banners printed up, I'll wave them. But you're moving too fast.''

''That's what Garnet says.'' A heavy sigh escaped him. ''And Stefi's dead-set against it. The three of you can't understand that the only way is to trip Zio off his feet and lasso his forelegs like a heifer for branding.''

''The three weird sisters have flashed you a red light. Hit the brakes.''

''Zio would see it as a confession of weakness.''

''That's the trouble with being a mutant,'' Winfield observed calmly. ''You're caught in a crossfire. From now on you'll keep clashing with Zio till one of you . . .''

''Say it.''

But she couldn't trust her voice anymore, with its cool cadences. Instead she bit into her lunch and chewed furiously. Both of them knew she didn't really have to finish the thought aloud, anyway.

* * *

The tall man and short man found an empty bench. The balloon man at the Zoo made a howling sound with his helium tank like a soul being expelled from Heaven. Nose Cohen munched mournfully on a hot dog with greasy onions.

He was too young to remember Gary Cooper in any but his middle-aged roles, notably as the *High Noon* sheriff. So many people had remarked on Cohen's resemblance that he thought of himself in terms of Cooper moves, expressions.

If he ever left the Bureau, he promised himself, in moments of despair, he'd do a memoir, "I was a Jew for the FBI," and try acting. He'd actually found another Jew in the Bureau and they had started having lunch.

Gordon Stuart was his name, or rather his first and middle names, the patronymic having been abandoned. Gordon was squat and Italian-looking, which gave him strong street credibility. "These are not Nathan's franks," he announced after chewing on his. "These are not even all-beef franks, goddammit."

"Another failure." Nose's mournful expression, brooding and closed-off, resembled Cooper's when the townspeople refused to help him capture the bad men. "I got my ass racked back," he went on in a low drawl. "I needed a make on a kid who blew me up with a smart-ass question. Goddard, the seminar director, swore everything was on video so it'd be no problem getting a few blowups and ID."

"Surprise," Gordon muttered into his second substandard hot dog. "No tape."

"Malfunction. And Goddard's too busy to help. Is that my fault?"

"Of course it is, Nose."

"I have a name. Stop calling me Nose."

"OK, Noah. OK."

Silently, they chewed on. Then Nose said, trying not to sound bitter, "When is the Bureau going to realize that the Hebes *invented* organized crime? Agents like you and me, we've got it in our bones."

"Whadya mean, invented? You forgetting the maf?"

"All the wops knew was how to fight among themselves. It took Meyer Lansky and Longie Zwillman and

Dutch Schultz to show them how to organize and invest.
Without Meyer, the goombahs'd still be laying for each
other in alleys."

"And with him, they now own the world?"

"And maybe Lutjens, Van Kurve and Armatrading."

"Nose, give it up. Noah."

"Not me, Shorty." Cohen's jaw set in a Gary Cooper
line, wrinkled but firm. "My blood tells me that kid is
one of the protected species. That's why the video went
bust. I know I'm hooked into something much bigger.
All I have to do is convince Suggs, my supervisor."

Gordon balled up his bits of greasy paper and scored
a long hook into a wastebasket ten feet away. "You're
the Bureau clown. That's your assignment. You go out
and josh the yulds. Leave the bad guys to mean little
fuckers like me."

The balloon man produced a loud moan, tied off a red
globe with a long string and handed it to a four-year-old
who promptly let go of the string. Brilliant in the July
sunshine, the crimson sphere shot high overhead. Nose
Cohen watched the child break into tears. He looked
down at his failed hot dog and, bettering Gordon's shot,
dropped an overhead into the same basket. As he did so,
a man consigned most of a souvlaki to the same receptacle. He walked off with a terrific-looking tall girl young
enough to be his daughter.

"My type," Gordon Stuart moaned. "Face to face I
stand high enough to nibble her tits without crouching."

"You agents," Nose muttered sarcastically. "So
sexy." He watched the free balloon disappearing high,
high overhead and wondered when, if ever, life would
cut him loose and give him a break.

Fourteen

At the far 54th Street end of the Museum of Modern Art,
the bright, high-ceilinged, birchwood members' dining
room had been roped off for a cocktail party.

Along a sunny, west-facing wall of glass, people milled

about or stood gazing at the garden below in which white birches bowed to the command of the great steel breasts, brutal thighs and leering belly of Lachaise's monumental dominatrix. Inside, along the walls without windows, hung several dozen oils and watercolors. "Native American Graphic Arts Since 1980," a placard read. They had a common source but looked quite dissimilar, each taking a different path away from "looking Indian."

At a table color brochures sold for $20 each ($15 to members). Another placard, quite small, announced: "Through the assistance of Richland Bank and Trust Company NA—all proceeds to the Hopi-Kiowa-Zuni Nations Charitable Trust." It was behind this table that Charley Richards stood against one wall, watching people come and go. He knew quite a few of them. If they'd spotted him, he would have had to make small talk about the art on display. But no one noticed Charley in the same room where Dr. Garnet stood. She was surrounded by people asking her to autograph the brochure.

Because she had burst on Charley like a comet he often forgot that she had already taken Manhattan by storm fifteen years before. Now she was beginning to assume again that special New York aura, the Flavor of the Year, not as a model but as one of the country's most respected ecologists.

She was in her element, people in the process of falling in love with her. Charley watched her face light up the room and the people with whom she spoke. A soft smile lingered on their faces. They had given her the power to enchant them and now they basked in that enchantment. Charley knew the feeling. No matter what kind of mood he fell into, she had the power of surmounting it for him. He had no idea that her power came from his faith in her.

Watching the growing circle around Garnet made him ache with joy. He had never felt this about anyone else. Winfield? She could inspire pride and tenderness and a responsible base of intelligence, a brain far brighter than his. Yes, that was love. Of course it was. And Stefi would always be his first. But what he felt for Garnet was all that, ignited by a longing so passionate it hurt.

Charley frowned. He was a tough captain of industry. He was locked in a macho battle to become independent

of Zio Italo. Was this the man to stand around mooning
like a love-struck kid? Suddenly, he was aware that Garnet was watching him over the heads of her circle of
admirers. She mimicked his frown, then produced a smile
so brilliant that, at a distance of many yards, Charley felt
it strike its bull's-eye, him, and him alone. "Just remember," she had warned him once, "garnets are redder than
rubies. We're the color of blood." Those Indians, he
thought; deadly with bow and arrow. He clutched at his
heart and mimed both death and transfiguration.

"But that's not why we're here this afternoon," Garnet
was saying now to an older woman. "You can hear me
on my ecology soapbox any time."

"You can't tell me native Americans aren't affected by
ecological issues."

"More than the rest of us?" People continued their
centripetal swirl, closing in on her, until almost no one
was inspecting the paintings. "When we try to estimate
how destroying the forests swells the world's termite population and bloats its deadly contribution to our methane
balance. Can you imagine . . . ?"

Charley's luck with methane hadn't been too brilliant.
Most of his sophomore listeners had no idea what it was,
how it polluted the atmosphere and how it could be
trapped and burned instead of petroleum products. But
then, these nineteen- and twenty-year-olds hadn't heard
of FDR, couldn't locate Vietnam, had no idea what the
difference was between an American president and the
Queen of England or how a lightbulb worked.

The crowd around Garnet was growing with new ar-
rivals every moment. It really didn't matter why they
flocked to her, Charley knew. It was their destiny, just
as it was his to love her and make sure she was protected.

It was a different world outside the museums and galleries. There was every reason for Richland Bank and
Trust to subsidize her. But there was no reason why others, whose interests she attacked, might not attack her.

"Oh, no," Eileen said. She slumped back in her desk
chair as if suddenly deflated. Her small thirtieth-floor
suite of offices, Hegarty & Krebs, lay in silence. "I interviewed you twice. I read your school transcripts. Margaret Krebs interviewed you. I even looked at those

sample briefs you gave me. But where was I supposed to trace your family tree? The FBI? Where?''

Both of them sat in silence for a long time. ''It's a problem, isn't it?'' Winfield went on at last. The day had been laden with problems, most of them unloaded at lunch by a father who had suddenly jumped headlong into midlife crisis. Winfield, like most Sicilians, took her family responsibilities with deadly seriousness. She saw her father as diverted from self-defense and thus perilously exposed to an enemy with the morals of a sewer rat. And she saw herself as the only Ricci more ratlike than Zio Italo.

''The risk is there,'' Eileen went on doggedly, in what attorneys who opposed her in court referred to as the Hegarty Death Hold, a kind of wrestling grip that never, never lets go. ''Not that you'd betray me, Winfield, I know you're a fine girl. But the risk is that Cousin Vince will have you snatched and dispatched.''

''Eileen, it could happen to you. And what's to prevent it happening to Lenore, your new mole?''

''She more likely than anyone else,'' Eileen agreed.

This time they were silent for several minutes. ''What the hell am I to do?'' Eileen asked. ''I'm getting ready to defend in what could become the biggest AIDS case to hit America. I don't need all these conflicts of interest.''

''I read the depositions you gave me,'' Winfield agreed. Her voice indicated she was unimpressed. ''But right now it's only low-level criminal action. The john is an orthodontist. He's asking millions in damages because his career is shot. Even so, the case is tacky. To tart it up, forgive the pun, I can see the possibility of us adding other prostitutes as co-conspirators. Still not enough. Nowhere as sexy an AIDS lawsuit as that Rock Hudson inheritance or the Liberace thing.''

''That's a pretty cold-blooded view.''

Winfield shrugged. ''Do you think we can get anything useful out of this Dr. Battipaglia? Some hint that he was under orders to say all the girls were clean even if he knew they weren't?''

''We can try. Then what?''

''One of my few female classmates at Harvard Law is here in the Manhattan DA's office. Leona Kane. She's an assistant district attorney.'' Winfield paused. ''The whole nature of the case would change if the DA got into this.''

''You'd throw your cousin to the lions?''

''You see,'' Winfield said in a casual tone, ''from the outside, mafia families look impenetrable. Monolithic. But everything in the mafia is fear-based. Inside the family, the women are kept in tranquilized terror. They know they're to produce meals and kids. One independent step and their life is over.'' She fell silent, her glance turned inward. Eileen had no idea what she was thinking, but it clearly pained her, this cool young lady.

Winfield blinked suddenly, as if a flashgun had gone off. ''And not just women. Anybody inside the family who wants to fulfil an independent destiny. A man, even one high up, even such a high-ranking person, for all his maleness, isn't exempt.'' She stopped and seemed to reconsider her words. But then she went on so quickly that new words tumbled over one another, rushing to be said. ''A man who wants to do something useful, to give back some of what he's appropriated. To look back on something positive, not just robot-like accumulation. What chance does he have?'' For Winfield it was an outburst. She sat in silence.

Eileen stared at her for a long time, trying to read her. When she began to speak there was a different note in her voice. ''You're thinking of someone specific.''

Winfield nodded. ''My father. He's in the most terrifying danger. Either he doesn't know it or he's play-acting to keep me from worrying.'' She paused again, as if shocked at such a personal confession. But the pressure to go on was too great to resist. ''He has this familial view of his enemies, people he's grown up with whom he can't bear to think of as humanoid pustules.''

Her voice sounded dark, almost hoarse. She stopped and very slowly pulled herself together. ''It's a pact that goes back to when Dad graduated into running the Richland interests. It blindsides him. But fortunately, I'm here to guard that side. And I will.'' Her voice had steadied and cooled. She took a long breath and recrossed her long legs quite calmly now. But Eileen would never again think of her without remembering this flash of the real Winfield.

''And you all live with this schizophrenia?'' she asked in a kidding tone. She threw up her hands. ''Oh, what the hell. You were hired on a trial basis. All juniors are. So you're still on trial. I may live to regret it. But, then, I may live to regret making a friend of Lenore.''

''No.''

''What?''

''You'll never regret either decision.'' Winfield got slowly to her feet and looked down at her petite boss. ''We Ricci women give value.'' She pulled the telephone toward her. ''I'm calling Leona Kane. OK?''

September

Fifteen

Shan Lao's Citation II jet, one of his own fleet, came in over the Gulf of Tonkin at only twenty thousand feet. Below, the jumbled spread of Hanoi, with its satellite town of Haiphong, lay in dusk. A few lights began to come on as the jet streaked west into the setting sun over Laos and the topmost border of Thailand.

Historic part of the world, Shan thought as he stared down at the darkening valleys, mountains and plains. Made historic by the idiocy of the Americans. He sniffed the deodorized interior of the jet and detected the aroma of pine.

This was the Golden Triangle, source of nearly all the heroin in the world. For this drug, tens of thousands of peoples once known as Indochinese and Burmese had fought internecine gang wars and died in government massacres. And then, beyond the drug wars, Shan mused, the political wars of the Americans in Korea and Vietnam. Yes, an historic, but bloody, land.

Anyone else in Shan's position, controlling great manufacturing and service corporations throughout the eastern Pacific rim, would be content to manage such an empire from behind a desk. It was more precise, less risky, more visibly authoritarian. The other style, which the Americans called "hands-on" management, was a concept more promised than fulfilled.

But Shan Lao enjoyed getting into the darker side of his profits. He would personally spend months softening up a trade union boss of no breeding or culture to make sure when he paid over the bribe that all of Shan Lao's auto plants were kept remarkably free of unionization. His business rivals delegated such workface effort to underlings and watched the bribes produce nothing but betrayals.

Tonight, Shan Lao, master of dustfree electronics plants, clangorous robotic assembly lines, intricate financial entities, would delve into the undergrowth of modern capitalism, some would say the bedrock upon which it was founded.

As night fell on the great Southeast Asian peninsula, the jet lost altitude and landed not in Rangoon but in Mandalay, 350 air-miles north of the capital city. A small helicopter of Chinese make, a Kai-3, was waiting. It smelled strongly of the thick, spicy stench of burning opium.

In darkness now, with two porter-bodyguards, Shan Lao was lifted a thousand feet over the Shan Plateau and ferried back almost to the Thai border. The mountains rose here to heights of seven and eight thousand feet. It was not a country for foot soldiers, much less motorized cavalry, which is why the Burmese army only pretended to try keeping it drug-free. That and the fact that, without the opium cash crop, the people of eastern Burma would starve.

Below there was no sign at all of Mong Kyawt, the deceptively small village near which General Khun Kwa kept his headquarters. Ten years ago, when CIA funding ran out, Khun Kwa had approached Shan for what he described as "development money." Originally as Chinese as Shan Lao, but now claiming descent from a hill tribe here in Eastern Burma, Khun Kwa had been a lieutenant, then captain in Chiang Kai-shek's right-wing Kuomintang army, known as the KMT. Defeated in 1949, the KMT found the CIA ready with money, weapons and transport and, with the exception of a few greedy American agents, seldom asking for a hefty cut of drug profits.

So grew the KMT and Khun Kwa with it. With the Laotian General Vang Pao, he now controlled most of the opium sold to American GIs in Saigon.

As his helicopter roared through the night, Shan Lao pictured the man he had first bankrolled, a lean, sharp-eyed hustler, lips locked most of the time in mean silence. He had that look that Shan Lao liked, a certain cast to the lower face, tightened corners of the mouth, locked molars, flared nostrils. Such a man bore an expression that told the world: I am on a mission of the gravest importance. If I fail the planet combusts and we with it and no one knows of my failure. If I succeed, nothing at all happens and none knows of my victory. Why do I do it? Someone has to.

Remembering the look, Chan smiled. Such earnest men made the best puppets.

For Shan the investment was less than the cost of establishing his Yokohama automobile plant. After five years his original seed money had been repaid, interest free, and he had gone on the books for a ten percent royalty payment. Khun Kwa would always and forever cheat him but even a thief's idea of ten percent produced millions of dollars a year for Shan. In cash.

Shan Lao had now changed into a sort of jungle suit, much-laundered American combat coveralls with many pockets and zippered closures. As he sat behind the wheel of an ancient Willys Jeep, he nodded to his porter-bodyguards, whom he left to guard the Kai-3.

He was alone now, no guides, no bodyguards. The true "hands-on" master, delving into the dark heart of cash flow. Switching to tiny slitted night-lamps, Shan set the four-wheel-drive vehicle along a dark trail that differed little from the rest of the undergrowth except for the hint of two tracks in the brush. He inhaled the damp night air. Something had died recently and whatever carrion lived in the area had yet to take care of its putrefying stench. It augured ill for his visit to be met by that charnel smell.

He could hear the cheap heavy-metal rock music even before he reached headquarters battalion. Khun Kwa claimed an army of forty thousand men. In reality he led about eight thousand, most of them boys under twelve being trained in the use of submachine guns, mortars, attack rifles, grenades and rocket launchers.

A boy sentry stepped into the dim headlamp glow, aiming an AK-47 at Shan's head. Shan identified himself. The child's eyes went wide. He had been warned that the man known to the boy army as "The Banker" was expected. Even so, it was a major event for him. Making himself useful, he perched on the hood of the Jeep, brandishing his AK-47 and shouting ahead in a loud voice, "Make way! Shan Lao approaches! Make way!"

The headquarters officers' club shook with raucous disco music. It stank of sweat and cheap alcohol. A few young men, lieutenants mostly, had brought girls from town. They did the usual apish arm gestures and cataleptic leg movements, sweating freely.

At an elevated table in the rear, just behind 100-watt amplifiers and huge loudspeakers, Khun Kwa sat drinking a particularly vicious local brandy labeled with five stars. This man, who could have bought the Hennessey or Remy Martin distilleries if he wished, had long ago declared himself a slave to the local stuff, a kind of grappa also used successfully in Zippo lighters.

He stared foolishly at Shan as the industrialist approached him. This was no meeting of equals, Khun Kwa's slumping posture announced. This was a subordinate he was allowing to approach the throne.

Seated just behind him, his young aide-de-camp, Colonel Tuong, made a little grimace of distaste. Shan had had no contact with Tuong, on purpose. He had left that to Baxter Choy, who had attended the same Irish Jesuit school with Tuong.

Shan saw at once that in the year since they'd last met, Khun Kwa had gone to fat. His small, close-set eyes seemed buried now in rings of flesh; his cheeks burned with the dull red of alcohol. That look of being on a global mission had disappeared, leaving him with the bland stare of a slab of suet.

The insolent murderer was not going to stand up, was he? Worse, he flicked a finger at a child hanger-on who now came forward, his holstered Uzi machine pistol dragging at his trouser-belt. "Hands up," he said in what was meant to be a crisp voice but only sounded high and frightened. He patted down Shan—Shan Lao!—for concealed weapons, then stepped back.

"Greetings, Banker," Khun Kwa called in a derisive tone.

"Greetings, General." Shan's voice could hardly be heard over the disco din. He sat down at Khun Kwa's table, nodded coldly to Colonel Tuong and laid his hands palms down on the damp table. Khun Kwa at close range looked and smelled like a roasting pig, oozing garlic. "Let us speak of the Caribbean," Shan began at once.

"Let us first drink." Khun Kwa slopped some five-star in a dirty glass and shoved it at Shan.

"Thank you, no," the industrialist said. "Tell me about the Caribbean. Have shipments been curtailed?"

"Drink!"

"No, thank you, General." Shan's voice had gone as dry as chalk dust.

"Then I refuse to monkey with your Caribbean shit. They get what they ordered. I don't play games with paying customers. Drink, Banker!"

Shan's head moved slowly from side to side, once, seeming as always a bit too large for his neat body. "Colonel?" he asked in a papery thin voice.

Colonel Tuong shifted slightly in his chair. A single outrageous roar deafened everyone temporarily. The S&W .357 Magnum took out the front of Khun Kwa's face. Those behind him were spattered with bluish-violet bits of the finest brain the CIA had ever trained.

For a long time no one reacted. Then someone with finer sensibilities than the rest thought to shut off the music. A lot of drinking had been going on—Khun Kwa forbade opium smoking—and by the time stunned people realized their leader was dead, Tuong had taken over with a barked series of commands. It seemed to Shan Lao that such a voice and such commands were all most people waited to hear. Life had to go on, after all. His man, Baxter Choy, had done well with his classmate, the young colonel.

The corpse was straightened up in its chair. Its ornately gilded hat was placed on its blasted head. The music began again.

In a corner two boy soldiers watched, wide-eyed, as if this were coming to them on a TV tube. Shan Lao splashed the full glass of five-star across the table to sluice any stray bits of Khun Kwa into the general's own lap. A rotting vegetable stench rose off the table top in almost visible waves. What was managing from behind a desk, compared to this? Shan Lao disciplined his face to show nothing, neither excitement nor disgust.

"Colonel Tuong. The Caribbean shipments."

"To the Ricci interests? I have ordered them stopped," the colonel assured him. He produced a bottle of Johnnie Walker Black and poured two clean glasses half full. "To loyalty," he said. "You may always be sure of mine."

"To loyalty," Shan Lao echoed. "As mine is pledged to you."

Both of them lifted their glasses to the corpse with the gilded hat brim. The neat, smoky smell of the whisky was a cleansing antidote. Shan Lao began mentally computing what his royalty would be once Tuong had agreed to up it to twenty percent.

He saw that a small sliver of brain had nestled between his thumb and index finger. He shook it off. And the band played on.

Sixteen

Manhattan is full of smart little bars and restaurants whose chief claim to custom is that one cannot possibly run into anyone one knows. This is a big-city delusion in which people committing middle-class adultery put a lot of faith.

Thoughts of this kind flickered through Lenore Ricci's mind as she sat in a tiny Second Avenue bistro not far from Dr. Eiler's 72nd Street offices. She nursed a long Planter's Punch made with Myers Rum while her escort finished his third very dry Noname Vodka Martini straight up, lemon peel, dash of gin.

Thy myth that vodka could not be detected on one's breath was not the only unscientific belief held by Buzz Eiler. Another was the pleasure of starting an affair with a patient. Lenore had never cheated on Vince with anyone. But autumn in New York signaled, to her mind, her last season on earth.

Vince was in the Caribbean tonight. As long as she got home in time for his usual check-up phone call, she was safe. Buzz had come on to her for this date, so her conscience was half-clear. The other half was racked with guilt; she would be cheating on her best friend. Over the summer months she and Eileen had created an alliance that, in Lenore's mind, was stronger than any formed during her school years. And now, she thought, watching Buzz's face get redder with drink, I'm panicking and trying to make sure Vince gets himself a kid. Panicking and destroying Eileen's marriage thereby.

"You *see* any of your other patients?" she asked suddenly. The use of the verb "to see" had its normal Manhattan copulatory meaning.

Buzz blinked. His kewpie cheeks looked inflamed. "You're not my patient, Mrs. Ricci," he said, quoting an old Thurber cartoon, "you're my meat." When she didn't smile, he rushed on suddenly, trying to lie his way back into her good graces. "I've never felt this way about any of my other patients."

"What way? Drunk?"

He managed to look hurt. Any further play-acting was cut short when his beeper began shrilling. He glanced at the LCD readout. "Have to get back to the office." He threw some money on the table and helped her to her feet.

Escorting her out of the bistro, he watched the way her long, slim calves tapered down to very narrow ankles on four-inch heels. A lump rose in his throat. He had to have her. Had to! Thank God the office was so close or he'd have had to lift her by the armpits and pin her against the checkroom wall.

God, what a thing he had for small women!

In Eileen's experience, when Buzz said he'd be working late, he rarely got in till midnight. She had, of course, long ago recognized the implausibility of his actually working that late. Patients had their own lives to live in the evening hours, even if he didn't. But, occasionally, he'd be called to an emergency case at one of the three hospitals which were happy to count him as a consultant. The rest of the time? Well, what sort of framework for a marriage could a wife construct around the central fact that her husband was inside other women all day long? He came home smelling of them. Eileen had learned not to insist on him taking a shower after work. A miner's wife had that right. She didn't.

This night, expecting Buzz late, she'd gone early to bed and was reading over the transcript of a pre-trial hearing with Salvatore Battipaglia, M.D., the incompetent who had assured her clients they were disease-free. Dr. Battipaglia was still on the Ricci payroll, but he turned out to be a painfully honest man: "You know how it is. You look at a hundred women a weekend, you get rushed, maybe careless. You don't always check your nurse keeps the specimen labels straight. Maybe once she doesn't. But that's just carelessness. That's only human, am I wrong? That's only to be expected.''

Running a pale yellow marker through this paragraph, Eileen heard the front door of their flat open. "Buzz?"

"Hiya-hiya-hiya."

Drunk, Eileen decided, although he was a floor below and several rooms away. She heard him blundering around in the dark and then the sound of the downstairs shower. He'd evidently had so arduous a day that even he knew he needed the aroma of women hosed off.

Ten minutes later he appeared naked at the bedroom door, his stocky figure looking pale beige, his blond body hair giving him the frosted look of a children's maxi-sugar breakfast cereal. "Evening, Mrs. Eiler."

"You're early," she said, putting her reading aside.

He glanced at a wrist bare of timepieces. "Ten-fifteen," he read there.

"You OK?"

"M'fine, Mrs. Eiler. Few marts witha boys."

She watched him advance on her slowly, uncertainly. Something other than sex was on his mind. He was standing now by her side of the big bed. "Looking mighty tasty tonight, Mrs. Eiler."

She watched in surprise as he slowly sank to his knees. "Gooda nuff to eat," he mumbled, trying to spread her legs to the gynecological angle. Eileen started to giggle as she turned out the light.

Lenore answered on the eleventh ring, just to give Vince a bit of a heart flutter. Nothing got a Sicilian male more upset than the suspicion that his wife was enjoying the same sex life he was. "What took you so long?" he demanded.

"I was asleep, Vince. How's the Bahamas?"

There was a pause, during which she visualized him giving a big wink to whatever totsy was sharing his bed at the moment. She would be a big one with tits like Volkswagens. "Humidity's near a hundred. See you tomorrow night."

"Looking forward to—" she stifled a yawn, "—it. Bye."

As she had earlier this evening, she got the distinct

impression that another thread had been woven into the fabric of her betrayal of Eileen. But, Christ, the stakes were too high to pause now.

Buzz Eiler was not overweight, just tended that way. His breakfast was black coffee, no sugar and two slices of Danish cardboard labeled health cracker. This morning, because he was feeling so godawful, he added an orange which he was mauling to bits as he sat there in his tartan plaid bathrobe. Hangovers turned his normally dextrous fingers all thumbs. He, the inventor of the Eiler Section, was making a mess of peeling a simple orange. "You sure these are navels," he complained.

"Ask the doctor, Doctor." Eileen was dressed for a date at the District Attorney's office first thing this morning. She wore a dark blue suit and an off-white blouse with ruching at the throat. She handed him some neatly peeled segments of her own orange. "You look horrible. Is that what sex does to you?"

His face grew warm. What did she know? His head began to ache. Had he let slip anything about Lenore Ricci? "Is that some kind of insult?"

"Buzz, we have two rare events in our family. One is hangovers. The other is sex. Last night we had the latter. This morning you have the former. It's not an insult. Just an observation."

Buzz winced as memory flooded in on him. He had had both petite women, with their smooth, succulent, boyish little bodies, delicious entrees on garnished silver trays, no more than an hour apart. He swallowed the lump of lust in his throat. He could almost hear the swish of something closing around him. "I am directing the jury to disregard that," he muttered gloomily. No wonder his cock had felt used this morning in the shower. Not sore so much as overdone, like a knockwurst left too long on the grill. "So," he said with mock brightness. "What sort of day lies ahead for you, Counsellor?"

"A day of ups and downs," she said with equally mock cheer, "of random sorties into the unknown. Of justice and injustice and the gnashing of teeth. And yours?"

"A whole lotta twat."

He sipped his coffee in dead silence. Dread dropped down over him like a mantle of heavy fabric. He had done something stupid last night, the feeling told him, for which he would now pay.

The District Attorney of New York County, also known as Manhattan, keeps fairly plain offices on that part of Leonard Street, downtown, which is now called Frank Hogan Place, after a former District Attorney. Its entrance is actually a side door to the unadorned pile whose main entrance is 100 Centre Street.

In an even plainer box within, very plain Assistant District Attorney Leona Kane did business. A dejected day-lily in a pot offered a faint splash of yellow-orange against the grim window sill. What emphasized the smallness of her office was her size, on the order of Winfield's, but without the good looks. When they pecked each other ceremonially, Eileen felt like a starling watching storks. Leona Kane was obviously hoping to make quick work of the idea that the DA might enter this cheapo criminal case.

" . . . we'd have to enter dozens of other cases, which we simply haven't got the manpower to do." Her plain face looked quite severe. "So, I'm very sorry, but—"

"Why?" Winfield interrupted. "Because there's no evidence Battipaglia warned Ricci the girls were diseased? Or that Ricci told him to lie about it?"

"Isn't that key?"

"Suppose we could produce such evidence?"

The assistant DA glanced at her watch. "Richards, call me the minute you have it." She rose from her chair like a rare marsh bird, seemingly balanced on one leg. Her unlovely face brightened momentarily in a small smile.

But Winfield remained seated. "Kane, I hope you know what you're turning down. The DA who puts Vince Ricci behind bars can be this city's next mayor."

"Who's turning you down? Evidence, Richards, evidence."

Out on the streets trying to hail a cab, Eileen glanced up at her junior. "What makes you think a brand new ADA, fresh out of law school, coud even remotely harbor political ambitions?"

"I know Leona. She's not just a pretty face."

This caused Eileen some moments of hysterical laughter. "All right. Granted."

"Her way is to help men till they depend on her so utterly she has to zip their flies for them. Taxi!" The tall young woman jumped out into Centre Street and physically bullied a cruising cab to the curb. As they bundled inside, she went on, "By now, or within a few months, she will have caused someone much higher up in that office to go all limp and helpless without her. Someone with big political ambition gnawing at his vitals."

Eileen turned to watch the passing streets. "You seem even more determined to sink Cousin Vince than I do."

"Nothing personal. A tactic in a larger strategy."

"You'd better tell me what it is."

Winfield was silent for a while. "I told you the trouble my father's in. It comes from my great-uncle. He's wily but aging. If I can put Vince in real jeopardy, I can force my great-uncle to shift focus and forget . . . well, neglect some of his other targets."

In silence the two women rode northward. Eileen chewed over the meager clues her junior had given her. It sounded, even in precis, too Byzantine for close analysis. Even so, she was beginning to feel sorry for the aging great-uncle.

She glanced sideways at Winfield's calm profile, eyes downcast as if in deep thought. But what Winfield was thinking, Eileen realized, not even God would know.

Seventeen

The Caribbean was not all Ricci property.

As he lay, curled up like a cat, in the rear seat of the small STOL-craft flying back to Miami, Vince reminded himself that even without a proper maf franchise he was the uncrowned king of the area.

The resorts dotted throughout the archipelago were divided by organized crime first as to whether or not an island allowed legal gambling; if not it was considered open market. Second, they were liege to ancient fiefdoms dating back to the Cuba-based hegemony of Meyer Lansky. But along the way families like the Riccis, as the mafia put it, "dipped their bill."

The connection between Meyer and Ettore Ricci, the father of Italo, began after the First World War. Meyer was in the molasses business. When he and Bugsy Siegel branched sideways into contract murder, their first customer was Ettore.

His son, Eugenio, late lamented father of Vince, had studied icepick under Bugs and Meyer while the newspapers started calling them Murder, Incorporated. So it was only natural that when Vince finished his apprenticeship in Las Vegas and was looking to set up in a franchise area, the Caribbean boys made an opening for him on Grand Bahama. That was all a shark like Vince needed.

The resort life suited him perfectly. He looked terrific in skimpy swimming shorts, could handle large amounts of long, sweet drinks of the Zombie type, did all the latest dances and had a way with wealthy female visitors that gave them something more than snapshots to bring back to Grand Rapids, Michigan.

More important, he knew how to run a casino so it spat up every cent of profit like one of his own slot machines gone berserk. As a result, he had management contracts with other mobs to run their Caribbean resorts.

"Zio," Vince had once begged his uncle, Italo, "more than half my profits are legit. Why can't I be like Il Professore, out in the daylight?"

"You want daylight, cretino? You want the light of day on your illegal gambling? How about the hookers? How about the coke?"

"I'll split that off from Ricci Entertainments."

"You'll listen to your Zio, Vince. I'll tell you when to let the daylight in."

"For my funeral," Vinch had groused. "That's when."

He wasn't looking forward to his flight back to Manhattan today. He didn't have his usual pilot on this short hop, which got him a little nervous. But he'd also found half a dozen things wrong in Eleuthera, Grenada, Mustique and Guadeloupe. He'd had to have a cashier in Virgin Gorda iced. The boys made it look like a surfing accident, which cost Vince triple. And there was still no sign of where the drowned cashier had hidden £100,000 in £50 notes. Vince could already hear Zio Italo's lecture: "Buco di culo, *first* the money, *then* the take-out. How can a man tell you something if he's already gone?"

Then the tall redhead Vince'd been shtupping had finished off his Caribbean visit on an embarrassing note. A death-wish roulette player, she owned a chain of better-frock dress shops in Ohio and Indiana. Vince picked the big ones—she was five-ten and 44 DD—because he could get all his rocks off before they started to come. Essential on a one-nighter. Instead she'd made a fool of him, shattering the night with howls of pleasure. Vince did not consider sex something for two people. Even as a kid in high school he knew that only perverts bothered about what happened to the woman.

Women could really complicate your life. Look at how that Indian chick was messing up Charley, wrecking the family. But it was built into Il Professore's mind that he had to go for respectability. The Indian nafke only triggered off what was already there. The redhead's orgasms were embarrassing.

But they were peanuts compared to what he'd heard from his "outside" manager, his cousin Lauro. "Outside" referred to the fact that, in response to mounting demands from his customers, Vince had made coke and horse available via bellhops and hookers. Lauro ran the operation. The profits Lauro shepherded had grown so quickly that in Ricci resorts, as well as those only managed by the Riccis, drug profits equaled casino skim—both being unreported cash. Seeing what immense profits the Riccis had come to control in so short a time the Medellín cartels declared themselves in for a cut of the retail take. Pushed, Lauro developed an alternate source at twenty grand a kilo. Vince knew it came from a new production area, not South American but somewhere in the Far East. It mattered not. Only the cut-rate price interested Lauro.

Vince curled in the rear cockpit seat of a four-passenger Mooney, flying him to Miami Airport from Grand Bahama. The light plane would land there and Vince would transfer to a Ricci-operated Fokker 128, designed to fly high rollers to various Caribbean resorts. He seemed to be sleeping but his mind kept racing.

Vince's head was in turmoil. His faintly Arabic coloring looked putty-colored. His aquiline face seemed lifeless. The mascara-like darkness under his eyes stood out. Lauro's bad news: the new source was crapping out. They had agreed on fifty kilos a week. Now they were being squeezed down to eleven because of start-up difficulties in a new processing laboratory.

The Mooney was a fast, noisy little aircraft. Eyes slitted, Vince could read the fuel indicator and saw that their reserve was hardly touched. That meant this model had been modified with more fuel tanks for long over-water flights.

Vince knew the plane but not the pilot. Usually a chubby guy called Norm flew the one-hour trip to Miami Airport. Today the new pilot was a slim gent in Ray-Bans of a green so deep they looked black. He'd said absolutely nothing.

Vince liked quiet on these trips. They gave him a chance to clear his head of all the crap his managers had loaded him with. In clear weather this was a pretty trip or a chance to snooze. He dug his fingers into his short-cropped black curls and gave them a brutal scrubbing to clear what lay beneath. He could try to come to grips with the drop-off in drugs which would diminish his profit nearly a third.

He stared over the pilot's shouler at the altimeter. "Twelve thousand? No wonder I'm breathing hard. Hit the deck."

"My assigned altitude, Mr. Ricci."

"I said lose altitude. What kind of assigned horseshit is twelve thousand feet? We don't have oxygen."

Vince watched the pilot start a series of banked turns. The altimeter needle responded by dropping. "Level off. I'm gonna catch some z's."

He resumed his catlike curl, knees in black denim pulled up to his chest, sharp-heeled cowboy boots hidden under him. In a moment he had entered that vague region of half-consciousness where the strangest ideas seem utterly sane. He could feel the plane's slow banking turns like his mother's soothing hand on his baby carriage, slowly shaking, shaking.

He felt as if he were being smothered. Lungs empty! Choking! His eyes flew open. The altimeter needle was back at twelve thousand. Vince's normal reaction would have been a howl of rage. This time he remained as if asleep. The pilot ahead of him was slipping a .9 Browning automatic from the deep righthand pocket of his scratched-up brown leather jacket. Vince watched him release the safety. Carefully, Vince freed his boots from under him. He coiled even more tightly. His curly hair seemed to bristle electrically, like a cat's tail. The twin controls of the Mooney waved in front of him. In a second the pilot would turn, aim the Browning and—

Vince's legs exploded in a double kick. The cowboy heels slammed into the back of the pilot's head. He jerked forward as if hit by a truck. The weight of his body on the controls forced the plane into a dive. The automatic pistol clattered to the floor. Vince grabbed for it.

The Mooney was in a headlong dive, gaining speed. The altimeter needle rotated wildly from twelve to ten to eight to six. The pilot's dark-as-night Ray-Bans clung to his face like an angry bird. Vince's ears began to ache. Vince grabbed for the control wheel before the pilot recovered. He slid into the righthand front seat and pulled the wheel back with all his strength.

The plane fought against gravity to pull out of its dive. Vince could feel the G's tugging at his face like a hand digging into his skin. There was a shift in the whole world. He could *feel* the tight curls on his head flatten. His stomach seemed to slam up into his throat. He could taste the sourness. Suddenly, the Mooney was flying level. Two thousand feet. He'd pulled them out without an inch to spare. Close, Vince thought, but I'm still here.

What to do next? He was no pilot. The amount of island-hopping he did, he'd meant to get a pilot's license. But something always intervened. Beside him the pilot stirred. His hand went to the back of his head and he groaned. Vince sorted out the sound for sincerity and decided most of it was put on. He'd shocked the bastard all right, but he wasn't out of commission.

Stripping the magazine out of the Browning, Vince let the chunky .9 cartridges drop to the floor of the Mooney. Carefully, he fished out the thirteenth shell inside the breech and let its glittering brass and toughened lead drop.

"Sorry about that," he said, handing back the unloaded gun.

"Man, that *hurt*!"

"I get a little paranoid at high altitudes."

"I didn't *do* anything, Mr. Ricci. You got me wrong."

"I know it," Vince lied, imitating an apologetic tone. His heart was still pounding. "I'm revved up so high I just went ape. Forget it, will you?"

"I'd sure like to. You got a kick like a mule."

"There," Vince said, as if the pilot had made a promise. "See? Just an attack of nerves. All over. I'm OK now. And there'll be a bonus for you, too. Oh, there it is, Miami airport. I just panicked, that's all. You won't tell anybody?"

The pilot's eyeless smile was meant to be reassuring. "Mum's the word."

He began speaking to Miami air traffic control, murmuring of an engine stall and recovery. Four minutes later the Mooney had landed and taxied over to the general aviation side where a large hangar labeled Ricci stood at one end of a row. "Roll right inside," Vince said.

Once in the hangar, the pilot shut down the engine. He and Vince got down from the cockpit. A man in coveralls was coming toward them. In the dimmer light, the pilot reached to take off his dark Ray-Bans.

Vince's cowboy toe, pointed like a dagger, hit his groin a sharp, upward punch to the testicles. As he doubled over, Vince brought his hands, locked together, down on the pilot's neck where he'd injured him with his heels. The violent action tied them for one instant into a single entity, Vince's curly hair shaking with the effort of his blow, the pilot's neck jutting forward under his locked-hand karate chop. Something clicked nastily, bone on bone. The pilot began to topple. The man in coveralls caught him as he collapsed to the oily concrete floor.

"Jeez, Vince," he muttered. "Gimme a little warning."

"I want this stronzo sewed up while we backtrack him to June. I want to know if he had a job out Peconic Bay on Long Island. A double take-out? You remember the one, don't you, Kenny?'' He held his hand over his racing heart.

"Hey, cousin, I'm hip.''

"This man has a date to speak with Zio Italo. Capeesh?'' Vince rubbed the injured edge of his hands. He squinted for a moment, as if in pain. "Meanwhile, get me two aspirin. We came down too fast for my ears.''

"I gotta get you on that Fokker.''

Vince's neat, slightly pinched face registered pain. "Home to wifey.'' His headache grew sharper. The excitement was dying in his veins. Why was it, after one of these punishing nights with some demanding bimbo screaming in your ear, after some maniac tried to ice you at twelve thousand feet, Lenore always wanted to be serviced, too? Just to prove she was trying for a kid? OK. No other excuse would do.

"Hey, Kenny, want some advice? Never get married.''

"Too late, Vince.''

Together, they dragged the unconscious pilot off into a small room, leaving his black-lensed Ray-Bans on the oily floor. They looked untouched.

Eighteen

"Kerry,'' Charley Richards said over the intercom, "we're ready.''

The young man picked up a legal-sized lined yellow pad filled with notes. He let himself into Charley's office. Around the big conference table sat three Richland financial people and Andy Reid. Everyone looked at ease except Reid, who kept loosening his tie.

This was a trial run, a mock-up of a meeting they would be holding later today with Richland Holdings' lead bank, United Bank and Trust Company. Although they were UBCO's biggest commercial customer, and had independent financial resources of their own, Richland people took these meetings very seriously. Richland interests would be presented by Reid, who had the proper

Wasp Establishment facade. What he didn't have was Charley's brain. Thus these rehearsals.

"We're going to be refinancing most of FoodUsa," Charley was saying. "All the refrigeration is out-of-date. Any day now listeria, salmonella, even botulism will escalate out of control." He frowned. "This is top secret. Our freezers are overcrowded and old. Our employees are poorly trained, functional illiterates who would have been unemployable a few decades back. Now they're all we have. Our rescue plan costs out at three hundred million. That's a real hit in the head, but better than being sued by the parents of children killed by food poisoning."

Andy Reid's finger went between his neck and collar. "I'm nervous about this one."

"You should be," Charley agreed. "They must never know that if we don't modernize we face catastrophe. We say we're being extremely foresighted and public spirited. We're anticipating trouble decades before it happens, understand?" He stared hard at Reid. "This is very important, Andy. They mustn't get the feeling that we desperately need the money yesterday. Is that clear? We want a straight fifteen-year loan at a point over prime. Kerry, begin."

A telephone buzzed. Charley picked it up and listened for a long moment. "OK," he said and hung up. "Sorry about this. Kerry?" He got up and motioned Kerry to follow him out of the office, through the computer rooms to the high-speed elevator. "Zio Italo wants a sit-down."

"Right now?"

"When in the annals of man did Zio ever want anything except right now?" He said nothing more on the subject but his face provided the sub-text, a clue to the immense irritation caused by having to drop everything to answer a summons from a man he could no longer contemplate without disgust. That old-country touch, the nobility commanding Il Professore. Come. Go. Fetch. Beg.

In the basement garage they got into Kerry's small white Peugeot 205. Fifteen minutes later they parked in a no-parking zone on Dominick Street. A young man winked as he took up surveillance of the auto. Inside the San Gennaro Social Club Italo sat behind his big rolltop desk, fingers steepled in front of him, head bent, great nose shielding his fingers, eyes closed, deep in thought. This, Kerry reminded himself, was Posture One, the "Abbot at Prayer." Posture Two, the "Whirling Dervish," was much harder to take.

Charley sat down across the desk and tried to keep his face neutral. Kerry, still standing until invited to sit, noticed that they were being given an additional moment of meditation. Something major must be afoot. He was aware of what Charley had asked from Zio. He was also aware that Zio had angrily refused. But why ring him into this clash of Titans?

Finally the deep-set eyes opened and the nose lifted an inch. Italo's index finger pointed first to Kerry and then to a side chair. The young man sat down. It was nonsense, this medieval protocol, but the old guy set great store by it.

"Ragazzi," Italo began in a harsh voice. It had that clarion rasp of Il Duce summoning Italy to arms: "Cittadini!" he would thunder. Like most elderly people of Italian origin, Zio Italo paid lip-service to the notion that Il Duce had brought his nation low. But in his heart he knew Italy had never been greater than when massacring unarmed tribesmen of Ethiopia and forcing pints of castor oil down the throats of communists.

"Ragazzi," he repeated, "the esteemed Professore feels he can handle his own business affairs." A bitter pause. "With his own personal advisor, this Indian lady guru. But only I can fix this baby, left on my doorstep." Charley's hooded glance shot sideways to read Kerry's face. The two of them were quite used to Italo's dramatics, but there was something different about today's performance. What was it? Perhaps . . . a note of triumph? A hidden sting?

Italo reached into a desk drawer and carefully centered a Thinkman on his desk top. "You know this macchina maladetta? Kevin downloaded from London. One of my boys translated. Kerry, verify what your brother told me. Now."

Kerry took the pocket-sized microprocessor and began tapping in access codes. As he did so, Italo addressed himself with almost mock sincerity to his nephew Charley.

"You know how I hate to involve you in this side of the family."

"I know."

"Especially now that you want to pretend you no longer belong to us.

"I know."

"But this is what you asked me for last Christmas."

"I know."

"Now I'm able at last to spell it out for you in detail. I, not your girl friend. I, your own flesh and blood."

"I know."

The antiphonal quality of their discourse had a soothing effect, as on celebrants of a Mass in some cool, impersonal cathedral, as different as possible from their previous heated encounter in this room. Both men had turned toward Kerry, punching in commands, the kind of altar-fussing a priest does. After a long time he looked up. His young, unformed face seemed grave.

"I don't know how Kev got this stuff, but it's dynamite. Somebody's been messing it up but they couldn't scramble the core data."

Patiently, both older men waited. After the Andy Reid rehearsal, Charley had a meeting of regional sales managers on closed-circuit TV. After that he had a date with the financial management of one of the country's top *Fortune* 500 companies on a new bond issue. At noon he was due at the Plaza as guest speaker.

As for Italo, who knew which crowned heads and papal nuncios he had penciled in for today? "Just accessing a calendar for 1987," Kerry muttered. After a moment, "Got the heart of it. We're back in October. Remember?"

"You were still in high school," Charley reminded him.

Kerry nodded. "Kev got this from a Daiwa database. You should know from the start that Daiwa wasn't the prime mover."

"Piu veloce," Italo rasped.

"OK. OK. Wednesday, 14 October, 1987," Kerry went on quickly. "Normal day's trading. No violent swings. End of day leak from Washington, DC that when the August trade figures are officially released, they will once again be poor."

"Leaked by whom?" Charley asked.

"Doesn't say. But, on this information, a major financial-manufacturing conglomerate in Taiwan and Tokyo jumps the gun and begins to unload U.S. Treasury securities of every kind. That's Shan Lao, Ltd. They use all of Japan's Big Four brokers, Daiwa, Nikko, Nomura and Yamaichi. In turn, the Four follow suit, trying to save their asses. Shan has already dumped at par, no loss. The brokers' sell-off isn't too damaging. The strategy is take a small loss now rather than wait for the full crash and mega-losses."

"Faster," Italo urged.

"As they dump, it affects all bond prices in all markets. By Friday afternoon, any computer-driven investment program is busy unloading whatever it controlled, turning a small waterfall into Niagara. Monday morning, this hemorrhage spreads to stocks. It moves west, hour by hour. The further west, the heavier the loss of blood. By the end of Black Monday the world's in free fall. Small investors are being cleaned out. Only later do the experts realize that Wall Street and the City of London have been clobbered and the French, German and Swiss bourses are lying there dead. In one country, however, the damage has been neatly limited. Right. Japan."

Both Charley and Italo had been leaning forward. Now they sat back. Kerry continued, "To cover the fact that he was the Judas goat who led the Big Four into the slaughterhouse, Shan Lao goes, on Monday, 19 October, to the Japanese Ministry of Finance—he has friends that high—to whom he rats out his brokers."

"That's crazy," Charley burst out. "He informs on them?"

"It turns Shan into a hero. The Ministry of Finance forces the Big Four to bolster the Japanese market. This halts the fall. For Japan. Nobody else."

Both older men nodded slowly, thinking. "But, Kerry," Charley demurred, "Shan would be making four of the toughest enemies in Asia."

"No Asian was badly hurt. Only people like us and our customers. He gave the Four the kind of pep talk you expect from a Notre Dame football coach. 'See what we in the East have created! We have shown the white devils our power! Now they must fear us.' Or words to that effect.''

"How could they swallow that hogwash?" Italo demanded.

"They're still digesting it. A note in the Daiwa files warns against more joint ventures with Shan Lao, Ltd. But that was rescinded three years later. You see, there's never been any question that all this was accidental. Nobody wanted a crash. Nobody's accused Shan of engineering one. In Tokyo's eyes he's only guilty of blowing the whistle. A Jap would never have done that. But Shan is Chinese and they don't expect the same behavior code from him. In any event, his crying foul helped Japan come out of this smelling like a rose.''

"And next time?" Italo's strident cry was that of a hawk deprived of prey. "He's a crook! The Big Four are crooks. They conspired to bring America to its knees. Next time it'll be fatal.''

Charley's anger kindled slowly, first at having his day interrupted and, second, by such stale news, the jist of which Zio had already reported to him. "OK." He got ot his feet. "Andiamo, Kerry.''

"Hold it," Zio commanded.

"Be reasonable. I have a full day.''

"Calma, Illustre Professore. I didn't get where I am being reasonable.''

In the silence that followed, Italo seemed to grow smaller within his own skin, as if preparing himself to fight. Charley recognized the movement. There was a sting to the tail of this one. Zio was getting ready to deliver it.

"To chase this down, that's what I'm here for. Count on me, not some hotsy-totsy popsy. Because I am *always* unreasonable, suspicious. We have some Chink looney out there who can turn on 1929 any time he feels like it.''

Charley remained on his feet. "The instant way computers react to market shifts, anybody could trigger another crash." He started to leave the oak desk. "I have to keep Andy Reid off the white till after this UBCO meeting. Kerry, you'd better stay by his side from now till then. Especially when he goes to the john.''

"You wouldn't start a market panic," Italo said, as if

Charley hadn't spoken. "What would be your motives? Now, looneys like Shan . . ."

"What would be his motive? He's a capitalist, the same as us."

"No, there's one slight difference," Italo corrected him. He stood up, too, as if agreeing to end the meeting. The sting was at hand. "He's the only capitalist whose son is fucking my grand-niece Bunny."

Charley sat down again. Stung.

Nineteen

After a particularly demented week, Charley Richards boarded a pontoon plane at the foot of Coenties Slip near the heliport approach where Pino had died.

The light had begun to die as they flew northeast. But as the tiny craft soared skywards over the Brooklyn and Manhattan bridges, Charley felt a lift of spirit. He knew Stefi was waiting at the end of the flight. It wasn't the wild, unreasoning lift he got with Garnet, but he could use any manner of lift these days. Fighting Zio was heavy work, even though he had followed advice and tackled the problem in small pieces.

After a week's accelerated phone and fax with Basel, he had taken ownership control of MACA, the construction conglomerate, out of Liechtenstein and into Richland Securities, London, where his brother-in-law, Jack, would make a public offering next month. It would be an easy job. Thirty-three percent of the issue had been retained for sale in Europe and held for Forward Holding Trust, a Channel Islands company. Thus a third of MACA's shares were placed outside the purview of the Securities and Exchange Commission. All perfectly legal.

Zio Italo, sole owner of Forward Holding, had listened impassively to Charley's explanations and produced a thin, icy smile. When Charley explained that another eighteen percent would be held for Forward in New York, the smile broadened by the thickness of a knife-cut.

"You expect thanks?" was his only comment.

''Try this,'' Charley said in a fed-up voice. ''Ben fatto. Well done, Charley.''

Both Garnet and Winfield had cautioned him to treat Zio with the usual deference, humility, reverence, servility and blatant toadyism he had grown used to during a lifetime of it. By now Charley was too disgusted to care.

Flying east toward Long Island, Charley supposed he'd gotten off lightly, considering. What was Zio's game in staying coldly sweet? Deception, of course, but for what purpose? To lull Charley into thinking he had a green light? He'd probably seen through the piecemeal strategy and now considered he was dealing with a complete wimp.

Keeping low, a few thousand feet off the ripples of the East River, the plane flew over the Williamsburgh and Triboro bridges, banked east over Hell Gate and Rikers Island. In a moment, with the sunset light coming from behind them, it traversed City Island, surrounded by tiny, white-waked boats.

Charley's mind, trying to shed his worries, leapt ahead of the seaplane. Beyond Oyster Bay, looking across the Sound toward Stamford, Connecticut, sat an island connected by a causeway to the main bulk of Long Island. It was here, in the 1920s, that Marshall Field had built a mansion, complete with pheasant hunts. It ended in a deepwater inlet called Lloyd Point. Almost filling this sub-island, a fitfully semi-developed Caumsett State Park represented a compromise between the desires of the State of New York for recreational areas and the desires of Carlo Ricci, one of the four original Riccis, to keep a tract free for his two daughters, Stefania and Isabella.

Time had passed. Both daughters had fiddled the last letters of their names to become Stefanie and Isabel. The house Carlo left them had been built early in the nineteenth century by a whaling captain called Crutch or Crutts. Picturing the house on the cliff, Charley saw it in his mind's eye as a fortress. Crutch's devotion to the sea, which had made him a wealthy man, was to be seen in his second-floor windows, virtually a wall of glass. They gave Stefi a 180-degree view of the Sound and its far Connecticut shore.

Charley's tiny plane glided low over the waves of Long

Island Sound. Whitecaps glowed hot orange in the setting sun. Ahead he could see Lloyd's Point. They were ghosting in quietly at five hundred feet, then two hundred.

What was Zio Italo's game? If he'd decided to oppose Charley, a family-wide chill would have ensued like an all-points warning. But nothing like that had happened. Then was his strategy to take ownership and wipe Charley out? It wouldn't work. Every transfer relied on the services and anonymity of Richland Securities. Eliminate Charley and he eliminated his protection.

Charley shifted unhappily in his passenger seat. The choppy waves of Long Island Sound lay only yards below now as the amphibian coasted to a landing. After a moment the cliff-hugging fortress came into view just as the pontoon kissed the whitecaps and plane became boat, bobbing violently up and down in a September offshore breeze. The pilot pointed toward a small pier.

"Right," Charley responded, the only word spoken since the trip began. "I'll be ready for you in an hour," he added as he stepped ashore.

"See ya," the chatty pilot responded. He opened a paperback.

Starting when they had been lovers, they were careful not to meet like lovers. But today Stefi had climbed down the flight of stairs to the landing beach and was neatening the small boathouse there. Charley saw the evening sun setting her classic, Grecian face ablaze with light. He engulfed her in his arms and lifted her high overhead inside the privacy of the boathouse. "Look at us!" she gasped, breathless. "Teenagers."

As they walked back up the steps, Charley looked this way and that. "I know this beach," she assured him. "If anybody's casing it I'd've seen him."

She had started a small log blaze in the living room fireplace, its walls made up of floor-to-ceiling shelves of books. "How's Kerry?" she asked then.

Every family had secrets as well kept as the twins' paternity. Sitting by the fire with their mother in this book-lined sanctuary recalled to Charley those early days when she had, indeed, been a teenager and so had he and Vince. Both had sensed in her the kind of eccentric streak that lurks in the Sicilian temperament. Both had tried to seduce their dark-haired cousin with the hot eyes and

blossoming breasts. "I sure as hell copped a solid feel,"
Vince had exulted once. "Came up behind her and
grabbed two full hands' worth. Charley, I nearly blew
the copper buttons off my Levi's. That girl is built!"
Tonight, thirty years later, Stefi's short black ringlets
glowed in the firelight. Her great olive eyes, Italo's color
but wider-set, were fixed on Charley.

"Kerry is fine," he told her. "We had a meeting to
discuss some information Kevin developed. He's fine,
too." In the silence, insulated by shelves of books, they
heard a sound like a tree falling, a kind of rustling thud.
He frowned.

"That's the surf," Stefi said, giving him a shove in the
shoulder. "What a city slicker you are."

"Surf? This isn't the Atlantic side."

"I know every sound of this place. We get Coast Guard
jets. We get foghorns. We get seagulls. When the wind's
right we get the shoal buoys in Oyster Bay. Nights like
this, with the wind rising, we get the pounding of surf."

"It sounded like a door-slam."

She shook her head. "Charley, I understand even better than you how isolated I am out here. Especially when
I give Erminia and her husband the night off. But nobody
is creeping up on you. Nobody's casing the joint. Please
relax."

"I think of this place as a fortress, Stef, a sanctuary."
Charley's glance moved deep in the heart of the burning
log fire. "None of us knows what it's like to live in an
ordinary family, unprotected, subject to the whims of the
world."

"You get used to having the fix put in." She shifted
position. Her skirt rode up on her thighs and Charley saw
that she wasn't wearing briefs. She gave him a sideways
glance, testing. "It lets you play with life. Be bold."

"Lay off. I was told to live my life prudently. Told,
hell. I was ordered."

"You did one terrific job of it, Charley. You even
fooled yourself." She touched herself delicately. "Where
do you get the balls to go against everything you are?
Against everything the whole world is?"

He felt his throat close up for an instant, but he decided not to comment. "The whole world? It's not too

choked with honest people. I know that. But the whole world isn't Zio Italo, either.''

She sighed softly. "I've watched my boys go their separate ways. My heart goes out to Kerry, but in here . . ." she touched herself with a strong, pointing gesture, ". . . down here where the truth lies, I know Kevin is the future of the world."

Charley smiled grimly. "As much as I love that little nest of truth, it's lying to you."

"Maybe it's been on its own too long."

Their glances met with that non-verbal interchange that, for Sicilians, represents a silent language. Her glance turned challenging. "What does it mean to be responsible members of a respectable family? It means you can get away with what you want. So here I am cockteasing and you're considering cheating on Garnet. Is she any better than I am? The truth."

He puffed his cheeks. "The truth? When did the truth ever concern a Ricci? Stef, the truth is I have to stop banging my first cousin. And tonight's the night to stop."

"It's not as if we don't have protection." Eyes wide, she was rubbing herself. "If we were little people we'd be afraid. Anyway, who said anything about a bang? A little head isn't real adultery," she explained. "Ask any priest."

"What do you mean, protection? Something your local priest offers? What does he tell you? Light a candle? Or use it?"

"I mean family protection. I mean, whatever we do, Charley, no matter what, the fix is in. We just have to be big enough for it."

"Then bring yourself off big. I won't tell." He gave her a grin, to show he was joking. In all their years together they had never squandered words on their sex life, just gone ahead with it. He suddenly realized how dismaying this was for Stefanie. Didn't she have anyone else? Someone in reserve? He began to feel he had betrayed her by falling in love with Garnet. But that couldn't be right, could it? It was something he could discuss with neither of them.

He kissed her lightly. "It's not that I don't want you, it's that I made a promise to myself when I met Garnet."

"Vince is right. You've turned into a total tight-assed Wasp."

"Is that what you two talk about?"

"It's pruned your balls. You used to be real mafia. It didn't matter what or where. You remember giving it to me in the confessional at San Silvestro's?"

She got to her feet. "Italo eats you alive. All he does is pick up the phone and you come running. Yes, Kerry talks to me. In the middle of an important meeting, you let Zio yank your whang like an organ-grinder's monkey."

She smoothed down her skirt. "He's shrunk you, Charley. I always thought of you as the family genius. Veramente Il Professore. I see you're just an ordinary guy who's had Italo's cash to play with for twenty years. Ordinary." He watched her anger start to recede. "What good is it being a Ricci?" she demanded, her voice rising again. "What good does a life in this family do? What was the point," she added, her dark eyes flashing dangerously, "of living the miserable, terrified life I did if it doesn't give me a license to steal? Here I am, Charley, Steal me."

Far away, dully, the thud sounded again. Charley's mouth tightened as a shiver shot across his shoulder blades. "That's the world knocking on our door, Stef. The fortress is surrounded.

"Living like a Ricci is living in jail. Can you see why I want the warden to sign my release?" He laughed, a short, bitter sound. "A fortress protected by a private army. We have our own alliances with other governments. Our own cardinals, senators. Christ, we've even had our own president!"

Her full lips parted for a moment, as if to speak. Then she sat back down in her chair. "Charley, that professor's head of yours. Give it a rest."

"The old contadini figured the bigger the family the more harvest hands. In numbers lay strength. A paisano might go through three or four wives that way, grinding them down by childbirth. But it's all changed now."

"That a fact? The babies come out some other exit?"

"The more people in a family the more chances for outside to break inside. Enemies tamper with your kids. They hook them on junk. They kidnap them for ransom.

They bribe them to rat out their family. They fool them into con games. They trap them in blackmail. They betray them to the cops or the IRS.''

"Charley!"

"What's worse, young people aren't trained for today's world. Two hundred years ago in Sicily all you needed was a strong back. Today you have to read, write, figure. You have to know a little history, a little science. Kids hit college with the training we used to give six-year-olds. Do you wonder why we won't hire them till they have a Ph.D.?''

"You're depressing me.''

"Once we had just a handful of honest cops to worry about. Now we have anti-trust investigations. Price-fixing. Insider dealing. And on Italo's side he's facing Chinese Triads and Japanese Yakusa. I know Vince's hurting because of the Colombia drug cartels. Stef, on all sides, the fortress is besieged.''

"All the more reason," she cried out, "not to go against your own blood.'' She had hurt him with her taunts about his subservience to Zio Italo, about being too unmafia to take her again, Garnet or no Garnet. But he was too mafia to show his hurt. Hers had been a cry of loneliness. She needed him more than he needed her, precisely because he had Garnet.

"That's how Zio Italo sees me, Stef. The traitor who opens the gates of the fortress in the night.''

He expected to hear a quick denial. But, finally: "Charley, he's right.''

Truly hurt now, Charley got to his feet, his face expressionless. He had to have his head examined, letting her get under his skin this way. He wasn't used to such raw family faith, such old-country blindness in the name of the family.

"Good night, Charley.'' She waved softly. "Sorry to speak my mind like that.''

"It wasn't your mind speaking.''

A mocking smile as she fingered herself again. "Any time you want to talk to it face to face.''

Both of them burst out laughing, teenagers once more. Far off, with a hollow thud of great force, something immense seemed to pound on the fortress door. The young grins died on their faces.

Twenty

In the back room of the San Gennaro Social Club the morning light filtered thinly through high bullet-proof windows. For the life he lived, Italo didn't need to look at the world. And he certainly didn't need the world looking in on him. His talon-like fingers gently touched a computer keyboard with great delicacy, summoning up from London figures on the MACA public issue and his share of it. Everything was exactly as Il Professore had promised. But it wasn't his nephew's honesty he questioned.

The question that shook the pillars of the earth had to do with loyalty. Like the militant abbot he most resembled, Italo demanded total loyalty. He had pruned away all pillars but family. He used them like makeweight in a negotiation, like shields in an attack, like scapegoats when pressed to, like almost anything but human beings. To do that, one had to have human feelings. That was why he'd avoided anything truly close like a son or a wife. He had never regretted it. Now, when he had to discipline Charley in a way that was final and irreversible, Italo's judgment could not be tainted by compassion.

It was best, perhaps, to set the matter in motion at once, before Charley engineered anymore of these SEC-proof reappearances. For this Italo needed a specialist. None of Vince's would do. A man as fastidiously feline as Vince might have been expected to show compunction about hiring common killers. But he had reasons. In Vince's line of work, the self-advertising take-out served many purposes connected with instilling and maintaining respect. Italo required the much rarer and far more expensive expert who could make it all look accidental.

He frowned. The history of the modern world was filled with turning points and watersheds created by specialists who could make things look accidental or the work of a crazed lone assassin. Still, there were only a

few Italo would trust. And one had just now come to
New York City.

Nikki Shan finished scribbling in his spiral-bound workbook. He hesitated to fax it to his father. The first time
he'd done that, back in July, it had stirred up a great
hornet's nest. His mother had had to go back home to
soothe his father's agitated mind. Poor Lord Mace, the
original Lord Hopeless, had caught hell. And his father
had penned him a one-sentence note telling him in very
stiff language that he thought the essay quite good, of its
kind. He re-read this one.

> Dear Father,
>   For centuries, first sons have inherited immense
> estates whether capable of managing or not. Lord
> Hopeless is a stammering, maladroit drunk to be found
> at one of his two pastimes: drinkin' or pukin.''
>   On the American side of the Anglo-Saxon divide,
> presidents have been able to ignore their duties by
> appearing to be stupid. Instead of being impeached,
> they are often re-elected.
>   Clever people are thus shown how handy it is to
> appear incapable of thought. You get a bill for
> something you paid long ago, or never bought. You
> ignore it. A second notice is couched in polite
> language. You write a polite note. In a month a third
> notice arrives, stripped of politesse. ''Deadbeat: we
> will forward your case to our Rottweiler Squad.''
>   It dawns on you that the ''person'' signing these
> letters is a computer. The budget doesn't allow for a
> human being to read your letters. But it *pays*
> companies to play stupid and harass you this way.
> You may finally cave in.
>   The need to outwit this takes time, energy and
> will-power. So if you're smart you pack it all in and
> join Lord Hopeless, drinkin' and pukin.'' And if
> you're dumb, you already have.

Nikki had since bought a fax machine, more for Bunny
than for him. She had a queenly habit of never respond-
ing to the ringing of a telephone. People who wanted

Nikki and couldn't get his phone to answer soon tired of the game. Now everyone would be able to reach everyone else.

It was dawn in Boston. Sometimes the two of them had put in such a late and active night that it didn't pay Nikki to go to sleep. While Bunny lay stretched out naked on the bed, nearly six feet of gorgeous flesh and all his, Nikki would sit by the window overlooking the river and scratch away in his workbook like a monk with an illuminated manuscript. If he could draw he would have sketched her svelte, slender body. If he could write poems, he would salute her a thousand times in this form. But he could do neither, so he wrote essays.

He closed the notebook and watched the sun lighten the east. A faint ray came in over the window ledge and ignited one of Bunny's great pinky-brown areoles, as wide across as an ashtray with a hotly smoldering cigarette end for a nipple. In a while Bunny would entice him back into bed for what she kept calling "a little equestrian dressage." Nikki had heard of something called hypersexualis, a male dysfunction related to fornication overload. It manifested itself in loss of vitality. No such symptom had appeared. Nikki opened his book and made a note to look into the possibility that hypersexualis created an insatiable urge to write more essays.

At that moment his fax stuttered into life. He padded over, naked, to watch it automatically answer an incoming query and open the way for a printout. A moment later it began to stutter out his name and fax number. Then:

Nikki dearest. Prepare for family visit, both of us.
November at the earliest, Christmas at the latest.
Remain available through New Year's Eve. Aussi le
p'tite lapin. Au'voir. Ta mere.

Nikki stood over the fax machine, re-reading. It sounded much more serious than the casual wording indicated. In all his years at school in England, in Switzerland and now here, the great Shan Lao had never come to the lowly son. That was not the way of the East nor was it his father's way. Something special was at work here, perhaps his mother, Nicole, with some half-dreamlike hope of reconciling Shan Lao to the union of Nik and Bunny.

Removing the message, Nikki walked back to his desk. Bunny had moved out of her apartment the month before, claiming that the telephone rang too much. Now her makeup was scattered over his papers. She had brought very little else with her. Nikki approved of traveling light but not of messing up his desk. He bent over, trying to clear the eyeliner, mascara and blushers to one corner when he felt himself seized from behind. Moreover, seized by the scrotum, but gently.

"Bun!"

"Steady, horsie. Steady. You know I have you entirely in my power, horsie. You cannot move," Bunny went on with some enjoyment. "You can neither pee nor fart, horsie. You can only obey."

"Bun, will you—"

"Quiet, horsie." She tugged on his testes, but still gently. He craned his neck around to see that she was on her knees behind him in order to get the proper leverage.

"Ma chère," he began, "something immense is about to happen."

"Yes, horsie, I am going to bugger you from behind, once I find something suitable. Where's your great big fat black Mont Blanc fountain penis?"

"My father is coming to visit us."

Reflexively, her grip tightened on his testicles and he winced. "Bun, please? It hurts."

She gave up her grip but continued to kneel there, staring up at his buttocks. "I wonder if he knows."

"Knows what?" Nikki turned around to look at her.

"I mean he's such a man of mystery and suddenly he's coming here? I mean you and your mom never even mention his name, he's such a sacred monster."

"That's a good French phrase for him." Nikki turned back to his workbook and scribbled it on an inside page.

"So I figure somehow the word got to him."

"Word of what?" Nikki asked.

"Word that I'm pregnant."

Twenty-One

It was after six o'clock. Most of the people in Richland Tower had gone home. Charley Richards was still meeting with the operating heads of Richland's food handling conglomerate, FoodUsa. No one knew it, but he was already in touch with Basel. Once the UBCO refrigeration-update loan came through—and not an instant later—FoodUsa would be freed from its Liechtenstein anstalt and launched as a public offering for Zio Italo's private taking.

To Charley's mind, once Garnet had opened his eyes, nothing better dramatized his need to return all these businesses to Zio Italo. Running even legitimate concerns had become an uneasy trade-off between legal and illicit activity. You delayed as long as possible the removal of offending items from your shelves, hoping that uninformed consumers would buy what you would have to discard.

Tonight, waiting to talk to her father, Winfield Richards sat in Andy Reid's office, making personal calls and worrying about breaking her news. That afternoon, Nikki had phoned from Boston to tell her Bunny was pregnant.

"Oh, Christ," Winfield responded. "Is that—? I mean, do you—?"

"Want it?" Nikki finished for her. "That depends. What makes it hairy is that I'm expecting a visit from my father." Winfield had never really thought about the clear possibility that Nikki was fully equipped with interventionist parents. The way he referred to him now made it clear that father played a major role in Nikki's life.

After a long giggle with Bunny, Winfield had agreed to break the news to their parents. Now she wasn't so confident. She and Bunny had always been close and thin at the same time. She loved her but understood what a terrible weakness she had for miming others, mainly her sister. Being flattered this way was good for Winfield's ego, but ultimately bad. If they hadn't been sisters they'd have had nothing at all to talk about since Bunny was playing clone. They did, however, differ sharply on sex.

It was possible that between them they represented the sexual orientation of their two parents, Missy's Dionysian devotion to the body and how it absorbed abuse, Charley's . . . Charley's what? Winfield had never doubted that her father could be as Dionysian as the next person, especially when that person was the smashing ex-model, Dr. Garnet, who now seemed to monopolize all his free time.

Not that she wasn't a good thing for him. But Winfield already realized that as Garnet's influence grew, her own would wane. Probably just as well. Probably that boy, Alec, had been right. Perhaps she was sexually obsessed with her father. She frowned down at her hands, with their long fingers. She knew so little about herself and kept fighting what little information came to her. She felt protective of her father, but wasn't that only natural?

In her life he had fully earned the nickname he hated, Il Professore. He had always been her mentor, bringing her everything from why you mustn't immerse an electric coffeepot in water to such news from abroad as the vanishing of the ozone layer. In many respects, not just the biological, he had created her. None of her teachers had ever had his input. Untrammeled by curriculum, a Sunday with him veered wildly from how soccer differed from rugby and football, to why left-of-center parties like the Democrats always put up loser candidates for president. She and Bunny had been lavishly educated in the trivia that counted, although little of it stuck to Bunny. In me, Winfield decided, he had established himself. The rest was genes, some deadly ones.

For instance, she alone could outthink Zio Italo. Well, Aunt Stefi could, too, but Aunt Stefi was in the enemy camp. Her father rarely talked about Stefi but his silences told Winfield all she needed to know: of those capable of defeating Italo, only she was on her father's side.

As for telling her mother about Bun, that could wait. Missy would be fairly high by this time of evening. She didn't have a dinner party or her lover to fill in dead air. So the white could have to come to her rescue. Winfield found herself wondering how empty one's life had to be that only a drug could make it bearable.

Reid's private telephone rang. Winfield wondered if she should answer, since it might well be her mother. Finally she decided on the coward's way out, lifted the phone but remained silent.

"Hello, there?" a man asked at a strange pace, a kind of brisk drawl.

"Mr. Reid's office."

"Is he there, please?"

"Not at the moment. May I take a message?"

"Tell him Mr. Cohen is returning his call."

"Does he have your number, Mr. Cohen?"

"Oh, yes. Tell him I'm out of town till next Tuesday. But please call then."

"Is that the seventeenth?" But the line had gone dead.

Twenty-Two

The weather had turned chilly. September was ending without a taste of an Indian summer. At the level of the thirtieth-floor law offices of Hegarty & Krebs the morning was dull and raw. It was one of those New York City days when the air is choked with the moans and yelps of sirens.

Eileen had asked Lenore Ricci to drop in. "It'd be a big help," Eileen was saying. "You have to eat lunch, anyway. I'd introduce you under another name."

"I never met this Battipaglia, but for sure he'd know who I was whatever name you gave him."

Eileen considered this for a while. "I need a goombah with me," she said at length, dispensing with politesse. "I need somebody who can read a man like Dr. Battipaglia from an ethnic base."

"What's to read? He's a quack?"

"There's a streak of honesty. I'm going to tape. I'm going to show him the recorder. That'll put a muffler on him. If I had a translator for Italian body language . . ."

"Not me, Eileen."

"What're you saving yourself for? You want to help

me put Vince behind bars? I won't pretend I'm not grateful. But when do you start?''

Lenore shook her head. "My own way."

"You'll let me know when you hit pay dirt?" There was a faint sarcastic edge to Eileen's voice. Two sirens, seemingly moving in opposite directions, sent their sound hurtling upward thirty floors. Neither woman heard them.

Lenore blinked. "Eileen, please. I'm new at this."

Which accounted for the fact that when she met Battipaglia, Eileen brought Winfield Richards with her. Eileen had been moderately careful about the rendezvous. The doctor had suggested a clam house in the Mulberry Bend area known as Little Italy. Eileen had shifted venue farther uptown to a French restaurant in the theatrical district west of Broadway. It had been Winfield's idea to telephone that restaurant and leave a message for Battipaglia to meet them at yet another location. Eileen watched her closely for a long moment. "I keep forgetting," she said then in an approving tone. "You're one-half Sicilian."

"And that one-half tells me never give the opposition so much advance notice."

At half past noon both women entered a small Mexican restaurant on First Avenue in the shadow of the United Nations Secretariat building. It had recently opened and was still spotless, with crisp newly printed menus. They chose a table near the front windows to have a view of the UN Plaza. Overhead the skies had begun to darken even more. On the far side of First Avenue a police sedan, siren howling, roof lights dazzling, sped northward, weaving in and out of traffic. Eileen winched and covered her ears. "Disaster Day," she announced.

Battipaglia arrived half an hour late. "Crosstown traffic," he murmured apologetically. "You should have given me more notice." He ordered a Margarita and sat back, a dapper man in his late forties, jockey-like, half bald, with big black-rimmed Porsche aviator spectacles that gave him a startled leprechaun look. "To the ladies," he toasted, lifting his glass.

"Where would you be without them," Eileen added wryly.

"Hey, Miss Hegarty, I don't put on airs. I'm an aver-

age OB-GYN who got lucky in terms of industrial contracts.''

''With Ricci.'' Eileen opened her handbag and put the
small tape recorder on the table where Battipaglia could
see it. Then she covered it with her still-folded napkin.
''OK?'' she asked.

''Uh. I'm not—'' The doctor considered for a long
time. ''Just remember, I'm not going to tell you anything
new.'' He gave her a polite, professional smile.

''You never know. I might trick some new answers out
of you. You and I,'' she went on smoothly, ''are both
people of short stature, Doctor. We know the art of ap-
plying just a little force with a lot of leverage. Whereas
my associate here, being of a larger race, might have to
resort to brute force.''

Battipaglia threw back his head and laughed delight-
edly, showing extremely well-cared-for teeth, the
porcelain-sheathed caps and fillings a tribute to the dental art. His laughter was blanked out as a hook-and-ladder
firetruck screamed up First Avenue. ''But first let's look
at the menu,'' he said then, returning to earth. ''Brute
force,'' he murmured reflectively.

All three of them began to cope with a menu in Spanish. ''Oh, wait,'' Winfield announced. ''If you keep
turning the pages you get it in French, Italian, German,
English and Russian.''

''Ah, the UN strikes again.'' Battipaglia sipped his
drink and settled himself in his chair. The brand-new
ambience was pleasant. He obviously liked the place-
ment since the two women were staring out at the dull
day while he was able to survey both of them and the
rest of the lunching ladies. Doing so, Dr. Battipaglia
caught sight of one of his patients in the rear of the place,
a British call girl named Emma with very long blond
hair. She freelanced through a phone-booking service the
Ricci interests provided. She was quite lovely, Emma,
and, as Battipaglia had reason to know, a true blond.

Behind him the main front window loomed, about ten
by twenty feet of brand-new plate glass. A squat man
wearing a beret glanced in the window as he unholstered
a stubby Ingram M-10. He checked his wristwatch: one-
fifteen. Swinging the fat silencer in a circle, he sent an
onslaught of .44 slugs through the window, chopping a

great hole out of the center. Sharp splinters of brand-new glass sprayed wildly.

In the roar of First Avenue traffic the Ingram's silencer turned this burst into a slight, prolonged waspish buzz. Winfield dropped below the table, yanking Eileen down with her by brute force. The Ingram operator holstered his machine pistol.

His associate lofted a double-barreled sawed-off 12-gauge shotgun and he caught it gracefully the way Fred Astaire retrieved his walking stick, on the fly. Both barrels went in a roar that stopped traffic on First Avenue.

Battipaglia had turned around to stare. His face got some of the blast. His chest exploded scarlet rain over most of the restaurant. The gunman paused for another leisurely look. Then he readjusted his beret and entered a small gray Ford waiting at the curb, motor running. His associate drove off at the same prudent speed with which the entire event had been staged.

Later, giving statements to the police and TV reporters, many of the diners mentioned the easy look of it, as if the gunman in the beret had all the time in the world and knew it.

Inside the restaurant, shielded by the table top, Winfield picked bits of glass off Eileen. "I p-promise you," she said, her teeth chattering. "That's not your blood." Unable to speak, Eileen pointed to the blotches of red on Winfield's long, slender hands. "N-not my blood either. It's all Dr. B-Battipaglia's b-blood," Winfield told her. Her lower lip was trembling. "It's the last thing he's ever g-going to g-give us."

Far away, sirens keened in mourning.

The day grew unseasonably colder. Homeless men wandered along Dominick Street driven like dead leaves by a west wind at their backs, blowing in from the Hudson River.

Italo Ricci had no idea what the weather was like on the streets. He was brought from home to office by car and returned home the same way without having to step into the spit and shit of the streets. "Hands-on" management was a policy he followed, but only at his old rolltop desk. In addition to day-to-day management, Italo had over the decades amassed a file of blackmail dossiers, the basis of the tremendous clout wielded by the night side of Ricci affairs. In terms of his subjects' importance, his personnel files rivaled the FBI's.

He had some reason to know this. In addition to what he and his agents had developed over the years—wiretap transcriptions, intercepted mail, telephoto surveillance and the like—Italo had managed to capture the most important single cache of confidential intelligence of the twentieth century.

Over half that century J. Edgar Hoover had held maximal power through voluminous blackmail information. That power, residing in his jealously guarded personal files, was willed to his longtime companion, Clyde Tolson. The world was told that, before he followed Hoover into death, Tolson had burned these. Unfortunately, there existed a kind of trump card that would have tarnished both their memories by branding them a pair of elderly closet queens. Italo, who held the card, made a simple swap with Tolson, who didn't have Hoover's backbone.

The files were contained in twenty-seven double-corrugated cartons. For some years now Italo had himself transposed those files onto floppy disks. He had young computer-heads for the job, but they would then know what he knew. Italo was halfway through his task. He already knew which Supreme Court Justice liked to be dressed as a girl and forced into fellatio—this had helped influence the outcome of interstate commerce decisions. Of the senators who required servicing from male hustlers, Italo had a useful list—defense spending could be channeled completely with such knowledge. He had intimate knowledge of every business executive from A through L. Italo's only problem was the age of the data. Many of the subjects had died.

He shut down his computer. In one of the Greenwich Village side streets a siren began yelping busily. Italo detested sirens. They symbolized the crude violence of this accursed city. The moan always put him in mind of the mourners at a Sicilian funeral, the grief-eaters, some paid to orchestrate their grief, some bowed truly down by tragedy. People! That was always the trouble with life . . . the people who lived it.

The church struck the quarter hour past one p.m. The

telephone at his elbow rang. He picked it up at once. "Onorevole," a husky voice began. "Iggy here."

"I'd heard you were in town, amico mio. An opportune moment, let me add."

The man at the other end coughed. "At your service, my dear old friend."

"Do me the pleasure of sharing my lunch," Italo suggested. "Right now?"

"Which restaurant?" the man with the hoarse voice asked.

"Restaurants kill you. Right here in my office, dear friend. Right now."

"Crude," Charley said. His face was white, his mouth grim. He and Garnet had been watching the evening news.

"But effective."

"It has the Vince Ricci trademark all over it."

They retained, not the stunned silence most people feel after watching the half hour of disaster and corruption pictured on almost any evening news program, but the heightened silence of intelligent people thinking furiously, a kind of electromagnetic field of rational thought waves desperately trying to make sense of the brutal and irrational. And, as always, losing.

She finished her drink and got to her feet, smoothing down her skirt, eyeing him as she ran her fingers through her cap of white hair. "And Winfield was sitting right there?"

He nodded almost vacantly. "When she called me she said neither of them were—" He stopped and a great sigh seemed to retch upward from him. "Vince must have known she'd be sitting there. He must have known she was at risk."

"Winfield's life . . ." She stopped. Then: "When you hire a murderer, perhaps it's like hiring an artist to do your portrait. You have to give him creative space to work in, make his own decisions, exalt his own hideous soul." She watched his face grow even more grave. "If so, the murderer is a self-portrait of Vince Ricci. Would you like to eat here tonight? Restaurants seem rather risky." He said nothing. "It really distresses you. It's Winfield's safety."

He drained his drink and poured a little more Irish whisky in his glass. Her face reflected his pain. "If I ask her to drop this case, she'll work even harder. But it will end up killing her. Vince is that way. He's hardest on someone he feels is not just an enemy but a betrayer. If you're a Ricci, and you oppose him, you deserve a special death."

"What would a special death be?" Garnet wondered somberly. "How much more dead would that be?"

"A special death." His voice had grown harsh. "A young woman, brimming with promise. That's a special death."

"That death takes place every day, everywhere, by the thousands. Oh, God, it isn't special." She started to cry, very quietly, shoving away the tears at the bottom of her almond-shaped eyes. Then she closed the gap between them and hugged his head to her breast. "She is being responsible, your daughter. She has found a tremendous job. It entails risks," Garnet added in a grave voice. "We are all in a high-risk period. Once the international political tensions relaxed, once we stopped worrying about communism, our true danger became clear. The political rivalries were only rhetoric. Now we're left with the realities. How many years before we can all breathe safely again?"

"And drink the water," Charley said with some irony.

She gave him a painful squeeze and let go. A small ketch ghosted downriver in the gathering twilight. "Oh, how beautiful!" They went to the window to watch.

"I love this house," he said then. He stood behind her, his arms encircling her. "I love the feeling it gives me of movement, of freedom to move, of everything being transient."

"Including me. It's not mine for much longer."

"Will your friend sell?"

"He doesn't own it anymore. He made it over to the Herman Foundation for all sorts of tax breaks."

"What's the Herman Foundation?"

"Non-profit." She waved her hand vaguely. "Education. Environment. You ought to get together with them. They feel the way you do about reforming teaching. Although you might be a bit too radical for them. But once you're a contributor, they'd overlook extremism." She laughed softly, "Anyway, they want me out by Thanksgiving." A siren coughed into life along Sutton Place, moving closer, then dropping in tone as it passed. She turned, kissed him firmly on the lips and started for the kitchen. "Get on the phone and talk to Winfield. See how she's taking it. Let her know you're concerned. You'll feel better about it if you do. I'll warm up something in the oven."

"She knows how concerned I am."

"Tell her again."

"I don't have to do that with Winfield. We understand each other."

"You have to do that with every woman, Charley. Do you want me to write it down for you?"

He laughed. "No. I'll remember." He stood there, sipping his drink, listening to her making small kitchen noises and trying to decide whether to phone his daughter at her apartment or her office. Far above, racing away from the city along the high, arching Queensborough Bridge, two sirens whooped and howled like wolves at play.

A heavy-laden lighter, riding low in the water, edged upstream, leaving a creamy wake that caught the dying light. At the bow, holding a coiled rope, a white-haired old man caught sight of him. He waved casually.

Charley raised his hand to wave back.

The rear of the house blew apart. The shock wave slammed him forward against the plate glass, which gave way. He and the window flew through the air. He hit the front garden, face spouting blood. He swerved sideways to look back. The whole rear of the house was in flames. Gas explosion!

He stumbled to his feet, blood running down his face, and waded back through the glassless window. The kitchen wasn't there, not really. She had been flung sideways like a doll. When he lifted her up, she weighed nothing, nothing at all. A Raggedy-Ann doll.

He carried her outside. The silence was total, appalling. The old man on the lighter had pulled in to a wooden bulkhead and was tying up. He started running toward Charley. "Hold on! Mister, don't move her!" he called. "Hold on."

November

Twenty-Three

"It isn't that people are having more babies," Buzz Eiler assured his less successful neighbor, a dermatologist. "It's that nobody has a baby unless they get it from Eiler."

The big white-brick apartment house on East 72nd Street provided a central entrance. The lobby walls were lit by their original Art Deco lamps of half-round, translucent plate glass, etched with greenish seaweed patterns. On glossy ebonite tables a miniskirted girl in a wind-blown garden hat was being dragged along by a Borzoi, each sculpture in a bronze patina that matched the seaweed.

Overhead, the twenty stories of the building were devoted to apartments of various sizes. Here below, to the left of the lobby, a group of doctors operated a small medical co-op. An internist, a pediatrician and a dermatologist shared more than enough space for their combined patient list and malpractice insurance.

To the right of the lobby, with three nurses and a physiotherapist, Buzz Eiler filled the same space and was hoping to buy more from the dermatologist. By now the doormen of the building were used to ushering through opera singers, television stars, the governor's wife and most of the social register.

It was with some doubt, therefore, that the white-haired doorman viewed the two burly young men who hurtled simultaneously through the front doors from the street, as if propelled forward by a double-barreled shotgun.

"Eiler's?" one asked curtly. He wore marvelously overwashed jeans and a white Shantung jacket with its sleeves pushed up past his elbows.

The elderly doorman looked perplexed. "Are you picking up your wife?"

"Pop, I couldn't budge that tub of lard. There?" He had caught sight of a door plaque, being the one, obviously, who did the reading.

The two young men threw open the door and peered

inside. "Yes?" the receptionist asked with the same odd look as the doorman's. She was a rather attractive brunette in her late forties with a professionally intimidating air of brisk hauteur. Her eyes seem to drag reluctantly over the white Shantung, condemning it as a fabric, a design and a way of life.

"Doc in?"

"I beg y—" Her voice died momentarily as the young man's pronunciation—"Daggin?"—caught up with her hearing. "Do you have an appointment?"

"In or out? Snap it up, lady." His voice was ragged, as if he normally shouted a great deal but in her case was making an exception.

"He's only in by appointment," she persisted gamely.

By now both young men were leaning over her like a pair of bullocks. "Is that a yes or a no?"

"Yes, if you have an appointment. Otherwise, no."

"Jesus," the one who talked complained loudly. "What would I have to do to get a straight answer out of you, Gilda? Lou, go tell him."

The silent Lou left the office and could be seen outside on 72nd Street conferring briefly with the passenger in the rear of a chauffeured Rolls Silver Dream. When he returned, he was moving bulkily behind a man whose catlike stride was that of a dancer's, heel before toe, precise, rapid, sure. Under his black curls, Vince Ricci's hot eyes checked the waiting women and the receptionist up and down. She got the distinct feel of the ambient temperature warming up, which a small filet mignon about to be forked might undergo.

"May I help you?"

"The doc's private office." Vince's hissing purr succeeded in alerting any of the women who hadn't yet looked up from their magazines. A hush fell over the waiting room, this place where the aftermath of sexual encounters rarely included the sudden possibility of a new one. Vince's shiny leather trousers fitted like a glove, cupping and separating his buttocks appealingly. The thin black leather jacket draped his shoulders like a torero's cape.

The receptionist, determined to repel this unusually male boarder, felt her hand lift against her will as her finger indicated a closed door. "But he has a patient in there."

"Decent?"

The receptionist's glance locked with his. "I beg your pardon."

"Still in her teddy? Up on slings? Split beaver? What?"

When he got no answer, Vince smiled charmingly and indicated the door to his two colleagues. They swung it open with a loud bang. One stepped inside, swiveled his head both ways and then stepped aside. "OK, Vince."

Beyond him, Buzz Eiler had been talking to a fully-clothed young woman who handled tax-free Triple-A municipal debentures for a downtown brokerage house. He started to his feet. "Hold it!" he barked.

" 'S'OK, Buzz!" Vince shouted, a tall dark menace with glossy curls moving inexorably down upon a short, sandy man with a kewpie-doll face.

"Who the hell are you?" Buzz demanded in a brave voice.

"Hey, baby! I am the happiest wop in New York! I'm Vince Ricci!"

The sound of Buzz's bottom sitting down on his chair was like the report of a small revolver. He blinked. "You mean you're Mrs. Ricci's huh-huh-hus—?"

"I am the future father of Eugene Ricci. My man, you are a miracle worker. Anything I got is yours, baby. Lenore told me the news this morning." He had his arms around Buzz, lifting him bodily out of his chair and shaking him in a gigantic bear hug. "Anything, Buzz, baby, anything at all! For a goombah good and true, I spare nothing."

"Wha-wha—?"

"Look inside your sexy little heart. See what's hiding there. What desires. The wildest, outta-this-world experience you have ever dreamed of? OK, it's yours."

"But I—"

"Starting with an invite this weekend for you and a broad. A small island in the Mediterranean. Not much to do but bare-ass gambling. You do gamble?"

"Uh. I . . ."

"Hey, Buzz, what's that Thursday night high-stakes poker game of yours? Knitting class?"

"Who told y—?"

"I do my homework, sweetheart. When I make a life-long goombah, I gotta know him inside and out."

"Inside—?" Buzz's throat snapped shut.

"Hey, some pal of yours showed me your med school records. The papers you wrote. The research stuff. High-class work. You got admirers, my man, and I'm one of them."

"That stuff is confid—"

"Not between goombahs," Buzz-buddy." Vince glanced at his watch. "Gotta run." He delved into his breast pocket and produced two folders. "Air tickets. Honeymoon suite. A voucher for a G's worth of chips. All courtesy of the future father of Eugene Ricci. See ya, Buzz, baby!" He blew a kiss to the doctor and then, carried away blew kisses to half a dozen ladies in waiting. As he left, followed by his goons, three of the women burst into applause.

Twenty-Four

Bloomfield was a Hoboken street whose 1890 row houses were filled with lovely century-old architectural details. Kerry Ricci lay fast asleep in his second floor bedroom facing his postage-stamp rear garden. During the night a light snow had started, dusting his bushes and two small trees with a floury bloom like powdered sugar on a Christmas ginger pfefferneuse. The snow stopped at four a.m. It was then Kerry awoke.

Fear had come to him in his dream. He had a sense of being invaded, of a breach in the wall and intruders swarming through. They were . . . ? He couldn't remember any more of it, just the awakening, prickling skin across his shoulders and chest, his hand reaching automatically under his pillow for the flat .25 Beretta he had been told to keep there.

He held his breath, listening. He heard . . . nothing. This disturbed him more than the dream. He slid silently off the bed, holding the small automatic pistol in front of him.

He froze. Someone was sitting in the easy chair by the window. No, not a trick of the light. A person, sitting silently.

"Sit perfectly still," Kerry announced. He was horrified to hear his voice crack. "Don't move."

"Why the fuck should I move?" Kevin asked in an irritated tone.

"You creep!" Kevin yelled. He chucked the gun at his brother and jumped on him. They wrestled for a moment, cuffing each other with ferocious snorts and faked pounding sounds. "Slam! Pow! Thud! Ka-runch!" Finally they calmed down. Kerry sat down across from his twin in a matching easy chair. This was, after all, Kevin's house as much as his. Everything in it was paired, even to twin breakfast tables in the kitchen downstairs.

"There must be an easier way of inducing cardiac arrest," Kerry observed. In the dark they could barely see each other. But they had no need to. Apart for months on end, their own mirrors were constant reminders of what their brother looked like.

"Hey, Ker, you were having one helluva dream."

"I dreamed my brother did one of his celebrated breaking and entering numbers."

"Hey, I used my key."

"Oh, my God, I'm so sorry," Kerry apologized with false sincerity. "What's up? What've they got you doing?"

"Breaking and entering, what else?" Kevin drummed fingers on the arm of his chair. "How about coffee?"

Kerry stood up. "I'll make some."

"It's made. I got here half an hour ago."

"Smooth moves, man." Kerry glanced out the window. "Look, Jack Frost on the job. You here through Christmas?"

"I don't know. Can you come out to the Island with me this weekend? I want to spend some time with Ma. In case I can't be here for Christmas."

"She needs stroking," Kerry agreed. Silently, they walked downstairs to the kitchen. Kevin poured two mugs of steaming coffee and they sat down, each at his own breakfast table, facing each other.

"A classic portrait, Mr. Bad versus Mr. Good." Kerry sipped his coffee. "How can Zio Italo be sure, when he sends you off to fight dragons, that we haven't secretly switched roles?"

"He gives us a math problem. The one who does it without his Thinkman is you. But if he wants to know what Shan Lao is up to, he has to call for me."

"Nobody knows what Shan is up to," Kerry said. "Cousin Charley—" He stopped and squinted at his brother. "You heard what happened to Charley and that Indian lady he's sweet on? Round-the-clock nurses, drip feeds, third degree burns, skin transplants. Charley has been sitting by her side all summer."

Kevin stared at him for a long moment. Then: "I see."

"You think Zio paid the gas company a bonus?" Kerry demanded.

"How many guys are loose on this planet who can produce a genuine, old-fashioned gas explosion?"

"I love that note of admiration in your voice. Maybe you can put a byline on the blast? Or to what happened to Winfield? She nearly got shotgunned."

Kevin nodded. "Schmulka Rubin."

"Schmulka what?"

"Escaped from the Soviet Gulag. Before glasnost. Wears a beret. Handles all Vince's Manhattan contracts. Didn't he first chop out a hole in the glass with an Ingram?"

"My God, a designer take-out, trademark, logo and all." Kerry made a mewing sound between pain and resignation. "The family is getting too big, Kev. Charley says we have too many hostages to fortune."

"What's that mean?"

Kerry lifted his hands palms up. "One daughter is there when Vince's kosher nostra opens fire. Another is hooked into the Yellow Peril's only son. Did I tell you? Bunny is growing Shan Lao's only grandchild. If it was up to Charley there'd be a retrospective birth control pill. A parent would take it and the kid would . . . disappear."

Kevin laughed out loud. "Especially where us two are concerned."

There was a long silence. The brothers had long ago stopped talking about their mysterious paternity, but that didn't preclude thinking about it. Kerry got up and walked to the rear door, facing the garden. Dawn had turned the white frosting pink. "He's never been anything but terrific to me," he said. It was as close as either of them ever got to guessing out loud. "Now he's going to change everything. He sees that he spent his whole life taking. Now he wants to spend it giving. Nobody will let him get away with that, least of all Zio."

Kevin produced an evil chuckle. "Who's enjoying Il Professore's terrific view, you?"

"Help yourself. Nobody's using it." When his brother failed to respond, Kerry went on, thoughtfully, "If the blast was meant to keep Charley in line, it failed completely. You know a Sicilian testa dura, Kev: a hard head that gets more stubborn the more you beat on it."

"Zio wants me to go to the Philippines." Kevin produced a heavy sigh. "I want to stay here for Christmas."

"What's this one?"

"Nothing for you, Ker. It's between Vince, Italo and me."

Kerry did a good imitation of his brother's sigh. "They say the Filipinas are all gorgeous. Kev!" Kerry said with sudden urgency. "Listen, Kev. What I said before. Remember? How would Italo know which of us he sent?"

Kevin sat motionless for a long time. "How? He'd never guess. Never. Only Ma knows about this," he added, touching the skin under his left eye. "And she tells nobody nothing."

Both brothers fell silent.

Twenty-Five

Garnet's way back? For a long time it didn't exist. Once she could hear them, the doctors' forecast about her never began with "I'm sure . . ." but always "We can only hope . . ." It was one long night, sleepless, cocooned in utter uncertainty. There were bandages on her eyes because of the stitching, but whether the eyes could see or not, only daylight would reveal. That sense was turned off. So was the sense of touch, with both arms splinted and taped. So was smell and taste. Four out of five senses shut down. Hearing was her only window. People spoke to her but she couldn't speak back. Even Charley grew silent in such circumstances.

Charley. She knew he was there because he spoke, haltingly, regularly. He was the floor under her and the sky overhead. His voice was bright or dull, eager or depressed. Charley was her whole world.

Charley's way back was another matter entirely. For the first two weeks after the explosion, he had been thankful for the Gestapo regimen of the hospital, which kept out reporters, TV crews, family visitors, everyone but himself and a few detectives and fire inspectors. He'd seen the last of the police the moment they agreed that the explosion had been accidental. How they had done this Charley didn't know, since Garnet couldn't speak and his own testimony had been less than useful.

His way back? Only a smashed nose and front teeth, superficial cuts from shattered glass. He was bandage-free by the third week: the packing was out of his nostrils, his sutures were removed. He looked like himself, recovered from a fistfight.

It occurred to him that the job of all police and fire investigators was to close the book fast and snip off any loose ends still hanging out. Charley knew this was a cynical idea, but the explosion had left him with few others.

He thought about very little but Garnet and whether or not the explosion had been accidental. If he had lost her then, his mind would now be coping with his grief. But as it was he only had room now for hope, a much more painful thing. Therefore he was prepared to keep his book open long after the police had closed theirs.

Italo had visited the hospital twice—unusual for one who hated to tread the loathsome streets—each time turned away but leaving a small, expensive bouquet for Garnet. After a while he stopped coming but the gifts continued, perfume, flowers, chocolates, magazines. A gentleman of the old school.

As Charley sat by Garnet's bed he watched her still body for signs of hope, something that could match his hope. Her only activities were respiration and pulse rate.

There was no expression to go by. Her dear, elfin face was swathed in a thick gauze-and-cotton bandage with no eyeholes but a sardonic, cynical slash for a mouth. Once a day Charley was sent out of the room while a three-person team changed the dressing and anointed it with unguents, a profane imitation of the extreme unction a priest gives to the dying. The various drips and feeds that surrounded her like a malign forest gave the battle-field a nasty science-fiction look. Charley had rejoiced the day they'd taken the oxygen tent away. He had cheered when they freed her right arm from splints and pronounced it healed. He could hardly wait for them to remove the traction and cast from her left leg and the cast from her left arm. That would be a hopeful day. When? With what results?

That she was conscious through most of this, he had some form of proof. When he held her cold, still right hand, where the bandages had left the fingers exposed, she felt it. Several times her fingers palped his hand.

Then a great forward step. When the right splint was removed and her arm lay free of restraint, she had held his fingers and squeezed them with the terrifying weakness of a newborn's tiny grip.

The hospital ambience had begun to grate on him, the officious nurses and doctors speaking badly in their foreign accents, the bustling orderlies squandering their tiny budgets of domination. Volunteer women who brought his food had their small power dramas to stage, moving him to a different chair, arbitrarily changing his coffee to tea. Small nastinesses to renew self-importance. How could anyone make any kind of recovery in this dismal concentration camp? The whole atmosphere of the place conspired to hold down one's spirit until hope choked and died.

He longed to get her to a private clinic Richland operated in a leafy area of northern Westchester County, a rich man's place with its own CAT scanner, every member of staff, down to the janitor, speaking English as his mother tongue. There hope would blossom. There Garnet's deathly passivity would end and a new life would begin. This hospital she was in had to be tolerated only because it had the best burn trauma teams in the nation.

One morning, when they renewed her dressing, they

thoughtlessly let him watch. The team of a doctor and two nurses cut away the thick wrap. For a moment all Charley could see was a flash of raw, oozing red. Then this was covered with a much thinner mask of gauze, buttered with a medicated gel.

Had her eyes fluttered? All her hair had burned away and, with it, her eyelashes and brows. But hadn't her eyelids fluttered? "Did you see that, Doctor?"

The young Venezuelan gave him a bored glance. "Say wha'?"

"Her eyelids fluttered."

"Di'dey?" he asked a nurse, as if Charley's lay report was untrustworthy.

"Din notice," an Iranian nurse responded.

The team cleaned up and left without saying anything else. Charley approached her bed, his heavy heart lifting at her new appearance. She looked more human now with the thinner dressing, less like a medieval knight in his jousting helmet or a hockey goalie repelling hard-rubber bullets. Not only was the new mask thinner, but it had diamond cut-outs for her eyes. "Garnet, I saw your eyelids move. I know I did." His voice had that hollow quality, unprojecting, of someone speaking his hopes aloud to himself. He watched her new, more human mask. She had been warned again and again not to try to speak or move her head in any direction. But had she heard? Did she understand?

Between plaster and surgical tape, only her right arm lay free. The rest of her remained immobilized. Her left side had taken the brunt of the blast. After a moment he gave up watching her "face" and glanced at the exposed fingers of her right hand. As he did so, she lifted her first and second fingers up and down several times, then again. It was a pitifully small movement, less than an inch in either direction, but it signaled immensities.

"Yes!" he shouted. "Yes, you're saying yes! You're back! You're with us!"

In the patient's lounge, half the people wore pajamas or dressing gowns. Charley was dressed in khaki slacks and a tennis sweater. "Yes, pretty hairy," Winfield agreed. "Eileen is still totally freaked out after all these months."

"I don't understand why you're not. You were both in the line of fire."

"Ricci genes. But Eileen's discovered she's pregnant, so it changes her choice of options when somebody gets shotgunned to death all over her."

Charley winced. "Hideous."

"What's hideous is that with one take-out Vince has destroyed the witness who could have sent him to the slams . . . and scared Eileen shitless." Winfield stopped and readjusted her face to get rid of the annoyed look there. "We were in the process of adding defendants to the docket, other Ricci hookers who'd been told they were healthy. In all, we can now go to court with ten co-defendants, the feminist trial of the century. But she's afraid to take the next step."

"Which is?"

Winfield paused. She gave him an embarrassed half-smile. "You needn't know that. You're targeted already."

"Me? I'm convinced it was an accidental gas explosion."

"Which box of chocolate creams from Zio Italo changed your mind?" She frowned at the annoyed look on her father's face. She had, after all, gone to some trouble to remove her own. "To one who learned skepticism at her father's knee you sound strangely believing."

He made a face. "A true professor never regrets instilling wisdom." He shrugged. "But I was never a true professor. So I regret passing along smarts. Yes, I do. You're too smart."

"Smarts? You mention smarts? Through a pal in the D.A.'s office, I saw the police explosion report," she told him. "It's not even proven Garnet lit the oven. Her fingerprints on the controls mean nothing. The explosion conveniently destroyed any evidence of a slow leak or gas buildup. It's a meaningless report. Why do you buy it?"

"Because . . ." he eyed her sideways, trying to judge the effect of what he would say, "because when you're my age you're sick of fighting lost causes over and over again. You forsake smarts for neat explanations. Because I really can't credit Zio with such murderous intent against his own family. And because, my dear, to hark back to those Ricci genes, if Zio had hired a specialist for it, Garnet and I would both be six feet under.''

''Had any time lately to continue transferring Richland ownership?''

''No. I've been waiting for some sign that Garnet is improving. I got it this morning. Let me tell—''

''Let me tell you. The organization of which Zio is a high-ranking figure only rarely resorts to death. For centuries they've known that the threat of death is far more powerful than death itself. Don't tell me Zio would've needed you six feet under. You're precisely, precisely where he wants you both.'' Her voice had risen slightly from her usual cool tones and her face, normally lacking in any great expression, had grown agitated. Now it lapsed back into the relaxed calm of an ivory Madonna.

''La Professoressa,'' he said, smiling weakly in case she objected to the nickname. But she didn't seem to. ''Have you noticed,'' he mused aloud, ''that all the doctors being trained are foreigners?''

''Hard to ignore it. Especially mysterious if you subscribe to the Charles Anthony Richards Theory of rotten U.S. teaching.''

''It gives you a clue as to how bad teaching is in other countries.''

Her face puckered. ''Third World countries?''

He looked worried. ''Where do American medical students go to school? New Guinea?''

''You're cracking up?''

''Could be.''

''You're realizing that Italo has you where he wants you.''

''Mmm.''

''Fear not,'' she said. ''Quite soon now, I'll have Italo where I want *him*.'' Her smile terrified Charley. ''And then we can discuss . . . Ricci genes.''

The second week of December, when Charley came back from lunch, he found that Garnet had gotten hold of a stubby pencil and some scrap paper. On it, in the loopy capital letters of a six-year-old, she had printed: ''IT'S ME!''

''Can you see me?'' he asked.

''Y,'' she printed, the computer stroke for ''Yes.''

"Remember, no talking yet." He bent over her, staring hard into the eyeholes of her mask. "You look sensational," he said, "like something a fancy butcher delivers for a Sunday roast. Are you still in pain?"

"N. LUV U."

He was kneeling by her bed now. Over the past days they had cleared away most of the tubes and drips. He kissed her bared fingers. "I love you, too," he said. "Stop wasting your strength trying to seduce me."

"3 PM," she printed.

He frowned and then remembered. "Is it today they take it off?"

"Y." She kept on printing until she had, "T MAN."

"T-Man? Treasury agent? Oh! You want a Thinkman? I'll phone Kerry."

"N. U GO."

Charley glanced at his watch. He had an hour before the dressing team arrived to remove the gauze mask, perhaps forever. In Hollywood this was the crucial moment. Played by a little-known actor, the fugitive—wanted for a crime of which he was innocent—had lived in bandages until this moment when Thomas Mitchell, drunken plastic surgeon, cut away the gauze and showed us the anxious features of Humphrey Bogart. "I'll be back by three," Charley said, getting to his feet. He blew her a kiss as he left. Ten minutes later the dressing team arrived. It had been a deception on Garnet's part; if the skin grafts had failed, she didn't want Charley to see them.

Italo looked out of a high, unwashed window at the sky. Snowflakes drove down in diagonals. Outside, on Dominick Street, they were using jackhammers to break up a trench for a new sewer line. The hammerman let off bursts of noise like a machine gunner.

Beside the big oak rolltop desk sat a tall, handsome man with a hairline mustache and black hair, going salt-and-pepper at the sides. He wore an extremely well-tailored suit of Continental tailoring that hugged his neck without gaping. His shoes were narrow and pointed. In one hand he held a long ebony-colored cigarette holder from which an even longer, unlit cigarette jutted. A diplomat, possibly? One used to luxury. More than that was unreadable, except that he knew Italo quite well. Italo was, first, an ascetic, and, second, a health nut. The visitor's cigarette remained unlit.

Nevertheless, from time to time, with an elegance of movement, he placed the holder to his lips and drew deeply and with some satisfaction. Italo turned back from the window, his deep-set olive eyes sparking anger. "My right-hand nephew hasn't left her bedside all summer."

The jackhammer erupted noisily. "Ah. How is your nephew's health?" the visitor asked.

"Charley? Never better. That was precision work, my friend."

"Nothing." The visitor's hoarse voice was accompanied by a gesture of his unlit cigarette, conveying pride. "Did I do right, opening contact with you again? I mean, after the, er, explosion?" He had an odd accent, harshly produced, the r's ulular as in French, but the rest of his pronunciation slightly British.

"Iggy, you did right. I am," he added, "in your debt. Again."

"It is I who am the debtor." The man took a deep drag on his cold cigarette. His hoarse rasp made it easy to picture him as a heavy smoker.

"Hey, any buddy of Meyer's is a buddy of mine."

Neither man spoke for a long time. Then Italo released them from further talk. He clapped his hands together as he stood up. "Iggy Zetz," he said, extending his right hand fervently, "you are a true pal. And an A-number-one professional." They shook hands for a long time.

Twenty-Six

Western Pennsylvania, between Pittsburgh and the New York State border, has always been a victim of industry. Petroleum was discovered here first. It has also been victimized by coal, iron, rail, carbon and paper. Almost every aspect of the Industrial Revolution has visited Western Pennsylvania like a series of biblical plagues. It was small wonder that the natives were touchy.

In mid-December, when the doctors told Charley that Garnet's condition had markedly improved, he scheduled a one-day visit to the area with Kerry in tow. It seemed fitting to him that he somehow atone for having almost drowned Garnet in the murderous undertow of Zio Italo's survival schemes. It seemed more than fitting that he concern himself with the last thing she had brought to his attention before the explosion.

World oil prices had started rising; new reserves of natural gas were needed; Richland was reopening holdings in the Adirondack Natural Forest that runs southwest from Salamanca, New York, to Kane, Pennsylvania. The object was to have been pumping crude and tapping off gas but, in his new frame of mind, Charley simply wanted to unload the leases to another company by demonstrating that the wells were live.

In a plague spot like this, any re-industrialization was welcome. A job was a job. But by the 1990s, Western Pennsylvania had awakened, somewhat, to the value of rolling foothills, unspoiled forests and meandering rivers. The national park drew skiers in the winter, picnickers every other season and money all the time. Rebuilding the old wells and refineries would bring in a swarm of itinerant drillers, welders and the like. But then it would leave the area jobless. OK to do that to Arab tribesmen with flies clustered around their eyes, Charley knew, not to native-born Pennsylvanians.

A picket line was the first warning. A group called KPG, Keep Pennsylvania Green, had mounted a twenty-four hour watch on Richland numbers 27, 28 and 29, wells that hadn't been worked since 1944. The national park had since overgrown them. Meanwhile, using tactics invented by Greenpeace, a fleet of huge, lumbering off-the-road recreational vehicles bearing signs and banners was shadowing Charley's limo. The usual slogans prevailed but one seemed specially devised to get under Charley's skin. "You toucha da forest, we breaka you arm."

Since most of the oversized vehicles were driven by 300-pound youths in baseball caps and thick beards, neither Charley nor Kerry felt too optimistic about a good old-fashioned yelling contest. There was simply no point in beating their way through the snowy underbrush around Richland 27, 28 and 29 while several dozen pairs of hostile eyes marked every movement and video cameras recorded the city slickers in action, presumably for broadcast on local TV.

"It's a no-win bind," Kerry told him. Charley nodded, wondering when Kerry had started using out-of-date nonce-words. His language was usually formal and downright conservative. They beat their way back to the locally rented limo that had picked them up when they disembarked at Du Bois airport. Between there and here lay the town of St. Marys, where some of these Paul Bunyan types had set up the KPG nerve center.

"Let's beard these bears in their den," Charley suggested. "You're more their age. Find a spokesman or chairperson and let's sit down and talk. Let them know we're not ogres, we're open to negotiation."

The limo was making its ponderous way southeast toward St. Marys, immense, fat-tired vehicles surrounding it on the narrow roads and keeping its speed down below thirty miles an hour. They passed through towns choking with waste acid gases from carbon filament and paper production.

More snow lay aloft in the gathering leaden skies. Kerry wondered why he had been stupid enough to get himself into this particular mess. He was carrying a Thinkman with him, programmed for oil depletion reserves and the like. He could answer any petroleum-related question. But that wasn't what he was being told to do. He was being told to listen, compromise, sway minds. Kerry would be up to the challenge, no question of it. But Kerry wasn't Kerry. It was Kevin beside Charley. The twins had decided on a dry run of their substitution scheme. If Kevin could successfully mimic Kerry, they'd do a trial of Kerry impersonating Kevin. If both went off well, they would give themselves a green light: Kerry would go to the Philippines and Kevin would get a rare Christmas at home with Stefi.

But, already the substitution was not doing well.

By the time they crawled into St. Marys the short winter day had ended. Night had fallen as the limousine pulled up to a funeral home on North Michael Street, not far from the St. Marys' library. As Kevin got out under the long awning, Charley stayed in the car, telephoning Garnet's hospital in New York.

In the basement of the funeral home a copying machine was producing letter-sized sheets that would fold into a leaflet. A smell of formaldehyde embalming fluid pervaded the area. Kevin, in his Kerry-styled financial clothes—herringbone wool-coat with velour collar, three-piece dark gray suit, white shirt and striped tie—felt entirely out of place among young people in jeans, sheepskin jerkins and plaid wool lumberjackets.

"Yes?" The girl was his age, about twenty, in a brilliant yellow oilcloth, wool-lined poncho. She looked up from the copying machine. "You're from Richland, aren't you?" Kevin tried to get the sense of her without seeming to stare. She wasn't bad looking, although a bit overweight. But they all were out here in the sticks. What else was there to do but beer up and shove in another load of potato chips? She had long black hair that looked clean enough and a sort of bright-lipped Irish face.

"Yes," he told her. "I'm one of the city slickers come to corrupt you honest conservation people."

"Really?" She stopped the machine. "How would you go about doing that?"

Kevin shrugged. "How about a check for a thousand bucks? Don't tell me it wouldn't be welcome."

She extended her hand out, palm up. "Let's see it, slicker."

Around them a few people began to collect. One of the gigantic bearded blimps guffawed. "Hey, Mary-Ann, cash on the barrelhead!"

Kevin had brought out his check book. "Who's it payable to? KPG?"

Someone in back produced a perfect rebel yell like the eehaw of a jackass. Kevin began to write the check. "One thousand bucks," he said out loud.

"And a case of Straubs!" a fat young man with straw-colored hair hollered, naming the local beer. He shouldered his way forward until he was face to face with Kevin. "Clear out. You stink up the place."

Kevin stopped writing the check. "OK, let's talk instead. No need for confrontation when we've still got negotiation."

Before he could duck sideways, the young man bent

him backward over the copier. He pried Kevin's mouth open and was stuffing the check inside. Kevin's teeth snapped down hard and the young man let out a deafening hoot of pain. "Sonofabitch bites!"

Later, trying to remember everything step by step, because Charley was asking him to, Kevin realized that he was no match for one of these outsized youths, let alone three. They pried open his jaw again, braced it with the handle of a whiskbroom and forced the check down his throat, past the swallowing point. They seemed to know instinctively where that was. Farmboys would. "Next time," the blond lad told him as they let him stand up under his own power, "we gonna make you take back your check through the other end."

"What I'd expect of an asshole like you," Kevin snarled.

It only looked like an offhand cuff, like a man slapping a fly but it sent him across the copier and into the girl. They went down together, rolling over each other like a mating pair. This produced such a chorus of whistles and boot stamping that Kevin decided he'd had enough.

"Thank you, ladies and gentlemen," he said, helping the girl to her feet as he brushed down his financial overcoat. "I have never before seen such a will to fail. We're willing to talk about reopening 27, 28 and 29. We're willing to negotiate. We're willing to hear your side. The world will salute us and think you people are a bunch of redneck troublemakers." He turned and left the funeral home. Would Kerry have handled it that way, he wondered. Outside the snow had begun again and there was no sign of the limo. He stood, rapidly cooling off. Then he heard footsteps behind him and turned to find the dark-haired girl in the yellow poncho.

"The limo's around the corner, gassing up. I'll walk you there. You'll be safe with me." She took his arm and started walking toward what seemed to be the center of town, where many streets crossed in a kind of grand junction.

"Don't tell me I'm in danger," he joshed her as they walked. Snow flakes were driving almost horizontally now.

"This is the boonies out here. You could disappear and never be found." With the arm she wasn't immobilizing,

Kevin slowly reached inside his herringbone overcoat and suit jacket to the shoulder holster where he had hung Kerry's flat .25 Beretta. Its icy metal made his fingertips tingle.

"Please don't frighten me, miss. I cry easy."

"They're serious. You better be."

They had turned the corner. Across the junction of streets he could see the limo and Charley. Before they reached the lighted area, however, he and the girl had to traverse a path leading back behind the library. As they reached that point, she stumbled slightly and pushed him sideways into the alley. Kevin caromed off one young mammoth into another. A third tripped him and Kevin went down on his rear end. All three young giants advanced on him. Kerry, Kevin supposed, would have talked his way out of it. Maybe. Instead, Kevin pulled the flat little automatic and snapped a shot over the head of the biggest youth. In the cold, snowy wind, it sounded like a dog's bark. All three paused. From behind them the girl called, "Come on, J.J., let's beat it."

"Yeah, J.J.," Kevin suggested, "listen to Mary-Ann."

As he sat on the cinders, something gigantic seemed to drop down on him, boot heels smashing into his groin. Kevin rolled sideways and fired off another shot. A fourth obese youth had fallen all over him, knocking his lungs flat. Kevin seemed to black out for a moment. When he came to, seconds later, the alley was empty and there was blood on his nice white shirt. Someone else's blood, but that didn't matter. What mattered was that Kerry would never have handled it this way. Never.

Charley and the limo chauffeur came running over. "You OK? What happened?" They stared down at him, snowflakes brushing past their faces.

"Let's just say we agreed not to negotiate," Kevin muttered, getting to his feet and brushing himself off. Fury washed over him like red waves of lava. When you were Il Professore's errand boy, you had to eat shit. They would pay! They would pay!

"Are you sure you're OK? Because I have to get back to Manhattan," Charley said. "You're welcome to come back with me. But I'd really like you to stay here a day or so and see what you can sort out with these kids. Try to explain our position. Try to get it across that we're not the enemy. See if that works.''

"What's the bottom line you want from me?'' Kevin demanded.

"Kerry, I'm as new at this as you are. See what they offer. Let them do the talking. Go see the sheriff. Let him talk to you. Something may develop that'll surprise us.''

Twenty-Seven

INJUNCTION HITS GREENS;
"WELLS OPEN BY APRIL"
RICHLAND EXEC PROMISES

The sheriff had been young, college-trained with his second child on the way. A man with pretenses and expenses. Kevin, only a few years his junior, in his guise as Kerry had guided him through the details of accepting a bribe masquerading as a vehicle maintenance subsidy. All this took another day.

Kevin had eaten dinner in a small, unclean coffee shop on the main junction that seemed to be the center of St. Marys. The proprietor had given him notice that he would close at eight p.m.

He felt jumpy, nervous, unsettled. He knew the feeling well. Il Professore, the original Mr. No-Balls, had taken away his chance to even the score by limiting him to negotiations. Kevin found it hard to believe that a man as soft as Charley could claw his way 130 stories into the sky and, what's more, maintain his perch there. Some day . . .

Gazing out the street-level window, not Charley's aerie, Kevin stared at the empty, snowbound streets. St. Marys went to sleep much earlier than eight, not in bed but before the TV set. He glanced back at the scrawny old man who ran the coffee shop, a cigarette dangling from his lower lip.

"How bad do they hate us?" he asked. "I mean, now that we won."

"You ain't won nothing," the proprietor assured him. "You got a piece of paper sez the Greenies have to leave you alone. That's all."

"You telling me the KPGs aren't law-abiding people?"

This reduced the old man to helpless laughter and a paroxysm of coughing that shook his frail frame. "My dear God," he marveled at last. "This town is as law-abiding as you'll get in Western PA. St. Marys used to be a Benedictine seminary called Marianstadt, for Christ's sake."

"So what gets you so choked up with laughs?"

"That a sharpie like you worries about people obeying the law." For the same obscure reason, this again tickled the proprietor but he limited himself to chuckles and thus avoided another coughing fit. He did, however, keep the pulmonary franchise by lighting a fresh cigarette from the smoldering end of his previous smoke. "That's what y'call the irony of life," he said then, blowing out a great sheaf of smoke while the old cigarette continued to smolder in its ashtray. "I mean, y'get to be my age you have to laugh, is all. You have to laugh."

Kevin shrugged. "Beats watching TV."

"Ho, yes. If I told y—"

Someone in a passing 1965 Chevy pickup heaved a cinder aggregate building block through the window of the coffee shop. The noise sent a jolt through Kevin's body. Both men ducked sideways as glass rained down on the booth next to Kevin. It isn't always possible to chuck a twenty-pound block with great accuracy, which was what saved him.

"Jesus!" the proprietor screamed. "Jesus H. Kee-rist!"

Without a word, Kevin ran out into the street, leaving the old man to pick up the glass. By now Kevin had memorized the streets that slanted into the junction. He felt on fire with rage. What he needed was revenge. Now! He wanted the funeral home on North Michael Street but he didn't want to approach it directly. Once again, he knew he was behaving like himself and not his brother.

But that was the result of having a cinder block thrown at him.

To his mind, Il Professore ran things much too loosely. He'd sent the limo back to Kevin. But the driver had disappeared with the keys. The damned limo sat there on the main street, collecting traffic summonses. Let's face it, he thought as he ran: getting an injunction against Keep Pennsylvania Green was not enough anymore to outbalance having a cement block dumped on you. It called for new punishment, especially in the mind of someone who had been forced to eat a check and was then stomped on in an alley.

Rage possessed him. He thirsted to hurt and humiliate those who had hurt him. Revenge was what Zito Italo operated on. It ran in his veins. It made him an object of respect and fear. Nobody fools around with a man who understands revenge.

By now Kevin had edged his way around a block of one-family houses and was in against the walls of the funeral home from a different direction. The place was dark inside, even on the second floor. But in the basement a light showed. He could peer down between bushes and see Mary-Ann, the dark-haired girl with the Irish face, still churning out leaflets. The table behind her was covered with neat piles of half-size folders, thousands of them. As far as Kevin could tell through the window, she was alone at her nightwork. Pretty soon she'd go home to her TV dinner in a warmed-up aluminum foil pan, or whatever she ate to keep that zaftig figure. Was it worth waiting for her to leave?

Kevin did a slow, thorough search of the funeral home grounds. As far as he could tell there were no bearded behemoths hiding in bushes, nor any of their monstrous balloon-tired off-the-road vehicles towering up on driveways and curbstones.

He let himself in by a basement door and walked along a corridor that had the morgue odor of formaldehyde. Kevin's nose twitched. "Need any help?"

She cried out and grasped her left breast in its bright pink sweater. "You scared me half to death!"

They eyed each other. "In answer to the question you haven't asked," he said then, moving sideways so as not to seem to be approaching her, "no, I don't hold it against you for setting me up in that alley. I figure you live here so you have to play ball.''

"And I'd do it again," she snapped back. "You know that second shot of yours creased Leroy's midriff. He's got a bandage over it.''

"To stop from leaking beer?"

"Don't," she said. "I know some of these boys let themselves go, b—"

"Trying out for the freak show, most of them.'' He was less than a yard from her now. "You could do yourself a lot better, Mary-Ann. Compared to these fatsos, you've got the only class I've seen in Western PA.''

"What a charming compliment.'' She moved to put the copier between them. "You still carrying that toy gun with you?''

He pulled it out of its shoulder holster and shoved it back. "Man can't be too careful in a big, bad, crime-ridden metropolis like St. Marys." Neither of them spoke while she unloaded the copier's OUT tray. Then she asked, "You here to try your charms on a simple country girl?''

"Figure I'll need the gun?"

"If you ever quit working for Richland, come on back to St. Marys." She smiled almost shyly. "You never know.''

"Why wait till then?" he asked, closing the gap between them.

"My brother's picking me up there in—" She glanced at her watch. "He should've been here by now."

"And how much does *he* weigh?"

She grinned at him. "He's the one who came down on top of you last night.''

"Say no more.'' He extended his arms as if she were holding a gun on him. "You win, Mary-Ann. Just do me one favor?''

"Why, sure."

"When I come back some day, to rescue you from all this, don't be as fat as Leroy.''

The expression on her face was precisely the one he wanted to see: hurt. He turned and walked out, down the corridor and into a mourners' sideroom. He felt great. Not revenged but great. He slammed the front door as if he had left and waited silently, almost as if in premature mourning.

It took her no more than ten minutes to finish up and leave. There was no brother, as he'd expected. He stared out into the snow-covered streets outside. An occasional eighteen-wheeler squealed to a halt for the traffic lights where the 255 headed north to Bradford and the oil refineries. It would not be a peaceful place for a good night's sleep.

He watched her hurry down the side lane and off into the night. Then he slipped back into the darkened room KPG was using. The smell of embalming fluid was strong throughout the basement but in this room the smell of copier cleaning fluid was stronger. He had no idea if formaldehyde would burn. But cleaning fluid was another matter. She had left a notebook on top of the copier. "MARY-ANN IANUCCI" she had printed on the cover. A goombah, Kevin thought. Now, why the hell hadn't she told him? What was a goombah doing in conservation, anyway?

The stacks of leaflets took the whole half-gallon of fluid, sopped it up and cried for more but there was no more. Kevin opened a matchbook and stuck the match-heads under a sodden pile of leaflets. He made sure his escape path was clear, then lit the paper flap of the matchbook.

Even the air might ignite. Fumes were everywhere. Kevin ran down the corridor and out the door, leaving it open to improve the internal draught. He drifted down to the corner near the wrecked front window of the coffee shop. He could just see the funeral home from here. Someone was hurrying down its entrance path under the awning. Time passed. It took so long that he was sure he'd failed. One minute. Two. Then, with a snap like a whipcrack and a sudden blaze of light, the whole basement seemed to blow.

Never underestimate the power of fumes, Kevin thought as he walked, unhurriedly, to the limo still parked across the intersection. He stripped the traffic summonses from the windshield and got inside. In a minute he had hot-wired the Caddy ignition and started the ice-cold engine. In another minute he was driving through slush, down North Michael Street past the funeral home. Its lower story was ablaze with flames. He waited lawabidingly for the traffic light to turn green and then sped out of town.

When Charley heard of this he'd think Kerry had gone crazy. Zio Italo had been right on that score: keep the two sides of the family separate and non-touching. He was right about a lot of things, including revenge.

Funny about Mary-Ann. She would have come on to him a lot stronger if he hadn't been from Richland. But if she'd known he was a Ricci from Richland, what then?

From the top of a hill, Kevin stopped the limo for a moment and looked back at the blaze half a mile behind him. In the distance he could hear sirens. But once you started a paper blaze that way, in a frame building and a strong wind, nothing on earth could stop it till it burned to the rafters. It would all go, even the memory of Mary-Ann.

He felt so much better now. The lava-like rage had cooled. Zio, he thought, how right you are.

Twenty-Eight

"As if Nikki and I were Royal breeding stock," Bunny told her sister, Winfield. "On display like prize heifers." Bunny had flown down from Boston.

The sisters were unpacking heavy corrugated moving cartons in the living room of Winfield's tiny new apartment on East 73rd Street, off First Avenue. A fifth-floor walkup, it was designed, as Winfield said, to keep her abdomen and her wallet perfectly flat.

Bunny suddenly clutched her back, grimaced and sat down on a wooden chair. "Nobody gets back pains this early," she announced triumphantly.

"Oh, Eileen does," her sister corrected her. "I'm surrounded by pregnant women. But nobody's laid a hand on me in months."

"It's not their hands you have to watch for."

"You, Lenore Ricci and Eileen. The 18-28-38 Club. That's your ages. And your IQ's. Bunch of oversexed penis worshippers." This reduced them to giggling. Winfield sat down on the floor. "When does the Great Shan arrive?"

"It's family protocol not to discuss itinerary. There are people in this world Shan Lao wants to keep in the dark about his whereabouts." Bunny settled back for a long talk. "Nikki is already feeling guilty that the pregnancy has forced Daddykins to divulge plans and be somewhere his enemies might figure out in advance."

"To assassinate him? What fun." Winfield stretched flat on her back, linked her fingers behind her head and did ten slow sit-ups. Then she did ten more.

"In honor of the summit meeting," Bunny went on, "Nikki has written another of those boring 'Dear Father' essays."

"I know what our Dear Father said about the essay I showed him." Winfield rolled over on her stomach and did a Yoga stance, the Cobra, ten times. Then she did the Locust ten times. Then she started to alternate between the two.

"Will you stop that shit?" Bunny yelped. "Not all of us are anorexia freaks."

"He thinks Nikki's a radical. These days, Dad's into that."

Bunny wrinkled her nose. "I would *never* put out for a radical. Not knowingly. That Indian lady; is she some kind of radical?"

"Since the explosion, Dad has discovered American Indian religious philosophy. We are all part of nature. We must adapt to nature. We must not force nature to adapt to us." Winfield stretched flat on her back and slowly, slowly, elevated her legs.

"Cut that out," Bunny snapped. "Do you see her?"

"No visitors allowed yet but Dad. But I hear the plastic surgeons are finished." She stared up at her sister. "I'm not putting down that Indian stuff. She believes we're all one great single force. You can see why she's such a big conservationist." She frowned. "I guess I'll have to know her better if she's going to be our stepmother."

"That's what Nikki said I should do with the Great Shan, know him better," Bunny said. "Is that an idea a radical would think of?"

"How could the only child, son and heir of Shan Lao be a radical?"

The two sisters glanced casually at each other and Winfield was reminded once again that for several years now, if Bunny had a role model it was not their mother, it was her sister. Winfield supposed there was nothing wrong with this as long as Bunny had a sister as superior, as talented, as accomplished as Winfield and a mother as spaced out as Missy. She chuckled "When're you going to stop mimicking me?"

Bunny's face darkened. "Me mimic you? How can you say such a thing? Are you knocked up by a half-Chink? Have you fallen sideways into some mysterious Oriental hoohah that reminds me of a Spider-Man comic book?"

"Just who is Nikki's old man? Really."

Bunny, although she didn't know she was doing it, produced one of Winfield's studied pauses, as if sending this question through a thousand microchip arrays with the speed of light. It was an intimidating posture to most people. It had always been enough to reduce their father, Charley, to putty. But sisters have stronger armor than parents; to Bunny it was simply adult behavior she liked to borrow because if it worked for Winfield, it clearly ought to work for her.

"I won't tell him," Lenore Ricci promised. "Buzz won't tell him. So how is he going to know that Mrs. Eiler is also Ms. Hegarty?"

"You mean he's that badly briefed?" Eileen demanded.

"Vince? This is Christmas vacation for the future father of Eugene Ricci and he doesn't want to know anything else." She laughed. "It's the first we ever had together. Carrying little Eugene converts me into being a human being." They studied their legs, already toasted by the hot sun. "I don't think," Lenore said in a thin, musing tone, "you really understand what the maf is all about."

"Oh, don't I?"

"I mean how they think about women."

A long time passed in silence. The faint Mediterranean surf made shushing sounds that would have lulled them to sleep, but Lenore had more to say. "Vince has spent weeks studying Buzz, finding his soft spots, looking for a way to set a hook in his hide. And never once asked himself, who is the little charmer Buzz married? I mean you're not exactly crowbait, Eileen. Vince would love to slip you the prong if you didn't belong to Buzz. But you're not some attractive female with a life of her own. You're goombah property: hands off. Does that bother you?''

"A little." Eileen frowned. "A lot, when you realize he isn't interested in checking me out. What sort of intelligence set-up does the mafia have? Carrier pigeons?''

"Part-time stoolies ratting out each other. There's nobody looking at the pieces and fitting them together. Zio Italo perhaps, but he's getting old.''

"So, in other words, to Vince I'm a non-person?''

Lenore made a sound very much like a malicious snicker. "Ah, but that is going to change." She raised herself on her elbows and grinned down at Eileen. "I have spent a life in the maf. To any maf guy I'm a place to shoot off his dick. My family had only one interest in me: making sure nobody broke my cherry till I landed a major fish like Vince. If such a man met me what would he want to check out? Only one question. Is that pussy intact? If so, don't bother me with anything else." She lay back down. After a while the soothing sound of the surf had reduced both of them to somnolence. In the distance a motorboat snored lightly as it dragged a waterskier across absolutely flat warm water of such saltiness that it was almost impossible to sink in it.

Northern Italians unkindly divide their peninsula at Rome: north of there is Europe, south is Africa. This is just nastiness. The dividing line is the Strait of Sicily that separates Sicily from Tunisia. Along this strait, too, are found Italy's southernmost possessions, tiny islands like Pantelleria, Limosa and Lampedusa. Perhaps the smallest is Grotteria, a volcanic "O" with one bit broken off to allow ships into the central lagoon. Around its inner circumference man-made beaches offer sugar-white sand, stark against black volcanic rock.

In the mid-1980s the commune of Grotteria signed a contract with Ricci Entertainments, Inc. It was now a hideout for the rich who liked to bathe nude, swap bisexually and chemically assist their orgasms. And gamble. Already the tiny atoll had traditions. One was Anti-Christmas, as the staff privately called it. They saw themselves as acolytes to a pagan celebration of the Anti-Christ.

Neither of the petite, dark-haired women was showing yet, although both of them had conceived on the same night. Only Lenore knew this for a fact. They lay on canvas chaises longues looking out toward Malta, both of them in bikini bottoms and nothing else. Their rate of suntan had been as closely matched as their pregnancies so that both women were now quite dark.

Their husbands, on the other hand, were still pale. Vince had introduced Buzz to the roulette table on their first night, shoving over a pile of chips worth a thousand dollars with some unconsciously grotesque comment about nothing being too good for the man who'd "made Lenore pregnant."

Vince dated the conception of Eugene Ricci from the night after it had happened, when he'd returned from Florida and, as he put it, slipped the fish to the missus. Since then his delusion had broadened into a guaranteed male embryo that would, moreover, bear the illustrious name of Vince's father, the icepick specialist. Vince didn't yet know that Buzz had blown the first thousand and a thousand of his own. Forsaking roulette, he had taken to the blackjack tables, recouped a thousand and gone on to lose two more.

In Buzz's mind he was ahead. Sitting hunched over his cards, a lone, rather distinguished figure of innate charisma, he felt himself being scrutinized by sheiks, tycoons, desirable women and even the lovely blond dealer as a man of mystery for whom the casual loss of merely a few G's was of no importance whatsoever. The fact that most of his fellow gamblers were clad in bikini bottoms and little else helped foster the illusion that he was among the élite of the world, obviously where he belonged. And when he lost big there was a strangely fierce surge of joy, as of a masochist being flogged. Take that, guilty one! And, Oh God, that!

At the bar, while ordering a Mummy's Curse, he could hear Bing Crosby singing "I'm Dreaming of a White Christmas." Grotteria's fake sand beaches provided the white but Buzz never got out to them. He was having too much fun.

For Charley Richards, Christmas came in three takes. This was the first, on the afternoon of Christmas Eve, sitting by Stefi's huge fireplace after lunch and watching the flames of beachcombed logs the twins had found on the beach. Soaked in seabrine and dried, the beachwood flamed brilliant yellow. The spines of her books that lined all the walls glowed like hot mustard.

The boys had given their mother a gag present of an electric sea-sled, a kind of amphibious scooter she had no intention of ever buzzing about in. She had given them paired sets of computer-theory books which they groaned about. She had given Charley an illustrated history of Sicily, published in London in the late seventeenth century with the kind of maps and drawings that usually end up expensively framed in print shops.

Very little of this registered on Charley. He sensed that the history of Sicily had set her back a few thousand. But his mind remained far away. Mostly it lived in Garnet's hospital room. He resented the time he had to spend away from her. Even a short separation started him imagining all sort of setbacks, accidents, things that might impair her recovery. It was going so quickly now. The stitches were healing. Her face was taking shape every day, almost unmarked. He hated to miss a second of it. She was being reborn. He wanted to witness every piece of the miracle. The rest of his mind bitterly regretted the day spent in St. Marys, not only because it took him away from Garnet. There was another, darker reason. He waited through lunch, saying nothing, but broadcasting such an aura of angst that none of them was in any doubt. Now he stared down into his wine glass and said, "You do know what happened to that girl?"

Everyone looked up from the illustrated history to stare wonderingly at him. "What girl?" Stefi asked.

Charley took a long, firm breath and vowed to be as objective as possible. "Kerry knows. She was one of the Green protesters. Mary-Ann Ianucci."

The two brothers glanced covertly at each other. There hadn't been time for Kevin to brief his twin on what had happened in St. Marys. "Oh," Kerry said, sparring for time, "that Mary-Ann Ianucci."

"No smart-ass, Kerry. She went back to the funeral home to pick up her notebook. Your goddamned delayed fuse trapped her. She burned to death."

Kevin winced. "You mean she—" He paused, swallowed. "Why didn't—?" He stopped cold, glancing around as if to see if any more blows were coming his way. "Look," he said at last in a baffled, angry voice. "We were going to tell you anyway, Charley. This was a kind of experiment to see if one of us could fill in for the other. That wasn't Kerry in Pennsylvania. It was me." In the silence a sea-drenched knot of driftwood exploded resin with a high, vicious hiss.

Charley blinked. The room smelled of church incense. "That explains why you torched the place. The Zio Italo system of revenge. You'd already tied them up with injunctions. I understand that eager-beaver sheriff even turned them in to the local FBI on suspicion of covert communist activity. But that wasn't enough."

"Charley?" Stefi asked. "You said a girl died?"

"Kevin, who I thought was Kerry, torched the headquarters of the local conservation group. Accidentally, a girl died. That's what a very expensive panel of lawyers would finally get a corrupt coroner to agree. The accident is that if it'd been Kerry, the girl would now be alive."

No one spoke. Charley poked at the burning logs. He stood with his back to the fire and stared first at Kevin and then Kerry—or so he hoped.

Stefi had draped greenery over the fireplace mantel, intertwined with gold balls and tinsel. "Italo murders his opposition," Charley said. "We used to get the authorities to do the killing for us. Never again. We always gave the *impression* of not breaking the law. Now I want more than an impression. I want the real thing, Kevin. We *don't* break the law. Is that too hard to understand?"

Stefi grabbed the ear of each son, bringing their heads together. "You remember when Kevin fell on that ballpoint pen? When he was three years old?"

"Ma."

She pointed at a small blue dot under Kevin's left eye. "It's like a tattoo, Charley. These two scimmoni will never be able to pull such a trick again."

Charley stared without passion at the dot. The mark of Cain, he thought. But kept silent.

Palawan is an oceanic reef thrust up, mountain-high, west of the main Philippine archipelago. One side faces southeast over the Sulu Sea. On a clear day you can see North Borneo.

It was on this sunlit side, across from Borneo's cedar plantations, old trees that until they were wiped out produced planks as wide as a table, that Lord Hugo Waismith Mace had convinced Ferdinand Marcos to bring in high-leverage mega-farming. It took very little persuasion, the profits were so obscene.

Palawan's main town, Puerto Princesa, lay thousands of feet below. The cash crop flourished in the heights, as it did in Colombia. It was not as cumbersome to produce as aromatic cedar planks, nor as wasteful of a natural resource. It could be replanted continuously. For shipping, its refined state was white powder.

Mace's British manager needed cheering, no question of it. "Broomthwaite!" Mace called from the mess shack, where he had secured a bottle of trade rum, a lime and some ice. "Broomthwaite! Over here, dear chap."

Broomthwaite was a cockney Mace had recruited in a Manila male brothel after a knife fight with two French sailors. He had a short, thin body which, in Mace's recollection, he never hesitated to throw into a fight whatever the odds. Like Mace, he made do with whatever boy or girl was handy.

"A bracer before the big slap-up Christmas dinner, Broomthwaite," Mace said, handing him a stiff rum-and-lime. The bar was decorated with palm leaves in lieu of holly. "The girls have baked a genuine long pig."

Broomthwaite's small, alert eyes widened. "Leave it out, Vicar. Long pig? These cannibals haven't barbecued one of their own in fifty years."

"Ah, not just any long pig," Mace said, clinking glasses. "This is Josepina."

"Come orf it, guv. I saw little Josepina this afternoon."

"A tenderer young piggywig you will never find," Mace promised, knowing he fancied the boyish girl whose boyfriend had recently disappeared. "They let her carry on unsuspecting and baked her alive, to keep the flesh tender."

People tended to disappear on Palawan. Marcos had shipped in hundreds of prisoners from mainland jails. Experimental crops always required more labor than anyone planned for and the coca bush had proved reluctant at first. Prisoners never got back alive to Manila to report slave-labor conditions. But the new government was beginning to nose into the Palawan death camps.

Two women set the table. Neither of them was the small Josepina with her boy's rear end and tiny breasts. The women brought out pitchers of local beer. One by one, Broomthwaite's civilian staff wandered in and sat down. His guards platoon had its own mess in another part of the enclave.

Mace could see that Josepina's absence worried Broomthwaite. Eating human flesh seemed much more gaudy a sin if you'd first admired the flesh for carnal purposes. But most sexual foreplay mimed cannibalism anyway. Mace calculated that if they'd been thrifty enough to eat prisoners, this Chan Lao enterprise would have shown an even greater profit. He nearly drooled.

When two of the men carried in the main course, a platter four feet long decorated with more palm leaves and featuring what seemed to be a whole pig, spitted and barbecued before being cut into juicy chunks, Broomthwaite seemed to rise slowly from his seat as if tugged erect by strings. "Look 'ere!"

"Yes, Broomthwaite?"

"Tell me it ain't 'er."

"But it is," Mace assured him. "Our own secret, darling, juicy, soft and tender and very tiny-assed, utterly edible Josepina. Dig in, everyone!"

Broomthwaite sank down, his head cradled in his arms. He lifted it to say something and saw the tiny Josepina at the other end of the table. "Is true!" she shouted. "Is my own recipe! My own pig! Eat!"

Broomthwaite laughed so hard the tears ran down his cheeks. "Happy Fucking Christmas," he chortled.

Manhattan is a city of hotels, from trademarked hostelries everyone knows to gruesome fleabags no one admits knowing. And then there is the Smythson, so exclusive that passersby can't tell it's a hotel.

Shan Lao rarely used Suite 14A, which fronted on Park Avenue, but paid a yearly retainer for it. Tonight Nicole had redone the post-modern decor of scrolled entablatures and Poussin reproductions with cachepots of holly in gold grosgrain ribbons.

The Shans, Nikki included, had invited one of China's UN observers, a Mr. Ho, and his wife. "Smythson's chef,'' Nicole began in flawless Mandarin, ''assures me that this is the traditional New England Christmas dinner: clear broth, breast of turkey *en beurre noire,* mousse of yam, galantine of oysters and chestnuts and chutney of cranberry and piñon nuts.''

Nicole's parents had been in the foreign service in the Far East, where Nicole had been raised by amahs and French missionary sisters. Tonight she had chosen a dark green knit that clung to her slender figure. The cheongsam split showed her long legs to advantage. Around her neck she wore bright coral temple ornaments from Japan.

One of Shan Lao's own armed guards, disguised as a waiter, checked their dining room every few minutes. It was a routine that armed guards hovered wherever Shan happened to be. They were not always disguised as waiters. ''You need these guards,'' Nicole had once accused him, ''in order to verify your own existence.'' The fact that this one was Chinese, while real New York waiters are always Turks or Iranians, seemed not to have attracted any curiosity.

But Nicole's Mandarin did, since Mr. and Mrs. Ho spoke a different dialect of Chinese. With that in mind, Ho had asked that everyone speak English, to improve his wife's rudimentary knowledge of that language. Nicole and Nikki acquiesced.

Mrs. Ho had said hardly anything, eyes downcast as she regarded each dish with the bemused attention of a health inspector. She failed to look up just before dessert when the Chinese waiter called Shan to the telephone. A day later, Nikki learned the call had been from Baxter Choy, in Washington, DC. But during the meal, as Shan slipped back into his seat, his grave expression gave the game away: bad news carries its own imprint. No armed guard can fend it off. In case anyone hadn't got the message, Shan said nothing more for the rest of the meal.

It fell to Nikki to draw out the silent Mrs. Ho. ''Have you been long in New York?'' Nikki asked, trained from childhood to handle these language pauses. When she failed to respond, he shifted to easier ground. ''And your children?''

''They are well.'' Mrs. Ho's pronunciation had the random unstressed rhythm and pauses of human speech as replicated by microchips.

"Are they in school here?"

"In Beijing. They are well."

"Then you have time for sightseeing in New York?"

"All is well."

For some reason this fascinating exchange pleased Mr. Ho. "Your son does you great credit," he told the silent Shan Lao. "It is by our offspring that we verify our value to mankind."

"And our existence on earth," Nicole added.

Two unarmed waiters wheeled in a white-frosted cake with green and red candles. It rotated slowly on a mechanized base, its music box playing Smythson's perfectly valid idea of a seasonal tune, "Santa Claus Is Coming to Town."

Shan and Ho regarded this Christian relic stonily. The J. Fred Coots tune was equally unknown to Nikki, his mother and Mrs. Ho. Therefore, in deep silence, the five diners watched and listened with puzzled suspicion as slowly, ping by pang, the platform slowed and the music box died a painful death in midphrase: *"You better watch out, you better n—"*

Christmas Day Charley Richards spent with his wife and daughters. As an act of simple Christian charity, as she told them all several times, Missy had invited Andy Reid as well. "The poor man's all alone at Christmas. Isn't it sad?"

It had been her idea to hold the lunch at Winfield's new flat, making sure that what Santa brought would be "household" in nature. Her own contribution had been twenty-four ugly Moser lead crystal goblets from Prague in a velours-lined walnut case far more attractive than its contents. Charley remembered it as a wedding gift twenty years ago, never unpacked. The economies of the rich were always enlightening. He recalled Zio Italo's mingy little habit of saving scrap paper torn from other people's letters.

Bunny had given Winfield a Monopoly game in Russian Cyrillic characters. Andy had arrived with a useful Lucite folding card table and chairs. Charley had brought nothing. He wandered about the small rooms as if caged.

The fifth-floor walkup faced south. Through sheer good fortune, no higher building masked Winfield's view of the Chrysler Building thirty blocks to the south. "Beginner's luck," Charley told her. "Of all the things I could wish you, the most important is luck."

"Do you mind if I write that down?" she asked in a kidding tone.

He grimaced. "That's all I do these days, deliver homilies."

"Is that what you delivered in Western Pennsylvania? Has Garnet seen that headline?" Before he could reply the telephone rang. "Yes, Nikki," Winfield responded, "she's right here." She handed the phone to her sister.

In a room this size, everyone could hear everything. It said something for their social graces that the two men—who loathed each other—instantly set up a conversation about convertible debentures while, in the kitchen, Missy noisily supervised an unnecessary third batch of Martinis, busying herself with frequent sampling.

Bunny hung up and came to the kitchen door. "Off the hook. The Great Shan had to dash to Washington. Too busy for little swollen me."

"Tough on him," Winfield remarked loyally.

"Nobody's in Washington," Charley pointed out. "They're all back home making speeches and self-destructing on eggnog."

"It's Christmas here, too," Winfield said. "Let's give business a rest."

"I only—"

"You only want to know what Shan's up to."

"Remember," Missy added, "when you do meet the Grand Shan don't let him weasel." She sloshed her Martini around recklessly. There was something to be said, Charley saw, for the East Coast Monied Protestant style in marriages and breakups. If one had never loved one's mate to begin with, but had only been following the dictates of financial prudence, then very little rancor remained afterward. "It takes two to make a baby," Missy sniffed. "Shan's got his responsibilities as we have ours."

Bunny leered over her mother's head at Winfield. "Is anything better guaranteed to send me straight to the abortionist?"

Winfield returned the fake grin. "Merrrry Christmas!"

The big Catholic church, Sacred Heart, was filled. Snow began falling on the town of St. Marys during the funeral

Mass. It fell on the countryside, the highways, the abandoned oil wells and coal mines, the fresh grave awaiting the corpse of Mary-Ann Ianucci.

The huge church was full. Old Father Heaney rarely saw such a capacity crowd even at major holidays. Once a fiery young priest, he had, over the decades, grown slow and easy within himself, fitting into the slumbrous Catholicism of the town and its people. Today, recognizing the special occasion, he had taken the rather unusual step of asking several members of the parish to help read the eulogies. They were long: Mary-Ann had achieved a lot for such a short life. Her hearse headed out toward the cemetery leading a cortege of private cars, many of them the oversized off-the-road vehicles popular in this part of the world.

At the fresh-dug grave, Father Heaney surveyed the hundreds who stood, heads bowed, in the falling snow. In his forty years at Sacred Heart he had rarely seen so many non-family make the trip from the church. He kept the interment brief.

To one of Father Heaney's Irish temperament, half asleep now after decades of disuse, it had been a curiously indirect tribute. No one had mentioned Richland 27, 28 and 29. The congregation didn't go for anything that direct. It wasn't their way. Then, too, a lot of the mourners weren't from his parish; many weren't even Catholics. So they wore a bit of green, a tie, a scarf, a shawl. It was a very suppressed occasion: symbols had to do the job.

Irishmen of Heaney's age could remember life in the old country during the Troubles, when wearing the green could get you shot, on the spot, like a dog. The British Black-and-Tans were nothing more than criminals recruited to terrorize the Irish. Even now, the injustice stirred his uneasy blood.

Father Heaney could see Sheriff's deputies and an FBI photographer making a video, as if this were a wedding. The local newspaper had summed up the establishment's decision:

"NO WAY OF KNOWING"
EXTENT OF LEFTIST PLOT
SHERIFF COX REVEALS

Father Heaney wondered if it was a color video they were taking. In which case, wouldn't the green look grand? Snow was turning to sleet now, slanting sideways. People were advancing to the grave to place small bouquets of bright green leaves. "Oh, Paddy dear, and didja hear the news that's goin' 'round? The shamrock is forbid by law to bloom on Ireland's ground." Heaney's old eyesight blurred. Sleet. He sniffed hard, wiped his eyes.

Surprising who came to pay their last respects to Mary-Ann; conservative elders of the community, a doctor, the boys from the brewery, the lady who ran the five-and-dime. And many of them with a bouquet. The priest wiped his eyes again. Busy shifting lenses, changing cassettes, adjusting parabolic microphones, the law men kept occupied. Sheriff Cox, in his Sunday best, trotted briskly from one group to the next.

In another part of the cemetery the Knights of Columbus had organized a Christmas memorial for the war dead. A choir from the ladies' auxiliary, high sweet voices, was singing:

> *Oh, little town of Bethlehem*
> *How still we see thee lie.*
> *Above thy deep and dreamless sleep*
> *The silent stars go by.*

To the war dead Mary-Ann's name was now added. With Sheriff Cox, a tall, rangy stranger showed his credentials to the FBI photographer. The local man pawed through his cases and came up with some photographs. He handed a few to the stranger, who looked like Gary Cooper. The women sang:

> *But in thy dark streets shineth*
> *The everlasting light.*
> *The hopes and fears of all the years*
> *Are met in thee tonight.*

March

Twenty-Nine

"Father, it's Nikki. Welcome to the States."

"How did you find out I'd be back in Washington?"

"It's a wise child who knows his father's whereabouts."

"Is that meant to be humorous? Good ni—"

"Don't hang up."

For Shan Lao, doing business in the U.S. was a sentence in Hell. Since Christmas he'd been back twice, a fireman putting out blazes. He loathed the role. He detested America, where a network of fax and telephone and gossip journalism enmeshed everyone in a spider's web of publicity. He particularly hated the jovial hypocrisy of America where all motives are ulterior and no one stands up as honestly corrupt, frankly for sale. It was impossible to deal with people who could never admit what they really were.

It was impossible to become *out of touch* in America. How had Nik known where to reach him? Shan had no family life. His wife and son were business credits. If Nicole suggested—as she occasionally did—that Shan sponsor some cultural event, he viewed this as a potential business credit and his wife as an associate whose task it was to locate such credentials.

"Did you get my latest letter?"

"I will respond to it soon. Thank you for calling."

"Please don't hang up."

"My life is hectic at the moment."

Crisis had become a way of Shan's life in Washington, even with Baxter Choy to run his errands and enforce his schedule. The air of crisis was exacerbated by a lack of armed guards. Too sophisticated, these people: the presence of armed guards alerted them to rich pickings. Shan felt particularly ill at ease knowing that the American style of doing business frowned at an obvious show of armed caution.

In any event, armed guards would not be able to protect Shan from the greedy members of a Congressional oversight subcommittee. These gentlemen had taken an interest in mask aligners, sophisticated machines for making computer chips. Costing millions each, these machines were no longer under the sales control of CO-COM, the seventeen-nation Coordinating Committee for Multilateral Export Controls.

Meant to keep strategic material from the Soviet bloc, COCOM was an awkward corpse left behind when the Cold War died. Those who had once exercised Congressional oversight missed the clout this gave them. A few still hoped to generate votes from an ignorant electorate out of one last gasp of anti-communism.

Shan's electronics subsidiaries bought mask aligners from manufacturers like Sony and Canon. Now and then one of these three-ton machines would end up in East Germany or Czechoslovakia, enabling the former Soviet satellites to leap forward into a higher state of the art.

Baxter Choy had been assigned the task of quieting the diehard Cold War warriors from constituencies where news of what had happened to Eastern Europe in 1990 had yet to reach voters still wallowing in 1980s Reagan rhetoric. Sensing undercover profit as well as votes, the greedier of the congressmen wanted to deal with nobody but Shan, who was at the same moment needed in mainland China. He was needed in a dozen other places as well.

"You sound unhappy I phoned."

"If you know where I am, Nik, someone could force you to tell them, too."

"Never thought of it that way. Sorry, Father."

"I will telephone you and your mother tomorrow night. In fact—" Shan paused. He had pressing reasons for seeing Nik face to face, pressing thoughts to impart. But on an unsecured phone line he couldn't mention the possibility that he would fly up to New York for a visit. "In fact, be at home tomorrow at this hour. I shall call."

Shan had been thinking hard—spread thin and racing to put out fires on both sides of the globe—of appointing a real number two. Lord Mace, of course, was a joke. Baxter Choy, whom he had educated, already functioned brilliantly in this hemisphere as Shan's assistant. In Asia, a lawyer called On Seong served as Shan's closest aide.

But this would be more than a niche in the chain of command. The number two Shan needed was someone to succeed him in some areas now and in all areas when he died. That person must be a Shan.

"I'll make sure Mother is here, too."

"Yes, do that." Shan hung up.

Nik was as intelligent as Choy. He'd infiltrated the Richards-Ricci fortress quite ably and would soon have a child to show for his troubles. And all this, mind you, without knowing anything of his father's grand strategy for the House of Ricci. There only remained the problem of Nik himself. His personality was entirely unsuitable. His word games with weighty matters disturbed his father profoundly. His most recent letter:

Dear Father,

Some years ago young blacks raped and nearly killed a young white woman in Central Park. In the *Los Angeles Times* William Pfaff wrote: "Fifty years ago . . . the élite that controlled the country's banks and industry nominated its government . . . blacks, Catholics, Jews, Asians . . . submitted to intense pressures to conform and assimilate.

"This America . . . will never be recovered . . . Americans of fifty and older know how profound a change has been produced . . . an America of morally isolated people no longer connected to a culture deeper or more responsible than that provided by the mass entertainment industry, a people for too many of whom 'fun' is what life is all about, if it is about anything."

What someone over fifty might also remember is an America where parents enforced hypocritical standards. Today's parents hand over "fun" instructions, e.g., how to con Blue Cross into paying for an abortion. They and their children are co-conspirators in "fun."

Fun in the J. P. Morgan era was gang-raping black women. Today, white. It's the same moral void America's always had, minus the camouflage of parental hypocrisy and, thus, more sharply perceived. As George Santayana said: There is nothing like having your face pushed into your own turds.

Smiling at some of Nik's turns of phrase, and of Santayana's, Shan Lao called an executive air service and booked a flight the next evening to New York under the name Charles Lee. He then called Baxter Choy to hire a plainclothes armed guard for the flight and the trip into Manhattan from La Guardia Airport.

Shan tried to relax. He would have to acquaint Nik with the truth about his family. He would have to "blood" Nik if the boy was ever to become his number two. Nik would be blooded precisely the way a hunting dog was, by being forcibly accustomed to, and thus made contemptuous of, blood. Santayana's formula worked for any body secretion. Shove Nik's nose in enough blood and he would soon learn to shed it profitably.

Shan Lao picked up one of the hotel's ball-point pens and a piece of stationery. In his youth he had been envied for his work with the plump, ink-laden calligrapher's brush. But this would not be a document, just an *aide-memoire* for his face-to-face talk tomorrow evening with Nik. "Hypocrisy between parents and children," he wrote, "can never build a long and fruitful relationship. For that truth must prevail, the truth of the family, of the father and of what is expected of the son." He smiled condescendingly at the narrow, greasy line of blue produced by the ballpoint. Rich, India Ink black would have suited him better. Or, considering what lay ahead for Nik, a dark, thick, fast-coagulating blood red.

Thirty

"Look at it this way," Eileen told Winfield. "We have collected eleven hookers, sitting at the defense table. Six are over forty. One is fifty. All are dying of AIDS. Two have the new penicillin-resistant syphilis. Three are incontinent with anal fissures caused by sodomization. One may die before we get a trial date. Only one speaks grammatically. Three are black. Four have such bad complexions that, without a makeup base, they look contagiously leprous. Seven have prior convictions, sometimes a lot of them. Five have done time for assault, soliciting, disturbing the peace, bunco game, shoplifting. They have been whipped, flayed, chained, punched, crushed, choked, stabbed, burned, kicked, raped, slashed and pushed out of moving cars. And that's only by their regular customers. Many have been gang-raped by cops, sodomized with truncheons or larger penis substitutes and, in two cases, shoved out of second story windows. There is a total of twenty-eight broken ankles or legs, forty-one broken wrists or arms, smashed fingers and toes, police fun. Among them nine have had several abortions, five are mothers of children they have never seen. One has an MA in philosophy. One was a mezzo-soprano with the chorus of the Metropolitan Opera. Ten are alcohol abusers. Six smoke crack. Four mainline heroin.'' She paused for breath. ''If you were a juror, could you believe anything they said in court? Could you even stand to be in the same courtroom with them?''

Winfield sat in silence for some time. Then she said, ''Tell me about a typical jury.''

Almost six months pregnant, Eileen shifted ponderously in her armchair. ''In New York County seven out of twelve will be black or Latino. My biggest problem will be the males who use prostitutes and want to punish them some more. We call that the Jack-the-Ripper syndrome. My second biggest problem will be female jurors who are daughters or sisters or mothers of prostitutes. They will also want to punish my clients. My third problem is jurors connected with organized crime.''

''They should be easy to weed out on challenge.''

Eileen frowned at her. ''You cannot be that innocent, Winfield. Not with your family connections. At the moment organized crime and its legitimate enterprises have become the single largest employer in America. Between eighteen and twenty percent of the workforce labors for them. Our job will be to get accurate background information on all prospective jurors. That costs.''

''We need more than that,'' the younger woman responded.

''These women are pariahs, Winfield. They have provided the most unspeakable services our society demands of women. There is no one to step forward and say: 'This was once a decent human being.' No priest, no doctor, no social worker. No one.''

Both women mulled this over for a long moment of utter silence. Then Winfield sighed. ''Then no jury will credit anything they say.''

''If I want your pal Leona Kane to add Vince Ricci to the docket, I have to present something better. Otherwise a jury could pin the blame on poor Dr. Battipaglia.'' This time the silence between them lasted even longer. Finally Eileen made a rueful sound. ''I realize now how much I was counting on his testimony. I can't tell you what a sly snake you have in your Cousin Vince.''

''You don't have to.''

''Vince and Buzz have become such bosom buddies that there is absolutely no air between the two of them. Father-buddies. Total contact. Buzz has been put on what they call a high-roller list. He gets flown to any gambling casino in the world and handed a free honeymoon suite and a thousand dollars' worth of chips. I have some reason to believe this includes the offer of hot and cold running blondes.'' Moodily, Eileen fluffed out her black hair. ''I did our personal accounts last night. Vince is killing us.'' She stopped talking. Winfield avoided looking at her. Finally, Eileen went on, ''We're eighty thousand in debt and hemorrhaging. Buzz is so rarely in town that other doctors have stopped referring patients. When I spoke to him about it this morning he stomped off in a snit.''

''Another of Vince's triumphs.''

Eileen nodded. ''Vince is more convoluted than anyone could dream. Lenore tells me he's admitted her to the human race because the amniocentesis confirms it's a boy and that makes Lenore temporarily male.'' Eileen stopped and shifted uncomfortably in her chair. ''How's Bunny doing?''

''About as well as you: still sick in the mornings, showing quite a bit. Filled with doubts, now that it's too late for an abortion. She says Nikki's no help. He and his father are dancing some kind of gruesome gavotte around each other. Bunny is a study in demoralization. She devoutly wishes it wasn't too late.''

''It's not!'' Eileen said in an agonized voice. ''Problematical, but Buzz swears it's still feasible.''

"Would he do it?"

"Not for me. Probably not for anybody. But someone else might. In New York State it's legal through the twenty-fourth week."

Winfield grimaced. "Remind me to stay on the Pill till well past menopause."

Another silence descended on them. "One thing, Winfield: I am *not* abandoning this case." When the younger woman said nothing, she went on: "You were quite sure the assassination of Dr. Battipaglia would have a chilling effect on a gravid creature like me."

"And it hasn't?"

"Try not to be deliberately insulting. It hasn't."

"Great!" Winfield responded. "Then it's time for Lenore."

"Lenore? She's as demoralized by pregnancy as I am."

"I remember once when you demanded to know what she was saving herself for," Winfield continued in one of her calm, inexorable tones.

"That was deliberately insulting of me."

"Not at all. I think it's time to ask that question all over again."

"Winfield, you have no idea how hard it is in this condition to focus on anything else but being huge with child."

"Nevertheless." Winfield sat back, her mouth a firmly pressed line. "Lenore has got to start helping. And I know how."

Between them they had decided an ambulance would call too much attention, a cab would be too small, so a large limo and driver had been booked. Winfield had been plotting Garnet's escape for several weeks, ever since a one-bedroom apartment in her building had opened up. Acting as Garnet's attorney, she had signed a two-year lease. The problem had been Charley, whom they had decided would be against this move as being an un-chic address, and a move not yet condoned by the doctors. By three o'clock, Winfield had helped Garnet dress, wheeled her downstairs to the limo and installed her in her new home.

"Careful lighting the oven," she murmured, deadpan.

Garnet's face, still kept immobile by sheer willpower,

grew even more deadpan than Winfield's. "I see you know my MO, torching kitchens."

"Whatever pays," the younger woman said. She looked over the woman she had elected as her stepmother well in advance of her father divorcing Missy or marrying Garnet. Her coarse white hair had grown back to a length of over an inch, giving her the new androgynous boy-look of rock singers and the more bizarre fashion models.

Her face looked flawless. The eyebrows still needed encouragement from mascara, as did the lashes. But even the joins around the eyes and mouth had smoothed away under dermabrasion. Her lips were different, no question about it, the lips of a much younger woman, inexperienced, a bit tremulous. She could walk a while if she had to, dress and wash herself. After months of exercise with weights, her left arm had grown as sleek and limber as her right. The fingers remained a bit stiff. From time to time, as she sat talking, she squeezed a tennis ball with some ferocity. She looked ten years younger. They had, willy-nilly, face-lifted her.

"Do you have a patent on that hair?" Winfield asked. "I'm thinking of having mine cropped down to that length."

Garnet felt the younger woman's long, dark hair, parted in the middle and regularly swept back behind her ears by a gesture that was now almost unconscious. "Too fine," she said. "You have to start out with a real Hopi horse-tail. You should see baby pictures of me: a back braid so tough I could swing from it." She picked up a handful of mail forwarded to her here. "Uh-oh, the Herman Foundation has tracked me down." She wiggled a finger inside the envelope. "After the way I left that house on the river, they probably want my head on a platter." She pulled out a letter and read it quickly. "Even worse," she said then.

"The explosion wasn't your fault. We'll fight 'em."

"Worser. They're rebuilding the place for their education fellowship. They do research on current teaching methods, the kind of stuff that gets your father's blood pressure jumping. And they want me to serve on the fundraising committee."

"Who said do-gooders weren't sly?"

"I won't have the time. But maybe Charley will."

As always, Winfield saw, Garnet had remained terribly thin. Now that she was on her own, except for weekly visits to the doctor, she had to begin to fill out a bit. Not for the first time Winfield wondered how her father would take this sudden independence.

"Charley's due at the hospital about now," Garnet reminded her, in her casual mind-reading way.

"I left word at his office to drop by my apartment first. He'll find a note on my door directing him to Apartment 2F."

"God, that Winfield deviosity. Where do you find the time to take care of a raggedy waif like me?"

"The Ricci clan is in remission."

"I don't understand."

Winfield stepped into the tiny kitchen and let the cold water run. "We're like a cancer. Sometimes metastasis stops for a while. My great-uncle is no longer trying to kill my father. My father has given up purifying the Richland empire. What would you call it, a cease-fire? An armed truce?" She filled a glass with cold water and brought it to Garnet. "You put your pills somewhere in your travel bag."

"Uh? Oh. Yes." Garnet opened her shoulder bag on her lap. She swallowed a scarlet antibiotic tablet with water. "Thanks."

Winfield retrieved the glass of water and finished drinking it herself. The two women fell silent, glancing about the large living room which made up most of the flat, mentally redecorating it. At the moment it had been hastily furnished with three plain Scandinavian teak things Winfield had found in a charity shop. The bedroom contained only a queen-sized bed that used up most of the space.

"You picked a perfect pad for me," Garnet said then. "Small but spacey. Your father has kept me on the Richland payroll all these months, so I have a nestegg to spend on redecoration. But it hardly needs any." Her left hand grasped the tennis ball and began kneading it again. "You seem to know my taste quite well. Whereas you are a very hard person to read."

"Me?"

"I have started copying some of your cool," Garnet went on. "The doctors want me to adopt a much less enthusiastic personality. No grimaces, shouts or grins for a while yet. Do you mind being my role model?''

"Not if you cut my hair your way." Winfield sat down in a low-slung teak sofa with dark beige cushions. "The person who's hard to read is really you."

"Woman of mystery."

"Veiled sorceress who phoenix-like," Winfield gathered speed, "emerges unscathed from the all-consuming fire to fulfill her destiny as the one person who can get my father back on track."

"The explosion more or less derailed him completely."

"It was meant to." Winfield paused. "He needs your grit. He had a great dream that would have killed him. I can't go into them but some good things have happened in the past months. I'm in much better shape to fend off Zio Italo now."

"How?"

The door-buzzer rang. Winfield got up and put her finger to her lips as she went to the door. She opened it slightly.

"Winfield," her father began in a harassed tone, "I'm supposed to be at the hospital this minute. What's so imp—''

"I wanted you to meet the lady who's cutting my hair." She stepped aside and he could see the woman in the wheelchair, nervously digging her fingers into a tennis ball.

Thirty-One

In Atlantic City, Vince Ricci always felt less secure than anywhere else he did business. It wasn't that the town lacked a comfortable history of crime. Despite the glitz laid on with a trowel it was still a sordid dump.

Once they had rammed through the New Jersey legislature the right to set up legalized gambling in Atlantic City, the various mobs had proceeded to carve it up among themselves, using legitimate hotel-styled fronts. Among them, they had created a gold mine.

But, and this Vince had never whispered to a soul, for all the money spent on dressing it up, Atlantic City was still a sewer catering to unemployed manicurists, Social Security wrinklies, small-time package-tour grifters and cheapo hubcap thieves of one kind or another. It hurt his self-image to spend time in this place, but he had to occasionally if only to keep his local manager honest. He was Al Zappavigna, his sister Lil's husband, not actually dishonest, just not very bright and thus easy for the help to hoodwink.

Al had greeted him on his arrival an hour ago with a whole sheaf of computer printouts, those wide greenruled sheets, folded on each other, the sight of which struck numb loathing in Vince's heart. He made a feline face of rejection, as of a week-old mouse. "Hey, Al, gimme a break. A quick summary, Al."

"Vinnie, every time I give you a quick summary we end up shouting at each other. The bottom line is this week was about five percent improved over last week. OK? Now for the bad news. I have run out of everything from outside."

This was Al's code phrase for drug shipments. Vince snarled, "Whadya mean run out?"

"I mean we ain't had deliveries in two weeks and my inventory is zilch."

Silently, Vince ordered him out with a twist of his thumb. He stared at the computer readouts and decided to take Al's word that they were all right. But the drying up of heroin and cocaine was not all right.

Vince had to kick the Far East pipeline hard enough to get it running again. His hand reached for the scrambler phone. This was a job for Kevin, who could slip in and out of places like a ghost. But as his hand touched the phone, a different one began ringing. "Yeah?"

"Vinnie, Al. I got a drunk down here claims he's your buddy so how come I don't cash his three-G personal check? Should I give him the heave-ho?"

"Not till you tell me his name."

"Some kind of doctor?"

"Short, sandy hair, rube expression?"

"Oh, you know him."

''What the fuck is a high-class pussy doctor doing in
Atlantic City? I freebie him to Macao, Monaco, Mauri-
tius. No, he's gotta mingle with the slobs. Where is he,
blackjack?''

''Yeah.''

''Cash his check. Tell him to wait there for me.''

Vince hung up. Shame about Buzz. Some guys could
take it or leave it. Not Buzz. Vince cradled his small,
neat head of tight black curls in his fingers and slowly
rubbed his temples. He was too damned tense. Buzz had
told him that, a little professional advice.

This drug slow-down . . . slow-down, hell, it was a
cut-off. In all the time he had been dealing drugs—ever
since his very moral father had been removed and, with
him, any objection to handling the stuff—he had always
been aware that with drugs he was never in control. If a
business was worth getting into—and junk was the
sweetest ever invented—then it was worth doing in a
businesslike way. That would never happen as long as his
product was plant-derived and grew in faraway places
thick with mosquitoes and banditti. The only way was
with ingredients supplied by DuPont or Monsanto or
Ciba-Geigy or ICI.

To do that he needed R & D. He needed somebody
with credentials to test out all the new stuff he was reading about, that medical science was producing, psycho-
tropic mood elevators and suppressors, synthetic
narcotics and soporifics, super-tranquilizers, muscle re-
laxants, all that feel-good shit that only required a prescription, not a corps of coolies chopping cabbage.

He found Buzz in the midst of losing a doubled-up
blackjack game. He had turned up his first two cards,
both aces, and was now sweating out the rest of the play.
The odds were good for hitting at least one ace with a
ten or a face-card, for a blackjack win. That's if he figured the odds mathematically, there being sixteen out of
fifty-two cards with a value of ten. But, as always, the
dealer was using a double deck, thirty-two ten-value cards
out of a hundred and four. This tilted the odds a little
more in the house's favor. But the odds were still attractive since, if Buzz didn't hit a blackjack, he might still
get himself a nice under-twenty-one lay to beat whatever
the dealer drew. This was the danger area for half-smart

bettors. He knew enough to figure odds mathematically, but never figured dealer odds. So when his dealer hit her own open queen with an ace, Buzz blew the whole doubled-up bet.

He turned away, gray-faced, and stared at Vince. "Hiya." His voice sounded pale, as if like his face it hadn't seen the light of day for years.

"That's all that's left of the three G's?" Vince asked, pointing to a smallish pile of white chips.

"I play hard, Vincenzo," Buzz said proudly. "When I work I sweat my butt off and when I play, I play my heart out. Vince, that girl pulled that ace out of her left ear." Buzz's voice sounded choked with suppressed rage.

"You telling me my best dealer with the most beautiful tits on the whole Atlantic seaboard is a cheat?"

Buzz turned back to stare at the dealer's cleavage. "Yeah," he said in a rattled way, "you're right about the boobs. Can I cash another check?"

"Why not?" He watched Buzz's hand, shaking so lightly only a pro like Vince could spot it, whip out his leather-cased check book and start scribbling.

"Five grand?" Buzz asked in a tone that wasn't at all questioning. He seemed finally to have understood his role in this transaction.

"Why not?" Vince repeated. He signaled a passing pit boss for two drinks. "Listen, Buzz, don't lemme butt into your fun, but lemme ask a question. A medical guy like you, I mean, you're entirely into females, right?"

"All the way in."

Another pit boss, summoned by Vince, took the filled-out check and disappeared with it. "But when you were younger," Vince persisted, "I mean you're the Eiler who invented the Eiler Whatever, right? That took research, right? A guy I talked to said you were probably *the* hot-shot research guy in your class."

Buzz's chest expanded almost visibly. "Did he tell you I was number one all-time winner in my poker game? Did he mention I once hung in all night and came out in the daylight fifty thousand richer?"

"From cards?" Vince sounded impressed. "So this now is just a short run of bad luck."

"I've had 'em before," the expert assured him. "They pass. So better lay aside a reserve fund, Vince, because

Buzz is going to blast your bank wide open one of these days.''

''Terrific!''

Slowly, Buzz's pale face was growing brisk and pink again. A balloon being expertly re-inflated, it assumed its original contour.

''So, like, you could do research if somebody made it worth your while?''

Buzz shrugged grandly. The two pit bosses arrived simultaneously, one with a pair of drinks, the other with a colorful array of chips on an identical tray. ''Don Vincenzo,'' Buzz said in an orotund voice, newly inflated with confidence bordering once more on arrogance, ''there isn't anything I couldn't do.''

Vince's smile was almost not there. Cats do not smile, even when a fresh, live mouse arrives, unwary, bristling with ignorance, having not the slightest suspicion that its destiny is to become catfood. Even then, cats know better than to smile.

Thirty-Two

''It was definitely him out in St. Marys, PA,'' Nose Cohen told Suggs. He had spread out half a dozen glossy 8 × 10 photos on his supervisor's desk. They sat in a cell-like FBI office big enough for one, with a narrow, unopenable window overlooking lower Manhattan.

''And the staff at Lutjens, Van Kurve and Armatrading confirm he's the one who gave you lip at the seminar?''

''The only one who could is Goddard, the guy who managed the seminar. He's been assigned to their Bangkok office.''

''Try him by fax.''

''I have. Waiting for a response.''

The supervisor, J. Laverne Suggs, swept the photos into a pile and shoved them back at Cohen. ''Meanwhile, you have another of these seminars coming up at Lutjens. Let's see if you can get through it without blowing sky high.''

"Look, I told y—"

"Calm down, Nose. You got a wild hair up your ass about this kid. Your idea, not mine. That Pennsylvania trip, that's out of your pocket, not the Bureau's. What do you hope to prove? That Kerry Ricci, grand-nephew of Italo Ricci, assistant to Charley Richards, attended a Lutjens meeting? So what?"

"I already proved it. That's not my point." Cohen took a long-suffering breath. "It's the Lutjens cover-up. The missing video cassette? The transferred Goddard? I think Richland Holdings owns Lutjens. And if they do, they have a secret pipeline into the heart of every business they compete with. We'll blow them out of the water," he went on as excitedly as Gary Cooper ever did. "Every honest client will quit them cold." He waited for Suggs to respond and, when he didn't, went on: "This is the same Kerry Ricci who was physically present when somebody torched that environment group in St. Marys, PA. Where the girl was burned to death. They call it accidental because the forensic capability of the sheriff's office isn't up to anything more sophisticated. But—"

"But you think Kerry Ricci set it."

"I think a case could be made. Right now our guys out there have run the sheriff's commie angle into the ground. There never were any commies. It was something he saw in a dream, right after this Ricci kid visited him." His grim smile tried for irony.

His supervisor lifted his shoulders in a gesture of futility. "Let's say you prove the Lutjens connection, Nose. What then? Suppose the Bureau circularized Lutjens clients with a Cautionary. Suppose, every time we found some company stepping out of line, we circularized it? Hey, folks! Sub-standard tomatoes in the catsup! Do you have any idea what a mafia-owned senator could make of that? We'd look like the Gestapo. Even worse, like the IRS." This attempt at humor failed to get a smile out of the grim-faced frontier sheriff now tucking away photo prints in a manila envelope. Neither man spoke as an internal messenger arrived and placed an envelope in the precise center of Suggs' desk. Suggs pushed it unopened to Cohen.

Nose opened it. In that closed-in, oppressive cell, his

face went stony in a strong, lawman manner. "Bangkok. Goddard died of dysentery this morning."

"Don't tell me," Suggs demanded, "they'd kill to hush this up?"

Cohen shrugged. "Wouldn't you?"

"This," Zio Italo said in a sepulchral voice, "would never have been a problem from the beginning if Il Professore had listened to me instead of that Navajo squaw." His grand-nephew, Kevin, sat across from the old rolltop desk, torso erect, feet on the ground, shoulders squared. The physical posture of a West Point cadet, if not the moral stance.

Outside, on Dominick Street, spring changed gears with every passing moment, drizzles followed by heart-warming sunshine. None of that warmth got through the dusty window to Italo. He seemed to radiate gloom, his deep-set olive eyes glinting in their caves of shadow.

"These Torella cretini out in New Jersey," Italo said with a heavy sigh, "they are from a very respected family. Not from our region around Castellammare del Golfo, but inland in Corleone."

Kevin decided to take a chance. The man who coveted Charley Richards' lofty aerie had to be more than Zio Italo's gopher. "Zio, what Corleonese has respect? They're all a little crazy."

The old man's eyes hooded even more in their dark caves. One corner of his mouth went up in sarcastic recognition of the grown-up truth the youthful Kevin had spoken. "And since when," he asked in a paper-dry voice, "is being a little crazy a bad thing?"

Kevin grinned. Normally he would nod politely at this point and, chastised, drop the matter. But the man who wanted to annex Charley's view had to keep on asserting himself. "So," he said in Kerry's dry voice, "when a man is a little crazy, it's harder to figure his moves."

"Un vero pazzo called Lucca Certomá runs Corleone." Zio Italo's narrow face looked pinched with pain. "Nobody in that accursed town challenges him except one even more insane, called Mollo. But that is Lucca's problem, not ours." He sighed impatiently, fastidiously, as if loathing the necessity of unveiling all these secrets

because they were distasteful. "Our problem is the Torella family in New Jersey."

"The shit shifters?"

Italo nodded gravely. "Hazardous and toxic waste removal. Gaetano Torella is married to Certomá's sister.
At this sensitive moment, one of Charley's subsidiaries,
which handles hazardous waste disposal, is bidding
against the Corleonese in New Jersey. Salt in the wound!
You find out how bad they need sweetening. Have they
involved Certomá yet." Zio paused and his eyes suddenly grew brighter. "This also has touched on your dear
mother and that vineyard of hers near Castellammare.
Where they make the Fulgatore wine?"

"Ma comes into this?"

"Lucca wants to buy her out."

"So? What's holding it up?"

"He is a bachelor. So is Stefania Ricci."

Italo sat back and leafed through some pages of a daily
diary as a sign that he had finished with the matter. "A
week to test the waters. Agreed? Now we have this other
problem. Cohen. We had to take drastic action on this
Goddard guy. Lots of people die from it each year but,
regardless, I want to let this all cool down."

"But, Zio, Cohen is still running around alive."

"Like a chicken with its head off," Italo amended,
smiling icily as if in pain. "He's not assigned to field
work, only lectures. I'm just surprised that Kerry opened
his yap like that. He fingered himself."

"I still think Cohen should go," said the young man
who wanted Il Professore's office.

"Oh, do you?" Zio Italo's wrath was hooded, like the
dark red glow Etna shows the night's blackness. "I wonder about both you boys, about your judgment. Right
now Cohen is an outsider inside the Bureau. He's got no
support, a supervisor who considers him a pain. But we
can raise him to the rank of saint, the law-enforcer of all
time and the subject of a vendetta, if we take him out."

"Cohen?"

"Any law guy. They might hate each other but ice one
of them and they freeze into a fist. And they never give
up. We don't. Why should they?"

"So how do we discourage this shithead?"

This time Italo's smile was real, no longer knifelike.

"Don't bad-name the yidlach," he cautioned Kevin. "They represent the kinds of brains inside the Bureau that could be dangerous. Instead, ask yourself: there are other sheenies in the Bureau. They don't behave this way."

"He's paid to."

"He was humiliated by that smartass brother of yours, publicly shamed. He smells a rat. And he goes for the rat. It's only natural."

"So what's the verdict, thumbs up or down?"

"Once in a while something of Charley's shows up in the open—like the New Jersey thing or the incident with Cohen—and the two sides of the family have to cross for mutual protection. Whether His Wasp Highness likes it or not," he added in a bitter tone.

"So we waste Cohen?"

"We let the Bureau forget." Italo leaned back in his chair and stared at the ceiling. "A long time. Then we hit him. I even have the take-out guy." He chuckled. "An old pal. A past master. He should run a college, this man. He's a professor in his field."

Kevin's smile was cautious. But as someone targeted by Cohen, he felt he had a right to ask questions he knew should never be voiced. "Is this the maestro of the gas oven?"

The fire in Italo's eyes was too deep-banked to flash. It glowed malevolently, but only for a moment. "I didn't hear that. Otherwise whoever said it would have his mouth washed out with lye."

Kevin sat back in his chair and tried to look relaxed. Zio Italo had just told him something. For the man who would one day sit where Il Professore sat, such information was terribly important.

Thirty-Three

Anywhere around Long Island Sound, March is a windy month, bringing squalls and sometimes sleet. This Sunday afternoon was no exception. Stefi and Charley watched the log fire slowly suffocate under downdraughts of chill, rainy air.

Still in her dressing gown, her bare feet tucked up under her, Stefi upended the Strega bottle. "Last drops." She got to her feet, her narrow-waisted body swelling upward to erect breasts and, below, into magnificent buttocks. Her gown swung slightly open. Charley swallowed once.

He would spend tonight with Garnet in her new apartment, but it would be to help her manage. The doctors had frightened both of them about making love. Some day they could resume being a man and a woman. Right now, after so many months of chastity, Charley was in a bad way.

"Charley," Stefi said in a warning tone. "I know that look, Charley."

He growled at her and lunged, snapping like a dog. When she sidestepped he fell short and dropped in a heap at her feet. He bit her toes. Then, glancing up: "Why, Miss Ricci, you are a natural brunette."

"I use the same stuff Reagan did. We are both natural everything."

"Never having seen Reagan's muff, I . . ." His thought died out as he stared worshipfully up at hers. "You know, I remember when you were just a skinny little teenaged delinquent with no ass at all."

"But did that stop you?" She padded off into the kitchen. Charley could hear her filling up the coffee maker. He poked disconsolately at the fire. The chimney rewarded him by sending a puff of smoke in his face. Then the wind moaned derisively.

He coughed and sat back on his haunches. Lately that was all he got, a mouthful of cinders to chew on. Once again, Zio Italo seemed to be in charge of his life. An FBI man, name of Cohen, had been sniffing Charley's spoor. The only good news was Garnet's recovery, but even that had a queer reverse twist. Living in her own apartment had produced a lot of progress. Then she had hit a plateau. Used to daily improvement, Charley felt vaguely cheated that it had all but stopped. He was paying maximum attention; why wasn't she?

All these frustrations seemed to combine to rob him of the will to act, even to shed more Richland subsidiaries. But, in its own remorseless way, what had finally taken the heart out of him was the death of the Ianucci girl. He blamed himself for leaving Kevin on his own in

St. Marys. Never mind that he thought Kevin was Kerry.
Mary-Ann's death roosted on Charley's front doorstep.
His guilt was so great he hadn't even told Garnet about
the girl. If she ever found out—

Mary-Ann stood for something. This girl he had never
seen had *gone first* along a way he had marked out for
himself, the path of separation from his criminal family.
Would her death have stayed with him this long otherwise?

Damn the twins! He had never seen a picture of Mary-
Ann Ianucci but he had forced a description out of Kevin.
Her long, dark hair and fine-cut face could come to him
at any time, but especially in sleepless hours, staring at
the ceiling at night, or now, staring at another dark Italian woman. Switching roles, the twins had made a mock-
ery of Italo's carefully drawn boundary between the night
side of the Riccis and what Charley did for him. To make
it even worse, Charley remained as haunted as ever that
they were actually his sons who had done this thing.

He had often tried to pry out of Stefi the secret of the
boys' paternity. He was going to try again. It came to
him with a force far stronger than a sudden whim that he
must, at last, know.

"Stef, you have to tell me."

She was returning from the kitchen. "About what?"

"The twins' father. I have real problems, Stef. Y—"

"What problems?" Stefi countered. She carried a pot
of coffee and some little half-moon cantucci, the almond-
and-anise-flavored sweet toast that both of them had
teethed on since infancy. "Charley Richards has problems?" she went on instead of answering his question
about the twins. "Il Professore, who has never even had
a traffic violation? Who files a model 1040 every April
15th? Who has been so laundered, deodorized and
tweezed that if somebody shouted 'Hey, guinea bastard!'
Charley would look around and yell 'Where?' That Charley Richards has problems?" He intended his frown to
silence this outburst, but it only seemed to open her up
wider. "Are you referring to the Charley Richards who
has had the best fica on Long Island for a quarter of a
century? Who gets the best toes to lick? The best breasts
to fondle? The best ass to bury his face in? The fica piu

stretta nel mondo, tight as a teenager's? That Charley Richards?''

''Stai calma, fica.'' He wanted to laugh at her irate expression and kid her out of her sudden flare of temper, but he knew she hadn't finished.

''The Charley Richards who can't even stay faithful for six months to his new girlfriend? What is it, Charley? If Garnet still isn't healed enough to put out you come sucking back between *my* legs? Is this the same Charley Richards we are discussing? The one with problems?''

''I knew I shouldn't've made that pass. Why are you suddenly Garnet's chief protector?''

''I would protect anybody against Sicilian manhood.''

''It won't happen again.''

''Not with me it won't. Some other fica, now that you're horny enough. That Wasp outside fools a lot of people, Charley, but I'm the one knows the secret of a Sicilian cazzo duro.''

He was silent for a moment. ''OK? Finished?''

''I have barely started. What sort of problems could a protected specimen like Il Professore have that would need me to dredge up the worst year of my life for him? Dredge up all the heartache of the boys' birth just to satisfy his idle curiosity?''

''Ah, that's what got you upset.''

''Your main problem is that because you are drowning in fica, you think you understand women. A high-powered mistress, a sexpot wife, me, who should have her head examined, two daughters. Everywhere you turn, beautiful women. And we all love you, Charley. Well, maybe not Missy. But, make no mistake, you are a lovable stronzo. My God, yes. That indirect approach, that understanding, sympathetic approach as if fucking was the last thing on your mind. It gets us all, Charley. With that anti-macho approach, you could be drowning in cunt. And if you have Vince's balls, you'd have killed each of us off . . . one . . . by . . . one.''

Charley felt a trap door was about to open if he took one more step. He moistened his lips. ''Care to explain that?''

''The natural relationship of mafiosi to their women?'' She poured two mugs of coffee and wrapped part of a mauve down-filled duvet around her so that only her face

showed, as if he was now officially denied the sight of
her body. "Why not," she went on then. "Know the
enemy, eh? You've had this coming a long time, Charley."

"What is this, Stef? You know I'm not mafioso."

"Once you told me the Riccis lived in a fortress like
royalty with our own armies and senators and cardinals.
What you were describing is the life of Italo and his
brothers and you and a few others who fought for it, like
Vince. You didn't have to fight. It was handed to you."
She passed him the plate of cantucci and a mug of coffee.
"Beve, mangia. Your whole life was handed to you on a
platter, Charley. If you and I hadn't already been fucking, Italo would even have pimped you another fica on
the side." She was silent for a long time.

"No proper Sicilian girl would have done the things I
did. I'm not a proper Sicilian girl. When my father found
out I was three months pregnant and no guilty name to
give him he started to throw me out of the house. My
mother was dead. My sister Iz was ten years old. He was
ready to put me *out on the street*. He sent me to Florida,
some clapped-up ex-mistress whore of Eugenio, Vince's
father. She was supposed to get me a safe abortion in
Cuba." Again she stopped but Charley knew better than
to interrupt. "I didn't want an abortion. That's one of
the ways you men work it. In the business we're in,
women have nothing unless they have children. We don't
exist until we're pregnant and we cease to exist when our
kids grow up. You men—" She broke off and stared
down into her own mug of coffee. "It's a male business,
the mafia. It always will be. Macho faggots, playing
power games: who's got the stiffest prick and wham! Up
yours, sucker! You circle each other face to face because
if one of you turns his back he's buggered to death.

"I wouldn't let them kill my babies. I ran away to a
retreat house run by the nuns. Eighteen hours' labor. I
had the medical care of a sharecropper on relief." She
nudged his mug toward him. "Beve. Mangia."

The words brought his nightmare back to him, Italo
offering the bloodstained Bens to eat. "Cut it out, Stef."

"When you ask dumb questions, Charley, you must do
me the courtesy of listening to the answers. I put in a
collect call to my father, Carlo. You're named after him.

His secretary, Miss Gonella, had the heart to accept charges. I told her I had had two boys, big healthy monsters. She and I cried over the phone. That's the same Miss Gonella who gave him head under his desk just before eating her own lunch six days a week for twenty-three years. Twenty-three years swallowing that manly antipasto.

"She was still crying when she put my father on. He was sobbing his heart out. Where was I? Why hadn't I called before? The two-faced, lying bastard. Anything for me and for the boys. You understand, Charley? I was back in the human race because I was the mother of boys."

In silence, both of them sipped their coffee. She handed him a cantucci cookie and he bit off half of it. "Are they mine, Stef?"

She took the other end of the moon-shaped cookie and dipped it into her coffee. "I was seeing three of you. You, a kid named Billy Mulloy, and Vince."

"Vince!"

"Billy went to Vietnam. He died there."

"You were putting out for Vince?"

"Everybody's fucked Vince. He gets it up even before he's unzipped. The first time it's flattering. Oh, wow, see what I did to this handsome fella? Otherwise it's a form of death. That's the mafia way with their prime enemy: hurt them, put them down and if they don't produce boys, kill them."

"But you must know which of us was the father."

"Single-minded, eh, Charley?"

"Stef, please."

"I've been your pussy for so long now, maybe I've turned cat. In heat we produce enough eggs to have one litter by two or three toms. Did you know that?"

"You have to have some idea who the father was."

"But telling it? Not even to the boys."

"I'm sure they asked you often enough."

"Not really. Thanks to my father dying when they were three years old, the boys had a very upper-middle class upbringing. In school they learned that a lot of boys rarely see their fathers.

"You remember that school. Your girls went there, too. You were an exception as a father, Charley. You existed. For most of the kids, the father wouldn't come home from work till after they were in bed. On weekends he'd be sloshed. In a few years, he'd be replaced by a new father. You would be surprised how easy it is not to miss a father when your peers don't have one, either.''

"That's some kind of joke, isn't it. Something to get your own back.''

"No, it explains how simple it was not to have to tell the boys anything.'' Mysteriously, she pulled the mauve duvet over her face. All he could see was one eye and a dark eyebrow. It regarded him unblinkingly. "Charley Richards has problems. Tracing sperm is not going to solve them. His longtime lay isn't going to cooperate. She isn't going to help him tap all the sperm he's stockpiled since his girlfriend went to the hospital. I'm sure you still remember how to jerk off.'' She stood up, draped in the duvet. "Wake up the pilot and fly back to Garnet. She must think she's got something special in you.'' She paused and her face softened for a moment. "Well, she has. We do all love Il Professore. And she's got her whole life to live with you, if that's the way it works out. But for me, Charley, you've fucked me enough for one life.'' She laughed and kissed his cheek as she shoved him toward the front door.

Thirty-Four

The seaplane let him off in Manhattan at the river's edge north of the Queensboro Bridge. Charley Richards shivered slightly, chilled after the flight. At this late hour nobody was on hand at the heliport or the amphibian base.

Charley walked over to First Avenue, looking for a cab. In his peculiar state of mind he had forgotten to radio ahead for a limo. He stood for a moment on the street, trying to get his thoughts together. Serve him right for digging that deeply into Stefi's real feelings.

Everything felt woolly, shifting like gauzy mist. There is a kind of depression in which no constructive thinking can be produced. Nothing coalesces. Alone, middle-aged, ice-cold, and standing still while throngs of active young people milled past, Charley felt the first stirrings of panic. New York was a jungle in which the lame and old, when they stumbled, were instantly culled by hungry young predators. He needed to focus on a reference point, something that would re-establish his identity, an anchor. He felt he had once been vital, powerful, even rich. Now, shivering, he was an urban ghost, pressing his nose against the show window of Manhattan.

Amazing, the power Stefi had to disrupt his own psyche. Then he remembered: Garnet was no longer around the corner in the blasted wreckage of her house. No longer far, far uptown at the hospital. She was much closer, in Winfield's building a few blocks away. Released from his frozen stance, he began walking north along First Avenue past the noisy, colorful places where young people ate or hung out or paused to make their retail purchases.

And as far as Charley could see, the restless youth of the Upper East Side existed mainly on video rentals and no-cal soda. The all-night supermarkets seemed deserted. The brilliantly decorated shops were closed at this hour but still using up thousands of watts of electricity, as were the banks and travel agencies. He found himself wondering how Garnet could remain as cheerful as she did in the face of such self-destructive waste.

He had never felt lower. Never more pessimistic, less in control of himself. He swerved west at 73rd Street toward the building where—his mind started clicking again—both Garnet and Winfield lived.

In his heart, although he hated to admit it, he thought of all these young people vacantly rushing from place to place as simply wasting time, no goals, no standards, hardly able to read or write, ignorant of history or logic, shunted between parental coddling and unemployment, the shrewd few performing minitasks for mega-money. But who was he to criticize the young? How much worse was someone who knew better and still betrayed his own goals, his own standards? Who was he, with lack of will and lewd treachery still tainting his icy breath, to complain about the morals of the young?

He let himself into the building and took the elevator up. Standing in front of Apartment 2F he saw a line of light under the door. Garnet's sleeping habits since her recovery were erratic, especially when a change in the weather produced aches.

She lay propped up in the big queen-sized bed reading a leaflet through spectacles with very large-area lenses. She smiled at him over the top rims. "Your cousin turned you down."

"Did she phone you?"

"Never. When it comes to you, I'm telepathic."

She continued reading the brochure, which had to do with something called the Education Research Fellowship. "Isn't that . . . ?" he asked.

"That's the Herman Foundation offshoot that owns what the explosion and fire left of my friend's house on the river. They've roped me in to raise funds. Can I put you down for a ten-dollar bill?"

He stood in silence, a strange series of thoughts chasing through his mind. The academic life, the library life—Stefi's life, really, in that book-lined hideout of hers—the research life. Dear God, how it beckoned. Small, discreet goals, reached after years of peace and quiet.

"What's the matter?" Garnet asked.

"Just that name, that peaceable, quiet name. Education. Research. Fellowship. Think of each word separately and then together." The look on his face was awestruck, as if he had discovered these words for the first time. He pulled off his tie, kicked off his shoes and sat down at the edge of the bed. She moved over to make room for him, masking the ache this caused her. He kissed her lightly on the lips, as the doctor had been cautioning both of them to do for so long now.

"I made a pass at Stef."

She kissed him back just as carefully. "We're both living very monastic lives. How'd you make out?"

He was silent for a long moment. With all she had to contend with, he hated to complain about his own life. "I'm very low. I'll get over it."

"Come to bed."

"No, I thought I'd—"

"Come to bed."

"But you wouldn't w—"

"Third notice: come to bed."

He undressed quickly and slid in beside her, feeling

the warmth of her body and the chill of his own. He had
no idea how icy he'd become as he brooded on the flight
back. He shrank from touching her as he made his confession.

"I swore a great oath to buy Zio Italo out of my life.
I haven't done anything about it for months. These trans-
fers take time. I had the time and I wasted it." He turned
slightly away from her. "I swore a great oath when we
fell in love that I would never betray you. Thank God
Stefi turned me down. Can you imagine how low I—"

"Making a pass at a former lover—former *is* the
word?—is not my idea of betrayal. Letting Zio Italo beat
you at your own game, that's another story." She laid
her warm fingers on his chest and recoiled. "This is the
corpse Stefi's left me? No wonder she turned you down."

"The reason she threw me out is that she had more
sense in her little finger than I do in my—"

She began stroking his chest and belly, which always
robbed him of the power of speech. "This little finger?"
she asked. "It's an icicle. What have you been dipping
it in?"

"Wormwood. Wormwood and gall." He sighed and
circled her head with his arm, hugging her to him. "It's
nice of you to take such a reasonable line."

"It's more than nice, it's angelic." She gave his penis
a flip and removed her hand. "I can see why even a first
cousin rejected you. Unidentified Birdseye Frozen meat.
You warned me." She lowered her voice in imitation of
him. "I'm very low," she quoted, foghorn style.

"No jokes."

She surrounded him with her legs, moving gingerly.
Once again she masked the pain of the movement. "Men
are different from women. You get the notion you've
failed, utterly, on every front, and the gloom is as thick
as cornmeal mush. You've failed as a leader of the free
world, you've failed to kindle Stefi's passion, you've
failed to stem the know-nothing tide of ignorance drowning the land. The next step is a leper colony but, Dear
God, you've also failed to find a leper colony. What I
mean is, you have failed."

"No jokes, please."

She began warming him up slowly, rubbing her thighs
against his trunk and legs. "I thought after this long I

really knew you. I know Winfield a lot better than you. She and I have a mutuality. You and I have a duality. It's not the same. Oh, boy, is it not.''

"Mutuality? With Winfield?''

"I was seventeen when Gerry sold his first shots of me to *Vogue*. I was on my way. Also I had missed two periods. I was thrilled. Gerry was not. I had an abortion. It was too early to know what sex the fetus might have been.'' She paused and tried to smile but it didn't come. "That was twenty years ago. If it'd been a daughter, she'd be Winfield's age. That's mutuality. Being women, we know what we are to each other. It's not a stereotyped relationship, but it runs in channels and women are comfortable with those channels. We make good use of them. But, as for duality, let me tell you—''

"It stinks,'' he cut in. "Two people trying to match up. No channels. No preordained roles. Like the horrible trouble you get into when you try to shorten one leg of a chair.'' He tried a small laugh. "Even one person can't always match up expectations with results.'' His version of a smile was only marginally better than hers. "I didn't ask that much, Garnet,'' he said in a voice he was trying to keep light. "I only asked of myself: when I set a goal, the one with Italo, not to slack off till I reached it. Yes, I might fall short in the end. But not give up after a few lousy months.''

She wriggled until she was sitting on top of him. She might have lost the knack of smiling, but she had grown quite adept at hiding the pain most movements caused. "You've been busy reviving me. You gave me six months of your life. That's why I'm alive again.''

"Good! All I ask is that you feel guiltily grateful.''

"That is *so* Sicilian.''

Although she weighed very little, he could feel her along the whole length of his body, warming and holding, as if he were in danger of spinning off the planet unless she kept him in place. He could feel himself harden.

"Uh-oh.''

"Uh-oh,'' she echoed. "What will the doctor say?''

"What does he always say?''

"Then we'd better not tell the doctor.''

"What'll we do for guilt?"

"Watch me."

Thirty-Five

Monday morning Winfield Richards got up at six and stretched wide her long, slender arms, naked before her window. Her newly short-cropped hair, dark and fine, radiated outward like a medieval squire's bowl-cut, from the top of her skull. She stared south along the narrow line-of-sight that led thirty blocks to the radiantly aluminum Art Deco top of the Chrysler Building.

The stormy weekend had cleared the air like a damp broom. She could almost see people in the small, sparkling, curved insets of glass at the top, surrounded by neon tubing, but she knew this was an illusion. She felt light-headed from lack of sleep. At this hour no one was awake in the topmost attics of the Chrysler Building.

Her answering-machine was winking at her. Funny, she hadn't heard any incoming calls, but then it had not been a night for answering calls anyway. She bent over and switched the machine to playback. "Winfield," Bunny began without any preamble, her voice high and fast, "I'm not going to have it. That's all. I will not surrender my independence to make Nikki and his father happy. Winfield, wouldn't you do the same thing? I love my independence as much as you do. What is this baby to me except a whadyacallit around my neck? Something to keep me from being my own woman, like you are. Something to keep me subservient to men. Something to put me off sex forever. Yech!"

The machine went silent and then a second incoming call, Bunny again. "I know I'm right, Winfield. You know I'm right. Us Richards girls have to stick together. Babies are for men. Why can't they have them and leave us alone? Give me a buzz when you can."

Winfield wiped the messages and stood up. She listened to them again in her memory, trying to assess Bunny's state of mind. Excited by the idea of getting an abortion, excited and needing reassurance from her role-model sister. How many women of her age had Winfield listened to these past few years, asking for the same reassurance. People somehow felt, well, if Winfield says it's OK, it's OK. People should know better. How could you tell them to do it, do it, stop stalling and do it, when "it" would haunt their lives?

Should she call her now? Knowing Bunny, the desire to be rid of the baby might have passed. She might be thinking of names for it by now.

She stretched and turned to survey the naked young man on her opened-out sofa, his hair almost as short as hers. Us Richards girls have to stick together. What would Bunny have to say about this liaison?

Saturday night had been their first date, ever. Over the past decade at the same expensive private school where, although they were only a year apart, they had never exchanged more than a "hullo." It would have been the simplest thing for either of their mothers to have whipped up cousinly camaraderie but this was not in the nature of either woman. A pretext for friendship could have occurred in the gymnasium when teachers at either end, shaping up basketball squads among the taller boys and girls, might have summoned a "Richards" from the girls' end or a "Ricci" from the boys'.

Kerry lay fast asleep, as well he might. The two former private school basketball stars had given each other a full weekend of workout. It was as if neither of them had ever before had intercourse with the opposite sex.

What it was, Winfield knew, was simpler than that. Both of them were used to working at words, quite the most articulate members of their family, to the point of glibness. But establishing sexual territory, planting the flag on new flesh and enjoying its exploitation with equal vigor, did not need words. It barely needed thought. Only one thing had remained hidden behind the weekend's sexual pleasure: the tacit understanding that both of them were refugees from their all-devouring family. They had shown it non-verbally for years by their choice of clothes, books, of the music they listened to and of their politics, leftish and Green.

Of all their family, who set such store by keeping "in touch," only she and Kerry kept in contact with the world. It came before everything. Grabbing the ninety-second TV newsbite that satisfied most people was nothing compared to keeping in real touch with the outside world. Did anyone else in the family understand this? Perhaps only her father.

Escape lay hidden beneath this entire weekend's sexual excess: an escape hatch for fleeing the family. Would they ever enjoy this so much again? Wasn't the first time, in its heedless, melancholy way, also the last? She felt dizzy with the insight.

Kerry's eyes had slitted. He was awake, watching her, just as she was observing him. "God, you have long legs."

"Arms," she corrected him, stooping for a lightning-fast gorilla imitation. She swiveled from a simian crouch to a high leap and a skyward shove of outstretched fingers which rapped the apartment ceiling. Her hair spun outward like a short skirt. "I could jump-hook a basket from four yards away." The move made her head spin.

"I saw you do that a lot in that game against Chapin. You scored a dozen baskets, no assists."

"Then why didn't you sidle up to me afterward and ask for a date?"

"In those days I liked small girls with big tits, like Ma." He wiggled his eyebrows. "Have we got time for another penalty shot?"

She stared closely at him. "How do I know you're not the notorious criminal, Kevin Ricci, whose exploits in faraway lands have earned him the most dubious of reputations?"

"How indeed." He stopped and thought for a very long time. If she had known him better she would have recognized this distinguishing trait. Kevin never paused for thought. "You know," he went on then, "that business in St. Marys, PA? That wasn't the first time Kev and I switched."

"Just as long as I have the real article lying on my bed."

He watched her through half-shut eyes against the window's growing glare. There was a moment when the thing that they had never said might have finally been said: "Let's opt out of Ricci-hood. Let's join the big world outside, the one the other Riccis never notice." It would never happen, Winfield realized, and certainly not after their first real encounter, leaving them so pleased with their own performance that the idea of running away made no sense. Perhaps later. When each of them had grown a notch.

She moved out of the window space, knowing that to Kerry she had been only a silhouette. "Italian women have it easier than Italian men," she said then. "And half-Italian women have it even easier. Bunny and I don't have to conform to any criteria. You, poor slob, have to maintain that tight, anal-constricted macho strut, unforgiving, forever erect and engorged with penile blood."

"It won't always be that way," Kerry warned her. He sat up, rubbing his penis and groin muscles as if they were sore. Which, Winfield suspected, they were. "You are fucking your father's ex-lover's son," Kerry said. "Without committing incest by any legal definition of the word, this has got to be the most degenerate coupling in the annals of Freud."

"Probably why it's so much fun." Winfield knelt in front of him and took control of his penis.

"Not if I'm also Charley's son."

Her hands dropped to her sides. "What?"

"Just something Kevin and I have wondered about now and then."

"Thank you for waiting till the weekend was over." She went back to work on him, feeling light-headed again, slightly drunk with the enormity of all their potential sins. "It's a suspicion that has crossed my mind now and then."

"It doesn't bother you?"

"Too late for that," Winfield said. Her head had begun to spin again.

"What bothers me," Kerry said, slowly rubbing her short-cropped hair, "is the hypocrisy. That generation has always been unable to tell it like it is. Especially a basic, like who my father is. I mean I love her and I love Charley, but Christ Almighty they are such a pair of hypocrites. Our generation . . ." He paused to begin enjoying what she was doing. Then, slowly, "We talk straight," he said in an almost dreamy voice.

"Heap old folk speak with forked tongue," Winfield

muttered. "Um. Um. Look how inflamed I can get you. It's like a billiard ball. Does it hurt?"

"Want to see me put the red ball in the corner pocket?" He lifted her onto his lap just as the telephone rang. "Christ!"

"Let it ring," Winfield said, fitting him inside her. The totality of their possible sinning was a flood of pure unhypocritical light, illuminating each sin and naming it, pouring down on them out of the open window. "He'll call back."

"Who?"

"Charley," she said, beginning to bounce up and down. She got a sudden, headachy vision of them, Hieronymus Bosch sticklike nudes, fornicating mindlessly while Hell shat a thousand translucent devils over their heads.

He matched her rhythm. "Answer the phone, you total degenerate."

"Um. Oh, lovely. Hello, Dad?"

A silence at the other end of the line. Then, "Weenfield, Nikki. Bunny is there with you?"

Slowly, her up-and-down strokes diminished. He felt huge inside her, huge and suddenly painful. "I—no . . . not really." She could hear how shaky her voice was.

"I've looked all ovair Bowstone and Cambritch." His voice sounded raspy with fatigue, his French accent thick and careless. "She is headeen for New York beck—" He stopped. "Beck—"

"Nikki, tell me."

"Beck-os, b-because she want abortion." She could hear him sobbing. She could feel Kerry ebbing inside her as he picked up clues from her face. Talk straight. Our gener— No hypocrisy. The wages of sin, she thought, is death. Wages of taking your sister for granted . . . ?

Why hadn't she telephoned Bunny? Because she'd put her pleasures with Kerry first. Instead of calming the kid down and exerting that steady, logical, boring Winfield influence, she abandoned her to silence. Us Richards girls have to stick together? All it took to split them apart was one stiff penis.

She stared hard at Kerry, "You dog."

"What?"

"Nikki," she said. "Stay calm. We'll find her."

"But . . . the bebe."

Ah, yes, Winfield thought. Bunny was her number one pupil and when she set her mind to it she could analyze things as well as her role-model sister. Babies, she had pointed out, are for men.

Thirty-Six

Charley turned them all upside-down, searching for Bunny: his right hand, Kerry, three operatives from a respectable detective agency owned by Richard Holdings. Garnet and Winfield had checked abortion clinics in New York, Massachusetts and Connecticut, the emergency wards of public and private hospitals. A tri-state list of gynecologists had been checked by Eileen Hegarty. But there was no trail.

According to Nikki, who was particularly vulnerable and useless since his mother had returned to the Far East, Bunny had been in bed when he had left for his morning two-mile run. She had walked out in an exercise suit and high-lace sneakers. Her wallet remained behind.

"A voluntary walk-out," as one of the private eyes told Winfield, "is the toughest. They may not even be thinking of it when they leave. They may be going down to the corner for a pack of butts and it suddenly hits them to lam out."

Winfield eyed him glumly, knowing in her heart that if she had phoned Bunny things would be different. She should have realized how serious Bunny's intentions were. Role models are supposed to understand such things. They are supposed to see that the purpose of abortion is not the death of the fetus but the freedom of the mother and, even more, her freedom from the father.

Apart from good looks, Winfield wondered, what did Bunny see in this collapsed stud? Nikki moped. Nikki moaned. Nikki hit bottom in the self-regard sweepstakes. Everybody had more important things to do than help scrape him up.

On the third day Charley gave in to a summons from

Zio Italo on another matter. EcoClean, a highly successful Richland company which handled the maintenance of
offices and waste disposal, had somehow run afoul of
Gowanus Cartage, Inc, a wholly-owned subsidiary of the
Torella family of Jersey City and Corleone, Sicily. The
details, which had to do with encroaching on Gowanus'
bid for the handling of toxic waste, would have been settled by now. But Charley, rapt as he was in chasing down
every lead to find Bunny, was making the Torellas angrier
by ignoring them.

A mysterious look of satisfaction lurked in Italo's narrow, hawk-nosed face. Charley had been avoiding his uncle for months now. Being this close to him, after so
long, made him acutely uncomfortable. Perhaps, he
thought, one is always miserable in the presence of the
puppeteer who pulls one's strings.

"You leave the Torellas to me." Italo's voice seemed
to come from far away. "There is more here than meets
the eye, much more."

Charley blinked. The depth of his hatred for this man
was slowly dawning on him. He collected his wits carefully, as if he had never before had to control hatred and
make it look like family cooperation. "Zio," he said,
"the problem with Gowanus Cartage is not one of your
turf battles. Whatever else the Torellas do, Gowanus operates on the legal side."

Italo's fierce dark-olive eyes seemed to hood slightly,
as if he controlled a membrane that could shield these
windows of the soul from too close a reading. "Gowanus
and EcoClean are both bidding on that nuclear contract
from Network Power and Light. You can't handle the
contract and the Torellas can."

"Who says we can't?"

"It's not a contract for Il Professore. It's clean-up rags
and waste. It's old coveralls and gloves and dungarees
loaded with radioactive crap. It's muslin hair nets and
canvas slippers and a ton of stuff each month that sends
Geiger counters off the deep end. EcoClean can't dispose
of such waste."

"Why not?" Charley could feel his control slipping.
"Why not?"

"Because it can only be handled by illegal dumping,
out in the boonies where nobody sees. Three a.m., Go-

wanus trucks with their lights off. They back into fill sites and dump. Another fleet comes along and hides it under ordinary fill.''

Charley slumped back in his chair. ''Enough,'' he retorted. ''Spare me all the high-tech bullshit, Zio. What you're saying is, let thieves handle it.''

''Like I said, leave the Torellas to me.'' It was as if Charley hadn't spoken. Italo's sharp, sunken eyes looked away for an instant. ''Their connection in the old country is very tight. To the Corleonese clan they stand like the fingers of the right hand.'' A long pause. Then Zio's smile iced across the space between them. ''And how is my little Bunny these days?''

Charley glanced sharply at him. ''You found out?''

''Found out what? That she's in the Bahamas?''

It caught Charley quite off guard. ''What?''

''She's in the penthouse suite at one of Vince's casino hotels down there. The Miramar-Athenee, suite three.'' He scribbled something on a slip of paper he drew from one of the pigeonholes of his old oak rolltop. Charley recognized a wide scrap torn from a business letter Italo had received.

Charley read the telephone number. He felt as if his blood was actually starting to heat up, to boil, to fizz with rage. ''Does she still have the baby?''

''Of course she still has the baby. You think Zio Italo would be party to the murder of an unborn Ricci?''

Charley closed his eyes and tried to count to ten but his anger was too wild for such measures. This egregious mafia asshole! This dried-up eunuch! ''You'd better,'' Charley began in such quiet, slow tones that Italo had to lean forward to hear him, ''tell me exactly what you did . . . before I phone her and . . . before I tell you . . .''

''How angry you are,'' Italo finished for him. ''She has been under twenty-four hour watch since we knew she was pregnant. I don't take the birth of a Ricci lightly, Carlo. Especially not *this* Ricci, who's half-Chink. So when she phoned Winfield and left a message about what she intended to do, we knew we had to intervene.''

''You have a tap on her phone?'' Charley's voice had risen an octave. ''Or on Winfield's?''

''It's Shan's phone, too. We put her on a plane out of Logan Airport to the Bahamas and she's been there ever

since with a nurse and an orderly in constant attendance.''

"You mean two keepers."

Italo's glance sharpened. "Watch the tone of voice,"
he warned his nephew. "I mean a nurse and an orderly.
Bunny is happy with them. She has taken twenty bucks
from the orderly in gin rummy and the nurse is showing
her how to knit small woolly things for the baby."

Charley sat back in his chair and struggled for inner
calm. He knew how pretty a picture Italo could paint
when it suited his purposes. He also knew his uncle rarely
lied to him. But the gall of him! The cheap, meddling
chutzpah! He reached across to Italo's private phone and
pulled it toward him to tap in the long-distance number.
It was barely nine in the morning and the phone rang for
a long time before a woman answered.

"Penthouse Three."

"This is Miss Richards' father. Let me speak to her."

"I . . . Who?"

Italo took the phone from him. "Nurse, you know who
this is? Put the girl on the phone." He handed it back to
Charley.

Christ, he thought, even to talk to my own daughter I
need this nasty bastard's intervention? "Hello?" Bunny
asked in a tentative voice.

"How you feeling, kiddo?"

"Dad! I'm fine. The baby is kicking regularly. Why
hasn't Nikki called me?"

"Why? Because none of us knew where the hell you
were."

"Don't blame me," the girl responded with great
practice. "I'm just an innocent mafia dupe. I figured Zio
Italo would tell you. Listen, tell Nikki we've got a huge
honeymoon suite and a guest room. Tell h—"

"You tell him. Doesn't your suite have a two-way
phone? You could've called one of us." He paused. "I'll
give Nikki your number. I'll give it to Winfield, too. Is
there anything you need down there? Besides a good
spanking?"

"Uncle Vince has somehow got me the famous Dr.
Eiler. You know, the Eiler Section man? He does the
research here. A real cutie."

"Research? In a casino?"

"It used to be a casino. Now it's a clinic."

"For what? Pregnant runaways?"

"Druggies. It's a very posh detox center. I know half the other patients from finishing school."

Charley paused. It had become abundantly clear to him in the last few seconds that they had all wasted their time and emotions on this infant-bearing idiot. "You want to say hello to Zio Italo?" Charley asked.

"Tesoro mio, come stai? How is the littlest Ricci?"

Charley closed his eyes and this time managed to get as far as six before anger dipped him back in acid again. The nasty meddling nutless shithead guinea bastard! He stared out of the unwashed Herculite windows. Somewhere in this world people lived a life free of Italo's overbearing domination. Equally, they lived free of his aura of crime. Charley Richards was supposed to be one of those people. But to believe he lived a separate life was the ugliest illusion of all.

He listened to some Italian endearments before Zio hung up. Then Charley got to his feet. He felt that all that he was about to say had been said before and now fell on deaf ears. "Zio," he said in that slow, quiet voice that masked rage, "when you sent me off to Harvard, you said I'd run the legitimate side and you'd run the rest. What do you call kidnapping Bunny? Stashing her away in one of Vince's detox centers? Butting into the Eco-Clean business? Warning me off the Torellas because their Sicilian connections are too insane to argue with?"

Italo started to stand up, too, then remembered what a shrimp he was beside this big, blond Norman Siciliano. "Charley, nobody guaranteed the two sides would never overlap. It's life. Don't let it upset you."

"Upset me?" Charley turned to leave. "When every day I get fresh evidence that the nature of legit business is illegality? You say I can't handle nuclear waste and stay legit? I say the Torellas are lazy scum who make their bucks the easiest way possible. To cut me off at the knees, you kidnap Bunny."

This time Italo actually stood up and came around his desk to pat Charley's shoulder. "You got a lot on your mind, Charley. But it's a mind I have always admired *because* Il Professore can handle a lot. This will pass.

You'll get some perspective on this and you'll wonder why it ever upset you.''

''Who's upset?'' Charley asked. He extended his hands, fingers outstretched and watched them shake with a series of fine and coarse tremors. To Charley they resembled the gestures a prisoner makes through his bars, grasping for freedom. In his mind's eye he saw his hands circling Zio Italo's scrawny neck, the uncle who dominated his life. He could feel the ancient flesh between his fingers as he squeezed hard, harder.

''Who's upset?'' he echoed. Then he turned and left the office.

April

Thirty-Seven

"Stefi carissima, it's Zio Italo. How is my favorite niece on this bright spring day?"

"Fine, Zio. What's up?"

It was unthinkable that he make the hellish journey out to Long Island Sound to meet with his dead brother's, Carlo's, oldest daughter to ask a favor of her. Even a major favor like this one.

Tragic news from the old country: a vendetta had already destroyed the leaders of two families of honor, one of which had American connections. It was bad enough, Zio Italo mused aloud, that here, in a New York turf war, mafia massacred mafia. Stupid. As always, drugs. Even clever Vince had succumbed. What could Italo do in the face of such profits but bow to the inevitable?

"Stefania, tesoro, I know you have been worried about that land."

Stefi's brow wrinkled. She glanced around her at the book-lined walls and out of the window at the sparkling water of the Sound. "Land?"

"Those three thousand ettari of vineyard near Castellammare del Golfo."

"Zio, would you believe? Sometimes a week goes by without me thinking of them?" It was Stefi's way of testing the old man. If he didn't laugh at the joke she was in for something heavy.

"Your mother's father, Ugo Fulgatore, tilled those vineyards. All over the world people see his name on the bottle. And what about the substantial check you and Isabella get four times a year from Fulgatore s.P.a?"

Stefi closed her eyes. What was it about old people that they had to start every conversation by recounting how much you owed? She hoped she would never be that way with her boys. Mind-reading by telephone, Italo went on, "And the boys, tesoro, what an opportunity for them!"

"Opportunity?" She tried to keep the sarcasm out of

Leslie Waller

her voice. "Between you and Vince and Charley, my boys get a surplus of opportunities." Stefi calmed herself and sat down on a bench near the phone. This might take hours.

"You can't say you don't need a vacation, all three of you."

"Ah. In Sicily, right?"

"Where else?" Italo demanded. "All expenses paid."

A chill shot across Stefi's shoulders. That last phrase locked her in and threw away the key. It meant she couldn't reject the "vacation." With a hanging judge like Zio Italo, there was no appeal from such a sentence.

"Now I know we're in for it," Stefi said.

Their Alitalia flight, four hours late, had been met at Fiumicino Airport by a chauffeured stretch limo which whisked them to the top of the Spanish Steps and a three-bedroom suite at the Hassler.

In the long living room she shared with the boys, Stefi leaned out of the window and watched the hand gestures of the cab drivers down below, killing time while waiting for fares. She hadn't slept on the overnight flight from New York. The boys had. Perversely enough, each of them was now asleep in his room while Stefi found herself unable even to nap.

That was always the trouble with Zio Italo's plans: you never got to see any of the hole cards. She squinted up at the noon April sun, coming in at a low angle. Down below she heard a whiff of shouting. The sounds grew fiercer, harsher. From the few words that carried up to her floor, Stefi knew it was soccer they were quarreling about, but at such a pitch that one might think the honor of a mother or sister were involved.

"Noisier than Manhattan!" Kerry complained. He wandered sleepily out into the room, dressed in underwear shorts and woolly white sweat socks.

"If I'd slept as long as you . . ." Stefi watched him at the bar, pouring himself some red-hued orange juice. "Me, too," she called.

They sat, sipping. "What did Kevin tell you about this so-called vacation?"

Kerry shrugged. "Just that there's been an offer for the vineyards. The man from Corleone who grows the grapes for Marsala. He wants to branch out and produce a classy vino da tavola. The hard way is to plant a new vineyard. The easy way is to buy up Fulgatore s.P.a.''

"I'm supposed to say yes? And get Iz to agree?"

"Does Zio Italo ever give you a straight-line story?"

"Does he ever show *any* of the cards in his hand?"

They sat in silence, thinking, while downstairs several more cabbies joined in a shouting match. Kevin appeared in shorts and socks, grimaced, poured himself some juice and sat down in the other easy chair with a thump. "You speak Italian," he said to his mother. "What's all the shouting?"

"Soccer."

Each of them fell silent in a jet-lagged way, staring into the blood-red juice squeezed from Sicilian oranges. "Did Zio mention the feud?" Kevin asked. "He's worried about this vendetta between the Corleonese and the Castellammare crowd."

Stefi was used to these telepathic cross-references between the two boys. Kevin might well have been asleep before, but somehow, without overhearing them, he knew precisely what they were talking about.

"It's a Corleonese who wants to buy our land," Stefi pointed out. "Are you beginning to get Italo's drift?"

"Somehow," Kevin responded, "he wants your sale of Fulgatore to end the vendetta. What're you supposed to do, give it away?"

Stefi's head shook slowly from side to side. "That's not how you bend a Siciliano to your will."

"Certomá is the guy's name. Lucca Certomá." Kevin looked up, puzzled that his mother was laughing softly. "Let us in on it."

"Certomá is not a very decisive name." She finished her juice and set the glass down with a click on a huge plate glass tabletop. "It means 'certainly, but.' I imagine he takes some kidding about it."

"Nobody kids Lucca Certomá," Kevin said. "He's the capo of the Corleonese. A very hard wild man who runs a bunch of hard wild men. They not only deal junk, they use it."

"How do you know so much about the old country?" Stefi asked. "When I was a kid only the old people all came from across the water. Starting with Zio Italo and your Grandpa Carlo, the Riccis were born in the States. To them Sicily became a kind of branch office, not the headquarters. And to my generation, Sicily is a sort of . . . holiday camp. It's a vacation spot, lots of Greek ruins, good food . . .'' Her voice died away drowsily.

"It's the source of the mafio ethos," Kerry said. "They worked out the system in the old country. The new world provided the markets. The Palermo-New York axis is still the core of the whole thing."

"Which is why," Kevin added with a faintly malicious smile, "we're here today."

The telephone pealed. All three of them jumped. Stefi got slowly to her feet and answered. "Pronto."

"La Signora Ricci?" a man asked. He had a gruff Southern Italian accent, slurred and dentalized. Ricci in his mouth became Reedgee.

"No."

"No?" he queried.

"Sono la Signorina Ricci."

"Mi scusi! Lucca Certomá qua."

"Veramente?" Stefi teased. "E certo? Ma . . . ?"

Frowning horribly, Kevin shook his forefingers sideways. "Be nice!" he whispered. "Wild men don't like jokes."

But Certomá was laughing already. He switched without warning into a bad English. "I am in lobby. We hava da drink, si?"

"Well . . ."

"We get acquaint, si?"

"That might be—"

"You anna you nice boyce."

"OK. In half an hour," Stefi promised. "How will I know you?"

"Simple. I am very handsome."

Stefi nodded as if she had known in advance what his answer would be. She hung up the phone and started for the huge shower room that served the suite. "Boys," she said then. "Italo's trying to marry me off."

Thirty-Eight

". . . Sure they're treating you well?" Charley repeated. In his right hand, the telephone had gone moist and slippery.

"Just fine," Bunny told him. "If you want to worry about something, how about getting Nikki to haul his butt down here?"

"He still hasn't shown up?"

"Neither have you," Bunny let him know. "Only Winfield, out of sheer guilt, has seen fit to visit the swollen one."

"I know, I know. I asked her to."

"I really want that fugitive father down here. I want him doing his bit."

Charley shook his head. "Nikki doesn't come over as any kind of family man. When they kidnapped you he went to pieces. You're the only one who can paste him back together and I'm not sure you should."

"Just what his father was moaning about."

"You—? Shan visited you?"

"No. He calls Nicole."

"I had no idea she was with you." His voice had an oh-well-that's-better tone. Charley could hear that soft coo of guilt-avoidance that silvers over words meant to keep someone peaceful. Shameful to know that your own child has let you off the hook, on her terms.

"I'd go nuts without her. She and the Great Shan are trying to get Nikki back in their family, let alone mine. Nicole says it's overlapping circles. If Shan wins, we all win."

"That's deep, kiddo. Deep." He looked up to see Garnet carrying in two bags of groceries. "Here's a very strong person who wants to say hello," Charley said, handing her the phone. "It's Bunny."

"How's it going?" Garnet asked. "Nikki there yet?"

"He's frozen in ice up in Boston. I can't thaw him out."

"My, my," Garnet told her. "I have a similar problem right here with your dear old dad. Why are men such dawdlers?"

"I can think of a better word."

"The plain fact is, Charley," Garnet said, "you have let Italo steal your immortal soul. In the last few months, when you had enough time to transfer three or four company ownerships, you've not touched even one. You've complained about not doing anything, but that's the exent of what you've done. Complain. You remind me of Nikki." She hadn't put the groceries away. The morning sun slid sideways into the large living room, eavesdropping. Later in the day, as it swung higher to the south, it would come crashing in on any conversation. Now it tiptoed.

"I can still—"

"Charley, are you the man who gives me lectures about living in a land of ignoramuses?"

"I can—"

"A nation of know-nothings who are too ignorant even to know how ignorant they really are?"

He stood silently, the lateral sunlight picking out his left side as if he were an onstage actor. But this was one of their rare arguments; it would never have an audience.

"Then what do you call what you're letting Italo do to you?" she barged on. "What do you call a man who lets his truly nasty uncle run his life? Zio Italo has altered my view of mankind. If the race includes someone like him, then . . ." She faltered and stopped.

Charley cleared his throat. "I had made a good start before he kidnapped Bunny."

"He will always hold hostages. That's how he uses family. He will always have you over a barrel." Her white hair, kept cropped at slightly more than an inch in length, seemed to bristle. "But, Charley, think. He isn't about to harm a hair on Bunny's head. There's no reason you should hesitate. You're reacting automatically with the disciple's brainwashed fear of the master." She was in full flow again. "By gestating that sacred baby, Bunny is giving you valuable time to be free of your uncle. You're angry with her for behaving like a dingaling. But until she gives birth to the child, and for a long time thereafter, she has a choke-hold on Zio Italo. She is doing what he cannot. He stands in reverent awe, staying his bloody hand. Move, Charley. Go for it.''

Garnet drew a long breath. "That's why, when you hesitate, I wonder if that evil old man has stolen your soul. I wonder if I'm looking at the whole Charley Richards or just the good-looking cardboard figure Richland Holdings keeps propped up to scare off demons.'' She had the knack of projecting her feelings without raising her voice or resorting to violent gestures. Someone at a distance where her words couldn't be heard would still feel her disapproval. Closer targets could only wish for the floor to open up beneath them.

Instead, Charley turned to look out the window. Now his right side blazed in an aura of sunlight. Earlier, when Garnet had touched on his struggle to get Zio Italo off his back, she had sounded understanding. But with the passage of time and his dithering, a note of urgency had begun to sound. The connection between this struggle and their future life together was so obvious it hurt even to think about it. It was precisely this crucial importance that slowed his hand, or so he told himself.

Charley squinted. Garnet had the same view as Winfield, on the top floor, but one could no longer see the Chrysler Building from this low in the building. Maybe Garnet was right. Maybe he'd let Zio's voodoo shadows frighten him. He turned back to her.

The two women had redecorated her small apartment as a natural extension of her apostolic environment, galleries and museums. The walls had been redone in a thick-textured chalk white. Posters were framed in narrow anodized aluminum bars and hung from long gallery rods descending from the ceiling cornice molding. Matte black plinths of various widths and heights jutted up from the black-rubber floor tiles. On each plinth a small object had been posed in its own overhead pin spotlight.

The shortest plinth held an immense ceramic bowl containing rose petals, small crushed pine cones and thin broken branches of mesquite. An old friend sent her fragrant fresh mesquite every month or so from New Mexico. The same bouquet perfumed the bedroom, with its queen-sized bed that left no room for any other furniture. There was no sign any longer of a wheelchair or a walking cane. Garnet usually sat, as she did now, in a black-leather sling chair made of white-enameled wood. She still squeezed the tennis ball in her left hand, but it had grown so much stronger that she now reduced a tennis ball to tatters in a month.

"Here's a confession," she said then, keeping her voice low. Her dark brown eyes fixed him so firmly he almost moved forward to be closer to them, like a frozen man with a flaming brazier. "I was dead wrong to think of Zio Italo as a normal old man. You know how I feel about the oneness of the earth and everything that lives on it. But that man has made me see that in every Eden there is a snake. No one plays a tie-game with Zio Italo. His Machiavellian brain is not programmed for cooperation or compromise. Either he beats you or you beat him."

He was silent, mainly because he agreed with her. He tried to smile encouragingly, a difficult thing if one sees nothing encouraging in view. "And I've been wrong, too," he said. "He dazzled me with his masks. You're right about Bunny. She's running interference for me. I have to get the ball back and run with it."

She got up from her chair and moved to him, maintaining an even gait, not slow but not yet completely limber. She put her arms around him and squeezed hard. "That's my old Charley," she said then. Her elfin face, half-buried in his chest, looked suddenly less guarded. "You don't know how worried I've been about you," she said, her voice faintly muffled in his shirt and tie. "To tell the truth, about us. The Charley I first knew . . . he'd gone on sick leave. As if . . ." She faltered. "As if he'd been the one blown up." She nodded. "An evil strategy: destroy Charley by destroying Garnet. Blow it all away, simply to keep an empire together. Blow away two people who have spent half their lives just *finding* each other. Business—" The word was a toad in her mouth. "Business is more important than people."

"He's not the only old man who believes that."

"And is destroying the other ninety-nine percent of the world to prove it."

To reach the dining rooms of the Yale Club, on Vanderbilt Avenue near Grand Central Terminal, anyone can take an elevator to the top floors of the elderly, block-like building. Noah Cohen had been sitting in the bar-lounge, acutely aware that he had come this far without any credentials but could not order the drink necessary to camouflage his waiting.

He had no idea how long it might take Farrington Ansbach Reid to appear. Their last telephone conversation had been desperately short and unspecific. "Same place," was all Reid would say. "Friday."

Since their only previous meeting had been here in this lounge, it was simply a matter of waiting. Cohen, like any seasoned Federal agent, was used to waiting. That wasn't the problem. What made the waiting anxiety-provoking was that it had to be done on hours stolen from the Bureau. No one had authorized this investigation. Suggs, Cohen's immediate superior, hadn't forbidden Cohen's interest, he'd simply told him it had to be done on his own time at his own expense. Cohen's time was now in conflict with what he owed the Bureau.

Nevertheless, Cohen found he could sit here almost at peace with himself. He knew he was onto something big; Richland's use of sensitive subsidiaries like the accounting firm as a sub rosa source of intelligence against competitors. Industrial espionage was flourishing. The laws against it were muddled, which made the Bureau's position unsure, and where unsure, in the great bureaucratic tradition of Hoover, the Bureau feared to tread.

At the far end of the lounge the clock showed the time to be just after one p.m. Around Cohen men his age, early forties, well dressed in tailored business suits and softly glowing ties, their cheeks exuding manly aromas, were finishing a second drink. Most of them seemed to favor sparkling water with a slice of lime, but a few of the older ones had gotten through dry Martinis. In the opposite corner from Cohen sat a gentleman of a different, more European look, with hair a bit longer and a hairline mustache out of the 1930s. He had chain-smoked perhaps a dozen cigarettes in the past hour, through a long filter whose internal tube of absorbent crystals he was now replacing.

It struck Cohen that the other man hadn't ordered anything, either. Like Cohen he could be a visitor waiting for his host. Waiting. The situation had only entered its second hour and couldn't be judged critical yet. Cohen crossed his long, rangy cowboy's legs, folded his arms over his chest, set his Gary Cooper jaw and focussed his attention all the way across the lounge at some distant and imaginary snow-capped range of the Sierra Nevadas where coyotes roamed and buzzards flapped their wings.

That was how he happened to see Andy Reid come out of the elevator. Reid made a tiny dip with his head before walking away. Cohen got slowly to his feet. He might not be the tallest man in the room, but he looked it. He followed Reid into the men's room, wondering why so many clandestine meetings seemed to end up in a place where it was so easy to eavesdrop. The tiled walls and floors made acoustics strong and precise.

Inside, at adjoining urinals, the two pursued a secondary mission in silence until the other man left. Then Reid said, "This was a lousy idea."

"We need a better place. You know that little park downtown near Richland Tower?"

"I can't be seen downtown with you."

"Do you take the subway to work?" Reid nodded. "I'll meet you on the 68th Street platform of the East Side IRT. Downtown side near the change booth. Monday morning? Eight o'clock?"

Reid zipped his fly closed. "It can't be any worse than this place." He walked out of the toilet room without another word. As Cohen followed him a discreet thirty seconds later, he almost ran into the European gentleman with the cigarette holder. They did a small doorway dance around each other, smiling politely. Cohen walked back, paused for a while, then rang for the down elevator. As he got on, so did the European gentleman. They nodded politely to each other, as if they were old friends.

Thirty-Nine

It was the wrong kind of evening for three jet-lagged Americans. Lucca Certomá, strutting with self-confidence, had laid on a late night of such excess that, as it began, Kevin had leaned past his date, a tall black model named

Ngamba, to murmur in his brother's ear: "This is like killing a fly—"

"—by ramming it with a Mack truck," Kerry finished for him. His date was a Yugoslav model named Annima or Ennima. Both were lovely girls in their late teens. Neither spoke any English but were in the early stages of Italian. Ngamba explained as best she could that Ngamba was a stage name, fashioned after her motherland, Gambia. Her real name was Xylzae, with a glottal click in it. Annima had to write her name twice, once for each twin, to make sure it didn't start with an E.

Lucca turned out to be as handsome as advertised, not tall or thin, but not fat either. In his make-do English he explained that most Corleonese looked like him: broadshouldered, big-armed, thick-thighed, powerful men who could—

On their way to the supper club off the Via Del Babuino, Lucca had paused and crouched in front of a white Mercedes coupe. He grabbed the front bumper and lifted the car a foot off the asphalt. This impressed everyone, but especially the attractive wife of the man he introduced as his partner. She nearly swooned.

Gli Amici offered dinner, dancing to a small Latinbeat combo and the chance to rub shoulders with anybody else who could afford the hideous prices. It had been gotten up as—or perhaps actually was—a catacomb of ancient Rome, complete with niches of bones and skulls and statues of nude slaves being whipped by nude mistresses. The rest of the decor was operating-theater modern, stark Italian twenty-first century styling, brilliant with halogen stars, matte black chairs and aluminum accents, which only needed an anesthetized patient to complete the picture.

As Lucca ushered his party in at ten o'clock, the manager bustled up, holding a radiophone in his hand, extended to Lucca. "Signore Certomá, una chiamata da Palermo. Ed anche un fax."

Lucca's bright, cocaine-sharp eyes flashed in reflected sparks of illumination. He took the radiophone. "Chi parla?" he began. "Ah!" His smile winked out. His face darkened dangerously. "Che tu voie, Mollo?" He turned away and lowered his voice. His partner, known only as Don Pancrazio, caught the sudden air of peril and rushed them all to a great oval table frosted in halogen brilliance.

From the occasional reading of the glossy gossip magazines, Stefi could spot a few celebrities already in place and being adored. They were all quite young, as was the crowd, and closely related to either pop music or TV, but here and there an elderly industrialist made a spot of iron-gray or bald-pink pate among the great bush hairdos, true explosions of hair on both men and women.

"Champagne first! Then your best Fulgatore. Madame?" the popeyed Don Pancrazio asked Stefi. "They say your 1990 vintage is stupendous."

"Not bad," Stefi admitted. Her heart warmed to Don Pancrazio, who resembled a frog, for trying to give her instant celebrity status as a leading vintner. She had been seated beside Don Pancrazio's wife, whose hair, long and dark, had been kinked to give it such body that she resembled something that had flown off after an automatic car wash had self-destructed.

"Such strength," she was still enthusing. "I once saw him lift a camion. Veramente!" It dawned on Stefi that the lady might or might not be married to Don Pancrazio but could accurately be described as Don Lucca's inside piece. The empty chair on Stefi's other side was obviously for the strong man. He was, even now, approaching slowly, looking as if his talk with the person called Mollo had permanently poisoned his insides.

The volatility of Sicilian emotions was hardly news to Stefi. She watched Lucca pause and master his anger—or was it fear?—before replacing his fearful frown with a bright smile. The man called Mollo and whatever doom his name summoned up, had been skillfully covered over. Instead, Lucca produced a sheet of paper.

"They 'ave faxed me 'ere," he said with such synthetic pride that Stefi couldn't help smiling. "Cugine in New Jercey. De garbage business, no?" He shoved the paper at her, a facsimile of some computer printout paper, lined. "Noborry lemme be in vacanze," he complained. "Il boss never has un vacanze. Is againce da law." His laugh was as pretty as his smile. All in all, and considering how fearsomely ugly most Southern males were, Stefi realized that her dinner date was a winner. He had a very strong chin, set on a neck possibly

thickened by years of lifting Mercedes sedans. His teeth
were awesomely bright in his dark face, from which pale
green-blue eyes stared like beacons.

"E il Signore Mollo?" Stefi teased him. "Lui non é
un fastidio ancora?"

"Mollo?" Underneath Lucca's voice something trembled. It could have been either rage or fright. People in
such intimate contact with their emotions often failed to
make the distinction. "You know 'im?"

"Only heard his name just now."

"Den fo'get di name, OK? Is bad name." Certomá
rearranged his face into a more becoming smile. "Da
boyce. I ged dem da nize girlce, no? You no mind?"

"They're old enough. Parla Italiano, Signore."

"No. I godda praddice da Inglese. Is no Signore. Is
Lucca."

In this way, and with the help of quite a lot of champagne, Lucca had soon established a family atmosphere
around the oval table, in which, whatever else any of
them did, sitting here they all loved and trusted each
other like brothers and sisters. The name Mollo was never
again spoken.

Stefi, who over the years had been matched by her
family with a variety of prospective husbands, began to
feel relaxed for the first time on this trip. Sure he was a
hood. It was common knowledge that no coke stirred
through Europe except via the Corleonese. Sure he was
unreliable. What Corleonese wasn't? Sure he wanted
something and so did Zio Italo. But, what the hell. Who
was the noted world class vintner Stefi Ricci to look down
on a hood, especially one who seemed read to turn himself inside out for her pleasure. Besides, she couldn't
give anything away but her pure, white body, unless her
sister Iz also signed the contract. So she had a cushion
of safety.

It was obvious, by midnight, as they finished their
zuppa Inglese dessert and thought about cognac, that her
son, Kevin, and his Ngamba felt the same way; they had
been dancing between courses. Kerry, on the other hand,
had been huddled with Ennima/Annima as they felt their
way through a conversation in what turned out to be a
common tongue neither spoke, German. Typical, Stefi

thought. Kev is out there rubbing pelvises. Kerry is brushing up on his language skills.

The band segued into a slow rumba and Lucca invited her onto the floor. They danced rather sedately, beside an elderly auto manufacturer and a young blonde who had recently starred in a remake of *Open City*.

"Is nize place," Lucca murmured. "You nize hwoman." He led her to circle around him. Then, "You fly Palermo inna my Bandierante."

"Your what?"

"Is one of my tree Brazilian airplanes, Embraer 110's, molto veloce."

"You mean you run an airline?"

When Lucca laughed, all his teeth, back to the wisdoms, went on display, seemingly under their own illumination. "Is for me and Don Pancrazio and my odder partner, Don Ciccio."

"Do they call you Don Lucca?"

He managed not to miss a beat while producing one of those southern Italian body gestures, part shrug, part lifted chin, part downturned corners of the mouth, part upturned eyes, that indicates the fact that something may be true but modesty forbids verification.

"I don't see why," Stefi heard herself saying, "we Castellammare folks can't be your close friends."

Instantly she realized the stupidity of giving the end-game away before tonight's opening moves had been completed. And there was the whole middle game to endure. Nothing progressed rapidly in these matters.

He fixed her with another southern gesture, one of those fierce, soul-to-soul stares, his eyes stern and penetrating, as if to read the innermost secrets of her mind and heart. It was a multi-purpose stare. Its main purpose was to establish hegemony, if not mastery, to seal their relationship and to warn that any transgression would be regarded as an act of treason. What made it so impressive, Stefi realized, was that the ice-blue stare came out of a sun-browned face, like rays of sun through a deep jungle. "More dan cloce friends," she heard him say. "Mucha more."

It surprised her to hear him close the gap that quickly. Was Don Lucca in a hurry? Were there deadlines for this romance? But the throb of utter sincerity made Stefi's mind jump sideways to wonder how, in the same suite with her sons, she could accommodate any further advances.

When they returned to the table, both boys had solved that problem by disappearing with their dates. Don Pancrazio delivered their apologies and their profound thanks to their host, who accepted the news with a businesslike air, as if checking something off a list. It was, after all, past one a.m. If the boys wanted to be alone with their girls, he, Don Lucca, understood perfectly. If in the process they had left their mother alone with him, suitably chaperoned, why complain?

"Bene. Nice boyce." This was said with a devouring glance at Stefi's body, encased in one of those travel suits, well designed and very chic, which one always believes will fit into any milieu but is never up to a place like Gli Amici. In any event, Stefi saw, Don Lucca's glance was stripping it off, down to her skin. "Dis place," he said then, "it's 'ow you call . . . tame?"

"You have a wilder place in mind?"

Lucca didn't understand this. He turned for amplification to Don Pancrazio, who said, eyes bugging, "Don Fausto's li'l club off da Babuino, no?"

"Per finocchii?" Lucca flicked his ear in the Italian sign for homosexuality.

At the far end of the Babuino, just before it ended in the Piazza del Populo, a tall, ornate iron gate defended the entrance to a "private" cobblestoned alley, the Vicolo di Borghetto. The limo let them out there and the moment Lucca approached the gate a slender man appeared out of the darkened alley and opened one ironwork door for them.

A piano blues was being played as they entered the basement club. They were instantly ushered to a ringside table. Onstage less than a yard away, a boy in his teens was slowly stripping, with large, camp, feminine gestures, as if tossing garters and G-strings to his idolaters.

The pianist shifted into a slower blues as a second boy arrived onstage and synchronized his act with the other. By the time the first boy was naked, the second was on his knees, reaching for his penis which sprouted from a pubic mound as luxuriant as his hairdo, loose-kinked in cornrows. Stefi found herself wondering how all these hairdos managed to exist in such a primal state of bushiness? Was all of Italy awash in keratin?

Lucca's powerful hand clamped down over Stefi's knees with great authority. He cuddled it for a second and then started moving up toward her groin. She took his hand and lifted it to the table as one boy began fellating the other. The audience was clapping to the slow blues beat.

"You are hwoman of honor," Lucca was saying. He went to some effort to pronounce both h's. "Forgive Lucca. Lucca is drunk wid you."

On the stage floor now the boys were masticating each other like Yang and Yin. Here and there in the audience people were making rude sound effects. One woman was emitting a steady, low series of yelps, controlled and self-indulgent at the same time. "Whaw-whaw-whaw-whaw-whaw."

"No hwoman do dis to Lucca before. Is wrong for you, dis place." He got to his feet. The table overturned and rolled sideways like a sawmill blade, threatening to cut Yang apart from Yin. Somewhere a woman screamed.

Two very big bruisers, both wearing fishnet stockings, high heels and red satin bustles, appeared out of nowhere. Each prepared to lift Lucca by an armpit. They towered over him. There was almost no pause. They started to lift. In the dimly lit room a blue spotlight reflected on a knife blade in Lucca's hand. The blade slashed the belly of one bouncer. The blade flashed blue and scarlet as it withdrew. It sank into the other man's gut. Again, without pause.

Alley. Iron gates. They were outside on the Babuino. Shrieking chaos within. Limousine bearing down on them. They were in the car. They were gone.

Lucca was wiping the four-inch blade with a Kleenex. He pressed a button, rolled down a window as the limo sped into the Piazza del Populo, and threw the Kleenex out. Then he folded the knife and pocketed it. He pantomimed a small, quick hand-washing gesture. Then he gave Stefi a big, handsome smile.

"Mi scusi," he said. He frowned, seeing a spot of blood on Stefi's knee. He bent over and slowly and with great relish, licked it clean. "Is good," he commented, making sounds of labial enjoyment, "da blood of enemies. Taste good, you skin."

His tongue had been hot and wet. She felt a shiver
course up her thigh and into her groin like a foretaste of
orgasm. Accessory to double assault. Hopefully not murder. Zio Italo would be angry. This pleasing killer had
sewn her up like a litter of kittens destined for drowning.

Forty

"Finally, this shitpot is starting to pay off," Vince Ricci
said. He was, for Vince, strangely garbed in long white
trousers and a shortsleeved white tunic buttoned to the
neck. With his silky movements, he resembled a society
cat who has strayed into an alien alley.

Buzz Eiler looked small, dumpy and worried beside
him. He, too, was dressed in white, which suddenly gave
the game away. They were playing doctors.

The Miramar-Athenee had been built originally as a
very rich person's casino, all fuss and gilt, for gamblers
who wore dinner jackets at roulette and whose wives lived
in ball dresses from afternoon nap onwards. It featured
European games like baccarat. Slot machines were
strictly forbidden. Naturally, it went bust long before
Vince took it over. Real death-wish gambling is not the
province of the very rich. But it is one of the major ways
in which the middle classes kid themselves into thinking
life could actually amount to something, some time,
somehow. Then Ricci Entertainments, Inc. took over the
Miramar-Athenee. Slots lined every wall. Fusty five-
course dinners delivered under silvered bells gave way to
serve-yourself buffets. Bars standardized on pitchers of
sangria and beer, included free. Ricci package tours arrived three a day from the east coast of the U.S. Business
boomed.

But it was still the gambling business and, even with
a heavy drug sideline, it had begun to bore Vince. Satisfying the obsessive personal demands of the infantile
was only a starting place. He was already in full pursuit
of his dream, a drug business that depended on nobody
but him, staked out along lines that he, and he alone,

had devised. In short, not something he had inherited from the family.

He understood the value of experimenting with a really big idea to shake out the bugs before investing serious money. Accordingly, he first converted the top floor of the Miramar-Athenee to a discreet sanitarium. It was not uncommon for a gambling guest, having crashed on a week of no sleep, to be moved upstairs for some feel-good recuperation. Word got around. By the time Italo had tucked Bunny away there, Vince had converted the whole ornate hulk to a clinic with consulting rooms, laboratories and one rather impressive show operating theater that, needless to say, was never to be used for anything more complex than the treatment of athlete's foot.

When it came time for Vince to make his move back home on the mainland, he had proved to everyone who mattered—i.e., Italo and himself—that the detox idea was as capable of removing money from the middle classes as was gambling. And without breaking a single law, under the guise of social good. All it needed now was to broaden its base and it would become one of those bedrock industries, like coal or steel, upon which an entire nation, rich or poor, could depend.

He had been pushing Buzz unmercifully. Vince's European contacts had skimmed the entire Common Market for prescription drugs with promise, powerful painkillers like DF118, also called di-hydro codeine, the British version of Quaaludes, called Mandrax, Mogadon, and one of the most powerful synthetic analgesics ever developed, known abroad as Palfium. He had also set Buzz the goal of hyping up existing prescription analgesics like Dilaudid, Demerol, Percodan and Mepergan. He felt sure ways could be found to increase the potency, and therefore the addictiveness, of the heroin substitute, methadone hydrochloride, and anti-anxiety agents of the benzodiazepine family. As for the anti-depressive drugs, he had given Buzz a list that ran right off his laboratory blackboard, including Thorazine, Elavil, Pertofrane, Sinequan, Tofranil, Vivactil, Desyrel and the fair Pamelor.

DF118 he reluctantly ruled out, since codeine was a derivative of opium; the whole idea was to free himself from botanical sources and base his supply needs on easily obtained chemical reagents. But for the rest he had high hopes of either elevating their power to irresistible strengths or, failing that, to hijack patented formulae and gray-market the pills.

He couldn't share such dreams with Buzz. Imagine his opener: "You medics have created a coast-to-coast constituency of prescription junkies that Ricci Medical Centers, Inc. will now kidnap. We will develop prescription dependency from a cottage industry into a national consortium, our labs, our factories, our clinics, your prescriptions. Tomorrow, the world!" Better that Buzz wasn't privy to what his research would produce. Not yet.

Vince was clever enough to know that, in Buzz Eiler, he had a talented research doctor. But he had another, higher, responsibility in mind for Buzz, one that required a senior man with a reputation. Moreover, a senior man whose will was totally broken.

At a nearby casino run by a different mafia family, the Dolorosos, Vince completed the breaking of Buzz Eiler. Although a rather elegant form of sadism, it still wasn't at all pleasant to watch. He arranged for unlimited credit. That was all. Buzz did the rest himself. Compulsive-obsessive types can get hooked on almost anything; the inventor of the Eiler Section was now totally addicted to gambling. If money had been at the root of his dependency, the fact that he was broke and in debt might have weaned him from the blackjack table.

But money was only a transactional commodity in his obsession. He rebuilt a new ego every night as he sat across from the prettiest dealer in the room, doing his elegant dance of gestures that silently signified "hit," "stand" and the few other commands available to him.

This dumb-show, done very deftly and with fierce eye contact, established Buzz in his own mind as a man of mystery, of importance, of power, of prestige. Around the room, he felt, financiers, sheiks, armament dealers, women more beautiful than real life, were watching the economy of his movements, the cool indifference to loss. He felt like Christ in a Passion pageant, scourged, bleeding, flailed, but immortal. Everything he did was imbued with significance, even to carefully scratching his ear. A signal? What did the mysterious surgeon mean by that gesture?

Meanwhile, somewhere in the masochist heart of him, he was hemorrhaging. He hadn't spoken on the phone to his pregnant wife in several weeks. Doctors he phoned in Manhattan didn't return his calls. His banks bounced all his checks. His credit cards had been canceled. Having overborrowed on his insurance, he had coverage no longer, neither for injury, death, fire, theft nor malpractice. The bank that held mortgages on his office and his condominium had been trying to track him down for weeks. He was six months in arrears on both loans which, together, totalled nearly two million dollars. He was over one hundred thousand in debt to Vince and forty thousand in the hole to the Dolorosos. He was being scourged, all right.

Secret pain. Secret triumph over punishment no ordinary mortal could withstand. But he was up to it, this attractive, mysterious physician, cool, elegant at the gaming table. Hit. Stand. Blackjack!

By mid-April, the Bahamas are in full bloom, everything rich shades of green, palms, ferns, a world renewed, bougainvillea cascading brilliant purple and tangerine. With the aid of Tony Rego, a young chemist cousin of Vince's, Buzz had finally found a synergistic compound that increased by tenfold its potency over its individual ingredients. So optimistic was his phone call to Vince, who was in the Mediterranean at the moment, that Vince flew in two days later.

"Here," Buzz began, standing at his blackboard like a lecturer. He tapped the word "MAO" chalked there. "Monoamine oxidase," he explained. "People past their youth produce this enzyme in such volume that it breaks down messages to the brain. Such people grow very depressed, suicidal."

"Get to the good news," Vince urged. He had slipped into his doctor suit and it was obvious that he felt the need of a stethoscope bulging his pocket, or some tongue depressor sticks peeping out. If not that, then some other badge of profession such as a golf bag in the corner.

"The good news is MAO inhibitors like isocarboxazid or tranylcypromine sulphate. They block the MAO and people get incredibly happy."

"Wild?"

"Very pleased with life." Behind him, Buzz's assistant, Tony, seemed to be stifling a giggle. "Now, we have another family of drugs called ergoloid mesylates. They are also used to lower depression but in a different way, by stimulating circulation of blood to the brain."

"Buzz, baby, get to the point."

"The point is we tried the two in combination."

"And like *wow*!" Tony Rego burst out.

"Yeah?" Vince demanded. "Yeah? Give!"

"Well," Buzz hedged, "we've only tried it on ourselves, and only in very small quantities. But if I could set up a real double-blind test over a period of, say, six months, I think we could show you a new drug that sends people right off the high end."

"Right. Right." Vince's dark glasses swiveled this way and that. His black curls bristled. "It needs a name. MAO. MAO," he mewed like a cat. "Something catchy and easy. MegaMAO! Tony, you know what I'm thinking?"

Buzz watched the two cousins do their silent Sicilian communication, which seemed to leave bystanders in the dark. "You thinking about that corner of Uncle Marty's at 117th Street and Broadway?" Tony asked.

"I'm thinking up there at Columbia we have a handy source of dummies to test it on. Students."

Tony was a thin, weedy, young man with no chin but a protuberant forehead. When he smiled, as he did now, he revealed a piranha-like malocclusion of phenomenal proportions that only an infancy of total thumb-sucking could have created. "Students!" he echoed. "Always broke! Never too choosy about conditions! Or pay! And, being young, not likely to keel over and die on you in the middle of a test."

"But not six months," Vince went on. "I don't have that kind of time, Buzz. One month. By that time you'll know."

"I can't possibly call that a test. There are too many complications in a new compound like this. Suppose MegaMAO turned out to be lethal?"

"Suppose you let me worry about it?" Vince paused and uncurled his legs. He stood up and removed his dark glasses. It was obvious that what he would say next was deeply depressing. "The Doloroso boys are making trouble, Buzz. They called me in France and told me they were blackballing you."

"What?"

"Your marker's no good there." His dark eyes bored in on Buzz, enforcing with their power the seriousness of his news. "You're over the Doloroso limit. You've been over mine for some time. Nowhere can you get any action anymore."

The silence in Buzz's small, cluttered laboratory was awesome. Behind him, Tony Rego shook his head slowly in commiseration. Taking gambling away from Buzz was like removing his spinal column. No blackjack?

"Hey, Vince! Hey! We're going to be new papas together, you and I. What kind of thing is that to do to your fellow papa?" Buzz could hear the overweening, over-eager note of pleading in his voice. Under ordinary circumstances it would have sickened him. But some things were more important than pride. He could feel the earth crumbling in on him from all sides, like a corpse in a grave. "Vince. One lucky streak and I pay them back."

"It's across the board, Buzz. None of us can carry you anymore. It's not just bad business, it's suicide if we keep cashing your markers. Hey, baby, I'm your buddy. This is for your own good. Look at it that way."

Buzz sat down on a high stool next to the blackboard. He stared down at the floor and, as he did, the chalk dropped from his fingers. "I can't believe this is happening, Vince."

"Who's your best friend, baby? Who's your fellow Papa-of-the-Year? Who loves you, Buzz? I want you to dive into this test. Give it a month. If it comes up roses, your bonus is, now listen to this for a deal: I eat all one hundred G's of your markers, I hand the Dolorosos their forty long ones and you get access to any casino of mine anywhere in the world." Vince stuck out his hand. "One month without the pasteboards! Deal?"

"But one month isn't long enough to test this stuff."

"Sure it is. Students are young, active people. Students," Vince echoed, his dark eyes shining. "Hey, you can test anything on students, even MegaMAO. In today's world, students are the new niggers."

Buzz shook his head. The dazed look around his eyes deepened. "No," he said in a sad voice, "I am."

As a round trip, it was a marvel of planning. Charley Richards had left La Guardia airport at nine am. By eleven-forty a helicopter from Miami Airport was setting down on the lawn of the Grand Bahama clinic-resort and Bunny, looking very front-heavy, ran across the grass to embrace him.

"There seems to be some sort of obstruction to hugging," Charley muttered in her ear as they squeezed each other. "Sorry I couldn't bring Nikki along."

"I have given up on that creep," she said, leading him by the hand to a glassed-in patio where one tried to enjoy the sun while being thoroughly chilled by demon air conditioning. "You're staying for lunch, I hope. They have this crab with mayonnaise."

"As long as my copter can get me back to Miami by two o'clock, I'm yours. Here." He handed her an important-looking shopping bag from F.A.O. Schwartz. "Winfield's present."

Bunny dived into the bag and brought out a series of soft toys for infants, plus a pocket-sized calculator that played bridge, poker and rummy. "I don't play any of those."

"You will. When's delivery?"

"Wouldn't you know it? Late July. He'll be a Leo."

"He will, will he?" He smiled at her. "You look terrific, kiddo. You look happy."

"Makeup."

"You don't look like you're pining away for Nikki."

"Expensive makeup."

"How often does Zio Italo visit?" Charley asked.

"Never." She gestured to a passing waiter. "For me, mineral water. For you?"

"Bushmills and soda."

"Yes, sir. And would you like to see the menu?"

Charley frowned at his younger daughter. "Is Nicole Shan joining us for lunch?"

"She's in town, shopping. Won't be back till—" Bunny shrugged. "I might as well tell you. She was looking forward to having lunch with us. I mean, really high on it. But when she mentioned it to Shan on the telephone last night, he put such a heavy thumbs-down she cried herself to sleep.''

"No meeting with the father of the bride?''

Bunny was silent for a long time. "Dad, did you ever get the feeling that your life was surrounded by a whole . . . a whole landscape you couldn't see? Invisible things? And not one of them was especially friendly to you?''

He picked up her hand and patted it for a long moment. "Bunny,'' he said "welcome to real life.''

The building had long been scheduled for demolition, a narrow, ancient five story old-law tenement just off Broadway, its facade laced back and forth by fire escape ladders like a badly stitched wound, its dozens of tiny bed-sit apartments renting to anybody calling themselves a student.

It had been everything in its time, but of late a welfare hotel supported by the City. Now it was a shooting gallery, a rock shop, a place where for an hour an addict could crash out of this world of woe for a life so chemically enhanced that it beat reality to pieces.

A brother-in-law of Vince, and an uncle of Tony Rego, had been the owner of it for some time. He found various uses for the street-level storefront, newsstand, tobacco shop, numbers joint. Now, on orders from Vince, he had evicted everyone and sent painters through the building from top to basement with liberal dollops of cheap matte white.

RICCI MEDICAL CENTER NO. 201. From the moment the sign went up, referrals were never a problem. The immediate area was peopled by mainly white students of Columbia University and its adjunct colleges, Barnard, Union Theological Seminary and the like. It existed as a quasi-white pimple on the vast black buttock of Harlem that lay to the east, north and south.

In this broad swath of Manhattan, and the South Bronx above it, it was estimated that more than half the males were addicts. But in many cases they were the only breadwinners a woman tied to small children could count on. This was quite impossible if the breadwinner was an addict. Most slum women, black or Latino, understood that if they could get an earner straightened out, life could be feasible again.

This was actually the theme of a poster Vince had commissioned from his cousin Pam. She had devised what resembled facing pages from a comic book in which, frame by frame, in garish color, the idea of rehabilitating a breadwinner seemed to become possible.

For the first month the testing of a secret drug—labeled "anti-drug miracle"—took precedence. Neighborhood women wanting to enroll their men in a detox program were registered, their $5 deposit accepted and receipted. But they were then asked to come back in a month, once the testing ended. They got a booklet in three languages—the Haitians required French—which explained that a man had to show up one day every week at five dollars for the whole day, therapeutic drugs not included. These therapeutics were not specified. Allusions to wonder drugs were officiously pooh-poohed, but the entire block of copy kept hinting at the fact that this detox program, unlike most, actually worked *because* it was based on new therapeutic support drugs. "Detox is not an overnight miracle," the booklet warned. "Detox takes time, sometimes several months. At $5 a visit, detox can be expensive. And detox doesn't promise miracles, even with new miracle support drugs. Most detox patients get clean on this new program. For most, a new life is possible."

It was a shame no advertising council gave annual awards for the most misleading message, one that told no actual lies, sounded honest, but was fashioned of half-lies. Pam's would have won hands down.

The harassed Dr. Eiler in charge of the clinic seemed quite mad with responsibility and stress. He rarely showed his face, even to those student volunteers who were paid ten dollars a day to take a capsule a day and spend ten minutes a day reporting to a nurse—well, a young woman in a white uniform. In the basement of the clinic Tony Rego had already set up the minimal laboratory needed to produce the capsules, a mechanical mixture of two powdered compounds. It was simple enough to turn out the few dozen capsules per day of MegaMAO needed for the testing. But Tony was under orders from Vince to start stockpiling. In the first week, using ingredients stolen in bulk—always a favorite mafia method for reducing overhead costs—he and a teenage assistant had produced five hundred gross, 72,000 capsules.

Like most large cities, New York tries to maintain controls over services offered to the public, including restaurants, bars, food stores and the like. Licenses and inspections are necessary. Investigators come and go, making notes and, when not bribed, issuing summonses for violations. In the case of clinics, more is necessary. The Board of Health takes a hand. Mere cleanliness is only one criterion. For the first few weeks Dr. Benjamin J. Eiler daily expected such visits, investigations and routine shakedowns. But, as if bought from a mail-order house, the necessary licenses arrived, already framed. No one poked about the premises. No one asked to examine the books or patients' charts or the planning of the test or what purpose it would serve. It was as if some djinn had draped a cloak of invisibility over Ricci Medical Center No. 201. Students looking to earn money as guinea pigs seemed to know exactly where to report. So did harassed slum women. But nothing attracted official attention.

Buzz, on Dalmane most of the time, began to hallucinate that none of it was happening; the flood of women with their five-dollar bills, the smiling students, spaced out luxuriously on MegaMAO, the beat cops, walking past with a neighborly nod, squad cars giving the block a wide berth. Was this 117th Street and Broadway or was it the far side of the moon?

Every evening, from somewhere in the real world, Vince would telephone for results. Knowing how it tormented Buzz, he would begin each call by describing the sex life from where he was calling. "You remember Grotteria, Buzz? Where the élite meet to beat each other's meat? Last night I had a widow and her daughter, like sisters, four of the biggest, shapeliest boobs on earth. They wanted me to walk barefoot through their tits. I said, look—"

"Cut it out, Vince. I've got a hundred volunteers on MegaMAO and a hundred on powered aspirin in a capsule. Nobody knows who's getting what, not even me. The confidential double-blind code is locked in my safe. I won't officially open it till the month is over. But I took a quick peek last night."

"And?"

"Get back to your widow and daughter, Vince. Good night."

"Hold it, crumbum! What'd your quick peek tell you?"

"The stuff is effective across all ages, male and female, black, white, Asian. But in the strength we're using, it could be habit-forming."

"Oh, dear me."

"I want to do a second test at half the dosage."

"Not half, double," Vince ordered. "Twice as strong. See how habit-forming it gets."

"You can't do that. It's unethical."

Vince's laugh was a spurt of pure joy. "You kill me, baby. Do you know what a gold mine we have here? Tell me, how much more would it cost to produce if we doubled the strength?"

"Almost nothing. But I can't do that, knowing it could be addictive."

There was a longish pause. "OK, babes. Listen, is Tony around?"

"I think so."

"Put him on. It's—," Vince broke off to gather his wits. "It's about his father's birthday present."

"OK. Give the widow and daughter a kiss where it'll do the most good."

"Just remember, Buzz, in two more weeks, if you pull this off, you're a free man." His laugh turned sarcastic. "Free to go into the hole all over again. Lemme tell you, buddy, I don't give a goombah advice unless I know he needs it. If you can manage to keep out of the casinos, you'll be like a new man."

There was a pause. "What? Oh. Buzz, Lenore just walked in. Big as a house. For the first time in her life she's got tits. She says to tell you hullo."

Forty-One

Ngamba and Ennima/Annima lived together in a tiny but sinister hotel on the Via Della Carrozze, five minutes walk from both Gli Amici and the Hassler Hotel up the Spanish Steps. That was how Kevin and Kerry got home so early the next morning. They had crept out of the girls' room at seven and were now gaping at a morning news report on the TV in their hotel suite. Their mother had not returned. ". . . Looking for two men and two women," Kevin translated roughly, staring at the two bizarrely cross-dressed bouncers, costumes bloody, lying on stretchers with paramedics holding bags of plasma aloft. ". . . In stable condition," he added after another excited burst of Italian voiceover. The video portion then reverted to normal Italian news coverage, endless views of building facades.

Kevin glanced at Kerry, who was sipping blood-red orange juice again. "And Ma not in her bed. The publicity alone is going to kill Zio Italo. You know how he hates—"

"—seeing the Ricci name in the papers," Kerry finished. "I have got to learn Italian, goddammit." He jumped to his feet. "Up and at 'em. Shave and scram before they come knocking at the door."

"The pig? Fat chance."

"That chauffeur is only a hired hand," Kerry reminded him.

"Say no more."

They finished a sketchy breakfast in the Caffe Greco down the Via Condotti, reading tortuously through a newspaper report. Although the police had supplied a lot of information to the Press, nobody had identified anyone. "Hard to believe the driver didn't have Lucca's name."

"He just wants to stay alive," Kevin mused. He had ordered "a toast," thinking to get an order of toast, but found it was a melted cheese sandwich.

"And Ma is now an accessory." Kerry took half his sandwich. "If I was Lucca, I'd be as far from here as I could get, preferably back home with the other looneys in Corleone."

"Then he had to fly. And he took Ma with him."

"Jesus." Kerry's voice went dark with thought. "A witness is also an accessory." He seemed to be speaking for both of them.

"Whatever," Kevin decided, "owning the Fulgatore

vineyard will keep her alive. But the bottom line has to be: marry me or die.''

The two brothers sat silently for a long time, brooding.

"In fact," Kerry went on slowly, "from what we know of the Corleonese, Lucca staged the hits just to get Ma under his thumb. Life means nothing to these people. Especially wasting two overweight faggot wrestlers.''

Kevin stood up. "We'd better call Zio Italo.''

"Sit down.''

"Ker, we're in over our heads.''

"Will you sit down and cool back? We hold a trump card. But we have to be in Corleone to play it.''

"What trump?''

"Ma can't sign away the property without Aunt Izzy's signature. First we phone Uncle Jack in London and make sure he gets Iz and the boys out of the way. Under guard. Is he bright enough to do that?''

"No.''

"Then bring in Zio Italo's London people," Kerry directed. "Make sure Iz and the kids are safe, even from madmen.''

"And then we go to Corleone.''

"And play our trump," Kerry said.

His brother sat down and did something unseeable with the newspaper. When he pushed it across to Kerry, the weight of a gun had been transferred from his shoulder holster to the table under the newspaper. "Gee, Kev," his brother said with mock gratitude, "just what I've always wanted.''

"You know which end to point?''

"Let me see the instruction booklet.''

They ordered a second espresso and drank it.

Moist after half an hour in a telephone booth, Kevin came out of the long-distance center in the Piazza San Silvestro, slipping his ATT credit card back in his wallet. He sat down at Kerry's sidewalk table. "Cousin Jimmy promises they'll be invisible by noon. What's with you?''

"We've got one of Vince's Fokker F-128s. It left Monte Carlo—'' he glanced at his watch, "just now. It'll pick us up at Ciampino in an hour.''

"Is that a jet or a turbo-prop?''

"Pure jet.'' Kerry pushed across a tall glass, half full of lemonade. He watched his brother gulp down the

drink. Passersby had started to stare at the identical twins.
It was time to move on. "If the pilot redlines it, we can
be over Palermo airspace about one p.m. We find a local
light plane in Palermo."

"Or two parachutes." Kevin slumped back in his seat.
"Have you figured how to find Ma?"

"Didn't I tell you? We're bringing the contract to
sign."

"How does Lucca Certomá know that?"

"I went back to the girls' hotel and used their phone
to make all my calls. By now somebody in Rome has
told somebody in Corleone—"

"—that we're coming with the contract," Kevin finished. "You know what Lucca'll do to us when he sees
we don't have any contract?"

Kerry smiled slightly. "Not if we do it to him first."

"My brother, the assassin," Kevin muttered. He neglected to smile.

The grim, arid hills south of Palermo, stingily decorated
with yellowing clumps of sawgrass and wild mustard, are
meant for traffic by mule and goat. Auto roads squirm
and switchback to accommodate the landscape. Three of
them converge at the village of Corleone, in the shadow
of the local mountain, called Scorciavacche; a small peak
only two thousand feet high, its name also derives from
the local traffic, signifying "shortcut for cows."

There is no airfield worthy of the name. Local pezzi
novanti like Lucca Certomá and his partners come and
go by helicopter. This creates a major nuisance by landing in the village square in front of the church, despite
the protests of both the mayor and the bishop.

Since no one had warned the Ricci brothers of this,
their hope of slipping unobserved into Corleone was
doomed. The only helicopter they could hire was piloted
by the same humorist who regularly landed in the town
square. He did it again.

Small boys surrounded the helicopter in the baking afternoon sun, all begging for the small aluminium coins
Don Lucca was in the habit of tossing them with a great,
sowing arm gesture. In truth he was sowing continued
respect.

Kevin got out of the helicopter first and looked around.

"Is this the reception committee. There isn't an adult in sight."

"Siesta," Kerry said, joining him.

The two tall men strode over to the bar and walked into its cool stench of ageing almond paste mingled with the odor of rotting lemons. A young woman, dark, squat, with big breasts and eyes, gave them a disapproving stare. Although she kept two yards away from them her body odor died hard. "Che c'é?"

"Don Lucca, per favore."

"Don Lucca?" Her face closed off. "Non conosco."

Kevin, the twin who had a minimal idea of Italian, ran over his poverty-stricken vocabulary and decided on simply glaring back. His stare was pitiless, contemptuous, dismissive, the stare one gave a strange insect. Turning, he led his brother back outside to a table. He called to the woman, carelessly, as to a dog, "Due limonate, subito." Then, as they surveyed the terrace, "No, that table against the wall. Between us we have the square cased."

Kerry held a finger to his lips, listening to the faint sound inside the bar of a telephone being dialed. Obviously the fragrant young woman would be alerting Don Lucca Certomá. Kevin concentrated on eavesdropping. But her voice was mostly a fast-paced blur of run-on words. The only sound that came through clearly was one name: Mollo.

Kevin's eyebrows went up as he heard her hang up the telephone. "You heard the name?"

Kerry nodded. "She didn't call Lucca, she called the guy who gives Lucca gastric distress." His smile was nearly a grin. "For the first time, I begin to feel we have a ghost of a chance with this."

"You think Lucca has a rival? My information is that he controls the precise amount of sweat each man, woman and child in Corleone is allowed to ooze."

"The bar lady must have a special permit."

Both of them mimed silent laughter. "Now, remember," Kevin said, sitting down beside him. The twins automatically turned at right angles to each other, commanding a 180-degree view with a stucco wall backing them up.

"Remember what?"

"Remember which end the bullets come out of."

Forty-Two

It was well known that Italo Ricci almost never left his dark little San Gennaro Social Club idly or for pleasure. Even traversing the city in a Buick limo he hated the streets, filled with the pollution and detritus of the living. But there were occasions when pressures were too great for even Italo to withstand. Vince had put it to him this way: how often did the President of the United States present an award to a Ricci enterprise?

Italo, whose mind went back more than fifty years to when he sent U.S. Navy spooks to Charlie Lucky in his upstate prison for help with the invasion of Sicily, knew that no president—even ones he had helped put in the White House, like Nixon—had ever had the balls openly to support a Ricci cause.

Richland was different. It was so deeply into defense work that Charley Richards was constantly hobnobbing with White House trash. Let him. Politicians gave Italo the itch, anyway. All whores did. But today was unique: not the doing of Il Professore, but a victory belonging entirely to Vince.

It was that nervy medical clinic scam. Vince had gotten Pam to do a poster about detox and now one of the President's useless-except-for-show committees or initiatives or drives against drugs was making an award . . . to Pam! Only something like this could have lured Italo onto the diseased, verminous streets of Manhattan, gutters running with AIDS and syphilis and the other plagues with which God punished sexual sinners. Italo feared no such punishment, nor God, but the odd chance that some dying faggot would sneeze in his face.

Standing here, awaiting the arrival of the President, eyeing nearby faggots with runny noses, Italo resented every moment of this torture. He was too old and too powerful to accept such treatment, too free from sin to be dipped carelessly into God's shitpot of vengeance.

Today he had a special reluctance to leave Dominick Street because he needed to stay close to the telephone. Something had happened to his plans for bartering off Stefi to end the vendetta. Incoming reports were worrying: knifings, the twins needing an aircraft, Isabella needing protection.

Regardless, to the outside world Italo's step was sprightly, his posture erect. Seventy years, plus, seemed to weigh lightly on him. He had already outlived his brothers—he, the oldest, had survived them all! Cause for rejoicing? No. Only Italo feared how soon the reaper could scythe him. And behind this fear lay a deeper one: America was unforgiving of age, a nation devoted to the appearance of youth. Whole industries were closed off to anyone as old as Italo. Walking the streets, vulnerable to a pothole in the pavement, lying face down in a puddle, he could die like a dog and an entire city of youth-worshippers would pass him by.

Seething with discomfort, Italo felt angry as well for having involved his favorite, Stefi, in a scheme as crass as marrying to create peace. One could not trust the Corleonese, certainly not with a woman.

However, finally, the size of the throng began to appease his anger. Vince had tried to have them stage the presentation outside the clinic on Upper Broadway. But someone in the Secret Service refused to take responsibility if he couldn't have the surrounding area sealed off, cleared of human beings and hosed down with a nice carbolic-base pine-oil disinfectant. So the stairs in front of St. Pat's had been chosen.

Three awards were being made. One was a posthumous medal to the widow of a New York City police lieutenant killed in a shoot-out the week before. By now there were rumors that his own men had drilled him for demanding they stop shaking down pushers and pocketing the proceeds. The second and third awards were commendation banners, one to CBS News for producing a documentary on the cocaine trail that doggedly failed to implicate the heads of three Latin American governments whom the President strongly supported. The third went to Pamela Scarlette, Creative Director, Riccidiscs, Inc. for the poster headlined, DETOX UNLOX YOUR LIFE.

Italo watched the way Vince kept eyeing Pam. The former Pam Scarfacci looked terrific in a black skirt hemmed high above good knees, a white puff-sleeved blouse and a black sailor's ascot that crossed in front of her nice, big breasts. Her makeup was stronger, more vivid these days. Even at rest, without any inner animation, her face was a come-on. Even Italo could feel her vibes. Whatever Vince was thinking showed all over his face, at least to a shrewd observer like his uncle, who had no objection to cousinly affairs.

Vince's glance darted to Lenore. Pam was not as beautiful as Lenore. But today, with her bulging belly, such a petite woman looked grotesque. Overhead the taupe Gothic pile of St. Patrick's Cathedral looked misty in the soft April day. The sun came through now and then, highlighting the expectant mother, a kind of divine stage direction rewarding a woman who so obviously followed the Pope's directions against birth control.

Fifth Avenue traffic, rerouted above 53rd Street for the next hour, hooted. Faraway sirens groaned and choked. In the distance a fresh howl of sirens announced the arrival of the President of the United States.

The first and second Cadillacs disgorged handfuls of agents and the third paused to let the President step out. He obviously expecting cheering but this was just an ordinary noonday Fifth Avenue crowd, people on their lunch hour, shoppers, tourists.

Italo noted the disappointment in the President's long, narrow face as he and the Secret Service agents trotted up the cathedral steps, like a subway crowd, close-packed, being released into the open air. They headed smartly for the lectern, which was decorated in stars and stripes with a blue-and-gold presidential seal on a plaque.

At the corner of 50th Street a Marine band struck up the boozy, barroom tune "Hail to the Chief," a song few New Yorkers knew. The mayor seemed to pop up directly behind the lectern like a dapper spring-loaded Punchinello puppet. The band swung into "New York, New York." TV lights flared on. Shoulder-braced video cameras with telephoto lenses began to swerve and dip, nozzling in and out as the mayor delivered one of his low-key but demented off-the cuff rambles.

". . . Army of sewer rats carrying destruction, infection, revolution," he was nattering. For a moment confused listeners pictured real rats, which flowed through every artery of the city like cancer cells, the true inheritors, with the roaches, of Manhattan's enduring glory. The correct mayoral metaphor finally emerged, ". . . And unless we crack the back of the crack rats, they will crack ours."

Having elected him, most New Yorkers then stopped seeing him as the minor-league time-server he had always been. They expected of their mayors not management but entertainment.

". . . No slack attack, I'll find the jack to crack the pack. Tell them their days are numbered! Tell them I will not rest until I have wrung their necks and sent them down the tubes with the rest of the sewage." Applause. "We're here today to honor our heroic New York dead, praise our fearless New York journalists and celebrate our talented New York artists-designers. To imbue these highest awards, on this New York occasion, with a national sense of pride, let me personally present to you now, the President . . . of the United States . . . of America!"

To cover a dearth of applause, the Marine band repeated one chorus of "Hail to the Chief." Italo watched the tall, skinny President beam at the audience and blow several kisses to people in the crowd, as if he knew them personally. Then Italo watched Vince's come-on to Pam again, trying to catch her attention. One could see that Vince was bursting with self-esteem at what he and Pam had wrought. He, with his 12,287-page FBI dossier, he with his feet firmly planted in gambling, drugs and whores, with the help of a demoralized gynecologist in deep gaming-withdrawal shock, had created a brilliant new future, the supreme scam of addicting a whole new generation of Americans under the guise of detoxifying the previous generation.

Italo smiled stingily. The horizons were unlimited. Working people, kids, old folks, the rich and poor alike, professionals, teachers, everybody would flock to MegaMAO, tested and developed within the street-smart detox centers of a coast-to-coast network of Ricci Medical Centers.

". . . Unlimited horizons," said the President of the United States, "beyond which lie a better, more joyous life for every American. Let me—"

Where could this happen, Italo asked himself, but in America? He watched Vince give Pam a great grin, sharp with teeth, whiskers twitching with lust. Smiling back at him, pert and proper in her nautical outfit, she winked. Had Lenore seen her do that? Who cared?

Where, but in America!

Forty-Three

The village square of the town of Corleone stood hot and dusty in the afternoon sun, devoid of moving shapes, of voices, noises.

Kerry had often wondered how he would handle the kind of stress Kevin faced all the time. He didn't envy his brother's exposed position as the all-purpose Ricci troubleshooter. Sitting at the table in the patch of shadow by the Corleone bar, sipping lukewarm lemon soda from a bottle—no glass had been offered—Kerry sat quite as calmly as his brother, both of them casually inspecting the afternoon shadows of the main piazza. From any direction, trouble would come.

Well aware of this, the helicopter pilot had flown off. He had been promised a lot of money to return and pick them up. Nobody expected this to happen. Moving as if lemonade also ran in his veins, Kerry consulted his watch. "Half an hour."

"It takes that long for Don Lucca to put on his belly corset and start over here. I'm surprised the man called Mollo hasn't shown up. After the bar lady phoned him it would only be good manners to welcome us to Corleone. Have you got that folded-up bunch of papers?"

Kerry indicated his inside breast pocket. "They may not look legal enough for an Italian. No ribbon. No stamps."

"Tough shit." Kevin's voice lowered considerably. "That piece I slipped you? There's a round in the breech and twelve in the magazine."

"You mean you're not carrying anything?"

"Your little old lady's gun, the .25 Beretta. Only good close up."

"So, in other words . . ." Kerry was astounded at how cool he sounded, ". . . either I drop them at a distance or get them to sit down at the table for my near-sighted brother to play with."

A heavy afternoon heat hung over the town square. Down a narrow street, three men moved toward them between patchy, whitewashed walls. One, a stranger to the twins, held Stefi's arm. She walked with her head up on her long neck, staring ahead for a glimpse of her sons. The other men moved casually, as if chatting about weightier matters while attending to this trivia.

"Also that side street by the church," Kerry pointed out. "Two clowns we're not supposed to see. Nobody's got anything long, like a lupara. Just sidearms."

"Ma looks jaunty."

The piazza had very little foliage. The winter rains should have turned everything green. Instead what leaves there were hung dusty in the side-slanting heat of the sun. A scorched smell filled the air as if a fire had ravaged this place, not recently but always.

Carefully, Kerry reached into his breast pocket. The man holding Stefi froze and showed them a nasty Spanish imitation Colt .45 pressing to Stefi's side. At this distance, under a hundred yards, his face looked set in a mask.

"Could that be Mollo?" Kevin wondered.

Don Lucca and Don Pancrazio, the other two men, their recent hosts, also paused. When they saw the sheaf of folded papers, they relaxed and continued walking forward.

Kerry projected a big, friendly smile across the narrowing distance. The two men in the side street drew nearer, doorway by doorway, infantry style.

"The guy holding Ma must be Don Ciccio," Kevin hazarded a guess. "We get the top brass for this little transaction. Lucca wouldn't entrust a prize package like

Ma to a Mollo. Did you ever suspect Ma was this valuable?''

"Priceless."

Teasingly, Kevin jerked one hand up, paused, and calmly used the hand to scratch the back of his neck. "Man, they are a tense bunch of ginzos. Hold tight." He turned and shouted to the woman in the bar so that all of them could hear: "Un bottiglia di vino. Sei bicchieri. Subito!"

Kerry got carefully to his feet. The three men and the woman were just across the square from them now. "What are we drinking?" he asked in a carrying voice, "your marsala or our Fulgatore?"

Don Lucca, laughing, showed his brilliant teeth. He seemed in good high spirits. "It don't matta, cugino. We are all the same now."

"Not till we use this."

Kerry again reached into his breast pocket. Once more the oncoming party paused, froze, all attention. The muzzle of the Colt pressed into Stefi's side. Kerry produced a grin as big as Don Lucca's as he withdrew a fountain pen. "Once we all sign the contract," he called, "we are all one family."

"D'accordo."

They moved forward to the middle of the square now. Neither of the twins had discussed strategy, much less tactics. Such advance planning was unnecessary between them. "You OK, Ma?" Kevin asked.

"Fine. They have behaved like real gentlemen," she lied.

Although by now the siesta should have ended, the streets that fanned out from the piazza were empty. No one peered out of windows. No one lounged in doorways. Only the oncoming party moved. The rest of Corleone had disappeared.

No. The plump, pouting woman with the reeking armpits brought out an open, unlabeled bottle and six glasses. Her big eyes, swiveling fore and aft from the approaching group to the twins, looked desperate. She set the tray on the table and added four dilapidated wire chairs around the circumference of the small round table. Then she disappeared, pausing to curtsey forlornly in Don Lucca's direction, like a serf or a body servant. She did not go inside the bar. She went off down a side street as fast as her plump legs could carry her. The heat seemed to press down on the town.

Don Lucca's party were now on the bar's terrace. The two men in the side street could no longer be seen. "I'm apologice," Don Lucca said then. "No good, kidnapping la Mamma. No nize. You unnastan, no?"

"Only business, Don Lucca," Kerry said. He escorted his mother to a seat beside him and kissed her on both cheeks. Then he indicated with gracious bows the other chairs. Once everyone was seated, he said, "Ma, will you do the honors with the wine?" He pushed the tray in front of her. She began pouring the tall, narrow goblets half full of a wine the color of drying blood.

The Southern Italian protocol for wine pouring is as precise as any command of the Koran: who pours left-handed will betray; who pours with the right, but at a backward angle, will betray; only who pours right-handed with the bottle in the same direction as the arm, will be loyal. Stefi poured correctly. As she started to fill the last glass, Kerry bent over casually and slammed her forward into the dust.

Kevin's first shot blew off the center of Don Ciccio's face. The imitation Colt clattered to the ground as a second shot pierced Lucca's heart. The third, in popeyed Pancrazio's gut, knocked him backward onto the pavement. Sounding like the bark of a Pekinese, the three shots seemed to merge.

A man appeared on the church street and dropped to one knee. Kerry's Browning roared twice. The man grabbed his shoulder and started running away. The sound, immense and hollow, set up massive reverberations around the square, as if a volley had been loosed by a platoon of invaders. The other man had already disappeared. Swiveling sideways, Kerry examined every open window or doorway. Far down the street two lights winked close together, the front lenses of a pair of binoculars. It was too far for an accurate shot, but Kerry raised the heavy Browning in two hands. Slowly, as if he had all the time in the world, the person holding the binoculars let them hang from their strap. Tantalizing in its leisurely pace, a wooden shutter swung shut. Nothing more.

"Addio, Signore Mollo," Kevin muttered. "The town is all yours."

Stefi got to her feet and began beating dust from her skirt. "Listen," she said in a suddenly shaking voice, "let's get back to Long Island. OK?"

Only one automobile preceded Italo's Buick. It was Kerry's overpowered white Peugeot 205 1.9 GTI, but with a cousin, Vito Colucci, at the wheel.

How Italo yearned for news from Corleone, where two of his brave grand-nephews risked their lives. He worried about the fate of his favorite niece, Stefania. The many young relatives who worked for Zio Italo knew very well how he hated to be out of touch. The whole family knew. In Italian, the word for any kind of nephew or grandson was nipote, tangled in the same roots as nepotism. An elder of Italo's importance was served by dozens of nipotini.

His Buick was being driven by his personal bodyguard, cousin Bob D'Angelo. Next to Italo sat another bodyguard, a great-nephew called Dino Ricci. That they were all nipotini somehow comfortably diminished them in Italo's mind to the level of servants. Which they were.

All of these good young men, all the careful planning, made an outing such as today's almost bearable for Italo. As much as he loathed leaving Dominick Street he had had to be on the steps of St. Pat's for the TV and the press to angle some of their photos so that he, the fabled hermit, Italo Ricci, was seen in the same frame as the President of the United States.

Italo sat back on the cushions and relaxed. They had just crossed 14th Street and were surging southward through Greenwich Village. A few more minutes and they'd be downtown, easing themselves into the parking garage beneath Richland Tower. And then Italo would be upstairs, trampling nipote Charley on his own carpet. The stupid bastard was up to his old tricks again, once more transferring ownership of legit Richland companies to one of Italo's own holding companies.

After a while the limo turned right. Ahead of him soared the great upthrust of the Tower. The erection closed his throat with a burst of pride. It shouldn't be nipote Charley showing the world his great erection, it should be the man who made it all possible, himself, Italo Ricci!

But it wasn't his style. Leave that to the young flashers he knew coveted that tower aerie, the young nipotini, people like Vito and Dino and Kevin. For Italo, Dominick Street was fine.

Ahead he could see the garage doors open for the little white car Vito was driving. His followed. The tail lights ahead sparked bright red. Italo could hear a squeal of rubber. Vito jumped out of the car, a small .38 automatic held in front of him. The Buick braked to a halt with such force that Italo was shoved forward onto the floor. Dino Ricco fell on top of him. "Stai calma, Zio," the young man said, shielding his great-uncle's body.

One shot.

Italo shrugged up sideways from beneath Dino. "Lemme see."

Vito was crouched behind a great support pillar. In the darkness beyond something moved. An arm? Flinging a ball? Italo's throat shut tight. A bright metallic green grenade rolled at Vito's feet. He shifted his gun to his left hand, snatched up the grenade and threw it with all his might. It arched overhead in a long trajectory that ended with a bright flash of light and a deafening roar in that enclosed, concrete space. Shrapnel rained down on the Buick. Vito had dropped to the floor, firing into the very heart of the smoke. Italo watched his calm, deliberate rate of fire. He paused, re-aimed, fired. He shifted, re-aimed, fired.

The air thundered with noise. Streaks of cordite smoke drifted across in their direction. "Get off, Dino." Italo shoved out of the car and ran to Vito's side. His small feet made a pattering noise, as of a child. He dropped down beside him. "Anybody alive in there?" he demanded. "If we can keep one alive . . . ?"

"There's two of them, Zio." A bit of grenade shrapnel had creased Vito's neck. He was bleeding into his nice white shirt collar. "One is hamburger. His own grenade finished him. The other is hiding in that doorway to the left."

Italo squinted. "You in the doorway," he shouted. "Give yourself up. Otherwise you are a dead man."

In the darkened doorway something flashed faintly, an

open-chambered revolver. By reflex, Vito fired one more
shot. A man toppled sideways into the light. "Shit! Sorry,
Zio."

"Sorry? You only saved my life about three times so
far."

"Hey," Vito said, grinning. "Anything for a friend of
the President."

They inspected the corpse. Italo knew him to be a torpedo attached to the Torellas of New Jersey and Corleone. He said nothing to his nipotini, fine lads. "Leave
these stronzi where they died. Back to Dominick Street,
piu veloce!"

As his two-car cortege sped north and west into the
Village again, Italo found himself smiling. Clean hits,
nothing for the cops but spent shells. Let Charley explain
them. Italo's scimitar grin widened. Good workers, these
nipotini. Family loyalty was everything! If, God forbid,
the Corleonese iced Kevin and Kerry, what a wonderful
replacement this new bunch would make.

Forty-Four

In her original plans for this weekend, Garnet had pictured herself with a small shoulder bag vigorously striding the ten city blocks from her apartment to the
amphibian aircraft base just north of the Queensboro
Bridge. It would be tiring, but body-building, and not
beyond her powers. After all, she reasoned, this would
be a very outdoorsy weekend filled with even more walking. She and Charley had been planning it ever since his
cousin, Stefi, had offered them her beach house while she
was in Sicily.

Twice that day Charley had phoned her, once to call
her attention to what he called "a really sick shocker"
on TV, the President and Zio Italo in one grand occasion
of mutual guilt. The resonances of that encounter almost
darkened her day, but she was determined to remain
"up." The second time, just a few minutes ago, he had
called to delay picking her up by an hour. "Cops all over

the Tower. Someone was using the garage as a killing ground and they think I know who.''

So, when the time came at last to leave the apartment, Garnet's afternoon mode had set in, a bone-deep tiredness that made a ten-block walk too much. She hailed a cab and went first for a quick look at what progress had been made on the house she had once lived in. It had had to be gutted after the explosion and rebuilt as a three-story brick facade that went well with the two-story house on either side. Behind the facade lay a patio suntrap like a miniature cloisters courtyard. The offices of Education Research Fellowship ran around all four sides of the center patio, watching the greenery through large picture windows.

To Garnet the progress since her last look a month ago seemed negligible. But that was often the way with final finishing details. A Richland subsidiary ready to be transferred to Charley's uncle had done the work at cost, which pleased the Fellowship people so much there was talk of asking Charley Richards to join the board.

The cab took her up a few blocks to the amphibian base just as a sleek but ancient little Grumman seaplane touched down. Charley, trousers rolled and no shoes or socks, waded out to carry her aboard. "Isn't this what Sir Walter Raleigh did for Queen Elizabeth?" he shouted over the engine noise. He got her settled into the seat next to the pilot for a better view of the land over which they'd be flying.

"He draped his fur cape over a puddle. She walked across on it," she shouted back. Her glance swept over the pilot's face, a welcoming look as if inviting him to join the talk. The arrival of a carefree Charley, the prospect of the flight, and of the weekend, energized her again. "If you remember what an Elizabethan puddle might contain, you know Sir Walter didn't dare wear that cape again, fur or no fur.''

Charley laughed, buckled in and tapped the pilot's shoulder. The little amphibian with its curved, boatlike aluminum hull and pusher-puller propellers, began to head out toward the center of the East River, a *café-au-lait*-colored, garbage-enriched foam creaming up under its bow. The roar of the engine mounted, drowning out conversation. In a moment they were aloft, slanting eastward toward Long Island Sound.

The sun was beginning to settle in the west, firing a false gold glow and casting long, velvety black shadows that exaggerated the contrast of the maritime city as it met its many waters. "It *is* gold," Garnet cried. "Everything they say is true!" Again, she tried to include the pilot, but he had yet to break his silence. He was Charley's regular man, which she had no way of knowing, but somehow she sensed that Charley had picked him precisely because he went about his work in utter silence.

For one disloyal moment of mischief, she wondered if the celebrated Ricci family clout extended as it might in the Medici or Sforza era, to having the pilot's tongue removed once he got his flying license. Just think of the surgery, Garnet mused, if he'd shown talent as a boy soprano. A moment later, flying low over the river, the scenery drove everything else from her mind. "Look! Triborough Bridge!" A few minutes later, "Look! City Island! Charley, I'm all goosebumps!"

Sitting behind her and gazing at scenes he had been seeing for many years now from the air, Charley found it hard to match her enthusiasm. He patted her shoulder and let his hand remain as a kind of reassuring link.

"How huge it is," Garnet shouted over the engine noise. "Like a great inland sea."

The aircraft grew tiny around them, dwarfed by the great expanse of Long Island Sound. "See that knob thing there, all green?" Charley asked. "That's where we're going."

"But that's only halfway," Garnet responded. "Look how the island goes on and on. And forks left and right."

"You want to go all the way out to the end?" Charley tapped the pilot. "How's the gas?"

He replied with a laconic nod of the head and a downward turn of the mouth, signifying a sure thing. "I beg your pardon?" Garnet asked him, teasing. "What did you say?"

"Sure," the pilot expanded grandly.

"Enough gas to get to the end and then come back?" Garnet persisted.

"Sure."

"And to get you home again?"

"Sure."

"Where'd you get such a talky pilot?" she asked Charley.

"Don't make him self-conscious," Charley said. "OK, let's try the north fork at Orient Point."

"Look! All of Connecticut. And look! The Atlantic! Can you fly any lower?" Garnet asked the pilot.

"Sure."

They dipped slowly and leveled off at two thousand feet. Ahead the wretched urban sprawl and acrid smoke of Bridgeport wheeled by on the left across from the crab-like claws of Port Jefferson Harbor. Ahead the north coast of Long Island began to curve north as Orient Point came into view. The land narrowed alarmingly now, a harpoon aimed at the whalelike underbelly of Connecticut. Just beyond this razor-honed pint, a tiny island seemed to squirm uncomfortably.

"What's that?" Garnet asked, pointing.

"What?"

"Little squirmy thing, like a spermatozoon."

For a long moment no one spoke. Then, suddenly, the pilot came to life. "Plum," he said.

"Plum? No plum looks l—"

"Plum Island."

Garnet frowned. "Plum Island. Oh, dear. Now I remember." Her eager face darkened. "The environmental groups have been campaigning for years out here."

"What's wrong with Plum?" Charley asked.

"I'll bet you know," Garnet suggested to the taciturn pilot. "What do your charts tell you?"

"Not to land there."

"I figured as much."

"Not that there's a strip," he added in a garrulous burst of explanation. "Or a dock."

"Nor ever will be."

His outburst seemed to depress them both. Garnet hunched forward, brooding, as they circled over the big-headed, tail-lashing bit of land. Sideways, she studied the pilot's face for more information, but it had gone completely blank, exhausted by wanton word squandering.

The light plane banked right, gained altitude and, with another right bank, headed back into the setting sun. All three of them squinted as the golden force of the sunset drenched them in light. In twenty minutes they touched down at Lloyd's Point and taxied in toward Stefi's beachside boathouse. "Sunday?" the pilot asked. "Around now?"

"Right," Charley confirmed.

"Thanks for the sightseeing ride," Garnet said.

"Sure," said the pilot.

Charley carried her through the shallow water, crested with sewage-laden spume, along the boardwalk and up the cliffside stairway to Stefi's great, weathered front deck. He put Garnet down and used the keys Stefi had mailed him to let them inside. On the hall table stood a bottle of Strega, a plate of cantucci cookies, a spray of blueberry branch and a note: "Benvenuto a la mia casa. I gave Erminia and her husband the week off so you can behave like honeymooners. Beve! Mangia! Auguri! Stef."

Garnet held the card in her hands and stared long at it. "This took some doing," she said at last.

"The note?"

"The whole thing, starting with offering us the house. She's telling us two different things. She's telling you you're finished forever as her lover. She's telling me I'm certified an Honorary Sicilian."

He started to laugh, then saw how serious her small elf's face was. "I don't get it."

She glanced around her, saying in an airy tone: "Kimosabe speak with forked tongue. My, but this lady is a reader."

"All year long. Reads these thousands of books. Gardens a little."

Garnet began walking slowly through Stefi's living room, a huge enclosure that anyone else might refer to as a library. The dark oak shelves lined three walls, floor to ceiling, the fourth being a wall of small glass panes, the colonial size which matched the dimensions of a paperback book.

"That view! It's almost as breathtaking as from an airplane."

"You should see the view from the bedroom upst—" He stopped and blushed.

"Look at that! There's hope for you, Charley. You're not the case-hardened businessman you pretend to be."

She removed a large, colorfully designed book of the sort known as a cocktail-table book, meant to look intellectual. "Gerry took these shots," Garnet said, sitting down slowly in a deep upholstered chair with a wraparound back. "See?" She held up a double-page spread, a black-and-white photograph of windmills along a country road. The girl with the jet black pageboy bob over a triangular face was herself. "We did this for one of the early environmental groups. This scene isn't far from here, but on the south shore around Watermill."

He began paging through the book. "You're in half of these shots."

"Gerry was very ambitious for me. In those days if he had to photograph a car battery or a garbage can, he managed to get me in it. People must've gotten sick of my face."

"Not likely. I wonder if Stef knows that this girl model—?"

"Stef knows everything," Garnet told him.

"Has she been talking to you?"

"Not once, ever." She paused for a long moment. "We're already disobeying the doctor's advice against sexual excitement, so let's see what a thimble of Strega does for my delicate condition."

"You're not—"

"Not what?"

"Not pregnant?"

"Sorry, no. Would you mind?"

He gave her back the book. "It'd be just like fate to present me with a third daughter younger than Bunny's child will be." He left, returning a moment later with the tray of liqueur and cantucci. She was watching him without speaking, her eyes seeming to drink up great gulps of information from the way he poured their drinks. "You're sure you only make girls?" she asked then.

"Not positive. But the odds favor it."

"That's what Winfield thought, too."

"Are you two gossiping ab—?"

"She asked me if we were planning to have a baby. This girl thinks big. You're not even divorced and Winfield is eager for siblings."

"She's putting you on," Charley said, handing her a

small liqueur glass. "It's typical vintage Winfield. Even her small talk is deadly serious."

"Well." They lifted their drinks to each other and sipped the heavily spiced liqueur. "I can still have a child. It would only be one more thing the doctor told me not to do."

This time he couldn't suppress his laughter. "That flight has done wonders," he said. "You're a different person. I guess we'll have to get you in a small plane more often."

She nodded. Slowly, she munched on a cantucci cookie, obviously without really tasting it. Her glance looked faraway, as if watching something outside the house, beyond Long Island. "I imagine . . ." She let the thought die away. "Living out here in deep nature . . ." Again she stopped. Finally, "I'm trying to get an insight into her mind."

"Stef's?" He sat down in a matching armchair across from her. "You think she's green-minded, like you?"

"She bought this book a long time ago. Long before you and I ever met."

He considered for a moment explaining that people often bought used books, particularly if they believed their ex-lover's current love was pictured therein. Instead, Charley got up and crossed the large room. "You'll get a better idea of her from this." He brought back a large framed photograph, taken this year on the twins' twenty-first birthday. The photographer had arranged them so that Stefi, almost a head shorter than her sons, looked much the same height. Since they looked nothing like her in features or coloring, they served mostly to highlight her good looks.

Garnet's eyes went very wide. "I had no idea she was this beautiful. A photographer's widow can read a lot into the lowliest snapshot. You're sure it's all over between you two?"

He grinned as he sat back down in his chair. "Since about the time I first met you."

"Protect me from Sicilian male blarney."

"That's what Stef says."

"And the boys have lived out here all their lives? It's a lonely spot."

"No, Stef had a place in Manhattan when they were

in high school. When they went to college, she moved out here. She—'' He broke off, watching Garnet examining the framed photo very closely. She had that questing look, as if she really could scoop secrets from their hiding place amid the silver particles trapped in emulsion. He could tell she was concentrating on the boys, one on each side of their mother. After a moment she looked up. Her glance seemed to engulf him, still searching.

''Charley?''

''No. I'm not the father.''

She laughed in embarrassment. ''How did—?''

''It's something I've worried about. The last time I saw Stef she told me enough of the story to make me think the father died in Vietnam. An Irish kid from the neighborhood.'' He paused. ''Stef's a loner,'' he went on. ''She loves it out here. Peaceful, relatively clean, devoid of people. It's her refuge against the whole rotten world.''

''A dangerous mistake.''

''What?''

''Charley?'' She got up and moved over to sit in his lap, cradling the photograph in her arms. ''Sometimes there's nothing to be proud of, being a member of the human race. I try to be up, no matter what, but sometimes people sink too low for redemption. Like your uncle. Of all the species, ours alone is destined to wipe out our world.''

He hugged her, feeling the difference in their body temperature. The flight had chilled her, but carrying her in from the beach had warmed him a lot. ''What brings this on?''

''Stefi thinking this is a refuge. The flight today. It's old hat for you. But as the sun goes down? As it sets everything on fire? As it adds long black shadows to everything? You get the feeling of a paradise on earth. And then you catch a glimpse of Plum Island. Hell swept under a carpet.''

He turned her face around to see it. ''What the hell is Plum Island?''

''No. First ask me, what the hell is the tri-state area around New York City.''

''It's what? Twenty million people? Twenty-five?''

''It's a major center of the arts, of publishing, music,

painting, the theater. Can you picture the U.S. without this tri-state corner?''

"People in LA and Boston will give you an argument. So will people in the District of Columbia. Chicago. San Fr—''

"Of course. But, Charley, whatever other riches we have, in this megalopolis sits a lot of our best hopes, our fondest ambitions, our highest claims to being decent members of the earth.''

He made a face. "What happens if I admit you're right?''

"Then I'll tell you the story of Plum Island." She pulled his arms more tightly around her body and held them—and the photograph—with all her strength. "Back in the First World War, long before we entered it, the greedyguts who supervise such matters had begun producing chemical weapons.''

"Is this true?''

"Is mustard gas true? Is phosgene true? That development continued during more than twenty years of peace that followed. When the Second World War was in the offing, the mad experiments went into high gear. Not just chemical anymore. Bacteriological.''

"That part I know is true.''

"Then you also know, from some of the things Jet-Tech International gets into, that during the forty-five years of the Cold War our scientists were insane. There wasn't anything they weren't allowed to tinker with. We gave them the same license Hitler gave his death-camp doctors. A permanent Federal license to kill.'' She stopped and got to her feet. "We don't know exactly how much is buried there on Plum Island. We only knows it's been a chemical and bacteriological dump since the First World War, a million canisters of hell, alive, potent, their containers rotting.''

The room had grown dark. He could barely see her. She had gone to the many-paned window as if seeking to escape into the light. Instead, she stood silhouetted, caught in a dark web. "Twenty years ago," he heard her say in a small, desperate voice, "we were trying then to get them to admit what Plum Island was, so that we could get them to destroy, safely, all that desecration of mankind waiting to be unleashed. Would you believe it,

Charley? Nobody was interested. Nobody wanted to know.''

"Oh, I believe it," he said. "What a blow to the vacation-home industry if the truth had to be faced up to. What a blow to all property values. How could you get anybody to work on Long Island and live there?''

"So many perfectly good reasons," she mused, "for sweeping evil under the carpet. That was twenty years ago. Imagine how much worse Plum must be today.'' Her face went very blank, remembering. "You get a different dose of fresh catastrophe every day, nuclear war, nuclear accidents, poisoned seas, global warming, acid rain, HIV-positive epidemics, the horrors of malnutrition, the death of the forests. How many of these can you keep in the front of your mind?

"I went out west where I came from. I led the academic life. Plum Island retreated to a pinpoint at the back of my tiny mind." She turned away from the window to face him. He switched on a small reading lamp beside his chair. "In worrying about other techno-deaths, it slipped my mind that we have something old-fashioned and far harder to keep under control. It's called plague. I suppose the government has Plum Islands all over the country.''

He patted his lap. "Come back. Sit down.''

"I will," she promised. Then, in an agonized voice, "I can't! Seeing that evil place. Seeing it waiting there in the golden sunset, ready to destroy a tri-state area of workers, children, scientists, artists . . .'' Her voice faltered. "What am I to do, Charley?'' she cried out.

"First? Sit on my lap. Remember, Plum's been safe enough for seventy-five years; it'll keep till Monday. Second, let's talk. Between us we have money, researchers, political connections. One of the Connecticut senators owes me big favor for making him a hero on that defense contract in New London. We can put together a campaign. We get our facts, we start legislation in motion. We set up grass-roots groups. In the spring a flotilla could sail around Plum Island and blockade it. Everybody on Long Island's always looking for something to do with the kids on Sunday? Hah!''

She stood in front of him, her head nodding, slowly at first, then faster. "A benefit concert in Carnegie Hall?

A marathon run from the Hamptons to Orient Point?''
Her dark eyes flashed in the half-light. "The churches
come in on it. The local politicians. The universities.
Everybody hates chemical and germ warfare." She
looked exalted, ready to take flight. Her great eyes devoured him, her hands gesticulated spikily, as if unable
to keep up with her thoughts.

He pulled her down on his lap. "Do you have any idea
how expensive it is to deactivate chemical weapons?" he
demanded. "There are hundreds of jobs in this boondog-
gle. This is the economically depressed ass-end of Long
Island. Cleaning up Plum will bring back prosperity. It
might have to be paved over with a billion tons of concrete, like Chernobyl. Bi-i-ig bucks!"

She snuggled in against him, silent for a long moment,
still hugging the photograph. Her voice sounded dark.
"Half an ounce of Strega. Wow. Charley."

"I hear a change in tone."

"Charley, I am already stretched too thin with a dozen
committees who count on me for a speech or an article.
Every day I get more involved with the Education Research people and that office they're building on the river.
And that's without what I do for Richland."

"Use Richland as a springboard to start the Plum Island campaign. We have a branch office in Greenport out
here."

"Charley."

"That tone again."

"Charley, without even a moment's research, you
know the same Department of Defense that showers lar-
gesse on Connecticut is the proprietor of Plum Island.
The moment the New London contractor and his senator
pal attack Plum they get kneecapped."

"For a good-looking broad you sure are cynical."

"Oh, Charley, that was a real rush to the head, all that
imaginary campaigning. Just exactly what the doctor
warned me against. The flotilla! The marathon run! Oh,
God, what a charge we worked up."

"On half an ounce of Strega." He reached for what
was left of his drink.

"That's why I love you so," she said in a small voice.
"You're as mad as I am." She curled up in his lap. "But
more practical. Charley, how did I ever find you?"

"Twenty times a day I ask myself the same thing."

"I would love to have your third daughter." Her elf eyes slanted sideways with mischief. "Or another pair of boys."

"You really are mad."

She sat silently, thinking. "I'm not sorry I saw Plum again. I can't do anything about it now. But I will. It's true, as you said: it's been here seventy-five years. It'll wait."

October

Forty-Five

His mother, Nicole, no longer visited him in Boston. She had rented a small beach house in the Bahamas, with Bunny and the newborn boy, a chunky infant named Leo. This was neither a Chinese nor a French name, Nicole had explained, but it was as close to Lao as she could get.

Meanwhile, Nikki had found himself a grim cell overlooking the Charles River, where he could keep his typewriter, his fax machine and a few books. But nothing calmed his unrest, not even isolation. He hadn't heard from his father, his mother or Bunny. Nor had he lifted a hand to telephone or fax them. It was not a breakdown in communication, Nikki told himself now, so much as a surfeit of communication. More words were anathema. More questions were odious. More truths would be the death of them all. His father's offer, tendered months ago, still kept him sleepless at night.

The central question was joined by others, equally pressing. Should he marry now? Should he give up Harvard? Nikki stood at the window and watched the autumn rain turn the face of the river to hammered pewter. Should he become his father's Number Two? Was some crime so cyclopean that it stopped being criminal and became the natural landscape of the tail end of the twentieth century?

He hadn't seen Bunny since a flying visit to the Bahamas after Leo was born. She'd changed a lot, from the funny, sexy, aggressive girl he'd known to a kind of fey sprite, not quite as old as Leo. Nikki supposed being isolated down there had detoxed her soul to the fetus level.

And who was he to criticize? Was he existing on any higher level than she? At least she was doing her duty as a mother while he was shirking his as a father. Was duty the right word? His role? But of course! With a role came a costume, a posture, a voice, a way of moving. Nothing came simply without its embellishments. If he was Leo's

father, the accompanying props were obvious: that he be
there and have a useful job, not the composition in faraway Boston of fugitive paragraphs.

He stared down, brooding, at the Charles River. In the
chill rain a two-man scull was slicing through the waves,
each rower in a bright orange plastic poncho. Together
they had the look of a water insect, the twin blots of
fluorescent color like wild, feral eyes. The image worried
him. Bunny's new personality worried him. His father's
silence worried him. His own failures in journalism, in
essay-writing, dismayed and depressed him. His neglect
of the father role produced the sharpest pangs of shame,
as if the curtain had gone up and he'd forgotten all his
lines.

His father had long ago asked him to make a decision.
He hadn't asked again. It was not his style to nag. Something had to be said, even if it was to temporize by sending his father his latest essay, which had a bearing on his
failure to act.

Dear Father,

This is the Imprudent Era. That an economy can
show life, long after running out of fuel signals the
death of the "Prudent Self-Interest Man" whose
motto was: "Build a better mousetrap and the world
will beat a path to your door."

After the Second World War it became apparent
that one could steal someone else's mousetrap,
cheapen it to an inferior product and, with the
proper advertising, still cause the world to beat a
path to one's door.

Making dunces buy a dud mousetrap is only one job
for advertising. Stocks and bonds, books for the cocktail
table, the bank account or church they choose, these
decisions are left to caprice, chance and the fallout from
media hype. The Imprudent People have lost whatever
grasp they had on cause-and-effect.

It is quite clear from a study of securities markets that
even "market forces" are now subject to whim.
Computer-driven probes monitor market direction and
react to change instantly. A broker's software kit allows
a robot to produce a consistent market profit.

But nobody wins big unless illegal insider

knowledge is fed into the machine. Stealing that information and unloading loser losses on little-guy chumps is another fact of life in the Imprudent Era.

As we stumble into the twenty-first century, it seems clearer and clearer that, while the Third World struggles simply to survive, the mendacious West refuels itself magically on effects without causes.

P.S. Yes, I know that isn't a commitment, Father. But these are some of the questions that underlie the decision you asked of me. I'm trying to see things your way but I've been educated in the West. We have so much poverty in the East that the worries of the West seem like children's idle complaints.

I did take your point about the definition of "criminality." It may surprise you to know that I agree completely that a "crime" is simply something the rulers of society have passed a law to forbid.

Criminalizing drugs, here in America, after the Second World War gave everyone what they most wanted: the mafia had an obscenely profitable replacement for its wartime black marketeering; the rulers of America had a new excuse for puffing up the nation's law-enforcement establishment far beyond levels actually needed.

In this way the United States is becoming an armed camp under martial law, the ideal state of control that Mussolini in 1922 or '23 first called the Corporate State. The Americans are developing their own brand of fascism.

And yet we still permit them to name the crimes, like Adam naming the animals. In such a context, Father, who am I to pretend any of us is any better than the next man?

A deadline will help me. Spring? It's lovely in the Bahamas then. I'd like to have a summit meeting there of the three Shans, Lao, Nik and Little Leo. March? I've stalled long enough. March it is.

Love.

Forty-Six

Broomthwaite awoke from his afternoon nap with a great sideways leap, as if someone had dropped a scorpion on him.

The island of Palawan did, indeed, have scorpions. Broomthwaite's girl, Josepina, might be playful enough to try such a joke, but never with a scorpion. The Palawan variety were too poisonous for anything but the serious baiting duel-to-death the local men staged in a small oval ringed by flattened tin cans.

Broomthwaite stared about him, wide-eyed, soaked with sweat. Some premonition? Something in his dream? A warning? A threat? As he sat up in bed, blinking away the sweat running down his brow, Broomthwaite listened intently, his wiry body still quivering. The overhead fan made almost no sound. He could hear a Jeep engine nearby and growing louder, but that was a common sound here in the highlands. Armed guards patrolled the coca plantations constantly, now that the cash crop had grown so abundant. The entire top of Palawan sprouted green gold.

He staggered out of bed and into the canvas curtained cold-water shower. Broomthwaite was a tough little man, hairy in unlikely places like the small of his back and the tops of his feet, bald where it counted most, on top. Ducking his head he yanked a cord and a spray of lukewarm water sluiced down over him. It had a soothing effect on Broomthwaite who still, after all these years in the Far East, retained the sparrow-like darting moves and head swerves of the typical cockney; a tightly coiled city-dweller to the core.

The Jeep stopped outside his hut. Broomthwaite shut off the spray and toweled himself. A moment later he heard footsteps on his verandah.

"Broomthwaite?" called the plummy voice of Lord Huge Waismith Mace. "I say, you old skiver! Wakey-wakey!"

Wrapping the bath towel around him, Broomthwaite came to his side of the screen door. "Crikey! It's 'im! Welcome to Palawan." He swung open the screen door. Mace entered. Behind him a tall young lad, good-looking in a nondescript way, smiled nicely as he entered with Mace. He was carrying a small khaki duffel bag rigged as a backpack.

"I see you sent Josepina off," the Englishman noted. "Too hot for naptimes?"

Broomthwaite grinned. "Haven't roasted her yet for long pig. Nice little bint, that. Wants it every day. But it's my afternoon off." He winked. Then his glance swiveled sideways to the newcomer.

"That experimental batch of seedlings seems to be doing quite well in the north plateau," Mace said. "Very encouraging."

"Once we got the hang of it," his manager added. "They make such a fuss over growing the stuff, don't they, those Colombian spics? All that balls about temperature and humidity. It only takes the right fertilizer."

"And a right old ton of start-up cash," Hugo reminded him. "I'm impressed at the quality of work you get out of your people, old man. Rum lot. But with a guard's riot gun trained on them, they do put in a day's work, do they not?" Mace turned to the young man. "Our field hands are all convicts. The government regularly clears out the mainland jails and ships the incorrigibles here. Or used to, under Marcos."

"The new government doesn't?" the young man asked in an American accent.

"They're not quite sure what we're up to here. This is a faraway, mysterious place," the Englishman explained. "We like to keep it that way. In Manila they've been checking over Marcos' bookkeeping without being any the wiser." He chuckled. "I suppose they're just waiting till we lose a man on Palawan."

"Jungle disease?"

"The only hands we lose are from guard brutality. A man gets beaten to death. Not too difficult a task, considering they're half-starved. Nasty but necessary to instruct the others."

"A lot of it?"

"It releases masses of the guards' pent-up needs. Reestablishes who's master and who's slave. Provides objects for their sadism. It's one of their major perks.'' He chuckled again. "No, I'm referring to escapees. We don't have 'em. Hypothetically, of course, we might."

"Not bloody likely," Broomthwaite demurred. "Any escapee fool enough to try it across Mindoro Strait would make shark appetizer."

"Unless he had friends who stowed him away in a freighter." Mace frowned. "A lot of these prisoners are politicals. Politicals always have friends. In any event," he went on with a sudden smile, trying for an airy note, "I said hypothetical and I meant hypothetical. But it never hurts to engage in a bit of what-if?"

Broomthwaite looked relieved. "I thought—"

"Yes, well," Mace interrupted, "say hello to young Kevin. He's an emissary from abroad, sent to check us out, Broomthwaite. We're famous. They'll be sending us teams from the BBC next."

The manager and Kevin Ricci shook hands perfunctorily. "That's a lot of sidearm there," Broomthwaite said, indicating the .9 Browning in Kevin's holster. "Looks like NATO issue."

"I wouldn't know. Nice cool place you have here." Kevin glanced around the big, high-ceilinged room. At the apex of the four-sided roof frame a long-bladed fan swept the room slowly. In the Palawan heat it sent lazy puffs of air across their moist skins, giving them the illusion of coolness.

"He's staying in the hut next door," Mace announced. "Just overnight. Perhaps," he went on to Kevin, "you'd like to unload your truck?"

The young man nodded politely. "I'll do that. Next door?"

"The driver will help you."

"I've just got this one small roll." Kevin started to leave, then stopped. "Oh, I've brought a sort of house present." He rummaged in his duffel bag and brought forth a sleek black Thinkman pocket computer. "Know these?"

Broomthwaite took it from him. "We actually don't—"

"What a thoughtful gift," Mace cut in. "Say thank you to the nice gentleman, Broomthwaite."

"Ta." They watched Kevin leave. A short, expressive

silence remained behind him. Now that the afternoon sun had grown less fierce, a songbird in a tree nearby unleashed a great burst of melody.

"Wot's the nyme of this gyme?" Broomthwaite asked in a cockney undertone. "We running the Shan 'ilton 'ere? Or Lydy Myce's English Tearoome?"

"He's been sent by a New York family," Mace murmured quietly. "That is, the East Coast and the Caribbean. We've been squeezing them down on their normal shipments. This was Shan's strategy to soften them up. They've complained bitterly, but now there's been a worldwide shift and they are well and truly dependent upon us. So they've lumbered us with this young troubleshooter type who obviously wants to know if we can be trusted. Incidentally, does the name Ricci mean anything to you, old cock?"

"Not half. That 'is nyme?"

"And 'is gyme," Mace responded teasingly. "I don't imagine," he went on in an even lower voice, "you get much newspaper reading done around here."

"With my schedule?"

"The Colombians are destroying themselves. Greed and hubris. But that's one of cocaine's predictable effects. I don't suppose they taught you at school what hubris is? No, of course not. Any idea how valuable Palawan white has become?"

Broomthwaite grinned broadly, showing a missing right canine. He hefted the Thinkman computer. "I've always wanted one of these since I heard Shan was making them in Korea or wherever."

"Just so our young guest doesn't get the size of Shan's tie-in."

"Then 'oo are we s'posed t'be? Princess Anne's Syve the Bleeding Children?"

"Anything you like, old man, so long as young Kevin doesn't twig Shan's now the number one source of white, moonrock and crack in the entire world."

Broomthwaite whistled softly. "Oh deary me." His eyes sparkled. "And when you say Shan, you mean Palawan."

"He has a sixth sense that tells him years ahead where to place his bets. And who to hire. You've become very important, you nasty old bugger." Mace wandered over to the bottle of dark trade rum standing on top of a dresser. "Any ice, old man?"

Broomthwaite began rummaging in a small refrigerator. He came up with a tray of cubes and a can of limeade. "Fancy a long 'un?"

"And one for our New York friend, too." The Englishman's glance grew shrewd. "Mind letting him have Josepina for the night? Or is she too small for him?"

"You know the old saying. Big girl, big twat. Little girl . . ."

"Yes?"

"All twat. But not Josepina, agreed? She's a clean girl and who knows where old Kev has been moistening the wick, eh? I'll find him another bint, one of the pros, real knee-trembler. Nothing spared in the way of hospitality?"

"Until he steps one inch out of line." Mace sank into a wicker armchair and let out a huge sigh. He mopped his forehead softly with small, dabbing gestures. "He has no idea of the extent of our plantings here," Mace murmured cautiously. "I showed him one stand. Lied and said it was experimental. Tomorrow, he's only to see shed three, which is small and negligible. He's especially not to see seven or eight. He hasn't a clue about that side of our business that isn't coke. We're not a pack of peasant prima donnas like those Colombian apes. We're businessmen. I want that lad," he continued in a very faint voice, "watched like a hawk. He's potentially dangerous. If we deem it necessary, he's also expendable."

"You mean . . . ?"

"I have it from Shan Lao, who has seen what this person can do to best-laid plans. He said he had never before seen such a natural assassin. Do you know what else Shan said?"

"He went and taught you the word hubris?"

Mace's deadpan face contorted in a sudden grin. "He waxed philosophical. That's how he talks when he's dead serious. He said to me: on Shan's close-mown lawn, grass becomes a sheet of green velvet."

"Bit of poetry, innit?"

"He said: then a dandelion springs up, marring its perfection. Do you know what we do to the dandelion?"

Broomthwaite's grin matched his, minus one tooth. "Gotcher, guv."

Kevin knocked at the screen door. "Just in time!" the Englishman called. "Come in. Sit down. Cool off."

Kevin entered, carrying another Thinkman. "Brought my own, in case you need coaching. When I get back to New York I'll send you an instruction brochure."

"Isn't that thoughtful, Broomthwaite? How're the drinks coming?"

"Just a sort of backwoods daiquiri," the cockney said, handing out tall drinks, dark brown with the color of the trade rum.

Mace lifted his glass in Kevin's direction. "Cheers, my boy! Welcome to Palawan. It's only a tiny outpost of our empire but we'd like to show you some real Shan Lao hospitality!"

Forty-Seven

The girl's name was Iris. She was taller than Josepina and, unlike that girl's stocky good nature, had the aloof, narrow-faced, swan-necked Nefertiti look much prized in the Pacific area. She and Kevin lay side by side in the narrow bed and watched the overhead fan flick slowly around.

Kevin knew she was a professional from the moment he bedded her. Not because her technique was much more advanced than one would expect of a local girl— even one this elegant—up in the high boonies, but because of her perfume. It was a provocative citified scent, part musk, part sandalwood, but that was not the real giveaway. It was that she never ceased to exude its sharp seductive aroma. Nothing clings that long, Kevin knew.

Iris had swallowed some. A whore's trick, it made certain every orifice of the night would be permeated with the same stench, modified by whatever other ingredients passed through. If she perspired, each drop reeked of musk and sandalwood. If she came, her orgasm released clouds of cloying scent. Wherever he kissed her slim, smooth body he got a mouthful of it.

There is a note in sandalwood of a low-banked autumn fire turning aromatic logs of ancient wood to dead ash. It's a dying odor, a church-incense scent hinting of the ice and snow that comes after autumn, funereal as a breath from the mausoleum.

By midnight, Iris had totally spooked him. Letting her mount him yet again was like succumbing to an Egyptian mummy filled with centuries of dry regret and shedding the shredded leaves of old linen wrappings. He felt confused by the fact that no whore had made this sort of impression on him before.

He edged out from under her and stood beside the bed. He smiled pleasantly. "Good night, Iris." He went to his bureau and found a fifty-dollar bill in his wallet. He stared hard at her mournful beauty. "Good night."

In the faint flicker of a low-burned candle, her flat Egyptian eyes widened. "That's too much." She moistened her lips, her tiny tongue darting like a snake's.

"Not if you leave right now."

"I came on too strong?"

"Not at all." He watched her as if seeing her for the first time. "It's just that I'm beginning to . . . uh, get all sorts of kinky thoughts about you."

"I do kinky," she offered. "Whips?"

"Mentally kinky. There's a word my brother told me once. Necrophilia?"

"I do whatever you like."

He picked up her short, flowered shift from a chair and pulled it down over her head and slim, odorous body. Then he tucked the fifty-dollar bill between her small breasts. "Anybody ever mention it before, Iris? There's a spooky feel about you."

"I do spooky, kinky, slavey, whatever. Just don't cut me."

The plea echoed inside his head for a moment, a sudden flash-picture of her life. *"Adios. Buenos noches. Hasta luego."*

Iris giggled. "I don't speak Spanish."

He led her to the screen door of his hut. "Be gone, fair maid, farewell."

He waited half an hour, listening to the night sounds

and thinking about his strange reaction to Iris. She stood out in this hideous jungle place, and her appeal for him was enhanced by the aura she wore of a life that no one should have to live. I do slavey, kinky, spooky. He shuddered.

How many times had somebody cut her soft, smooth skin, for the perverse pleasure of seeing blood well up? She had the kind of refined elegance that some men would long to throttle, rip and slash. He shook his head to clear his mind for the night ahead. Silence. No birdsong. No breeze through leaves.

The guards would have locked up the field gangs at sundown. Jeeps no longer patrolled the area. But it was possible Iris would have reported what had happened to her boss, or whoever had sent her. Whores had loyalty, of course, but you didn't always know to whom. She had stayed with him three hours. Fair enough. Perhaps she had been expected to keep him immobilized all night. Nevertheless, no self-respecting whore would report the evening as anything but a roaring success. Three orgasms, the scorecard would put it. Value for money.

He found himself wishing there were another way out of this hut. Only a front door and big screened windows on three sides. Easy to keep under surveillance even in the dead of night. On the fourth side stood the bathroom and canvas shower stall. Kevin entered it silently. Bingo. The stall could also be entered from outside. A man, dirty with a day's work, could get clean before he entered his cabin. Thus, a second exit. Smart.

By one in the morning, Kevin had repacked his duffelbag, leaving behind dirty clothes he had collected en route. The Thinkman he packed. Some months ago Kevin had had it, and the one he'd given Broomthwaite, specially adapted to use a new insert card programmed by one of Il Professore's computerheads. Each Thinkman, with the card, could function as a subminiaturized transceiver. It had a two-kilometer range. So listening in to Lord Mace's briefing of Broomthwaite in the next hut had been almost too easy.

Sheds seven and eight were off limits, were they?

By one-fifteen he had eased his way out of the compound in the general direction of sheds he had glimpsed this afternoon from an incoming helicopter, big, open-sided, tin-roofed monsters. If Mace wanted him to be-

lieve that Palawan was just a small test set-up, the sheds
gave away the game. They were processing sheds for
something truly immense in volume, much larger than
Zio Italo had dreamed. He had also glimpsed other buildings from the air, including a kind of great pig-pen where
the prisoner-workers were held, two sturdy buildings that
probably housed the guard detachment, a helicopter pad
and a nearby bungalow-pagoda-styled structure with gardens which could have been an infirmary.

But what was so special about sheds seven and eight?
The sample shed he'd been shown was typical of ones
he'd seen elsewhere in the world, with simple machinery
that macerated and stewed the coca leaves, mixed in reagents, and, after several more processing steps, produced the white crystals of cocaine hydrochloride so
prized by connoisseurs.

Mace, faggot fruitcake that he was, had put his finger
on what had caused the Colombians' downfall. The white
stuff did something to your head. From understanding
what you were doing, from knowing the consequences,
you graduated under coke to a power state in which whatever you did was right, right, right. No matter what, you
knew you would win.

By two o'clock Kevin had examined most of the sheds.
He judged they could easily produce enough of the refined powder to supply anything any drug trader wanted
in the Western hemisphere, even as fast as traffic kept
mushrooming. As for the crack market, one shed was
obviously devoted to preparing this cocaine derivative in
a form that could be smoked for that special high crack
produced, the stuff of heroes which left one emptied of
every human emotion, fear, remorse, pain, even hunger.
He had also found heroin which was being mixed with
crack to produce a new sensation called moonrock, more
highly addictive than anything in the history of street
drugs. Everything's up-to-date in Palawan.

Kevin had been working by moonlight, stopping when
the moon was obscured by clouds. The pale half-disc
overhead gave him all the light he needed. It also gave
any sentry the same light. But the quiet of this place was
reassuring. Nobody patrolled such areas at night. It
wasn't the sheds that needed guarding, it was the slaves
who worked there by day.

The next two sheds were tucked off by themselves in a small patch of aboriginal jungle that still survived after the whole mountain ridge had been re-cultivated for coca plants. This squared-off area of slender twenty-year-old trees managed to hide the two sheds in the dark of the moon. But when the cloud passed Kevin could see them quite easily. He could also see that a twelve-foot-high cyclone fence enclosed the area. The gate was secured by three bolts at three different heights, each with its own huge, vanadium-steel padlock. Savage twists of razor-wire topped the enclosure. His mouth felt dry. He moistened his lips and tasted Iris' body again.

Kevin wished now for the dirty underwear and shirts he had jettisoned back at the hut. He needed something like that to throw over the razor-wire. Just before another cloud obscured the moon, he inspected the fence for signs of electrification or an alarm system. Nothing that so-phisticated was necessary up here in the back of beyond.

As he looked it over he saw that where one roll of razor-wire had ended, and another began, there was a gap several feet wide. Someone with an eye to econo-mizing had let the gap remain, rather than start a whole new roll of razor-wire just to fill in a two-foot length.

By two-thirty, Kevin was up and over and prowling sheds seven and eight. So far the essence of their secret eluded him. It was true that they didn't contain any of the normal machinery used to reduce coca leaves to mush and extract their active principle. But the place was ob-viously some sort of lab. The heavy glass carboys in wooden crates were neatly stacked beside fifty-five-gallon steel drums.

In high school and college, Kerry had been the whiz. Kevin had just about squeezed through with Ker doing his homework for him. He had never before regretted this misspent youth. But now the names on the labels of these containers were exactly the kind of jawbreakers chemis-try teachers had been spouting off at him for years. As he read the labels, Kevin's lips moved. They felt dry as paper. He licked them and once more the animal musk and sandalwood odor drenched through his tastebuds.

What he should be doing was recording these names in his Thinkman, but he had booted it up in its trans-ceived mode. He'd have to unboot, locate a new card

and start it off again as a notebook. In the dark, without
a handbook? Not too feasible. Maybe he could just mem-
orize the names? Dimethylamine. Phosphoryl chloride.
Sodium cyanide. Ethyl alcohol. OK on the last two, he'd
heard of them. The first two needed some concentration.
Di. Methyl. Amine. OK. Phosphor—

The snick of an AK-47 being set on automatic fire is
very distinctive. Kevin's neck hairs bristled. He dropped
down between two wooden counters. Over in the doorway something moved, something short and manlike.
Kevin tried to ease the Browning out of its holster. The
Browning barrel wasn't that long but to it had been fitted
a four-inch silencer. It took forever to move into play.

The clouds deserted the moon. Its bright half-disc
shone down with sudden brilliance, silhouetting the man
in the doorway as he raised the AK-47 to hip height.

Starting to sweat, Kevin's thumb eased off the safety
catch. Everything seemed to progress in excruciating
slow motion. Did the man see him on the floor? How
could he? And yet . . .

The automatic came free of the holster. The movement
made absolutely no noise. But the man in the doorway
raised the submachine gun shoulder height and sighted
directly at him. A lucky aim. He would have no idea that
Kevin had dropped to the rough wooden floor. But you
couldn't leave it to chance.

Kevin put one round into Harry Broomthwaite's nose
and, as he dropped, a second into his chest. After firing
two rounds the silencer wasn't really guaranteed. Each
additional shot would produce a louder sound. But, at
least, the important shots had been silent. It was the first
time he had taken life since Corleone. He felt nothing
special. As usual. It was only business. And this lush
place, teeming with plant life, certainly didn't resemble
the Sicilian hill village which still, Zio Italo had told
him, figured in the transactions of the Honored Society.
Someone else, perhaps the invisible Mollo, had picked
up the pieces after the organization had been decapitated.

Di. Methyl. Amine.

He moved at a crouch around the counter, past the
sprawled corpse. Pausing only to take the AK-47 with
him—who knew what the rest of the night would hold?—

Kevin eased slowly out of shed seven and inch by inch into the moonlight. Broomthwaite had left the gate open.

Not smart, icing your host on the first night. Definitely a social no-no. He whistled silently, surveying the landscape for movement. He took a long, careful breath. The mausoleum smell almost overpowered him. He clenched his jaw. It was simple from here on. Lord Mace hadn't impressed him as what was known in the mafia as a war capo. The war capo lay dead in his own blood in shed seven. Mace didn't have the balls to lead a successful search for Kevin. Not at night. Anyway, all he had to do now was get off this ridge.

Get off this ridge, get off this island and somehow remember the names of all those chemicals.

Kerry Ricci arrived at Richland Tower long before anyone else and stood by Charley's window. He gazed down at the city as the morning sun sent slanting yellow rays across the awesome view that his brother Kevin coveted so much.

Something had kept him awake most of the night, something to do with Kevin. Given the life his twin led, in and out of scrapes, it was surprising the telepathy between them didn't disturb his brother more often. In a dream of Kevin his brother turned to him pleadingly. The face looked hollowed by stress. Pleading. At six a.m., Kerry had left Winfield in her bed and paced her small apartment slowly, afraid of waking her. He hadn't been very fun-loving the evening before. Kevin's absence had bothered him. It was something he didn't share with Winfield. She had her own troubles, which she spared him.

Dressing silently, he got himself out of her apartment and pushed past sleeping men and women on the subway station platform at Lexington and 72nd Street. The atmosphere stank of old grease, exhausted air, the raisiny stench of cheap fortified wine and dirty feet airing shoeless and sockless.

"Vanity," an old man cackled. "All is vanity." In the early-morning silence, his cracked voice reverberated. He had no teeth, no shoes, no overcoat, just corrugated cardboard wrapped around his midriff. His eyes stared up from the concrete floor, rimmed in dirt and wrinkles but unblinking, merciless. 'Looka that topcoat," he said accusingly. "All is vanity."

Hearing the approach of a downtown local, Kerry dropped a dollar bill in front of the old man, a votive offering to a sybil in its cardboard cave. "How will the day go?" Kerry asked him.

"For me? Or for you?"

The train pulled into the station, already full this early in the day. Kerry had the idea, over the shrill squeal of the wheels as the train sped downtown, that the world was trying to get through to him with a message.

Sitting at his desk now, he flipped on a small Japanese color TV set. " . . . Forty-three dead, including sixteen pre-school children. Meanwhile, in New Jersey . . ."

He turned down the sound and watched the tiny announcer's eyes hardly shifting as he read other grim news from his TelePrompTer. He looked neat, well-groomed, combed, alert, eyes sparkling with whatever varnish he dropped into them. All is vanity. Now the screen was showing a bombed-out Beirut street. A woman held up an infant, eyes staring, blood running from its neck.

Kerry resisted the urge to telephone Winfield. Their affair was not a mutual gripe session. Besides, her mind was much tougher than his. He wouldn't, he felt, like whatever advice she might give him.

He glanced back at the screen just in time to see the face of the FBI agent he had had an argument with last year at an accounting seminar. There was no mistaking that rangy, Gary Cooper look. He turned up the volume. " . . . Cohen, forty-four years of age. Roosevelt Hospital emergency ward doctors told Channel Seven News he had apparently suffered a massive heart attack while at the wheel of his automobile crossing George Washington Bridge from New Jersey. The car caromed off the guard rails, vaulted over the side and disappeared in forty feet of water under the Hudson River." The picture changed to a night scene illuminated by floodlamps as a crane hauled up a car, weeping great torrents of sewage-laden water, while the announcer continued: "At the Federal Bureau of Investigation, no one was yet available for comment. In Alaska this morning, the clean-up of a massive new oil spill is proceeding at a—"

Kerry flipped off the TV set.

Was Cohen's death what had kept him up most of the night? In the dream it was Kevin, not Cohen. But perhaps it hadn't been either. Perhaps the man in the dream had been himself, freed at last of Cohen.

By four in the morning, Sergeant Uisendonk had found Broomthwaite's body. He and Sergeant Van der Merwe were the two guard non-coms, both former torturers for BOSS, the South African government's terror squad, both cocaine addicts, which was why BOSS had fired them, finicky about who was allowed to murder suspects.

Under Broomthwaite's command, with a Lance Corporal Le Clerc, they ran a squad of two dozen guards, refugees from the French Foreign Legion's earlier adventures in Indo-China. As Kevin had seen from the air on his arrival, the guards lived in two brick barracks. A helicopter pad sat nearby and, beyond it, Kevin recalled a garden-graced bungalow-pagoda he had thought to be a dispensary or clinic. It was not. It was the pleasant lair of Angelique, a sixty-year-old madam from Saigon, and five hard-working whores, of whom only Iris showed any real beauty or elegance.

Uisendonk, whose mind was overstocked with useless military furniture, on finding Broomthwaite's body instantly assumed the entire compound was under siege. He started the sirens. This awakened Lord Hugo Waismith Mace in an absolutely foul humor, compounded of too much trade rum and no opium whatsoever.

By five o'clock the morning sun had appeared on the horizon to the east, toward the main islands. Birds greeted it with a burst of song and siren imitations. Mace and the guards convened in the clearing outside shed seven like an impromptu wake for a comrade only Mace had liked.

"See hyeah," Lord Hugo began in his fruity fake Home Counties drawl, "it's quite obvious the Ricci bloke's the assassin. We hold all the cards. We have all the transport, including a helicopter. The entire ridge is cordoned off by electric fencing and sheer drops on all sides. If you can't find him within the hour you're a pack of hopeless idiots. Get hopping."

Sergeant Uisendonk frowned. As a pep talk Mace's speech put the men's backs up. Still, he wasn't wrong. "You men on my left, Sergeant Van der Merwe takes you north. I take you lot on my left to the south. On the

double!'' The roar of Jeep engines filled the area. Overhead, the helicopter and its pilot hung noisily in the sky
as he started a long series of out-spiraling reconnaissance
flights. Lance Corporal Le Clerc, left behind to keep an
eye on the prisoner's compound and monitor the helicopter, walked back to the barracks alone.

An elderly specimen, tough as a whip, he sported an
iron-gray mustache attached to side whiskers. Prisoners
shook with fear in his gaze. For Le Clerc prisoners existed to be tortured in new and sexually satisfying ways.
It was Le Clerc who had developed in Dien Bien Phu, at
the age of eighteen, a method of flaying a man alive in
small patches liberally doused with alcohol to drive his
screams higher than a soprano's. When newsmen stumbled across such corpses, rotting under a live blanket of
flies, Paris decided to make Le Clerc the scapegoat who
alone indulged in such soul-slaking practices. Le Clerc
didn't mind the opprobrium but when they sent him into
prison for six weeks, he managed to escape. He had been
at large ever since, roaming the Far East in search of
legal victims for his pleasures.

He seated himself with a pack of cigarettes and a
sixteen-ounce bottle of beer and fiddled with the radio
equipment. *"Ecoutez-moi,"* the helicopter pilot was saying. "Faneuil here. Who's at base, Le Clerc?"

"C'est moi."

Le Clerc could hear guards charging past the barracks
toward the whorehouse. Feminine squeals. Laughter. The
sound of a bottle smashed on cement. Furniture being
pushed around. A quick, rough search. The squad moved
on.

If only, Le Clerc mused, one of those whores would
step out of line and Broomthwaite would order her punishment. His mustache quivered with the thrill of it. Soft
female epidermis, much easier to peel back centimeter
by centimeter and watch the face contort into a mask of
madness. If only Broomthwaite would— But he was dead,
nasty old bugger. And even in death he was causing them
all this trouble. Typical Brit.

"Corporal?"

He whirled in his chair. It was the one called Iris. He
didn't fancy any *putain* that skinny. Her tits resembled a
baby's. And she gave herself airs, did this princess. This

morning she had drawn an exaggerated line of eyebrow pencil that swerved outward in a dipping curve and then back to the outer corner of each eye. It reminded Le Clerc of a drawing on the wall of a Cairo brothel.

"Who gave you permission to leave the whorehouse?"

An indescribable smell wafted from her body, part perfume, part semen. She produced another bottle of beer. "Angelique thought you might want this."

Mollified, Le Clerc took the bottle from her. As he turned to place it beside the open one, the American stepped into the radio room, aiming his .9 Browning level at Le Clerc's gut. He advanced silently and shoved the muzzle of the automatic into Le Clerc's mouth. Blood spurted from the Frenchman's lower lip. Kevin relieved him of a .45 Colt sidearm. He leaned forward until he could switch off the radio transmitter.

"Listen," he said in a quiet voice, his face inches from Le Clerc's. "Anything at all could cause me to pull this trigger. Have you seen the exit wound a .9 slug makes? Show me you have brains, or I will show them to the world."

Le Clerc's eyes bulged slightly, but not with fear. If his feelings could have been analyzed, perhaps he was transfixed with sexual satisfaction, the torturer tortured. He managed to nod very, very gently, the soul of cooperation. The muzzle of Kevin's pistol clicked against his back molars.

"Tell the copter man to land and report to you here. Now."

Kevin removed the muzzle with such force that it cut Le Clerc's lip in a fresh place. Blood had somehow made its way along his mustache and was dripping neatly from one curled gray tip. The Frenchman dabbed at his mouth with a screwed-up paper napkin. He switched on the transmitter. "Faneuil. Report to me in the radio room. Out."

"*D'accord.* Out."

Kevin switched off the transmitter and jerked the automatic up and under Le Clerc's chin. He rose in his chair. "March over to the doorway."

As he moved past Iris, the Frenchman glowered at her. "Traitor."

"She's as much my prisoner as you are," Kevin told

him. "I forced her at gunpoint to hide me in the bun-
galow when the men searched it."

The look Le Clerc gave him indicated how little cre-
dence he gave the alibi. They stared out of the radio room
across a dusty clearing, marked by a large X of whitewashed rocks. Already the sky overhead thundered with
helicopter noise. Dust began to swirl as the tiny machine
settled down over their heads.

Kevin stood directly behind Le Clerc to hide the gun.
He pressed the muzzle into the Frenchman's kidney. As
the pilot cut his engine, noise and dust settled around them
all. In silence they watched the pilot trudge toward them.
It is in the nature of tension that it prolongs itself, or seems
to. The pilot was moving at a normal rate but, to Kevin,
he seemed to be crawling, dawdling, delaying matters
when there was literally no time left for delay.

Once he was inside, Kevin slammed the door of the
radio room shut. "Tie him up," he ordered Le Clerc.

"Y-you—?" Faneuil's eyes grew wider. "You are the
American!"

"What a spotter," Kevin remarked. He watched Le
Clerc handcuff his comrade to a heavy metal chair. The
state of Le Clerc's nerves was obvious. He had been ordered around too much, threatened too intimately. His
blooded mustache and whiskers seemed to bristle like a
badger's cornered in his sett. In a moment, he would do
something un-clever.

"Now do the same thing to Iris," Kevin ordered the
corporal.

"I have no more cuffs."

"Then rope."

"Here in this locker," Le Clerc said. His eyes had
gone muddy brown, like sewage water. Silently, his body
posture signaled: say yes. His eyes had gone dangerously
blank, stones set in rawhide.

"OK, open it."

Later, Iris told Kevin, everything seemed to move as
slowly as if she had smoked too much marijuana. Le
Clerc snicked open the door catch. He opened the locker
door. He reached inside. When he turned toward Kevin,
his hand came out of the locker. But it wasn't holding a
rope. It was holding an Ingram machine pistol without
its silencer. The stubby barrel looked like the snout of a

tiny porker. A patch the size of an Eisenhower dollar opened up at the front of Le Clerc's throat. The Browning in Kevin's hand jerked back. A great spout of blood arched forward from Le Clerc's carotid artery, pulsing like an ornamental fountain.

The helicopter pilot screamed. "I did not," Iris bragged later. "Not for a moment was I afraid with you protecting me." Instead, she and Kevin ran for the helicopter. Kevin got it started. The overhead rotor swung mightily. The craft shuddered. In the distance Jeep engines roared, closer, louder. A crackle of rifle fire punctuated the rotor noise. Kevin nudged the throttle forward and the helicopter lifted high in the sky like a soap bubble in a thermal updraft.

"Wonderful!" Iris screamed.

In a moment, they were a thousand feet over the compound and heading southeast. "In my backpack," he shouted. "Small little black box?"

She found his Thinkman and gave it to him. At this altitude, its range would be greatly enhanced. It might get as far as Brunei to the south. He had the name of an exporter who did business there with Richland Oil.

"Iris, do you read and write?"

She drew herself up quite erect. She had filled the cockpit with her powerful smell. "Both," she announced with pride. The Hatshupset eye design she had drawn around her flat-almond eyes gave her the look of a much younger girl, playing with her mother's makeup.

"Take that pen and that clipboard," he said. "Write down the following." One eye on his airspeed indicator and one on the coastline wheeling below him, Kevin squinted mightily. "Sodium cyanide," he said, spelling it. "Ethyl alcohol. Got it? OK. Next. The next words." A bead of sweat rolled down his forehead and spattered on the pad of paper where Iris was writing. "The words are, uh, Di. Got it? Methyl," he spelled it. "Amine. Phosphoryl. Hah! Got it. Chloride. Iris," he went on as she scribbled down the words, "how long does it take for that perfume to die away?"

"About three days, Kevvy."

"Will you make me a promise?"

"Anything, Kevvy."

"Never swallow perfume again?"

"But gentlemen adore it."

"That lets me out." Kevin squinted down at the coastline of Brunei ahead of them. He had iced two men for those words the girl had written down. And, without thinking, he now had her on his back till he could figure out what to do with her. Maybe Vince had a place for someone with such exotic good looks?

Forty-Eight

As the launch sailed across Hong Kong harbor, a brisk breeze ruffled the waters. The powerful craft began to surge up and down very slightly. Shan Lao, always a good sailor, ignored the new motion. Lord Hugo, hung over, began to feel his meager breakfast trying to rise in his gorge.

Doing business with mainland China had never been easy, but with another fully Chinese community on Taiwan, dedicated to free enterprise and superprofit, dealing with the immense bulk of the motherland had become even more difficult.

At heart, all problems stemmed from greed. A market of one billion Chinese, scattered across a vast piece of Asia from the borders of the old Soviets to the Sea of Japan, represented a window of opportunity no capitalist could resist, least of all the striving face of greed presented by business leaders in Taiwan, Singapore, Seoul, Bangkok and Tokyo.

The first problem: in what currencies could China pay for this deluge of goodies? Certainly not its own. Therein lay the heart of the matter. The second problem: which of these cities would become the aperture through which the wealth of China was tapped? Or would it be Hong Kong, soon to be subsumed into the body of its motherland?

Half a dozen leading financial-industrial giants pursued mainland China through a miasma of unrest, riots and crude military crackdowns. None had found a solution for the first problem. At least in his own mind, Shan

Lao felt he was ahead of the pack because he *had* found a solution.

He had gone about it in normal Shan fashion, cultivating top-level Chinese political leaders but not with the usual number nine envelope stuffed with ten-thousand-yen notes. Shan's control of electronics was his strength. One of his companies, with the attractively Western name of Topp Electronics, was prepared to produce virtually any equipment the Chinese lacked. Since mainland China was an inchoate swirl of poor communications, the political leader who could carry his message and program to the farthest reaches, who could thus jump the gun on his Politburo associates, could count on the support of the Army.

Based on circuitry plagiarized from the best Japanese firms, Topp's miraculous turnkey installations, state-of-the-art prefab television, radio and radar stations, below-cost receivers by the tens of thousands with a limited selection of channels, enabled an ambitious leader to blot out everything but his own messages. And hard currency with which to repay Shan? Here he showed his true genius.

Unlike other entrepreneurs wooing mainland China, he didn't offer long-term loans through which China could buy his products with his money. That made no sense to Shan. Instead, he opened more tempting vistas. In drugs, for example, Latin America had shown the way, providing political cover beneath which drug profits reached astronomical size. But why stop at drugs when thinking of forbidden items that could be sold for hard currency?

This particular yacht happened to be owned by a British consortium whose top executive had gone to school with Lord Hugo Waismith Mace. This was not a public school but a slum school in the East End of London whose alumni stuck together. The Mace connection was too important to risk a meeting aboard the yacht without Mace in attendance. Otherwise, Shan had no use for him in today's negotiations.

Mace had been summoned overnight from some sort of mess on Palawan. He'd arrived in such a state of high dither that Shan had had no time to find out what had gone wrong, except for a hurried exchange on board the launch taking them to the yacht.

"Apart from Broomthwaite, all is well. Production continues."

"I did warn you about that boy."

"I assure you every precaution—"

Shan's eyes swerved sideways, to indicate the crewmen handling the launch.

Aboard the old school chum's yacht, the three mainland emissaries were already there, having arrived under cover of darkness. In the tangled world of the Far East, it was imperative that they not be seen conferring with any one entrepreneur. The mainland posture was always: we play the field. But Shan Lao had reason to believe he had finally put together a cocktail of ingredients that he alone could offer. The market would be his.

It was more than the billion Chinese who constituted this market. The fact was, through colonization or diaspora, the Chinese as an ethnic people were spread around the world. Estimates put it succinctly: one out of four people on Earth was Chinese.

Zio Italo had given standing orders to anyone, wherever he was, to phone him at any hour, if necessary. "My line is always open," he told trusted associates. "At my age, three a.m. is the same as three p.m."

When the telephone call came through from Brunei, it was five a.m. in Manhattan but still the previous day in Borneo, distinctions Italo ignored. Even at this early hour he had his first visitor of the day, the distinguished, impeccably dressed man who sported a cigarette holder and cigarette from which he occasionally inhaled without having set the cigarette alight. "His name? M'sieur Charmant."

"Iggy," Italo was telling him. "My nipote cretino, Charley, thinks he's pulled a fast one on me. He's transferred a dozen companies into my control."

"How bad could that be?"

"That's not the p—" The telephone rang. "What? Brunei? Kevin?" Italo demanded.

"Scusi, Don Italo," his telephone caller said. "Sono Renzo Capra. Ricordi?"

"Kevin, say something."

"Don Italo, here is speaking Renzo Capra. I am the Richland representative in Brunei."

"Ah! Renzo! Mi scusi. Is Kevin Ricci there?"

"No, purtroppo. He has crashed his helicopter. In the sea. But he and the girl are safe. I have put them in a private infirmary. An infection in the lungs."

"Kevin? In a hospital?"

"But all is well, Don Italo. They were in the water a bit, is all. You have my word for it he will be out and walking around as—"

"Stai zito, Renzo!" Italo's voice trembled with a kind of impotent rage. He stared across his desk at his visitor and, with a facial tic and a movement of his shoulders, silently conveyed the message: what could a man expect to do over tens of thousands of miles? "He must be removed from the hospital, Renzo. Do you understand? At once. Now!"

"I have a message for you from him."

"I want him taken to your own house. I want him under your roof."

"It shall be done, Don Italo. And the girl?"

"What girl?"

"The— Never mind. Don Italo, do you have a pencil by your side?"

"Give me the message. Then run! Remove the boy to safety at once."

"Si, claro, sicuro. Have you the pencil?"

"Speak!" Italo thundered down the line.

"D, I," Capra read off. "M, E, T, H . . ."

"Wa-wa-wait, godammit!"

When he had transcribed the words, Zio Italo sat forward. "Renzo, stai attenti. Get that boy under your roof. Call me back the minute he's safe with you. Get his lungs cleared up. If your call don't reach me in the next hour, you're finished."

"Never fear!"

"Renzo, whaddo I do with these chemical names?"

"He say give 'em to Kerry."

Italo hung up and looked at his visitor. "You heard? Such crises. Such idiocy, putting a nipote of mine in a hospital where the most ignorant kind of hit man can get to him as easy as swatting a fly." He stopped. "With all due respect, Iggy. You understand I don't classify a maestro like M'sieur Charmant with the riffraff of the profession."

The distinguished, well-dressed man nodded. "From the little I hear of that Corleone matter, your nipote is

among the best. Nevertheless,'' he said in his funny British accent with the ulular r's, ''I have done my share of
hospital take-outs. You're right to move the boy. In Corleone, people die on the village square. Elsewhere, in
hospitals.''

''I have thought long and hard about that afternoon in
Corleone,'' Italo confessed. ''How two nipotini managed, in the very heart of the enemy camp, with their
mother to protect, to do what they did.''

Charmant shrugged eloquently, a surrendering-to-God
gesture as if the will of the Almighty was always, reli-
ably, unknowable. ''I am sure one or two thoughts have
occurred, my dear old friend.''

Italo's smile was as crooked as a lizard scampering out
of sight. ''One,'' he admitted. ''And that one puzzling.''
The man holding the unlighted cigarette inscribed a capital M on the desk between them. Italo's smile flickered
for an instant, the tail of the lizard disappearing. ''You
know this Mollo?''

''I know that he has been a stone in Don Lucca's
shoe.''

A tight sigh escaped Italo's lips. ''Mannagge, one more
thing. Is it any wonder,'' he asked in a low, dramatic
tone of self-pity, ''that a Wasp flyweight like Charley
thinks he can end-run me these days?''

''How could he?''

''With all the shit they heap on my desk, he thinks:
'Zio Italo has his hands full; now's the time to shaft
him.' '' He sighed tragically, thinking of himself as a
giant assaulted by pygmies. ''As for Mollo, this is not a
simple matter a—what do the newspapers call it?—a turf
battle. This Mollo has won himself Corleone only to
dismantle it.''

''I don't understand, old friend.''

''Nor do I. Mollo seems to be moving the entire operation, men, supplies distribution routes, refineries, everything.''

''To where?''

''To hell, for all I care. I am waiting for a sign that he
is honorable enough to avenge the welcome deaths of his
rivals. Is he a new man who cares nothing for revenging
three murders? So be it.'' Italo made a flicking motion

with his fingers, as if removing a bit of dirt from his desk. "You were saying, before the phone rang . . . ?"

"I was saying it's a new drug of the aflatoxin family. Occurs naturally. Mimics a coronary perfectly. Even if the, er, object is at the wheel of his car." M'sieur Charmant sucked hard on his unlighted cigarette. "The Feeb had no—"

"Mi scusi, old friend, but I must call my nipote Kerry with these chemical names. Perhaps you might wish to step outside and smoke that cigarette?" Both elderly men chuckled as Charmant got up, bowed and left. When he came back ten minutes later, beating the last vestiges of smoke out of his suit jacket, Italo was still on the phone. He beckoned him in.

"Si, Renzo." Italo glanced at his watch. "Si, less than forty minutes. I appreciate your concern in moving so quickly. He is safe in your home?"

"Under my roof, Don Italo. I can personally vouch for his safety and that of the girl. The finest of antibiotics are being used."

"What girl?"

"Non importa. He asked if perhaps you had had time to discuss those words with his brother."

"This time, Renzo, you need the pencil. Do you have it?"

"Si padrone. Mi dica."

"Tell him they are producing Tabun. T, A, B, U, N. Got it?"

"And what is Tabun?" the man in Brunei wanted to know.

"Ask the Iraquis. They love it. It's a nerve gas."

"Mamma mia."

"Cheap to make, like Dago Red," Italo went on. "One drop. One drop on your skin. You start going blind. Piss your pants. Cough up your lungs. Convulsions. Coma. Finito."

"Dio mio. Who buys such gas?"

"Somebody is obviously buying it from Shan Lao." Italo paused, wondering if he should add his own thoughts on the subject, that only a government can get away with peddling nerve gas.

"Che peccata," Capra mourned. "What a world, eh, Don Italo?"

"Si. But it's the only one we have." He hung up and turned to his distinguished visitor. "Iggy, is there anything you need?"

"I'm taking the day flight on Air France. Be in Paris tonight. After last night, I can't afford anymore chances. Could I impose on you to have someone drive me to JFK?"

"It's a pleasure, not an imposition. Anybody who could take Cohen out that neat, a plain ordinary car accident, and not get the Feebs upset enough to start a crusade, that man has my heartfelt thanks and my Buick to the airport." He stood up and came around his desk, clasping his arms around the much taller Iggy Zetz and hugging him roughly. "Whatta world, huh? As Renzo Capra says. But, Ig, it's true friends who count. True friends like you and family like Kevin."

They kissed each other on both cheeks.

Presumably none of them would want anything alcoholic before lunch. Even so, when the yacht's steward arrived with small porcelain cups and a great urn of tea, Shan Lao waved him off impatiently. He and the mainland people watched until the steward had left the room. Lord Hugo immediately missed him. He had, after all, been another white face. There came a time when one grew tired unto death of facing up to Orientals.

Mace watched the three men from Beijing. The youngest of them looked about fifty. That he was the most ambitious was easy to spot for an old China hand like Mace: he who is least eager secretly yearns most.

Exasperating. This was only the second of these high-security meetings Mace had set up. It was through his old school contacts that such hush-hush meetings were even possible. And did either side take advantage of his good work? No, they wasted valuable time posturing stonily for each other's benefit. It would help, Mace admitted to himself, if he knew their filthy lingo better. In several decades out here he really only knew the sort of restaurant and opium-den Chinese necessary to place an order. Well, damn them, they spoke English perfectly well, at least Shan and the fifty-year-old did.

By one of those shocking coincidences that disturbed Mace for a long time thereafter, the elder Beijing man, somewhere in his eighties but still fairly spry, suddenly switched into English. " . . . Come to our attention that the Palawan situation has grown problematical. Your esteemed associate, Lord Mace, can perhaps . . . ?" The old soldier's voice rose and faded out on a polite note of inquiry.

"Yes, of course," Mace jumped in, delirious at the chance to speak. "We are always aware that what we do carries risks. Most of the time these are technical. Once in a while, there are human risks. But the basic work goes on. No delays. No shortfalls. The production line is perfectly intact."

"We find it alarming," the younger Chinese said, with no tone of alarm whatsoever, "to learn that with such tight security, a saboteur was still able to infiltrate the compound."

Mace could feel moisture between his neck and the hard-pressing collar of his white shirt. "Not a saboteur, I assure you. He had arrived with credentials to act only as an observer of our other activity on Palawan." Mace's glance shot sideways to Shan Lao's impassive face.

"Lord Mace refers to the purely pharmaceutical side of our production," Shan picked up smoothly. "In short, the incident had nothing to do with you—" He lapsed into Chinese again, just as smoothly.

Mace sat back and listened to the words, unable to pick out even a few clues. Damned sneaky foreign muck. The fifty-year-old interrupted Shan, and in what he asked, Mace thought he could recognize two syllables. He started to lean forward but stopped himself from giving away his rekindled interest. He waited. Then in replying, Shan's seamless flow of Chinese also included the same two syllables.

The skin encased by his collar seemed to grow damper, not with heat in this air-conditioned yacht, but with sudden fear. There was nothing wrong with Lord Hugo's hearing. He had, indeed, correctly heard the word.

He had always known how Shan managed to give the Chinese what they most required, hard currency. Supplying forbidden chemical weapons enabled the Chinese, in turn, to sell to any buyer who came up with hard currency. Only a government could do that sort of thing and hope to get away with it.

But that wasn't the word Mace had understood.
It was the word anthrax.

Forty-Nine

Autumn often brings great peace and beautifully cooler
weather to the mountain towns of Sicily. To Corleone this
year it brought torrential rains and the kind of upheaval
none of the locals would ever forget. All day, in a steady
downpour, six-wheel camions slithered and churned
through mud, loading up carton after carton.

Everyone knew that the vast works of Don Lucca Certomá and his two associates would have to change ownership and control. No one suspected they would also
change locale. No one could have foreseen that all of it,
even desks, filing cabinets, centralino telephone switch-
boards, everything would be crated and removed.

Corleone was losing its one industry. The village was
being returned to its cows, its sheep and its goats. Having
been dragged, howling, into the tail end of the twentieth
century as the core and crux of a worldwide high-tech
business venture, it was now being stripped of the whole
thing, all its employees sacked and a whole group of new
and even uglier faces running around playing boss.

The plump young woman with the large eyes who still
served locals at the bar in the village square—the scene
of Don Lucca's sudden departure so recently—claimed to
know what was happening. She had managed to eavesdrop often when Mollo had discussed plans with his new
henchmen. "And not one of them Corleonese!" she
would yelp, agitating her arms in such a way that her
aroma spread far and wide. "Not even Siciliani. Foreigners!"

"Ma, da dove?" people would inquire. "From where,
these foreigners?"

"Calabria?" the woman would suggest hazily, naming
the next province to Sicily, separated only by the Straits
of Messina, but an even more lawless province with its

own mafia posing under the local dialect name of 'ndrangheta. It suited Mollo to let her spread such gossip.

Now the rain stopped. The sun came out. The trucks
left. The mud dried to dust. The village felt more peaceful. It slumbered.

She was right about the new faces belonging to Calabrese, most of them on Mollo's wife's side, hailing from
what had once been one of the largest Greek cities of
antiquity, Locri. It still bore its Greek name proudly, but
the Locrese 'ndrangheta was nothing to brag about; a
ratty collection of kidnappers and terrorizers of small
merchants for protection money.

Mollo kept quiet his plans for the marsala grape vineyards he had liberated from Don Lucca. The government
in Rome—which to a southern Italian is a great money
cow to be milked mercilessly—would cheerfully give billions of lire to anyone establishing what the trade called
agriturismo. This was a bucolic holiday venue of self-
catering huts in which tourists booked weeks of sunshine,
fondling of growing grapes, harvesting in the vendemmia
season and, of course, steady intake of wine produced
the previous year.

Like other mafiosi whom Zio Italo called new men,
Mollo had long ago understood that frozen Brits and
Scandinavians, Germans, Dutch, all of them paid good
money for the Southern sun. But not to live in a place
where people got shot or kidnapped. Not where the
carabinieri were always searching for drug shipments
or missing victims. Ecco. Move the dirty linen to Calabria. Let Sicily become a profitable island of peace and
quiet, credit cards and traveler's checks. Let Calabria, in
short, become the pozzo nero, the shitpot, of Sicily. The
Calabrese didn't mind. Nothing made them sick. And let
Sicily purge itself and become as sweet-smelling as the
flowers of the field.

This the woman at the bar never did fathom. And since
the vineyards were many kilometers from the village,
neither did anyone else until it was too late to realize
that, the twentieth century having passed them by, there was
nothing left for them to do in the twenty-first.

The first thing Lord Hugo Waismith Mace learned when
he arrived in Locri was that there was no decent hotel.

The town was the biggest along the Ionic Coast between Reggio CaCalabria and the provincial capital, Catanzaro, but if one sought clean sheets and working toilets, one had to leave for another town.

The province was almost entirely coastline, backed by a spine of mountains and alpine meadows. To any outsider it seemed the ideal place for tourism, much more scenic than Sicily. But, as Mace soon learned, terrain alone could not overcome the inbred fatalism of the Calabrese.

Did foreigners like Mollo establish refineries and entrepots here, making heroin available locally? So be it. Did English lords provide obvious financial support, guaranteeing Mollo's success? So be it. Did local families, potential competitors, die nightly, victims of Mollo's death squads? So be it.

Having lived and worked in former British power centers like Singapore and Hong Kong, Lord Mace was used to a lively, chattering local population which easily provided alert office workers and manual labor and, moreover, kept itself and its environment clean. This dispirited, glum, filthy population depressed him mightily.

He woke early this morning, damp with his own perspiration in the mush-mattressed bed. Damn Shan. Once more the air conditioning had failed during the night. Why, in October, did one need artificial cooling? Another of Calabria's delights. Damn Shan. He watched a small swarm of flies circling listlessly as if they, too, needed air conditioning, and couldn't function properly without it as the national bird of Calabria.

Mace got up, his back sore from no mattress support. Damn Shan! What a sadistic son-of-a-bitch, sending him to this benighted backwater. Damn Shan. Why must he have someone on the scene? Oh, Mace knew he was being demoted, and in a most insulting way. Morover, until opium base arrived, Mace was cut off from his chief recreation. Another sadistic twist of Shan's mind, exiling him to this garbage-strewn land.

Mace showered, dressed informally—his idea of being informal being an oyster-tan safari jacket and knee-length shorts—and took a caffé lungo at the hotel's bar. Then he got in his borrowed Fiat Uno and drove southwest toward Locri.

As he slowly negotiated the heavy traffic along this two-lane national highway, he noticed bright orange-red flowers along the way. What, poppies? At a turnoff toward the mountains, he stopped to examine a stand of them, tissue-thin petals quivering. Papaver somniferum, Mace wondered, or just some terribly ordinary roadside poppy? Too bad he didn't speak the wretched dialect, throat-hawking rasps and cowlike moos. An elderly, straw-hatted shepherd was driving a mixed flock of sheep and goats along the road up from the sea. He'd know.

Mace got out of his car. Too much was worse than too little, he thought, fingering the change in his shorts' pockets. Finally he waved a one-thousand-lire note at the shepherd.

"B'yorn," the man responded, taking the worn note.

Mace pulled up a handful of poppies. He mimed biting off the heads and swallowing them. "Buono?" he asked.

The old man, his lined cheeks whitened by a four-day growth of beard, lifted his head once, sharply, and made a tschk noise. He selected one of Mace's poppies, threw away the petals and chewed the rest of the head. Then he held up all ten fingers. "Deege," he announced. He held them up a second time. "Deege oncor." He rubbed his abdomen, pantomiming satiety. By now, unassisted by his hoots and whistling trills, the flock of sheep and goats was almost out of sight up the road. The shepherd lifted his battered straw hat.

Mace produced another one-thousand-lire note and they parted company. For the equivalent of a pound, Mace realized, he had suddenly acquired the power to make Calabria, if not pleasant, at least bearable.

He sat down on the hood of his Fiat and began chewing poppy heads. The old man had indicated twenty of them? Horrible taste. Damn Shan.

J. Laverne Suggs arrived at Roosevelt Hospital as soon as he got the message. He carried with him an extract of Noah "Nose" Cohen's Bureau service record with next of kin and home addresses out on Long Island. Suggs reported to the morgue, his only thought to send the body on its way with a minimum of delay.

He waited while time passed.

At JFK Airport the Air France day flight to Paris an-

nounced its final boarding call. The distinguished man
was already comfortably resting in his first-class seat.

At Roosevelt, the paging system lisped steadily: "Dr.
Aziz, Dr. Mulsindergee, Dr. Farmajanian." Then, mysteriously, Suggs had been redirected to Intensive Care,
where he'd shown his identification once again. He was
fuming, but concealed it. The nurse hadn't reacted properly. She had kept him waiting some more. "Dr. Sassar-
ian, Dr. Moon Sing, Dr. Bok." Intensive Care at
Roosevelt Hospital was always crowded.

At JFK, the Paris flight took off. The pilot turned off
the "No Smoking" signs. The man lit a cigarette and
inhaled with great pleasure and a certain air of relief.

Suggs, however, sighed with boredom and more than
a little peevishness at the trouble Cohen was causing him.
To the day he died, Cohen could be relied on to make
problems. But his last physical exam hadn't shown a weak
heart. Just like the dumb cluck to play his cards that close
to his chest. Joke. Suggs produced a wintry smile. Close
to the chest.

"Dr. Watanabe, Dr. Aw Hoon, Dr. Brosicevic."
Poor old Nose and his obsession with the Richland
Riccis. Not that their dossiers weren't growing all the
time down at the Bureau. There had been an attempted
rub-out right in the basement garage of Richland Tower.
And some sort of massacre back in Sicily that some people thought involved the Ricci side. Maybe Cohen had
got hold of something. Some people felt his death proved
he had something big in his sights. Too late now. Suggs
heard footsteps behind him and turned to find the nurse
with two doctors, one black, one white.

"Mr. Suggs," the nurse began, "Dr. Raglyn, Dr.
Shapiro."

Suggs started to stick out his hand, then thought better
of it. No sense making a goddamned jolly block party
out of this. "First I have to ID the body. Then I need
the usual forms for shipping a corpse. It's routine."

"No, it isn't," Dr. Raglyn told him.

"I beg your pardon?"

The black man eyed him for a moment. "First of all,
let me explain that the TV and the newspaper boys are
always jumping the gun, but never this bad before."

"Pardon?"

Dr. Shapiro's smile produced a frown on Suggs' face. Like Cohen, the doctor didn't look Jewish. "There was the usual air pocket as the car submerged," Shapiro said. "So oxygen deprivation wasn't immediate."

"We had total cardiac arrest but no suffocation," Raglyn added. "Maybe one of those aflatoxin attacks stale peanuts can produce. You guys are the detectives." His face went deadpan. "Shapiro is our Jewish heart man." He waited for a smile, but didn't get it. "He got it ticking. After a while it took."

"What the hell are you saying?" Suggs demanded.

"We're saying," Raglyn explained, "smile up a little. Cohen's alive."

December

Fifty

When she came back to Manhattan after a fifteen-year absence, Garnet had noticed changes in the way its people coped. In her last stay, business was transacted over a three-martini lunch. Dinner was normally reserved for account execs to try their luck at seducing her. Breakfast intake was restricted to drops of Murine in bloodshot eyes.

But today, she mused as she looked around the table, decked with floral displays and four crystal goblets at every place setting, decaf power breakfasts now kicked off the morning. Lunches were fueled by mineral water. By dinnertime, power players were too exhausted for food and too AIDS-spooked for sex.

Today the Herman Foundation had booked a major dining room of the Plaza Hotel for its annual awards in conservation and the awards of its offshoot, the Education Research Fellowship.

Garnet, seated on the dais, wondered why Charley's place next to her was empty. He rarely attended these gatherings but today she was accepting, on behalf of Richland Bank and Trust, the coveted Herman Trophy. This obliged her to make a small speech on any relevant topic.

The Foundation sponsored public service television programs. It was in the habit of adding to its on-screen logo a line saluting that year's trophy winner. Considering that PBS was the only television viewed by anyone with an IQ higher than his body temperature, winning the Herman was a public relations coup.

Luncheon was half over and two of the four crystal goblets had been put to use—for white wine and charged mineral water—when Charley slipped into his seat as the waiter removed his vol-au-vent of seafood and replaced it with very thin medallions of meat the size of jar tops.

"Do you have some suitable remarks in case they call on you?" she asked.

"Why does Richland have a philanthropic officer, if not to stand up and be ogled?"

"You're in a frisky mood. What kept you?"

"Ah!"

"Just 'ah?' "

"Ah-ha!" he added. He fixed one medallion with his fork and began cutting it with his knife as it swam in very dark sauce. "What's this? Venison?"

She tasted a piece. "Orlon?"

He tasted his. "Is there a rabbi in the house?"

"Why a rabbi?"

"They have to keep track of whether something's meat or not-meat." He tasted another piece, chewing very thoroughly. "Christ! I know what this is!"

"Don't sound so terrified."

"It's FoodUsa's newest synthetic. Mycomeat." He cleared his throat dramatically. "A matrix of threadlike fungus laced with hydrolized vegetable protein. Botanically it's lichen. Pork, chicken and beef lichen. That vol-au-vent was probably Mycomollusc. As Bunny always says, oh, yech."

He sat there playing with it, cleaning off the gravy, testing the "meat" with the side of his fork but never again eating any. All the while he kept humming. Finally he leaned closer to her and in a low murmur said, "I'm late because I sold FoodUsa back to Zio Italo this morning."

"But not before they created this stuff."

"My father's old concern. The final transfer. Italo now owns everything except the financial companies. Oh, and a small Japanese subsidiary, Richtron. It goes next week. That deserves a toast." He lifted his mineral water goblet. "Free at last."

"Charley. What great news." They touched glasses and sipped. "But why has Italo let you do it?"

"What I get is rumor. Italo's side of the family brings him nothing but worries. His agents have eradicated a whole echelon of enemies, or potential enemies, in Corleone, creating a new generation of dedicated enemies. One of his killers has gone berserk in the Philippines, escaping by the skin of his teeth. Italo sits at the center of a vast web of informers. I understand one of them has just given him premature Alzheimer's. Some flunky in the Manhattan DA's office. He says they're onto something with Vince.''

''No wonder you want out of that clan.''

''Italo knows it's too late to reverse what I've done. When I hand over control of Richtron in a week or two, that's it. He's become, under concealed ownership, the proprietor of a profitable empire that *he* has to run, not me.''

''You think he's finally accepted this?''

Charley was silent for a moment. He broke off a corner of a roll and sniffed it. ''Real bread?'' he wondered. ''What the hell.'' He sat munching the roll for a moment. ''I moved too fast for him while he was distracted. That doesn't take me out of danger. It only elevates me to the top of his shit list.''

''You already own that space.''

''The family.'' He sat brooding for a moment. ''Eventually it does itself in. It grows too big. It gets out of one man's control. Italo can't run all those companies. It's too much for him and he already knows it.''

''Thank you,'' Garnet said as the applause died down. ''While the Foundation has been kind enough to award our bank for its support of environmental issues, I've had the chance to watch the work of its satellite organization, the Education Research Fellowship.'' She stopped and sipped at her water for a moment. ''I've heard people wonder what education has to do with the Foundation's main commitment to protecting the environment.'' She gazed out at them and, Charley saw, they all seemed to draw closer to her. He supposed they always would. And so would he.

''To explain that we must face the fact that we really *are* a democracy. We really *do* get the man we want in the White House. The world wonders why we keep electing, by landslide majorities, such an odd and self-defeating assortment of ex-spies and former movie actors.''

The audience stirred. Figuring them as moneyed folk, Charley mused, they had to be largely GOP supporters. Throwing some of her own pet peeves at this crowd was probably suicidal for Garnet. It was the mistake a well-loved person made, thinking that everyone's regard for her would automatically extend to her opinions as well.

"The answer is what's happened to our electorate. It's our guiltiest secret: we have produced three generations of teachers who have grown increasingly more ignorant and less competent to teach." The hall was bustling with whispers now. "The toughest part of the problem is that neither these teachers, nor the unwitting ignoramuses they turn out, have any notion how uneducated they are. These are not stupid people!" Her voice rose. "These are misinformed, uninformed, mentally lazy, inarticulate people. They are the voters of America." Mutterings now. "No one senses this more keenly than they do. Will the mass media ever treat them as adults? Will the political parties ever trust them to choose a candidate on the issues, not homilies that sanctify greed?

"It's as if all of us were in a very leaky boat. None of us dares rock it. If any of you wonder how fads sweep into government the least qualified and most corrupt people, how foolish enthusiasms like oat bran, the death penalty or recycled toilet tissue masquerade as real issues . . . then you understand why the Education Research Fellowship's work is vital to saving our environment. Thank you."

Some hard-line Garnet fans began applauding. It grew to a sort of grudging halfway level. A few more GOP supporters joined in because it was the sociable thing to do. The increased sound level heartened a few crypto-supporters too afraid to expose their feelings. The overall American feeling that effort should be applauded finally produced what sounded a lot like an enthusiastic response. Whether it was for what she said, or the charismatic way she looked while saying it, Charley didn't know. And he was too proud of her to care.

And he realized, in America as long as you looked good, what else mattered?

Overhead a wintry sun shone coldly. Adjusting the back bows of her hairbun and kimono, a black waitress dressed in Japanese geisha garb placed tall Cokes, crammed with ice, in front of two elderly visitors to Manhattan. They glanced around them at the manicured jungle that spoke of tropical heat and, despite winter's chill, began sipping their frigid drinks.

"Whoof," the man said. "These New Yorkers are sure crazy."

"Amen," said Lenore Ricci as she happened to walk past.

A mendacious quirk in Manhattan's zoning ordinances, meant to control the overweening altitude of office buildings that hide the sun, had made it possible to build even higher by donating lower floors to a kind of God's Barbecue Pit. Manhattan had several of these glazed lanai, once described by an architectural critic as "a mafia funeral parlor in the Amazon," and Lenore Ricci knew most of them. It would have been one of her relatives who had built it.

Footloose in Manhattan, she had already had coffee in one such atrium, where immense bamboo trees, chopped live from their tropical homes, had been boxcarred north to die alongside Park Avenue. It now being the lunch hour, she was wandering in another synthetic patio among potted gingkos and dwarf figtrees while the December sun winked coldly down through a weatherproof glass roof. The ball of the sun, just visible in its low winter altitude, loomed a bleached-out ecru, like failed margarine.

Young Eugene—who had turned into a determined crawler—was old enough now to be left for a day with his nanny. Lenore was working hard to make this day's freedom meaningful. She had by now bought a suit and a blouse which, with several pairs of shoes, had cost Vince five thousand dollars. But she still felt there wasn't yet enough meaning to the day.

Flashguns began exploding in one corner of the Japanese-styled garden. An ambulatory flower, Lenore migrated toward the great bursts of pseudo-sun, meanwhile pondering her purchases. Five thousand was peanuts to Vince, she reminded herself. It represented sixty seconds of income from the 114 detox clinics he was operating coast to coast. He had bragged that the whole network was grossing three billion a year. Lenore had done the rest of the arithmetic herself.

A great poster as large as the twenty-four-sheet variety used on highway billboards had been erected against one

wall of the atrium. The poster represented a copy of Pam
Scarlette's new paperback called *Surviving the Century*.
A publisher of schlock bestsellers had suggested she expand her presidential award poster into a cartoon handbook for alcoholics, depressives, AIDS sufferers, battered
wives, rape and tobacco victims, sufferers from herpes
and penicillin-resistant social diseases, heroin and cocaine addicts and even a stop-press chapter on handling
the up-and-coming wonder drugs: "ice" from Hawaii,
"moonrock" from the Philippines and "MegaMAO" on
every urban American streetcorner.

"And now . . . h-e-re's Pam!" The TV camera lights
bore down on her. Lenore stood in the background, feeling proud. Never mind that the original poster and this
book were speaking out of both sides of their face. Never
mind that the impetus had been Vince's. Lenore knew
that kind of reality never counted, only the glamour of
how it looked.

God, Pam looked great. She was ten years' Lenore's
senior but her anorexic new body, her back-swept shock
of coal-black hair, chopped short in the rear, gave her
the punk hustler look. In short, a very now, very envia-
ble, woman.

Afterwards they embraced and decided on a quick
lunch in the lanai. Her publisher, one of those formidably
blond Manhattan magnates who singlehandedly keeps
Chanel in business, took a fast glass of Perrier with them
before running on. "Hi, I'm Imogen Raspe. We're devoting ten percent of our profits on Pam's book to charity."

"Does that cool IRS?" Lenore asked.

Imogen Raspe got to her feet, smiling with such power
that the winter sunlight etched each of her capped teeth
on the retina of an onlooker. "You two must have gobs
to discuss. Bye."

Pam watched her leave. "Great gal," she said, toying
with a small plate on which some raw vegetables, cut
fine, had been mingled with four slivers of smoked
chicken the size of pencil shavings.

"I was standing there, so proud," Lenore enthused.
"Proud for you. Proud to be a Ricci. It's a great family.
I know us Cianflones are only cousins, but—"

"But, hey, you *produced* a Ricci. That little Eugene must really be something."

"Active." Lenore decided not to amplify the thought.

"Like his Dad," Pam suggested.

Lenore considered this objectively, with her more focussed knowledge of the boy's paternity, and decided to agree. "You bet."

"Everybody was so proud when you conceived," Pam went on. Her voice was very low, almost a cello note. It rarely rose in pitch but often seemed to plumb darker, richer depths. Her publisher, the Raspe woman, had an even lower voice which Lenore suddenly realized Pam was striving to match. "You really proved what a winner you are. I know how crazy Vince was for a child."

Lenore's smile was slightly crooked. "The whole family knows about that."

"Frankly," Pam said, "and I hope you don't think this is being too frank, a lot of us wondered if he *could* have a child. I mean, Vince has been some wild fella, you know."

Lenore thought for a moment. "Does that affect the semen?"

"So they say." Pam's giggle had such a bass quality to it that people at nearby tables looked up. "Also, you know the kind of kinky tricks men get up to. I imagine . . ." She paused, delicately, and when she spoke again her voice was a downdropping chord of agonized pleasure.

"Imogen gives me all the inside stuff on kinky sex, head jobs, buggering. If you could believe her, men take one look at her and collapse at her feet, ready for slavery."

"Vince doesn't do that."

"Not with you," Pam pointed out.

An odd silence settled between them, as if Pam had spoken out of personal knowledge. "Now that you're Eugene's mamma, all Vince wants is a second son. There's only one receptacle for that. Giving head won't do it."

This time her giggle and Lenore's were a double bass cadenza beneath a sharp oboe passage. What it meant to Pam, Lenore didn't yet know. What it meant to her was that Pam was on a fishing expedition. She was trolling the waters for information on Vince's sexual preferences. How many reasons could there be for that?

"From whom," Lenore asked in a mock prim voice, "would I get head, I ask you? From sex manuals and magazine articles. From Vince, never."

"There's always somebody. You're a very attractive woman, Lenore. I work with models all the time, actresses. Men get some of the raunchiest fantasies about beautiful women. Imogen, who thinks of herself as hot stuff, showed me letters she gets, all the things men offer to do for her. There isn't anything too filthy for them. You begin to wonder about men's sanity, when they go ape over a woman. You have that same quality, piccola cugina."

"But no offers to go down on me."

"Just goes to show how stupid men are."

"Or afraid to mess around with Vince Ricci's wife."

"I know. I know. Cowards."

Lenore got the feeling that she had been cast as the soloist, to which end Pam was providing those little runs, chords and single throbbing notes by which the cello filled out a melody, those touches of bass harmony that trembled just beneath her own notes. High time for a shrill one.

"I'm surprised Vince never came on to you, Pam."

Pam's bright, strongly made-up eyes bulged very slightly as she considered her smoked chicken salad. The brown-red highlights on her cheekbones grew faintly darker. She sent her fingertips quickly backward through her short-cut schoolboy pompadour. "Oh, of course," she went on with the smooth mesh of an automatic clutch, "but that was a long time ago."

"When he was married the first time?"

"Before."

"When he was romancing Stefi?"

Pam frowned. It put ageing verticals between her eyebrows that Lenore was sure she would hate to see. "Was he? My God, who hasn't that lady put out for?"

"But, like they say," Lenore responded, "all in the family. The latest gossip is her Kerry and Charley's Winfield."

"But—! That's—!"

Lenore saw that she had finally gotten past Pam's all-purpose, heavy-duty skin of sophistication. "Everybody wonders," Lenore told her. "Stefi has never told anybody who the father was."

Pam dodged sideways into humor. "Could even have been Vince who sired those twins."

"No way." The words were out before Lenore realized. Anything else she said wouldn't help matters much. She began eating her salad.

"So." Pam looked around the huge, leafy space with a kind of proprietary air. "Stefi will never tell who the father is. I don't blame her." She laid her cool hand on Lenore's. "Or you."

The law offices of Hegarty & Krebs seemed deserted. There was no receptionist at the desk. It was five o'clock by the time Lenore walked in, during which time Vince's budget had been tapped for another three thousand.

Lenore hadn't visited for some time now, little Eugene being so demanding. She supposed Eileen's Benjamin, born two days after Eugene, was another demander. Coming from a large family, Lenore understood that all babies demanded but a special few had mastered the knack of driving you insane with their demands.

"Hullo?" Lenore's four-inch heels clacked down the corridor. She could see Eileen's office at the far end. The door was open and the office was empty. She knocked on Margaret Krebs' door. "Yoohoo." She swung the door open to another empty office.

"She's in court," Winfield said behind her.

Lenore wheeled around, huge eyes wide. "Buona sera. Come stai?"

They pecked each other's cheek. Winfield, who towered over her, extended her hand, palm down, fingers spread, and rocked it from side to side. "Bene. E tu?"

Lenore's mouth opened wide to emit a cackle. "You can't talk Wop worth shit. I have to give you lessons. E tu isn't A-2. Listen, who died around here? It's like a morgue."

"Not like. It is a morgue. We had to fire Betty and Delores. Eileen can only afford a mother's helper part time, so she's only here part time. Margaret handles the court appearances. I do the briefs and type them myself."

"I thought you guys had plenty of clients."

"We do. But our cash flow has dried up. We're half paralyzed." Winfield led her back to her room and sat Lenore down across from her. "I can't tell you how much time Eileen has to spend fending off Buzz's creditors, setting up a chapter eleven bankruptcy or whatever she's working out for him."

"No-good bastard."

"Time she's been devoting to this AIDS case. She and I were supposed to be out there finding more Ricci-connected hookers. We have a few. We were going to put together a kind of class-action affair and dump it on the DA's desk."

"Instead of which she's bailing out Buzz?"

"And I'm typing briefs. Half paralyzed."

"While Buzz bums around with Vince, losing still more."

"Vince is his biggest creditor. But Vince isn't calling his notes due because Buzz is making Vince so rich it's indecent."

"At the casinos or the detox centers."

Winfield sat back and put her long legs on her desk. "When the principals are away, I get to put my feet up. Go ahead, you do the same."

"Too short. Listen, I want to invite everyone for a Christmas party, you, your Dad, Stefi and her twins, Buzz and Eileen and your sister, Bunny. My mother, some of my sisters and their kids. That lets the three little boys raise hell and get acquainted."

"A ghastly mistake," Winfield responded the instant she stopped speaking. "First of all, Bunny is so spooked by the responsibility of raising the future King Leo that she refuses to leave him alone more than five minutes at a time. Second, there is no way, at such close range, that Vince will not finally understand that the woman he knows as Mrs. Eiler is also the ballbusting Eileen Hegarty."

"It'd give him a real heart attack, knowing how much she actually knows about his operation through that no-good, Buzz."

Outside the windows, traffic began to hoot at some obstacle that had developed. In the silence of the deserted office, the horns reverberated without competition from typewriters or copying machines.

Winfield shook her head. "Eileen had one hell of a time getting their credit cards shifted into her own name. Some of the companies wouldn't do it. They'd rather have a male deadbeat. As for a party, too risky."

"Vince won't be there."

Winfield sat forward. "How do you know?"

"Vince will be giving it to some big-boobed bimbo in Agadir or Monaco or Grotteria or the Bahamas or if he can't get out of the country, Atlantic City. He's not choosy where he picks up his AIDS from."

"I'm sure he takes the usual precautions."

"Not with me. I get pronged bare-assed naked every time."

"You? But you're not a fuck. You're a madonna. You produce holy infants. It's you the Pope told Vince to poke and keep poking."

Lenore's cackle echoed through the empty office. "I am the victim of my own—" She stopped and switched subjects so fast Winfield almost didn't notice. "What's happened with the idea of including Vince in that lawsuit?"

"Thanks to Buzz, Eileen has her hands full with other matters. Two of our hookers just died. We only have nine now and a couple of them are in bad shape, too. It's taken the heart out of Eileen. That and the fact that she knows she hasn't got a winner yet. Lots of publicity, but she'll lose."

"And Vince wins? Hey! He gives me a household budget now that I'm the mother of Eugene. He doesn't argue about a cent. I can subsidize you guys out of petty cash! A few cees a week? Five? Pay for a typist or two?"

Winfield sat there, dumbfounded. "You'd pay us to take Vince to court?"

"Winfield." Lenore dipped into her bag and brought out a check book. "Or maybe cash is safer?"

She laughed but Winfield didn't. Instead the tall young woman slowly removed her feet from her desk and sat forward, staring at her. "I have had something in mind to ask you for a while. When I told it to Eileen, she said never, never ask you. She said it was too much to ask of anyone." Once again the horns outside punctuated the

unnatural quiet of the office, like clarions heralding the
arrival of something unusual. Winfield stood up. "I have
to take some papers over to Eileen's house. Have you got
half an hour to come with me?"

Lenore got to her feet. "What's the thing you want to
ask me?"

"Eileen has to do the asking. It's her decision. You
and I have to talk her into it."

"Is this something to do with nailing Vince?" Lenore
demanded.

"It's everything to do with it."

"Let's go!"

Fifty-One

The moment Winfield brought her to Eileen's apartment
and Lenore saw Benjamin J. Eiler, Jr., for the first time,
she realized it would be suicidal to invite the Eilers to a
Christmas party where the two baby boys would meet.

Benjy and her Eugene had the same short, pudgy
bodies, the same broad faces, the same sandy hair. Could
anybody miss their resemblance to Buzz? Neither she nor
Eileen had had the time to bring the two boys together.
Now that both were six months old, there would be no
more excuses.

But Lenore prized her friendship with Eileen above all
others. Like many an Italo-American, her circle of
"friends" were really her own kin. To have struck up a
close, successful friendship with someone as distinguished
and respected as Eileen gave Lenore much-needed self-
confidence.

The distinguished Ms. Hegarty had poked her left nipple
in Benjy's eager wet mouth. He went to work emptying her
breast. "I guess I should've gone for the whole thing," Lenore mused, slowly sipping a glass of white wine. "But I
weaned Eugene to bottles. Vince has such a thing about big
tits. Yours look super."

"It's temporary," Eileen said. She seemed distracted

and kept glancing from Lenore to Winfield, as if silently asking the purpose of the surprise visit.

Winfield took the baby from her after a while, burped him with brisk professionalism and laid him face down in his crib, where he soon fell asleep. "Nice timing, kid," she said, walking back into the big living room. Eileen hadn't had a chance to clear up the usual litter, nor had the mother's helper, who was actually a seventeen-year-old cousin of Margaret Krebs.

Buzz Eiler's college rowing oars, crossed, decorated one wall. Otherwise there was no trace of him in the apartment. Winfield sat under a Daumier drawing of a fat French lawyer accepting a sheaf of franc notes from an extremely emaciated client. "Cause and Effect" was the caption.

She watched the two petite, dark-haired women and wondered as she often did what life would have been like for her at five-one instead of her full height of six feet. First of all Kerry would never have seen her in action against Chapin's or Brierly's basketball squad. Second . . .

Eileen and Lenore had settled into a low-pitched threnody of complaints concerning both of their husbands. "Where *is* Buzz tonight?" Winfield cut in.

"Where? Actually haven't seen the celebrated Dr. Eiler in weeks."

"Doesn't he come home for clean socks?"

Instead of making her laugh, the remark caused Eileen's face to screw up. She started to cry. "Oh, God, Eileen!" Winfield exclaimed. "I'm sorry. I didn't—"

"You couldn't know." She wiped her tears away with a corner of Benjy's feeding bib. "Until recently, that was the only time I saw him, when he ran out of shirts or underwear. But he's obviously got a stash somewhere else."

"Eileen," Lenore said, "this is your chance. Have the locks changed."

Perversely, this sent Eileen into a fit of laughter. Lenore frowned and turned to Winfield. "This girl is half off her rocker. What about popping the question?"

Eileen dried her eyes a second time. "What question?"

"You remember?" Winfield asked. "Months ago? I

said there was something Lenore could do? Something to break this AIDS case wide open? And you—.''

"Forget it," Eileen interrupted brusquely. Her eyes grew brooding and sullen.

"Listen!" Lenore burst out. "Is one of you going to tell me?"

"This lady has offered to find hundreds of dollars a week for our office expenses," Winfield said. "If she feels that strongly, why not give her a chance at something a lot more important than money?"

Eileen's face had closed down, its sharp-edged features congealing like ice. "These are marriages we're talking about, Winfield. Bad marriages? OK; Lenore and I are Catholics married to a pair of shits. But they are the fathers of our sons. Right, we've dropped into a Papal trap as surely as if a cage had been slammed down on us. But if we did what you suggest, we couldn't live with it."

"Oh. I see." Winfield nodded politely. "They can murder every tenet of the marriage ceremony. They can bankrupt the family. They can close down your office and all the cases you're trying to represent. They can destroy our career. And Margaret's. They can fuck their balls off with other women. But you two saints are just going to turn the other cheek. I get it."

None of them spoke for a long time. In the other room they heard Benjy mutter something and fall silent again.

Lenore stared down into her wine. "I want to hear it," she said then. "I want to know what I could do to Vince that is too horrible for you to ask me."

"Look, Lenore," Eileen began.

"I want to know," she reiterated. "I had lunch today with my dear cousin Pam. She's fucking Vince. I don't care. She deserves whatever punishment she gets. That's not what sticks in my throat. It's phony Mr. Ricci Medical Center, hooking a whole generation and getting awards from *the President* for it. That cunt, Pam, putting her name to a book about how to live with all the drugs Vince peddles that Buzz invents. All the diseases I'm always afraid Vince brings home to me. It's already sold two zillion copies and it isn't even out yet. I bought a copy. She's got a blurb from *the President* of the Whole Fucking United States of America. It sticks in my throat till I could throw up. Vince can have Pam. She can have Vince. But how do they both rate *the President of the United States*?''

This time the silence lasted much longer. Finally, Eileen folded Benjy's spit-up bib, put it away and nodded to Winfield. ''Tell her.''

Winfield got up and began pacing. She walked as far as the door to the terrace, turned and walked back to Lenore. Somebody her height created a definite draft as she questioned the witness. ''Tell me, first, Lenore, how often you've visited all the various luxurious and expensive resorts of Ricci Entertainment, Inc.?''

''Like once. Christmas last year. Eileen and I still weren't showing much yet. Grotteria.''

''Before then?''

''Never. Vince hates me anywhere around where he works.''

''But since Eugene arrived?''

''Ah, that's another story,'' Lenore explained. ''He likes the idea of the kid visiting him. He's asked me twice now to bring the kid down to the Bahamas. I've stalled. Eugene's too young for all that travel.''

''But you're now *persona grata* in Vince's empire.''

''Is that Italian or Latin?''

''Speed it up, Counsellor,'' Eileen urged.

''So, in the next month or two you could get to two or three of Vince's resorts on the pretext of escaping a Manhattan winter?''

''Sure.''

''No problems?'' Winfield pressed her.

''In the name of Eugene, I can write my own ticket.''

Winfield turned to Eileen. ''Suppose she does Atlantic City, Grand Bahama and Monaco? Just those three?''

''Finish telling her the whole idea.''

Winfield picked up her attaché case and removed something from a buttoned flap. She handed it to Lenore. ''What do you see? Trick question.''

Lenore fingered the pale blue matchbook. It advertised a brand of cigarettes. She turned it over several times, opened it, stared at the matches. ''It's a little too thick, right? What is it, a bug?''

Winfield's smile was broad. ''Eileen, did I tell you? This girl is a natural.''

"You mean?" Lenore brandished the matchbook. "One of these in his desk drawer, in each of his resort offices? Vince doesn't smoke. A matchbook could stay there forever. What's the range? Are these matches real?"

"Yes. They can be used as matches. The range is about a hundred yards. As long as you're there, you can monitor and record it. But when you move on we have to find someone else."

"And meanwhile," Lenore said, "we're hearing everything he says?"

"It's good for three months."

"During which he may never mention anything," Eileen pointed out, "relating to our case, that is. Be prepared for failure."

Lenore tucked the listening device into the front of her blouse, wedging it under the edge of her bra. "Failure? Look, I'm wired. Let me start asking him questions tonight."

"And end up in the family plot next to the previous Mrs. Vince Ricci?" Winfield paced back toward the terrace doors.

"My dear," said Lenore in a haughty tone, "you are not speaking to any old Mrs. Vince Ricci. You are speaking to the mother of the Holy Infant." She grinned at them both. But when she looked at Eileen, she saw that she could never, never tell her the truth about Eugene. Babies changed appearance all the time. Maybe the two boys would stop looking like twins. Meanwhile, to be frank with Eileen would be to destroy the one friend she had come to love.

"Give me," she added, "as many of these cute little bugs as you have."

Fifty-Two

The colorful French magazine, all lithe legs and bare buttocks, hit the stands in Monte Carlo on a Monday morning. It was sold out before lunch. Sitting beside the pool Vince Ricci leafed through its cover story with a feline smirk of satisfaction.

Back in the 1970s, before the murder of Princess Grace, when Monaco was undergoing a tremendous property boom, someone inside the gambling syndicate, the Société des Bains de Mer, opened a franchise for the American hotel group, Loews. This gave the Société new volume without spending money on new facilities. People thought the Société very clever.

At the start of the 1990s, when another franchise was issued, this one to Ricci Entertainments, Inc., people thought the Société mad.

Monegasques, who had by then had a bellyful of mafia control, brutally re-established after Princess Grace was terminated, wondered in their cynical Mediterranean way why the Honored Society even bothered to apply for its own franchise, since its people now operated all the gambling anyway. But they reckoned without Vince Ricci, whose ideas of true resort glitz were so far ahead of competition as to blind the world.

The hanging gardens, for instance, the cantilevered Olympic-sized pool beside which he now lounged, the restaurant which had already won its first Michelin star, the helicopter ferry between the Cote d'Azur Airport at Nice and the Ricci landing pad that jutted out above the harbor. This nicely calculated mixture of sheer excess and unbelievable ostentation had made Le Refuge even more fashionable a watering hole than Vince's pilot scheme on Grotteria. On the whole Mediterranean coast, where drugs from simple hash to complex cocaine/heroin moonrock were freely available, Le Refuge alone offered trendy, powerful MegaMAO. It was, in a real sense, a proprietary drug.

Perhaps the greatest mark of Le Refuge's success was when one of the weekly French color magazines had sent a team of sociologists and psychologists to investigate the "internal contradictions of the haute bourgeoisie, namely, for people who have everything, why this need for chemical escape?"

It spoke authoritatively of Vince's own sense of control that he cooperated fully with the investigation, made the eminent Dr. Eiler available for scientific background and then reaped today's cover story. It would create a demand that Le Refuge, fully booked for a year ahead, would find hard to meet.

"The New Hedonism. 21st Century Plumage . . . Now!"

"Le Refuge . . . the Naked Shape of Things to Come."

Vince thumbed slowly through the story with the help of Buzz's shaky command of French. "Here it is," the doctor said, "in the caption of the three models. I didn't give them this idea. They made it up. Here . . . 'le MegaMAO rehausse le vigueur sexuelle.' Meaning MegaMAO recharges your balls."

"It's true, Buzz. I go all night on it."

"You promised me never to get hooked."

"I can take it or leave it," Vince assured him.

"You shit can. MegaMAO is totally habituating. I warned you at the beginning." Buzz stopped, his attention distracted by two paunchy gentlemen with two tall young women in very high heels and not much else. They clattered along the far side of the pool in the wake of their protectors' cigar smoke.

"Two of yours?" Buzz wondered.

"Imports." Vince retrieved the magazine. "Recharges your balls, huh?"

"Something like that. Vince? MegaMAO is the ultimate enhancer of life. Nothing is ever dull again. You take it and you're Emperor of the Universe. That's why it's habituating. Its effect is so precisely calculated that—"

"Can the sermon."

"How long have you been on MegaMAO?"

Vince turned over on his stomach, as if to dodge any more such questions. His nearly naked body, bronzed under a slick layer of sun block, lay absolutely flat, face elevated slightly by a doughnut-shaped pillow, short black curls glistening. "Few months. Hey, Buzz, my mother you ain't. No sermons."

"No sermons. No sermons." Buzz's voice had gone dreamy. He lay on his back, his fair complexion reddening in the strong sunlight they were enjoying this close to Christmas.

It was so long since he'd functioned as a real doctor that he found the grooves in his brain clogged with disuse: symptoms, behavior, appearance. He squinted against the sun as he tried to unscramble what observations he could remember of Vince these last months. Lethargy? He couldn't remember a time when the hyperactive Vince was content to lie in the sun half a day, somnolent, quiescent. A winter sun at that, not the all-smothering furnace of summer.

A rare opportunity, Buzz realized, for the creator of MegaMAO to study its side effects. He eyed Vince warily. "Do you ever go without it for a while?"

"A few days."

"Any withdrawal symptoms?"

"Buzz off."

"I suppose . . ." Buzz's voice went dreamier with scientific speculation. "I mean, I suppose if you have an unlimited supply you wouldn't know a withdrawal symptom if it came up and bit your nose."

"Will you can it?"

"Just wondering . . ." Buzz sighed and rolled over on his stomach. "I mean, it's been a long time since I had a MegaMAO high, back when Tony and I were developing it. It's something you never forget. I wonder . . ."

"Can it or I'll break off your arm and shove it up your ass."

"Hey."

Vince's eyes blazed as he stared in menace at his fellow sunbather. Curled up from the waist and twisted sideways as if to strike, his whole body quivered. His short-cropped curls vibrated as if electrified.

"One more word, stronzo!" His voice had gone high with . . . with fright? "One more word and I dump you over the edge to the rocks."

Between them fear flickered like a scorpion, tail lashing. The heat in Vince's eyes! Buzz held up his hands, palms out, in a silent shrug of capitulation.

He lay back and gave himself over to the sun. Whatever Vince wanted was okay with him. The past months had been hectic and harrowing. When he'd been black-balled from everyone's casinos, he had felt like a dying rat at the bottom of a deep shaft, no light, no air. Vince had rescued him. That gave him the right to act now like a cornered but poisonous animal.

Yet another MegaMAO side effect: unreasonable fear. The white schlera glaring all around the iris. The rictus snarl of the mouth. The baring of teeth. A flee-or-fight stance and, knowing Vince, he would always choose to fight.

Buzz entered that half sleep where the past pours in over the present. Vince had always been his pal. He had the right to a small shit-fit, after all. Buzz owed him that. He owed a lot everywhere. He owed Eileen most of all.

Anybody but Eileen would have had the cops after him, but it was only through her legal intervention that he was still able to circulate freely in society. This whole year seemed a fantasy, like Le Refuge, a place of horrifyingly seductive excess, in which real things like a wife, a son, a career, even self-respect, were ghostly shadows of a past. It was for this bad dream come true that Vince had saved him.

Suddenly, he was crying, softly, the tears running down his cheeks. "Hey," Vince said. "Sorry I sounded off like that. You know me."

"It's not you. It's Eileen. I've wrecked her life, Vince. I've ruined her."

"Is that a typical broad? The first thing they do is make you feel guilty."

"I *am* guilty. You . . . I never told you—"

"Spare the sob story, goombah. It's always the same. One more broad has got one more good guy feeling he's a bad guy. Forget her."

"You don't . . . I mean, she's got her own work that I've—"

"The only work broads have is collecting come. That's what they're on earth for. It's the only reason we let 'em collect all that guilt with it. Shit, I don't even let 'em do that."

"I envy you, Vince."

"Don't envy. Be a man, Buzz." He punched him so hard in the shoulder that Buzz winced. Then Vince settled back down for another snooze. Buzz's view of his savior was a mixture of gratitude and hatred. Here lay the man who had hooked him on gambling and helped him ruin Eileen's career. Who tied his fate to the fate of suspect detox centers, a masquerade for pushing MegaMAO. Here was his buddy, who would always be grateful for Lenore's conceiving a boy. Here was his mortal enemy, if Vince found out how the conception had been arranged. In short, here were two men lying in the sun, Buzz knew, whose lives had grown so close together that they could end up killing each other.

Strange that Vince, so strong against booze and tobacco, would fall to MegaMAO. But the new drug meant everything to him. To its growing army of addicts it gave power and peace, not for the usual rush of ten minutes, but for solid periods of time. But for Vince, the eternal businessman, it meant much more. It gave him his dream of being free from every source of supply, of being totally in command of the entire process, right down to street sale. It cut him loose to prey on every level of society. And now, in his veins, it was freeing his very soul.

With a network and a clientele so highly placed, by this time next year there might yet be a senator from MegaMAO, just as there was a senator from Boeing. Great corporate achievements required representation, too, if this was to be a true democracy.

'Your back is bright red!'' a woman screamed.

Buzz turned over and found himself staring up into the lovely face of Lenore Ricci. She wore no top, but seemed content to shield her small, naked breasts behind a small, naked boy of six months.

Vince turned over at the same time. "Jesus H. Christ!'' he exclaimed. "Who let you two in?''

"I got sick and tired of Manhattan snow, you bums. I figured Eugene deserved as good a Christmas as his old man.''

Vince sat up and reached for his son. "Hey! Big Eugene! It's Daddy. Give Daddy a kiss, you little gangster, you!''

Lenore smiled down on the two men. Watching her gave Buzz a stir. This woman had the power of life and death over him. And he had the same power over her. His head seemed to whirl abruptly, as if the pool had spun around. All remorse had gone, all regrets about Eileen, all self-pity over the wreckage of his own career. He watched Lenore slowly massage her breasts. In his lethargic state it took him a moment to realize that she was coming on to him in front of her own husband. Was she under some pressure to have a second baby? In which case . . .

"Eugene," Vince was cooing. He lay on his back, lifting the boy in the air and bringing him back down with a plump smack on his chest. "Hey, Eugene! Gimme a smile! That's it! That's it! Gimme another," he demanded, nuzzling the boy's tiny genitals, "or I'll bite your balls off."

Slowly, Lenore settled herself crosslegged on the mat between the two men. She watched Buzz's gaze move longingly from her toes up her calves and ankles to the tiny strip of bikini concealing her side-shaved pubic muff. Lenore opened her bag and withdrew a pack of cigarettes and a pale blue matchbook which she handed to Buzz.

"When'd you start smoking," her gynecologist inquired in a hurt tone. "You know it's bad for you," the inventor of MegaMAO added.

"Oh, I don't inhale," she assured him as he struck a match for her. She retrieved the matchbook and carefully, slowly blew smoke in both their eyes.

Fifty-Three

Dear Father,

I'm low. I haven't spoken with Bunny, nor seen her and little Leo, for so long I am sure he wouldn't know me. If we met, would *you* know me?

There is a new me, as you can see from the essay that follows. In some ways I have changed completely. I want to show you how complete the change is.

Just as people make a business of committing crimes, other people make a business of protecting criminals. Governments rise to power in part on slogans about stamping out crime. Billions a year are squandered but all crime does is grow in scope and power.

With it, the size of the law-enforcement establishment—the police, the Army, the secret police, the prison staffs, the parole personnel, the courts, the juvenile centers—balloons out of all proportion to the actual rise in the crime rate. Why?

Basic collusion. Both sides have joined to create a true growth industry.

Crime isn't totally risk-free—what is?—but from its grotesquely immense profits a percentage is tithed to the government. Nothing in this world is perfect. There will always be a few honest congressmen, cops and commissioners. Accidents happen. But the rule is this: by and large everyone gets a piece of the action.

America is well past the point of no return to the old demarcation between law and lawless. When it comes to the war against crime, as in Vietnam, America has lost. We see the defeat all around us. It is bearable only with the help of drugs. It's silly, under such circumstances, to complain about crooked cops. Where there are no standards, who's to say what's crooked and what isn't?

As some ancient skeptic once said—I believe he was talking about Prohibition—"where everybody's guilty, nobody's guilty."

You have been very patient. But I am aware that your lack of contact with me indicates your displeasure at my failure to respond. Very well. I have responded, and considerably before my deadline, in the affirmative.

Yes. Yes, I am ready to take my family responsibilities seriously. Yes, both of my families. It was all a matter of motivation. Conflicting motivations between my urge to make my name in journalism . . . but that's a thing of the past.

Events have hurtled ahead. New responsibilities have emerged, supplying new motivation. I long to be with Bunny and Leo. I long to play a part in your business affairs. Yes! Yes!

Please, Father. Mother tells me there is an untenanted cottage next to the one she shares with Bunny and Leo. She can reserve it. Say the word, either to her or to me. We needn't wait for March. What about Christmas together!

With my fondest affection,

* * *

If Winfield hadn't been working late, typing up affidavits, Bunny wouldn't have reached her by telephone. The younger sister's grasp of time, never very strong, had grown even hazier in the life of the tropics.

". . . Mangoes and breadfruit and yummy organic goodies," she was saying.

"Which you have to prepare yourself," Winfield pointed out. "You and Nicole spend most of the day on the *hausfrau* bit."

"We love it."

Winfield paused. Something basic was happening to her sister's personality, never more firmly pinned in place than her sense of time. "You like the kitchen-and-apron routine?"

"We love it."

"Stop saying we. Nicole loves it."

"We love it," Bunny repeated. "What're your days like? Pressure and stress and over-achievement?"

"Nothing compared to gestating a baby. And waiting on him hand and foot."

"We love it, Winfield." Her voice had grown mulish. "We're trying to make a home here. Nicole and Nikki have lived all over. Shan spends most of his life on jets. We're trying to pull this together, get the men focussed on it as a real family base."

Her older sister paused again, recognizing a brick wall when she'd been shown one. "Has Nikki knuckled under? Is that what's happened?"

"Do you have to use that word? He's finally accepted his responsibilities."

"We *love* it," Winfield snapped in a mocking voice.

'Nikki and his father are the problem. If you think either one of them can be tied down to a base, you don't know Asian peacocks. But they can be teased into it. In tandem, sort of. If one sees the other inch forward, he inches forward. I should think," Bunny added sniffly, "coming from a broken home, we would both appreciate what it means to have a solid base."

Winfield sighed. Her own dingaling baby sister had outmaneuvered her. "OK, you're right. More power to you."

This abject surrender had the effect of shifting Bunny's

attention away from her own navel. "How's the big case going?"

"Stuck. Eileen's financial problems have pinched us down to worrying about paying the rent. To buy type-writer ribbons we have an anonymous angel, but there is no money for grand legal adventures. Morale around here is about as low as it can get."

"You need a break. We've rented the cottage next door. There's plenty of room."

Eileen appeared in Winfield's doorway, looking upset. "Who is that you're talking to?"

"Bunny." The two women eyed each other. Eileen's appearance was an artlessly disheveled variation on Sandbox-Attendant, her black hair yanked back in a rubber band that had come loose.

"Winfield?" Bunny asked plaintively. "You there?"

"Yes. I've got to sign off. Thanks for the call."

"Remember, you're always welcome."

"Not sure that was wise," Eileen began once the phone had been hung up. "That girl is not always discreet."

"I didn't tell her much. What brings you here this late? How'd you unload Benjy?"

"I didn't. He's asleep in his stroller behind my desk. Winfield, I don't think we can keep this office going much longer."

"I was afraid of that."

"Lenore's money is a Godsend, but she can't keep raiding her household budget forever. Vince will even-tually notice. And you have to admit the bugging strategy is a huge gamble gone sour."

"We should start getting results pretty soon."

"Not my idea," Eileen said, "of a firm base on which to keep a law office going. It's like betting on one of B-buzz's b-blackjack deals." She burst into tears.

As if agreeing, from the other room, Benjy Eiler awoke and began crying, too.

Fifty-Four

"Anybody who schedules his Christmas in Atlantic City," Imogen Raspe said, "automatically earns a World Class Death-Wish citation."

She and Pam Scarlette sat in the lounge of one of Vince Ricci's better hotels and finished their second Planter's Punch, a drink with such a delayed kick that users often didn't feel it till their fifth. Pam, with her svelte punk appearance, contrasted brilliantly with Imogen's bleached-Swedish-wood look.

The publisher's middle-class Jewish parents had bought her a B.A. and M.A. in American Literature, plus doctoral work at Wittenberg, like Hamlet. There she met and married the neo-Nazi poet Udo Raspe from whom she separated within a year. Her separation from literature took longer.

"Actually, I can only spend tonight with you and your gorgeous mafia lover," Imogen was saying in her basso growl. "I have a serious heavyweight New Year's Eve party to supervise back home. So to business, lovey. What's your next bestseller? Incest? Child abuse? Do mafiosi make lousy lovers? My life in the Famiglia Ricci?"

"I thought . . ." Pam's dark, low voice sounded like a trombone after two Planter's Punches. "What about cannibalism?"

"Old hat."

"Come on."

"An Imogen Raspe book never treads in the same schlock as its competitors. My readers demand new schlock, fresh schlock, or freshly dressed schlock." She finished the long drink and signaled the lounge waiter with two fingers. "You didn't realize you had signed a pact with Beelzebub."

"What about satanism?"

"*Ancien chapeau.*" Imogen's expensive power suit, her Hermes carefully slung off shoulder, indicated even to the hapless hayseeds who filed through Atlantic City pushing their lives into slots, that here was one of that élite breed of old Manhattan mammas who managed most of the city's fashion, advertising and publishing.

"Child abuse?" Pam recalled. "I wouldn't know where to begin. My father used to cuddle me, of course. But he—"

"Dear child," Imogen honked, "now that I've positioned you in the market, your personal expertise doesn't matter. Your next five books are guaranteed runaway blockbusters. Ideas! There hasn't been anything on aphrodisiacs lately. Illustrated profusely. They tell me MegaMAO is a real turn-on."

"They tell you right," Vince said, coming up behind Imogen and cupping his hands over her monster 44-DD shoulder pads. "You ready for a personal demonstration?"

"Not in front of my favorite author."

"Listen," Vince said, "I jetted over from Monte just to meet Pam's fabuloso publisher. I expected one of those dried-up librarian types. Instead . . ."

"Instead you find yourself suggesting a *menage á trois*, enhanced chemically by—" Imogen's deep drawl stopped short. "Got it!"

"Pardon?"

"*The Pam Scarlette Book of Bisexual and Bizarre Behavior!* One hundred ways for three to reach heaven glued into a single squirming lump. The book that gives bondage a good name, frottage a strong boost and daisy chains a rave. 'Favorite Fantasies for Major Masturbation.' " Her small brown eyes slitted as her voice rolled on: "The sin that speaks its name from the penthouse-tops. The sure cure for male impotence and female frigidity. Gives new meaning to bed-wetting. If variety is the spice of life, meet Miss Cayenne Pepper. Buggery made simple in three easy—"

"Listen," Vince cut in with brutal joy, "it smells like money!"

The nearest Caribbean island to mainland U.S.A. is either Bimini or Grand Bahama. Power boats from West Palm Beach make the brief crossing routinely. They usually end up at the Miramar-Athenee in Lucaya on Grand Bahama. But some come around the northwest point of land called West End and speed along a lovely stretch of wooded beachland where impressive mansions and secluded cottages are barely visible in their private splendor.

None of these boats is as fast as the airplanes that make the crossing. But, among the power boats, probably the fastest is Li Brothers' fifty-footer, powered by twin Volvo marine engines providing quiet turbine-assisted water-jet propulsion. The craft is called the *Robert E. Li,* after one of the brothers killed in a running gunfight last year with the Coast Guard. Shan Lao, using the name Henry Shiu, always had first call on the boat, as now. He was an honored benefactor of the Li Brothers' many enterprises in these waters and his New York man, Mr. Choy, was a concealed partner.

"Not enough has been made," Shan once told Barton Li, "of the Chinese of our planet. Hard-working, reverent of family values, good citizens of a hundred countries but loyal always to the traditions of their motherland. Take your family, for example," he reminded Barton. "What great work you have accomplished, first for yourself, then for your adopted land and, in the long run, for China. You are a resource as yet untapped by any Chinese investor but me. I am remedying that, all over the world."

"Right on!" Barton enthused.

He was at the wheel when the power boat landed Shan Lao on Grand Bahama on December 24. The small dock served a cottage his wife Nicole had rented for his grandson Leo. Nicole, in a sleek cheongsam skirt split up the side, was waiting on the dock, waving to the oncoming boat.

Shan disembarked, dressed still in his stiff banker's dark gray, his protuberant eyes swiveling from side to side, absorbing information in great swoops. Barton Li off-loaded two suitcases and a large wrapped package with the "chop" logo of a prominent Tokyo department store on its wrapping paper.

"Greetings, my dear." They embraced, then turned to wave as the boat shot off. The *Robert E. Li* left behind it a plume like a rooster's tail as it returned to West Palm Beach.

"You are thinner," Nicole said.

"I am thinner," Shan agreed. "My schedule has been punishing this year." He glanced around. "A servant for the luggage?"

"We have no servants. I'm the cook and the cleaning lady. And," she added, picking up the Tokyo package, "the porter."

"Hello!" Bunny advanced toward the dock. She carried Leo in her arms. "Welcome to Palm Shadows!"

"Ah," Shan said in a discreet undertone. "How terribly tall she is."

"As Leo will be."

"And Nik?"

"He flies in today."

"Welcome!" Bunny said, coming up to them. "I'm sorry we haven't met before."

"That is soon cured," Shan said in his most cultivated Oxbridge accent, his huge eyes in his too-large head seeming to bulge. He ignored her outstretched hand and, instead, took Leo from her arms. He held him around the midriff, a fat baby who smiled a great deal. "Leo Shan," his grandfather murmured. "See the eyelids, my dear?"

He turned to Nicole. "Of all the genes we carry, this trait is the most irrepressible. The boy looks exactly as Nik did at this age." Still holding Leo he turned with solemn courtesy to Bunny. "Miss Richards, it is a conspicuous honor for this elderly person to be made the grandparent of such a jolly young boy by such an attractive and talented young woman. I can only count my Christmas here with you as already blessed by fate."

"My goodness," Bunny said as he lifted her hand and kissed it. "Nobody told me what a great flatterer you are."

"Of flattery the world has an oversupply," Shan pointed out. "I hope to make my approval of this young man, and you, more apparent than can mere words." He led off the parade, carrying the baby, followed by Nicole with the gift package and Bunny, silently recruited to carry both suitcases. They made their way along the pink sand of their private beach, through palms and a garden, to a frame cottage, shingled in cedar, with a large verandah overlooking the sea.

Shan Lao, Leo Shan in his arms, stood on the verandah and watched, in the distance, the plumed wake of the

Robert E. Li suddenly swerve landward. It drifted to
shore, letting off half a dozen lithe young Chinese dressed
in jeans and T-shirts. As they hopped off into the pleasant surf they held over their heads items wrapped in waterproof tarpaulins. The week before, Baxter Choy had
hired them from Barton Li for three days of bodyguard
duty while his boss, Shan Lao, was enjoying the Christian holiday fate had dealt him. During this vacation, Nik
would join them. And Shan would begin the fateful business of blooding his own son. Shan's Christmas might
well be blessed by fate, but there was no point in not
giving fate a hand.

The cough wouldn't go away. When they'd ditched the
helicopter, Kevin and Iris had picked up a virus no Brunei doctor could manage. Zio Italo had sent them both
to a sanitorium west of Tucson, Arizona, operated by
Richland Caring.

Where a finger of the Pacific reached up from Baja
California to the U.S. border, drug smugglers shipped
mexishit into Arizona east of Organ Pipe Cactus National
Monument, past tiny Indian villages like Chukuk Kuk
and Wahak Hotrontk, before redistribution to gateway
markets like Scottsdale and Phoenix. The same places
also attracted lung patients who were recovering. Kevin
arranged, on the first day the doctors let them out, for
Iris to shop in town while he met with her next protector.
She had mentioned a Hollywood screen test. If Ricci
clout meant anything, this man would get it for her.

The three of them met in the foyer of one of Scottsdale's glassed-in shopping malls, all green garlands, tin-
kling red-and-gold holiday ornaments and overstocked
franchises of nationally trademarked stores. On display
was enough merchandise to supply ten Scottsdales. Most
stores were empty of customers. At the far end of the
enclosed vista, refrigerated to Arctic levels, a Santa Claus
was entertaining kiddies on his lap even though their orders would have to be relayed to the North Pole by fax
to get them down the chimney tonight.

The talent recruiter was young, short and as straight-
sided as a garbage can on legs. His small face would
defeat any witness's attempt at identification—a sort of
. . . nose. Eyes were, uh, two. Hair was . . . there.

He glanced at Iris, looking quite elegant in the same flowered shift Kevin had pulled down over her body a month ago on Palawan after their sandalwood drenched evening of cold passion. She had already begun to refurbish herself with American makeup products that were capable of altering the look of her face. She had bought an entirely different perfume, more floral, and remembered never to swallow any.

A Muzak voice sang:

> *You better watch out.*
> *You better not cry.*
> *Better not pout.*
> *I'm telling you why:*
> *Santa Claus is comin' to town.*

The man couldn't seem to stop watching Iris. Finally he tore his glance away and grinned sheepishly at Kevin. "There's a car," he said in a vague way.

Kevin handed Iris his credit card. "Go for it," he murmured and sent her on her way to the nearest outlet. He turned back to the man. "Lead the way."

Slowly, the station wagon circled the area, pausing in huge parking lots, loafing past neon logos of American businesses. "That your girl?" the man asked after a while.

"Not after tomorrow when you take her to LA."

"Maybe do more than that."

"She's a solid kid," Kevin said. "We're giving her a good crack at Hollywood. She's got letters to half a dozen talent agents."

"She's special stuff, huh?"

"I owe her."

"So, hands off?"

Kevin frowned. "Am I her father? She's got smarts. You got smarts. Your spare time is no business of mine."

"You got it." Another thoughtful pause as the station wagon circled through its fourth parking lot. "It's a pleasure doing business with Zio Italo's nephew."

"Great-nephew." It reminded Kevin that this man was not a family member but a sort of franchisee of the family. From loudspeakers on masts:

You better watch out.
You better not cry.

Kevin did not like to do business with franchisees. All around him stood the franchise mall shops of I. Magnin, Burger Queen, Levi's, Sock Shop, Taco-Bell, JC Penney, names that, like Ricci, had made America great. If all you wanted was a pair of jeans and pizza, fine. But in a delicate matter like a career, doing business with a franchisee was not the same as doing business with a family member, even a remote cousin.

Kevin found himself hoping Iris would, nevertheless, make out all right. Knowing her, he felt she would.

Charley Richards poked the slumbering logs back into flame again. He stood in front of Stefi's fireplace, a glass of marsala in one hand. Normally he didn't drink the sweet, burned-flavor wine but he loved dunking the small cantucci di Prato in it, the crisp, double-baked, anise-and-almond cookies. Marsala turned them into chewy mouthfuls.

He smiled first at Winfield and then at Kerry. Both of them had opted for coffee in which to dunk their cantucci. Charley thought he knew what was coming, but he was wrong.

It had been Winfield's idea which she'd sprung on him the day before. "Aunt Stefi's invited me out there for Christmas Eve and since she's the only one of us with a proper fireplace and chimney, I said yes. I said I'd bring you."

Well, why not, Charley thought now. He'd invited Garnet to accompany him but she begged off without explanation. But he hadn't bargained on Winfield and Kerry as a couple. Until now they'd had the kind of cousinly relationship that consists of pecks at weddings.

He was the only one standing, Charley saw now, and this was a mistake. Stefi was curled up, as always, in a corner of the fireplace sofa with a duvet over her legs. The two young people sprawled on the floor, endless lengths of long legs and narrow torsos. Behind him the logs snapped and spat as flames shot higher. The backs of Charley's calves were growing uncomfortable. If this were going to get off the ground as a happy, family

Christmas, he'd have to sound the first fanfare. "Well," he said, raising his glass of marsala, "good health to us all."

They all sipped their drinks. They had no way of knowing that the marsala was from dead Lucca Certomá's grapes. Nor would they know that the vineyard was now under the absentee control of Mollo as a feature of agriturismo; elderly platinum-blond Scandinavians, retired machinists from Stuttgart and suet-cheeked burghers of Holland crowded eagerly at vendemmia time, paying money to be allowed to help with the more back-breaking pressing of grapes.

"Cin-cin," Stefi echoed. "Sit down, Charley, you're making me nervous."

"Sorry. I had no idea." He looked around for a suitable place to sit, feeling that Garnet's closest female friend, Winfield, would not appreciate him sitting close to her Aunt Stefi. Why were family occasions so crammed with pitfalls?

"Good," Kerry said, getting slowly to his feet like a fireladder unkinking skywards. "Winfield and I have a question to ask."

Charley frowned at them. "On Christmas Eve? Before the presents?"

"Before anything." Kerry shifted nervously from one foot to the other. Such lack of social grace was unusual for either of the twins. Charley stared at his face, looking for the telltale dot under the left eye that identified Kevin. There was none.

"Ma," Kerry said, turning to her. "I've never bothered you with this before. It never bothered *me* before. Now it's become critical."

"Uh-oh," Stefi murmured.

"I have a strong enough reason to insist on an answer. Tell me who my father was."

Charley winced. What he noticed immediately was that Winfield kept her glance away from him. To him it was a clear accusation of complicity in the matter of the twins. Stefi merely smiled. "After twenty-one years you come down on me like a ton of bricks?"

"You're a very smart lady, Ma. You knew you'd have to answer some day."

"I knew," she responded with sudden emphasis, "I never would. And I won't."

"You have to. Winfield and I have been seeing each other a lot." He looked embarrassed for a moment and younger than his age. "It's nobody's business but ours," he went on bravely, "except for one thing."

The right hemisphere of Charley's brain started to ache with tension. He didn't want to live through this all over again, the three potential fathers, the aftermath with Stefi's brutal father. It was a story he recalled with pain. "That's one helluva stupid way to celebrate Christmas," he blurted out.

"Don't fight it," Winfield spoke up suddenly. "We have to know."

"It's my business," Stefi said. "It might be the boys' business, it might not. But it is definitely not yours, Professore."

"What about me?" Winfield demanded.

Stefi's lustrous dark eyes surveyed her closely. "I haven't been through a lot with you. With the boys I've been through everything from chicken pox to a triple take-out in a town square."

"I understand," Winfield persisted, lawyer-like. "The boys are closer to you than anything, Aunt Stef. But you're still holding back, even from them."

"I'm hard-hearted. Ask Charley."

"Why they're asking is obvious," Charley snapped. "Embarrassing, too. Do they have the same father." He turned to his daughter, his cheeks reddening.

Her glance finally met his, not heavily, but with intense thought. He watched the computer behind her eyes as it clicked back and forth through variations of the problem. Then she grinned at him. "You're blushing!"

Infinitely relieved, Charley turned back to Stefi. "I know you in this mood. Una vera Siciliana. You don't listen to reason. But these two must have an answer or they run a needless risk."

"Worse than being cousins?"

"If they're siblings, the law is very clear. Look. I'll leave. You three will be alone. Don't tell *me* but for Christ's sake tell them."

Charley's phone rang early on Christmas morning. He reached under Garnet's bed and answered it. "Merry

Christmas," Winfield said. "You're off the hook. We're only cousins."

He swallowed. "Somebody named Billy Mulloy? Died in 'Nam?"

"So she said."

He paused and, although drowsy, refrained from saying what was on his mind, that Stef would think nothing of transferring responsibility to a dead man. Besides, with Winfield, you knew she'd already thought of that possibility herself. "Well, good. And thanks for not making a drama out of me and Stefi. Garnet doesn't, either. I sometimes wonder why I do. Where are you?"

"We're still out here. It's nice."

"Your mother wanted us to visit her today at Doctors Hospital."

"I'll get there. She won't be detoxed for weeks yet. Meanwhile, they allow her half a fifth of wine with lunch and she wheedles another split out of the orderly. She's trading one drug for another."

There was no reasoning with her in her greatly relieved frame of mind now that she was sure she wasn't enjoying an incestuous affair. But it was good of her to carry the visiting burden for the family, Bunny being laid-back organic in the Caribbean. "No, I'll meet you there," Charley insisted. "Say five o'clock?"

" 'Kay. Bye."

Charley switched on Garnet's bed light and glanced at his watch. Still half asleep, Garnet turned over and muttered: "Wha's time?"

"Seven. I apologize. But it was important to Winfield—" he broke off, laughing,"—that she wasn't having an affair with her half-brother. I'm sorry, I shouldn't laugh, but I'm more relieved than she is. What time is it in Basel now?" He ticked off his fingers. "Oh, but Christmas Day. I won't be able to raise anybody whatever time it gets to be."

"Mm?"

"There's been a hitch in the Richtron transfer."

"Merry Christmas."

Christmas Day in Atlantic City, New Jersey, dawned cloudy. The eastern sky turned a paler shade of gray than

the leaden skies to the west. Imogen Raspe woke up in
Vince Ricci's king-sized bed. She glanced around her
and sniffed the sheets. Then she sniffed Pam Scarlette,
asleep beside her. The yeasty aroma of intercourse was
unmistakable, even when dry.

She hadn't dreamed it. On a combination of Planter's
Punch and MegaMAO, she and her author and her author's mafia lover had previewed the next blockbusting
bestseller, *The Pam Scarlette Book of Bisexual and Bizarre Behavior.* She desperately wanted to be removed
bodily from this low place and allowed a night's sleep in
her lovely old, huge-roomed apartment on Central Park
West.

But there was an attractively louche side to Pam and a
brushstroke of mafia menace that made her the perfect
celeb-figurehead to front whatever outrageous bestseller
Imogen would devise. Real writers were no good at it.
They worried about motivation and tax avoidance.

Imogen pulled back a corner of the curtains to examine
the gray day. A baby squealed. She turned in time to see
a bellhop swing open the outer door and admit a small,
attractive brunette carrying a baby boy on one arm.

"Vince! Wake up! Here's your personal Christmas
present!" Lenore's eyes hadn't yet adjusted to the bedroom gloom. "Vince? Who's here with you? The Red
Army Women's Auxiliary Chorus? Eugene, say hello to
Daddy!"

Imogen snatched up a corner of the bedsheet to cover
herself, thus exposing Pam, who was rapidly coming to
life. "Lenore?"

"Pam? My God, you don't have Mr. Penis all to
yourself?"

"Lenore Ricci," Pam said, sitting up in bed and shoving back her shock of black hair. "Imogen Raspe, my
publisher." She paused in confusion. "Lenore is my
cousin. I mean, Vince is my cousin. Lenore is Vince's
wife. That's his son she—" She lay back, exhausted by
relationships.

"Why do I never have my camera with me?" Lenore
asked, putting little Eugene on the couch.

"Mrs. Ricci," Imogen said then with basso profun-
dity, a voice of utter authority. "This isn't what it looks
like."

"But it is Vince's suite. The bellhop said so. Where's Vince?"

With some nonchalance, Imogen dropped the sheet and pulled on what turned out to be Vince's dressing gown. "We've been hard at work on Pam's new bestseller."

"Hard at work, I buy." Lenore clacked over to the window on high heels and sent all the curtains flying open. Atlantic grayness filtered into the room, making the rumpled bed seem even less promising a venue for literary discussion. She picked up the telephone. "Mrs. Vince Ricci in Suite A. Lots of coffee and three breakfasts. Also a bagel? Stale, for a teething baby." She smiled pleasantly at Imogen. "You look like the more responsible deviant in this set-up. Will you keep an eye on Eugene for a minute? I have to see Vince in his office."

"You're not going t—?"

"Keep my coffee hot." Lenore wiggled her fingertips and left the suite.

She found the door to Vince's office ajar. He and Cousin Al were arguing roulette take. "Surprise! I left Eugene in your suite!"

"Sonofabitch!" Vince screamed. It was more a rising shriek. "I left *you* in Monte!"

"Eugene was asking for his Daddy."

"Hullo, Lenore," Al said, using her entrance as an excuse for his exit. "Good-bye, Lenore," he murmured, backing out of the room.

She sat down across the desk from her husband, opened a pack of cigarettes and lit one. "Hey!" Vince complained. "You know I hate smoking."

"Scusi." Lenore ground out the cigarette in a wastebasket. "Come on up to the suite. I ordered breakfast. Eugene's there with some nice blond lady publisher." He got to his feet and headed for the door. She slipped the matchbook into the center drawer of his desk and shoved it shut with her knee. "Isn't this terrific?" she asked. "Little Eugene so wanted to have a Merry Christmas with his Daddy."

February

Fifty-Five

He found it hard to think about anything at all. He found it hard to focus his mind, impossible to follow through. He would wake up late in the morning and look about him to see where he had spent the night. It was usually a luxury suite, air stale but cold, in one of Vince's hotels; that was no great mystery. But a hotel . . . where?

In the period since Ricci Medical Centers had burst upon an unsuspecting world, dealing and denying drugs so boldly that the authorities and medical boards still hadn't caught up, the career of its chief medical officer, Benjamin J. Eiler, M.D., OB-GYN, had gone into total eclipse. A turning point had to come. All common sense, all mathematics, said so.

Hauling himself out of bed now, he stumbled toward the big picture window and made several grabs at the curtain cords. This was a new feature of his condition, Buzz realized, increasingly, more inaccurate depth perception or motor coordination or whatever the hell a real doctor called it. He finally grasped the cords and pulled open the curtains. A painfully hot sun lasered down into his bleary, squinched-shut eyes, the tight wince of some cave creature exposed to light for the first time in the history of its species.

No, not Grotteria, where the sun shone 365 days a year. No, not Monte Carlo. The absence of sampans convinced him it wasn't Macao. It had to be Grand Bahama. It had to be here, perhaps today, that the turning point came.

He took in a great breath of stale air and when it came out he was sobbing. The shivering in his chest shook him as if he were constructed of paper. He collapsed on his knees by the side of his bed as if about to pray.

Symptoms, he told himself. It was so hard to think at all, about anything, but he must, must do his history. Patient is forty years of age, ten pounds overweight, suffers from light-aversion, tremors, inability to ratiocinate,

faulty eye-muscle coordination. Abuses alcohol but not
routinely. Other drugs in regular use: Ibuprofen, Dalmane.
Non-existent libido. Patient is proud of not succumbing,
as so many in the caring professions have done, to a
hopeless dependency based on his ability to prescribe for
himself a Devil's encyclopedia of forbidden or controlled
substances.

He is a fool.

Buzz felt the sobs ebbing. But it was comfortable here
on his knees in deep-pile carpeting, head resting on the
bed, eyes shut against the ferocious light that tried to etch
chasms in his retinas. Might as well pray.

*Dear Lord, make today the turning point. Over and
out.*

Only a fool would have forgotten his chief dependency, blackjack. Buzz tried to get up but found he
couldn't, not yet. He had two dependencies, gambling
and Vince Ricci. Thus it was Vince and his works that
encapsulated Buzz from head to toe: Vince's detox money
paid for the gambling; his casino dealers removed the
money. He didn't need women anymore. Whatever else
Buzz had wanted them for, they had no rôle in his dependency.

*Oh, dear Lord, light my way to a turning point. Roger,
10-4 and out.*

He hadn't seen Eileen in six weeks and then only by
bad luck when he'd sneaked into their apartment to get
some heavyweight winter things. Little Benjy looked
amazingly healthy, didn't know him, of course. There
was no bond at all between him and his son. How could
one have been forged?

He had postponed this raid on his own closet, fearing
her admonishments. So he staged it when she was out.
But she came back from walking Benjy and caught him
in the act. "Not the tweed overcoat," she had said in a
calm, matter-of-fact voice, finding him in his closet. "It's
at the cleaners."

"Oh. Thanks." An awkward pause.

"As long as you're here, say hullo to Benjy."

"He wouldn't know who I was."

"No, he wouldn't. But neither would you."

He crammed his clothes into a big brown Blooming-
dale's bag and started out of the apartment. "I'm sorry,"

he said as he left. It was as close to "good-bye" as he could get.

Perhaps the crowning humiliation had been a month ago when his mail caught up with him, forwarded by Eileen, and he saw that in their graduating class at college she had been chosen for an honorary degree. "Leading feminist attorney and champion of . . ." It was as if he hadn't graduated in the same class.

But he was cut off from all of that, from old charge accounts, old credit cards, old mortgages, old acclaim, old honors. With clinical precision she had severed him from the whole bankrupt mess. How she coped with the debt he didn't know. He didn't want to know.

Oh, dear Lord, who maketh all miracles, get your teeth out of my ass. Release me. Stop the punishment. Let me turn the corner.

He struggled up from the floor and went to the bathroom for a pee. As he stood there, aware that he was missing the toilet bowl as often as not, it occurred to him that he really ought to see a doctor. If this was Grand Bahama, he knew of a GP in Lucaya. He needn't give a real name—Yes, Mr. Jones, no doubt about it. You require a major overhaul and a solid month away from the whirr of cards being shuffled. It's the whirr, Mr. Jones, that has unseated your centers of reality. The vibration has detached you from your mortal shell. Where you used to be defined as a husband, a father, a revered doctor, you are now only a squat, stinking turd fitted with fingers for turning hole cards over.

He glanced at the clock, set into the big TV set. Only half-past six. Today he would get down to the tables when the casino opened in half an hour, just as Alex, the assistant manager, opened the doors. He would brush past to the cashier's window and cash a hastily written check for five thousand dollars. The cashier, Elaine, would smile and say: "Good morning, Dr. Eiler." Or it might be Denise, who was British and called him "love."

That many chips would certainly last till lunchtime. With luck, perhaps all day. But by lunch, winning now and then, replenishing, he would know if today was his turning point day. No one had ever heard of a losing streak as long as his. All the laws of average, all the math was on his side.

He closed his eyes and tried to still the tremor that made him want to start sobbing again. Nonsense. It *could* very well *be* today. He got up and limped into the bathroom again and turned on the shower. Yes. Why not today? What had he done that made still more punishment necessary? Hey, Buzz, he told himself as the water poured down over him, the history of science is founded entirely on the question "why not?" The Eiler Section was based on it. Everybody from Archimedes to Einstein flourished on "why not?"

He found himself down on his knees, the shower cascading over him. The porcelain of the tub pressed cruelly into his knees.

Dear Lord, I am washed in the blood of the lamb. Janet Leigh's life ebbing down the drain. Lay off me, You heartless bastard! Persecute someone else! Make today my turning point!

The sobs welled up so fast it felt as if someone were choking him. Kneeling, he let the shower sluice his tears away. And away.

Fifty-Six

"Not a bad life, for a multi-billionaire," Nikki Shan told his father. "Why not think of this as your ultimate destiny?"

Yes, February on Grand Bahama was balmy, as it was nowhere in Europe or the Far East. Shan Lao had hired adjoining cottages and, from Barton Li, a twenty-four-hour bodyguard of tough young Chinese who lurked in the palms and made faces at the baby, Leo, when he discovered them during his crawling expeditions.

"Remember," Shan responded, "we are in the lion's den here. For me it is no retirement home."

Nikki suppressed a sigh. Business was what he had promised his father he was ready for. But on such a sunny morning? Bunny, the baby and Nicole had gone to Lucaya for shopping, that left the men to their male affairs. A breeze rattled the palms, their long, tough fronds batting against each other in varying tones, like the dark wooden marimba bars when struck by mallets.

"Naturally, I have a life-goal," Shan Lao proceeded. "To gain and hold as much of the world as possible." He saw he had shocked Nik. He tried a small smile, but it came out twisted. He touched the back of Nik's hand. It was a contact so unusual that the younger man jumped up straight, as if a current had passed through him.

"It has taken time to select a project that integrates you into my structure. If my son is destined for leadership he must point to accomplishments more substantial than a series of 'Dear Father' essays. That quotation from Santayana? About having one's face pushed into one's own feces?"

"Made it up," Nik confessed.

"You mean—" For once, Shan felt a real sense of pride in his only offspring. There was hope for Nik after all. Then he sipped his tea and made a face. This was not the tea he had brought, it was one Nicole liked, with a more robust flavor. The idea of robustness in a green tea was ridiculous. But what could one do with the French?

"My laboratory people have reproduced MegaMAO in less than a week, since the drug is merely a combination of two others."

In the distance a small bird chirruped. This close to the beach, without too much strain, one could hear the surf's silky swish. Closer, something moved in the underbrush, either one of the small geckos or an armed guard.

"You're muscling in on Ricci's turf?"

Shan Lao produced a small, neat grimace as a reaction to the slang. "We are expanding an existing market." A wintry smile came and went.

"Ricci will do anything to keep us out."

"He has a head start," Shan admitted. He grew warm at Nik's use of the word "us." "But his market includes consumers in conflict with the Establishment. We should not find it hard to portray the Ricci network as *part* of the Establishment. Our capsules, just as strong but half the price, strike a blow at the entrenched druglords and their corrupt political allies."

"And do we still make a profit?"

Shan's answer was slow in coming. He was afraid his
son would ask this. But it was Nik's asking that labeled
him a worthy successor. "For some time now," Shan
said slowly, "a number of our activities have been designed to hamper and constrict Ricci activities."

Nik frowned, as someone who had fathered a child
with a Ricci. "Why?"

Behind Shan Lao's neat, scholarly facade—diminutive,
bookish, utterly cool—he could feel his own nature twist
away from the next step. Secrecy was the armature of
everything; to reveal one of the master cores of that armature? He especially shied away from disclosing it to
an untested boy like Nik. And yet some of it, not the
overall strategy leading to the new Depression, but perhaps some tactics, had to be disclosed. In the distance,
as if cautioning silence, the surf made a deep shushing
sound.

"Nik. To monitor our conversation here is technically
simple. Let us continue our talk along the beach." He
got to his feet. "Now!" he commanded.

"What I resent most of all," Missy complained, "is being unable to see my one and only grandchild."

Charley Richards got up from the visitor's chair in her
large room at Doctors Hospital. Despite all the wine during this, her official detoxification period, his wife had
lost that puffy, drugged face. But talking to her was an
effort. One of her doctors had discoursed learnedly about
rebuilding brain receptor areas ravaged by massive drug
abuse. He was full of such nonsense.

Charley glanced at his watch. "Winfield will be here
shortly. She's seen the little boy. She says he's just fine."

"Andy says—" With a visible effort on her gaunt face,
Missy stopped herself. Andy Reid had dropped off the
face of the earth. Charley dated his disappearance from
the week in which that FBI fellow had had his accident.
Perhaps the same subtle hand . . . ? There had been all
sorts of theories about the vanished Mr. Reid. The companies in which Charley had required Andy's facade were
now the province of Zio Italo. Perhaps Zio had ordered
his demise. Only one person felt the loss, and she was
losing the memory fast. Sad. One side of the Sicilian soul
can wax sentimental about loss when it is someone else's.

As he gazed down at his wife, Charley felt hurt that
she had quoted the missing lover, even if the reference
was only a dismal bit of floor sweeping caught in what
was left of her mind. He resented the heritage Andy had
left with her, the look of her once beautiful nose, now
collapsed from within.

"What does Andy say?" he asked.

"Oh, please, you know he's dead." Her still-handsome
face looked like a piece of petrified wood. "You know
because you had him killed."

Her cool New England voice with its odd vowels carried almost no emotion at all. But it had the power to
ignite Charley's temper. "I don't have people killed,"
he said in that low, deliberate voice that signaled his anger. He fumbled inside his briefcase and withdrew a thin
packet of forms Kerry had brought back this morning
from Basel. Signatures were now needed from the two
correlative owners, Charley's wife and his oldest daughter. After all these years, the anstalt was being liqui-
dated.

A strange moment in the secret history of Richland
Holdings. Its hidden ownership was being transferred to
a Delaware corporation whose books would be available
for inspection. Vastly reduced now to a financial-services
holding company, Richland would even have a name
change. Garnet had suggested New Era.

"Although the way we're pouring money into the Education Research Fellowship, New Bankruptcy would be
a better name," he had countered.

Missy eyed the papers. Then her small, thin-lipped
mouth pursed provocatively. "What a glorious thing to
have a family as extensive as yours. You can always claim
ignorance if someone disappears. Do you know what my
brother Jack told me when he last phoned from London?
He said your Uncle Italo had thrown a bodyguard around
Isabel and the boys last year and the men were still there.
He asked me to intercede and have them called off."

"News to me," Charley handed her the forms and a
pen. "Sign at the X, please."

"Why should I?" Her eyes squinted fiercely, trying to
focus. "New Era Services? What's that?"

"Just sign it, Missy," he said in a weary voice.

"And what's in it for me?"

"Peace. Quiet. Unlimited expenses." Charley chuckled. "Oh, and I'll make sure Italo's boys stop bothering
Jack and his family. Fair enough?"

But she was already signing her name, rushing, im-
petuous, like a roulette player blindly plunking down
chips. "Andy says I—" She stopped and this time her
face looked pathetic as she pushed the signed papers back
to Charley.

He left them on the pale blue bedspread. "Winfield
should be here any minute." He shrugged into his topcoat, as if about to leave.

"Don't go." Her voice was tiny, abashed. She resembled one of his girls when they were babies. Her girls.
Oh, what a dissembler she was. What a manipulator. He
made a show of consulting his watch. Behind him the
door opened and Winfield arrived, rushing in as tempes-
tuously as her mother had signed the anstalt documents.

"Sorry I'm late." She sat down in Charley's chair and
began trying to unfold a shrink-wrapped sandwich.

"You know you're welcome to a full, decent, hot lunch
here," her mother said in an exasperated tone. "You
have no idea who made that sandwich. What sort of diseases . . . These days . . ." Detox was turning Missy
into an old lady again.

Winfield pulled over the packet of papers and glanced
up at her father. "These the ones?"

He nodded. "Right under your mother's name there.
Triplicate."

But Winfield signed nothing in the roulette-player fashion. She abandoned the struggle to open her sandwich,
sat back, crossed her legs and read fine print for more
than ten minutes, frowning. Over her head, her parents
glanced at each other, knowing how useless it was to
hurry her along. Then she signed.

Charley collected the papers and placed another packet
before her. "This is the status change for New Era."

She scanned the sheets. "Garnet's already signed."

"So have I. If you sign, we're empowered to convert
the corporation at any time to partial or full—" he
glanced at his wife and saw that she wasn't really listening, "—eleemosynary purposes."

Winfield gave him a solemn look. "Oh, well. Eleemosynary. One of the words they taught you at the Education Fellowship?''

She signed without reading and Charley put all the papers back in his briefcase. "What was that all about?" Missy demanded.

"In case we want to change what New Era does any time in the future."

"What's New Era to me?"

"You're very astute," Charley said. He pecked Missy on her gaunt cheek, gave Winfield a warmer version and started for the door. "A pleasure doing business with you charming ladies." He was gone.

Outside, he stood in the chill Manhattan winds of February as they whipped in off the East River. He found himself wondering if Missy would ever be right again.

Charley watched his driver pull out of a rank of Cadillacs and Lincolns to halt smoothly in front of him. He let himself into the back of the car and felt it surge forward heading for the FDR Drive that led southward to Wall Street.

One day, he heard Garnet's words repeating in his head. Meanwhile, he inflicted Missy on Winfield, making her take some of the burden of her mother's detoxification. There was no one else. He couldn't ask Garnet. Or Stefi. Between them there was very little milk of human kindness on behalf of Missy.

He allowed himself to sit back and relax. Almost the final act in dismantling Richland Holdings had passed so quietly, and with so little fuss, that it was hard to realize he was nearly free. It was as if, in that big Doctors Hospital room, by deft strokes of the pen surgeons had removed a gigantic hump from the back of Charley Richards.

The limo surged south past New York Hospital. Its telephone buzzed. "Richards here."

"Italo Ricci here. Ricordi?"

A sharp chill shot across Charley's shoulder blades. He hadn't heard from his lethal uncle in so long he had convinced himself he never would. "Buona sera, Zio."

"How's the wife?"

"Zio, I would've thought you had better things to do than have me shadowed.''

"That's true." The limousine picked up speed. "Listen to me," his uncle said, his voice sharpening, "maybe you should be watching your own ass, too."

"A guessing game? Give me a clue."

"A clue?" Zio Italo's voice sounded like a lookout on a whaling ship shouting "thar she blows!" He paused, probably for dramatic effect, and then said: "Here's a clue. Look at your calendar for next Monday and you'll see a meeting that's just been canceled on you." The line went dead.

Charley replaced the phone and found himself sitting forward again like the jockey in a steeplechase whose horse is approaching yet another hazard jump. One last fragment of Richland remained, Richtron Electronics, a Japanese company of the Crayette kind, providing micro computers whose speed rivaled that of the immense Cray machines the Pentagon loved. Monday's calendar popped into Charley's head: Washington, D.C.; Pentagon meeting just before and during lunch. Canceled?

He called Kerry immediately. "You're psychic," his daughter's lover told him. "They've just postponed, not ten minutes ago, without giving us a new date."

Charley's forehead wrinkled.

Richtron should by now have been transferred to Italo's domain, the last transfer, the final link severed, except that being a Japanese concern, it required much more paperwork to unload. Was it an accident, Charley wondered, that the papers of transfer had been delayed? Accident, hell.

His limo dropped him at the East River site where Garnet had once lived. Most signs of construction had been removed. Charley found the front entrance unlocked and wandered inside, worrying over the treachery of Zio Italo.

This place, he knew, had a soothing effect on him. The courtyard-patio had been planted with a dreamy willow and shrubbery. Two ordinary park benches sat at right angles to each other to give whoever sat on them either the south or west sun. Now, in February, its rays came in at too low an angle for warmth.

A watchman came hurrying up, recognized him and produced a casual salute before walking off. Charley supposed, as he sat down on one of the benches, that for the amount of contributions he'd made, they'd give him a set of keys. Staff were due to move in next month. Flat and co-ax computer cables ran under the floorboards, ready to tackle research projects now being done mostly by hand.

Garnet's idea, that the education of a nation set all its standards, had begun to haunt Charley. It wasn't just that he saw all about him the boundless confidence of the uninformed, or the ignorant hatred of ideas. It was that he refused to believe it couldn't be stemmed, turned around and made good. Instead of the silly "self-esteem" projects around the land, in which morons told each other they were terrific, there had to be a way of getting people angry at being cheated of intelligence, angry enough to grab for it. One of the people at the Fellowship had introduced him to the idea of entropy, the thought that everything, the planet and the universe, was decaying. So why not education?

He stretched his arms out on the bench and let a sense of non-Riccihood infuse him. Big issues, not Ricci greed. Big changes, not screwing some Pentagon brass hat. What the people needed, not what Italo Ricci demanded.

For the first time that day, he began to relax.

Fifty-Seven

It was rare for Italo Ricci to make a wrong assumption. But when a report had come to him many months ago that the wife of Vince's medical director was the lawyer for some of Vince's whores, he naturally assumed that Vince had matters under control. A classic ploy, hiring Dr. Eiler's wife. Similarly, when it came to Italo's attention that this Eileen Hegarty was a close friend of Lenore Ricci, his assumption was that Vince had sent in Lenore as a spy or, possibly, that the two women were going through the motions of a lawsuit to defuse and dissipate any danger to Vince. Anyone might make those assumptions. Anyone used to power and the exercise of it, anyone whose manipulative skills had accustomed him to such schemes.

But then, before Christmas, a legal secretarial service

had complicated matters. Only one miniature tape had
been given the service for transcription. No one on the
tape was identified. It ran for only half an hour and the
quality was marginal, but it was obviously from a clandestine device in someone's office. Someone called
Vince.

The woman who did the transcription thought enough
of the almost meaningless conversations to make a Xerox
of the transcript and send it, via a cousin, to Italo Ricci.
She had done this in the past.

As society grows more complex, illicit means of short-
circuiting its coils becomes more widespread. Mafia
technique is always basic: to get valid airline tickets, steal
validator plates and ticket stock; to erase violations on
driver's licenses, break into the Motor Vehicle Bureau
and demagnetize whole reels of tape records; to enforce
monopoly control of an industry like construction, capture companies *and* unions; to launder money, buy banks
and brokerage houses—everything at these levels is
straight-line.

Italo re-read the transcript for a long time, marking
certain words and phrases. He did not want to alarm
Vince, knowing what a hairtrigger temper he had. He
was not at all sure the "Vince" of the transcript was his
Vince. If he had heard the tape he could have settled that.
But all he had was typing.

". . . Twenny-tree t'ousan' a week," one phrase ran.
". . . Buncha Boy Scouse."

". . . Take care'v'it. No probs," another phrase went,
". . . won' even know."

". . . damned sure he knows," a voice labeled Vince
said. ". . . Whole neighborhood's crawling widdem."
Twenty pages of this added up only to one unhelpful assumption: someone called Vince was being bugged by
someone in the habit of using a legal secretarial service.
Now, Italo goaded himself, it was time to put his mind
to work.

Clearly the easiest way was to present all this to Vince
and learn if that actually was him on the tape. Italo hung
back from the single most possible assumption: that the
Hegarty woman was fleshing out her defense with eavesdrop evidence. It made no sense. No court would admit
private surveillance material as evidence. Like most hu-

man conversation it was repetitious trivia, legal proof of nothing. Italo made sure the woman who had gotten it to him was properly rewarded. He suggested, if there were a next time, that she send him a copy of the tape, not the transcript.

He went on to more pressing matters. From time to time, as a crossword addict might return to an unsolved puzzle he assumed to be of only theoretical importance, Italo would puzzle over the transcript yet again and decide no action was necessary.

That, of course, was another wrong assumption of Italo's.

"Hearsay, circumstantial, irrelevant." Eileen Hegarty's voice sounded dragged out with fatigue. She paced the window wall of her office while Winfield sat at her desk. "No attorney could get it into the record unchallenged. None of it is persuasive enough to show Leona Kane at the DA's office. The one moment it bore on our case was when Buzz was in Vince's office in Monaco and Vince just happened to ask him about AIDS carried by prostitutes."

Winfield looked unhappy. "We have another month's life in those little matchbook bugs. Lenore's on the tapes now and then. Why can't we brief her to ask Vince some leading ques—?"

"Stop right there." Eileen's diminutive figure had paused, the thin February light from the windows silhouetted her for a moment. "You are surely not going to ask her to put her life any more at risk than it is now?"

"What harm is there in asking?"

"Winfield, sometimes you worry me."

The silence between them went on as Eileen resumed her pacing. With more than half her time spent on little Benjy, her way of dressing had changed over the past months—low-heeled shoes, skirt-and-blouse outfits, easy-brush hairdo had turned her from the rather intimidating power figure of a feisty crusader into something closer to a housewife doing part-time fill-in work.

"OK," Winfield gave in. "Let's say there's a man who once knew greatness and is now ground down into the slime, as low as only a mafia medic can get. Sound familiar?"

"You want me to dangle rehabilitation in front of Buzz?"

"You're not asking him for much. He's already had that one gyno chat with Vince. Let him initiate a few more."

Eileen sat down across from Winfield. "The last time I saw Buzz he looked like something from a Gogol tragedy, piteously pawing through old overcoats. There's nobody there, Winfield."

"Rehabilitation," the younger woman mused, "resurrection, reformation. My, what a lot of 're' words. Even the lowest sinner craves resurrection. But, why not make it easy for the two boys to get down to cases? Why not have Buzz open up with a blockbuster show of total loyalty?"

"Like what?"

"Vince, I just learned something awful. You know this lawsuit against your hookers? You know this Eileen Hegarty? You remember my wife, Eileen? It's one and the same woman!"

"Insanity."

"Good confidence ploy," Winfield calmly contradicted her. "Vince is grateful for the warning. This gets Vince talking about the case. Our little bugs are grinding away. Unforced direct testimony. And if Buzz works it right, no hint of entrapment."

"How does Buzz do that?" Eileen laughed unhappily. "How does Buzz do anything these days?"

"You have to motivate him."

The sigh that escaped Eileen was so profound it chilled the atmosphere between them. "Winfield," she said, "if someone as accomplished as you can be said to have a flaw, it's how little you understand the human heart."

"Don't. My mother lectures me on that."

"Does she. There's *chutzpah* for you, eh?" Eileen shook her small, neatly drawn head. "That's two people close to me you're prepared to throw to the lions, Lenore and Buzz. Try to remember th-that—" When she stumbled on the word, it surprised both of them. Winfield could see her eyes brimming with tears. "You haven't a clue about Buzz," Eileen went on. "He's unreadable. He has no interest in Benjy. I haven't barred his access to us. But blackjack is his choice because blackjack diminishes him to the point of non-existence. He's on a suicide course using a very slow poison.''

Winfield nodded vigorously. ''What's a better suicide than doublecrossing Vince Ricci?''

''I don't want him dead!'' Eileen's voice had risen almost to a wail. ''He doesn't love me anymore. But that's no reason to see him killed.''

''See how he reacts. All he can say is no.''

''Resurrection is the word. He'd be coming back from the dead. It's only been done once and it took divine intervention.'' Eileen's lips pressed in a tight, despairing line. ''I can't ask a man with so little regard for me to do such a thing.''

''Reaffirmation.''

''Redemption,'' Eileen added. ''Regeneration. Restoration. Winfield, shut up, will you? You know nothing about the heart.''

''All he can say is no.''

''He's had a lot of practice saying no.'' Eileen stared down at her hands. ''You have no idea what this man was like when we first met. What he was like even a few years ago. What we had between us. You have no idea what he's like today. It's . . . he's . . . destroyed.''

''Ask him anyway. You're the only one who can.''

''The way he looks at me. Dead eyes.''

Winfield came around the desk and hugged her. ''It's his only chance. And yours.''

Fifty-Eight

Nikki Shan had been told to be on the cottage dock at six a.m. A mahogany and bronze motorboat, the Dragon Lady, would pick him up. He was to identify himself as Arthur Dumont, based on the initials A.D. The other man would use an alias employing the initials B.C. That was all Shan Lao would say. The rest was in Nikki's hands. This was more than a trial run. This was being thrown in at the deep end to sink or swim.

At five-thirty Bunny wakened him very gently. Every-

thing she did lately was with the gliding gentle movements of Nicole. She had taken to wearing her hair
Nicole's way, combed high on each side and pinned back.
She wore the same skin-tight cheongsams, some of them
made for her by Nicole. She spoke softly, melodiously,
in a muted tone. And, like Nicole, Bunny had taken to
treating "her men," meaning Leo, Nik and Shan Lao,
as alien beings from another planet, to be cossetted,
served, met with smiles, plied with little chirrups of
pleasure, spoken to only when asked.

Only Nikki found this disturbing. Leo and Lao considered it their natural right. To be babied and catered to
was, perhaps, Leo's right for a few more years. Nikki
had never even noticed how subservient to his father Nicole had been, not until he found Bunny mimicking her.

He stood alone on the dock now and watched the mahogany motorboat coming toward him. Something had
been done to muffle the engine's exhaust. Although the
craft moved very quickly, it made almost no sound until
it was on top of him, engines cut, coasting slantwise into
the dock. A Second World War cartoon of a sexy Chinese
charmer, almost nude, decorated the bow with its
"Dragon Lady" lettering. A young man stood there, a
short cigar clamped in his rather moonlike face. He held
out his hand and plucked Nikki aboard. The engine cut
in again and the craft moved off in a muffled, bubbling
thrust of speed.

"Baxter Choy," the man said.

"Arthur Dumont." They shook hands.

"Sweet Jaysus . . ." The newcomer paused, eyeing
Nikki. He was half a head shorter and his coloring was
quite different from Nikki, whose skin had an olive cast.
Baxter Choy's was reddish-tan, an almost American Indian look. "Sweet Jaysus," he repeated in an Irish
brogue, "they told me you looked like a Frenchman."

"And I don't?"

Choy laughed. His cigar bobbed up and down. "Shit,
no. But do nayther the pair of us look Chinese?" He led
Nikki past the young Chinese helmsman and down into
the galley. "Milk with your coffee? Sugar?" Nikki could
barely feel the forward thrust of the high-speed craft
through the ocean. "Do you know," Choy asked him

suddenly, dispensing with the brogue, "how valuable a face like yours or mine is in a city like New York?"

"The kind the cops like to chop down."

"I'm not talking cops," the other man demurred. "Cops we always have with us. I'm talking Ricans, Dominicans, Haitians, Cubans, Mex, people whose only common denominator is that their ancestors came across the Bering Straits ten thousand years ago or over the ocean in slave ships. They take one look at my face and I'm a brother. You, too, if you could do something about that Froggie accent."

Nikki sipped his coffee. "I'm OK till I get tired or too excited."

"Hey, that's the story of my life." Baxter Choy glanced forward, over the shoulder of the helmsman. "Left five degrees." He turned back to Nikki. "Your father picked me because I went to college. Which he paid for. Other than that, let's not have any role confusion. You're the manager. I'm the enforcer."

Nikki grinned. "Everybody's got to be something. What university?"

"It's a missionary college in Hong Kong, run by Irish fathers." Choy puffed cigar smoke into the air and patted it away gently. "Shan Lao 'bought' me when I was six years old. The Jesuits told him I was bright. So he left a wad with them to make sure I had the proper clothes and books. You know the old Jesuit saying? Give me a child before he is five and I care not who has him thereafter?"

Nikki examined his new helper. Baxter Choy looked like a light-heavyweight, undershirt displaying tremendous shoulder and biceps development. His roundish face, even in repose, seemed set in a slight sardonic smile, a "Have A Good Day" happy-face gone skeptical. About his face, Nikki saw, Choy was absolutely correct. It could be anything from Iranian to Eskimo. He only needed a line of chatter to flesh out a nationality and it was already pretty obvious that Baxter Choy had a way with blarney.

"You run?" Nikki asked. "I try to do two miles a day."

"You mean, like jogging? I do weights."

"Have to try that," Nikki mused. "Enforcer, huh?"

"At your service."

"Is that like a bodyguard?"

When Choy got serious his face lost its "Have A Nice Day" contour and grew rather lethal. "Not really. When you muscle in it's a question of surprise." He pointed to a small puddle of coffee on the galley Formica. As Nikki watched, he dipped his finger in it and drew: $S = S$. For a moment they both stared at the equation as if it had appeared by magic. "Surprise equals success," Choy explained. "Surprise is a secret weapon available to everybody. You don't use it, you lose it."

"You are a great one for slogans," Nikki shook his head helplessly. "Isn't there a better place than New York City for us to start this new enterprise?"

Baxter Choy laughed. "Have no fear, Choy is here. My orders are to help you get this started. The strategy is classic: any entrenched establishment is vulnerable. An attacker, using surprise, can cripple it. Look at Li'l David and his sling. In the process we both want to stay alive, right?"

"That would be nice."

Choy examined Nikki's rather glum face. "Smile! We're going to do something that has never before been done: beat a Ricci on his own turf."

Charley tried never to overnight in Washington, D.C. No matter where Kerry booked him in his national capital, whether prohibitively expensive or only insanely costly, he found precisely the people he was trying to avoid, competitors, old Harvard pals, lobbyist vultures and the most gorgeous hookers east of California.

He also found that whenever he thought to bring along one of Kerry's Thinkman computers, booted up to locate eavesdropping devices, he found a bug in every phone, under every table and behind half the pictures on the walls. He wasn't paranoid. He didn't jump to the conclusion that the heavy surveillance was for him, exclusively. But having it in place, for the use of anyone from the FBI to a business rival, could easily spoil a night's sleep.

Worst of all about this particular trip was that he had almost been able to avoid it by shifting responsibility to Zio Italo. By some black magic, the old man had delayed the securities issue of Richtron so that it clung to Charley like a bloodsucking leech, demanding attention when it should long ago have been transferred.

Charley snapped off the late-night news on the TV screen. Outside the immense picture windows of his suite, against the dark indigo sky of Washington, he could see the phallic thrust of the Washington obelisk, brilliantly lit. His door chime produced a three-tone summons.

"Yes?" he called.

A murmur, muffled by the brushed oak door.

Charley strode to the door. "Yes?"

". . . Mumnumb . . ."

He unlocked the door. She was as tall as one of his daughters and about the same age, with blond hair that fell below her shoulders. "Charley Braverman?"

"Wrong Charley."

Her eyes, rather small, had been shadowed outward to resemble immense pools of forgetfulness. Unsmiling, she displayed herself in an almost topless ballroom gown of snowy white with a Lurex thread, Arthurian samite. She carried a sable wrap over one shoulder.

"I guess I'm supposed to provide Excalibur," Charley mused out loud.

"Mr. Braverman?" Her glance raked past him, searching the suite for the other Charley. She was still not smiling.

"Sorry." He started to close the door. "Good night."

"Charley Braverman, Topp Electronics?"

"Try the desk again." He closed the door. Then he placed Charley Braverman. He'd been a middle-echelon Richtron designer two years ago, then lured away to the Far East by a salary double what Charley was paying him. Was he back to sink the axe into his old employers? Topp Electronics, of Seoul, was a major competitor of Richtron. Product by product, Topp knocked off every new Richtron design, undercut the price and swiped customers.

It was bad enough competing with a quality leader like Cray, Charley thought. He'd just spent the day stroking middle-aged Pentagon colonels and generals with children to send through college, explaining that the Richtron 030 computer wasn't trying to put Cray out of business, just offering a low-cost supplement. It was disgusting work. What made it even more hateful was that

Zio Italo had somehow trapped him into it. Finally a compromise deal had been worked out.

If Topp now appeared in the picture, today had been wasted. Topp's Charley Braverman would be offering Richtron 030 features at one-third discount, that third earmarked for bribes. Charley turned and opened the door. She was standing in the middle of the wide corridor, her eyes dull with confusion. "Come in."

"Mr. Braverman?" He got the distinct impression that, though beautiful, she was not amazingly bright.

"Why don't you call the desk and find out where he is."

"Thank you," she said, still gravely unsmiling. "If he isn't with you he's in Mr. Cheong's suite."

"Mr. Cheong of Topp Electronics?"

When she shook her head, the fine blond hair flew out around her like a full skirt. "Mr. Cheong of Shan Lao, Ltd."

Fifty-Nine

"It's so funny, being without Benjy," Eileen said. She and Lenore were swinging along the boardwalk at Atlantic City, glancing in the windows of cheap souvenir shops and echoing squeals of horror. "Tacky. Yech."

The February gloom camouflaged nothing, concealed no splayed wad of blue bubble gum stuck to a railing, candy wrapper, plastic Big Mac tray dripping lettuce shreds, used condom, brownish banana skin, Diet Pepsi can. A tramp fished a crumpled popcorn box out of a crack in the broadwalk. He felt around inside it for abandoned kernels.

"Not that Benjy has to see this place."

Lenore reminded herself how essential it was at this stage of the boys' lives that they never meet. She had placed a series of calls worldwide early this morning and had tracked down Buzz Eiler to either Atlantic City or one of Vince's new casinos on Dominica. Lenore and Eileen had put on walking shoes and boarded one of the many buses that cruise Manhattan whisking bettors off to Atlantic City. They hadn't located Buzz at the glitziest of the Ricci emporiums. This next was quite down-market but, as Lenore pointed out, blackjack was blackjack.

It was a lucky choice. They stood behind Buzz for a full two minutes while he lost four hundred dollars on two hands. The dealer, a pert redhead, had noticed Lenore and Eileen the moment they arrived.

"These your guardian angels?" she asked Buzz.

He turned around and nearly fell off his stool. Seeing the two of them together was not just a vision of petite twins, it was double guilt. In Buzz's mind they were twin time bombs, fated to destroy him. To find the mothers of his sons in this place blanched his pudgy cheeks to an even more unhealthy shade of off-white.

"You—" His throat closed with a click.

"Dr. Eiler, I presume," Lenore said. "Have you got a pad in this fleabag place?"

By way of answer, his glance darting from one to the other, Buzz scrabbled in his pocket and fished out a room key, triumphantly, as if this would save him. He brandished it about until Eileen picked it out of his fingers. "I'm taking five minutes of your valuable blackjack time," she said. "Then you can come right back down here."

"You—" He swallowed. "What's—?" He glanced pleadingly at Lenore, whom he considered to have the power of life and death over him. All she had to do was talk and either Vince or Eileen would kill him with their bare hands, depending on which got to him first.

"It's between you and Eileen," Lenore said. "I'll be waiting at the first slot near the entrance door. It's always rigged to pay off a shade better than the others. Dr. Eiler," she added, lowering her voice in a sinister way.

"You wa—"

"Let me tell you . . . something very serious." Lenore waited for a long moment. "I'd like to tell you . . . that I advise you . . . to cooperate." There was a slower pace to her words, no longer flip or conversational. She had picked up the knack of uttering a mafia threat not from her family of brothers and certainly not from Vince, but mainly from films on TV. The trick was the slow pace, the steady eye contact and the utter deadpan cool.

And while you spoke, you had to think of sharp knives. "Whatever Eileen asks," Lenore told him, "I'm also . . . asking. Does that . . . register?"

"You two m—"

Eileen took his arm and they went to the elevator shafts, stacks of glass in which cylindrical cars ran up and down, twinkling. Through the glass, as they ascended, Eileen waved to Lenore, who waved back.

In Buzz's room the bed had not been disturbed. He had evidently just checked in. Apart from a small carry-on bag, unopened, there was nothing in the room to identify its occupant, nor would there be. Buzz had cut down his gambits to a very small chess board, with hardly a square in any direction, somewhat like a king trapped by four rooks.

"You know what this is?" Eileen began, showing him one of Winfield's light blue matchbooks.

"A matchbook?"

She perched on the window ledge, a small, crisp figure silhouetted against the February gloom outside. "It's a listening device. One like it sits in the desk drawer of each of Vince Ricci's main offices. We have been tapping him for several months."

"Eileen!"

"The material we've been getting is next to useless. But I have heard you on these tapes, usually something to do with MegaMAO, once with AIDS and prostitutes. And I'm reminded that Vince has never tumbled to the fact that your wife is Eileen Hegarty, who is defending a Ricci prostitute against Murder Two, reckless endangerment."

"He does . . . does . . . doesn't kn—?" This time his voice died away of its own terror, its own fatigue. He hadn't shaved. Obviously he'd just come off a flight from somewhere and barely had time to dump his bag in the room before yielding to the lure of the blackjack tables. The cruel February light, shadowless, brought out every bruiselike discoloration in his face, the puffy eye bags, the budding jowl-droop, faint slivers of white in his two-day beard.

"Oh, God, Buzz!" Her cry pierced the sullen anonymity of the room. Her voice, like an arrow, impaled his heart. She needed no words to convey what he looked

like to her, or the sorrow of it. She only needed that one
outcry.

He began waving his hands, palms out, before his face,
shielding himself from further hurt. "I know," he gab-
bled. "I know. Need a shave. Night's sleep. You don't
h—"

"Buzz," she cut in. "You look like such a loser. Dear
God, it's hard to recognize the man wh—" She stopped.
Slowly, her face grew stony. "Buzz, it's time you warned
Vince Ricci who your wife is. I'm suggesting you find
time for a short talk, using that as an intro."

"He'll murd—"

"He'll thank you. He'll be grateful. You'll draw him
out, buddy to buddy. We'll get whatever he has to tell us
on tape. If you do the job right, if Ricci is incautious
enough, if, if, if, we may then be able to mount a case.
Right now, we're stymied."

"I can't d—" His throat clicked shut with fear. He
coughed convulsively. "You can't exp—" Once more it
shut down with a sound as of a single hand clap. "Eileen, listen, I could never, ever . . ." His mind seemed
to die out on him.

"Not even for your own self-respect?" Eileen asked.
There was a steel ring to it she instantly regretted. This
wasn't a courtroom. He wasn't a hostile witness. "Not
even for what's left of our marriage?" she asked. "For
your family? I know we don't mean much to you, Benjy
and I. But . . ." She gestured, almost hopelessly.

"Not me, Eileen. Somebody else. Not me."

"He talks to you. With no one else is he that much at
ease. Because you have made him a father. Because you
have made him the number one drug dealer in America.
Because he knows how burned out you are. Oh, how well
that bastard knows it. Get him to talk about Dr. Battipaglia. About the women. You can do that. Only you."

His glance brimmed over with hurt. "You think I've
sunk that low?"

"Low?" She got to her feet. They faced each other
across a yard of anonymous tweed carpeting. "Low? Betraying a killer is lower than betraying your wife and
son?"

"I can't."

"Will you do it for me, Buzz?"

"I can't."

"Oh, yes, you can." She took a deep breath and her eyes flashed. "If he wants to, Buzz Eiler can do anything."

His eyes widened and to Eileen's horror, a tear ran down one of his cheeks. "That's the old Buzz," he mumbled.

"The Buzz I fell for."

He was sobbing now. His face had gone damp and he shook with short, trembling sobs. "The d-dead Buzz," he cried.

"Will you do it for me?"

"Eileen . . ." The sobbing wracked his chubby body forward and back. "Eileen, you know I will."

They were holding each other tightly. The flat February light cast an overall grayness. She inhaled his odor. There was nothing to smell, no scent of tobacco or sweat or booze. The man wasn't there, not yet.

"You're a wreck, Buzz Eiler," she said. She shook him gently. "You've hit bottom." She released him for a moment to put her fingers under his chin and lift his damp face up. "And I'm still in love with you. Will you tell me something, Buzz? Which of us is more pathetic?"

Sixty

"No, thanks, Honey. Not tonight."

Charley Braverman had put on weight. On Seong, Braverman's boss, looked as emaciated as a survivor of a Japanese death march. They sat at a large glass cocktail table in Charley Richards' hotel room while the tall blond hooker—excused from normal duty—made drinks and filled ashtrays with peanuts from the minibar.

Since Braverman had rarely spoken with his former boss, Richards, in the days when he worked for Richtron, there was a freer air about this conference, no recriminations, no grudges. If there had been, Charley Richards felt, On Seong would have been offended. In his skin-and-bones way, the Oriental gentleman exuded wiry repose and a lifelong dedication to peace and quiet. Hard to think of him as heading up the Far East's most cut-throat electronics holding company.

On Seong beamed at the tall glass of sparkling water the hooker presented him. "Ah," he enthused, "what a tall drink of water."

"Isn't she," Braverman agreed. "You from Texas, Honey?"

"Holly," she corrected him, not smiling. "Lubbock."

Charley Richards smiled at the hooker. "Holly," he said, "if Mr. Braverman agrees, I think you can be excused. Yes?" He glanced at his opponents.

Braverman fished his room key out of his pocket. "Let yourself in, Honey. Have a nightcap. I'll be with you soon." He glanced questioningly at On Seong.

"That," the Asian said, "depends on Mr. Richards."

"Soon," Charley told him.

"Soon, Honey."

"Holly." She took the key and left the suite, trailing her sable wrap behind her. "Mm," Braverman grunted. "Mm and mm again. What turns me on is that she *never* smiles. Let me explain what we're after, Charley."

"Yes, Charley?"

"We can either lowball you out of the Pentagon contract or we can start to live together in sin. It's up to you, Charley."

"Lowball us on the Richtron 030's, Charley?"

"The Topp 500, we call it. Or cut a deal." Braverman sipped his whisky. "I don't care what deal. You give us a consultancy fee. Or we sell our 500's relabeled 030's and pay you a fee. Or we halve the order and sell both." Braverman continued sipping. His intelligent eyes never left Charley's face. "Naturally we'd share any, uh, subsidies any of the generals want on their personal retirement pensions. The main thing is we hop in bed together."

Charley Richards turned to his magisterial Asian competitor. The empire controlled by Bunny Richards' future father-in-law was larger than the Richland Holdings' enterprises newly transferred to Italo Ricci, but didn't include a financial operation. The information Kevin had stolen in Singapore made it clear why. None of the Japanese Big Four trusted Shan Lao anymore. Without their confidence he would be ill advised to branch out in any major way as a bank, a brokerage or any other kind of financial institution. But if he affiliated with a going concern already operating nearly 200 bank and brokerage offices around the world . . . ?

In other words, the financial services Charley had reserved for himself and kept away from Zio Italo would be the ones On Seong was looking to—what was Braverman's felicitous phrase?—hop in bed with. But even now they had changed shape and name. New Era Services had registered this morning in Delaware. Even Shan Lao's worldwide network hadn't gotten the news yet.

"Is that the case, Mr. Seong? Are you that eager to join forces with us? Even to sharing the bribes? It's very flattering."

"Eventuarry," On Seong said, making a valiant effort at handling the l-sounds, "we most preased with a merger." No matter how mispronounced, the m-word sent a ragged chill across Charley Richards' shoulder blades, even though Richtron existed in a paperwork limbo between an anstalt that no longer existed and a Delaware corporation no Far Eastern pirate would ever want to buy into. "A merger of Topp and Richtron?"

The Asian waved his skeleton-like fingers in the air, sketching yet another gesture of peace and quiet. "Whatever prease you, Mr. Richards. Your daughter and Shan Lao son have point the way."

"Mergers are in the air," Braverman reminded him. "Size is the key to success. Little guys get eaten alive. Only giants survive. Big is better, Charley."

"Is it, Charley?"

"And Richland is one of the partners we've targeted, Charley."

"Targeted, Charley?"

"That's a no-no word," Braverman agreed, swallowing too much Scotch and choking. "But between old pals like us, why not be candid, Charley?"

"Charley, if you two will excuse me." Charley Richards got to his feet. "I have to catch some sleep. I'll keep your offer in mind. I'll get back to you very soon. Good night, gentlemen."

He succeeded—by not turning them down flat—in

shepherding them out of his suite. He waited until his visitors were off his floor, left his suite and went down a flight of stairs. He paused within view of the public telephones in the lobby, wondering how many were bugged. He decided on a brisk walk.

The Washington Memorial stood behind him as he walked in a southerly direction. His notion of District of Columbia geography was hazy. Ahead, he knew lay the island known as Potomac Park, formed by the river branching northwest and the Anacostia River striking out toward the northeast. Ten minutes later and frozen, he found a phone booth and placed a call to Kerry's Hoboken home. Only an answering service responded, giving Charley the telephone number of his oldest daughter's Manhattan apartment. He dialed it.

"Halleluyah," Winfield said. "What's the problem?"

"Kerry's answering service tells me you have a visitor."

"Now there's a diplomatic statement if ever I heard one. Kerry? Then give him back to me."

"Uncle Charley? What's up?"

"Sorry about this. Tell me whether Basel's broken out shares in Richtron Electronics? Could that have happened already?"

A long pause. "I can't answer for other markets till I access the files. But neither Basel nor Liechtenstein has so informed us."

"Let's suppose they didn't get through to us today. Let's suppose someone wants to assemble a controlling interest. They still couldn't, could they, because they'd have to place orders with Richland Securities and our people haven't been issued instructions yet on Richtron Electronics?"

"Right."

"So if you wanted to force a merger by takeover tactics, you'd fail?"

"By normal tactics," Kerry agreed. "But who knows what other tactics are possible?"

In the distance Charley could still see the Washington obelisk, bathed in light. He stared hard at it, an icon of everything that bothered Il Professore, a symbol of arrow-straight, rock-hard priapism, of always having the sword ready and out of its scabbard. "Go back to bed. Put Winfield on."

"Dad? You sound terrible."

"Daddy's little ray of sunshine. Sorry to intrude."

"We were having a fight."

Charley's teeth were beginning to chatter in the February breeze. "So am I," he confessed. "I'm just beginning to realize how stupid I've been."

"About what?"

"About Bunny's baby's other grandfather."

When he left the booth he turned in a direction he thought was east and then north. Charley Braverman, trading off Pentagon corruption for a slice of the defense pie. On Seong, representing an empire that made no distinction between legitimate and criminal profit, offering to buy everything up into one neat straight/bent consortium. No illusions. No Zio Italo niceties about respectability. Just raw profit, no matter how.

Charley's steps quickened in the chilly night. Ahead he could now see not only the Washington Monument but the Pennsylvania Avenue side of the White House, both symbols brightly lit, shining beacons of democracy.

He definitely did not hear footsteps behind him. There was definitely no warning. It was certainly not the normal District mugging, a quick chop with a crowbar, watch, wallet, rings, so long, suckah!

One masked man stepped in front of him while the other tripped him from behind. Charley fell hard on his face, arms outstretched to take the shock. The masked one pulled a gun. "Freeze!" Charley lay spreadeagled on his face, arms outstretched. Automatically he registered that the man was white and his idea of "Freeze!" sounded like "Fridz!"

He watched the man's finger tighten on the trigger. Charley's neck muscles bunched, as if the bullet would thus bounce safely off. So, the last sound Charley Richards would hear would be the bark of a handgun. Instead the sound was small, neat, a snick and a pop, like a beer can tab pulled open. The dart hit his wrist near a vein. He stared at it for a moment. The man in the mask reached down and yanked it out of his flesh. Beyond his legs, from Charley's supine angle, the White House glittered in the cold night air.

Pretty soon Charley started to black out. His last thought was two words: designer take-out. Or was that three?

He slept.

Sixty-One

There are adages about months, particularly March, which comes in like a lion. Nobody has yet described a February that goes out, as Baxter Choy put it, "like the Second World War." But, in the blooding business, upheaval is to be expected.

In the drug business, everyone wears extra hats. Ricko, who handled West 96th Street to 110th, was salesman, courier, bookkeeper, treasurer and enforcer. Anybody with that much responsibility drove, in his case, a seven-passenger Cadillac Fleetwood with orchid metallic finish and cerise trim.

Precisely at eleven-thirty p.m., typical of the discipline of an entrenched organization, he met Speedo, who handled West 110th to 125th. The meeting was always at 96th and Park, where the railroad tracks emerged. Speedo drove a black Daimler limo with tiny gold stars cemented all over its skin.

A third party, from downtown, met them in a bright orange Rolls, collected cash and filled tomorrow's projected orders. The rendezvous was so well established and so free of police interest that small boys gathered on the corner to break-dance for the hundred-dollar bills the drug dealers threw them.

This Thursday night, as the three conspicuous automobiles converged, a passing motorcyclist blew them a kiss. Something rolled unseen across the asphalt as he sped off in a raucous blast of exhaust. The dealers continued counting.

A white-hot flash lit the corner. The tall buildings below 96th Street flared in its evil spark. Then a gigantic roar as if Earth had collided with Mars. Colorful bits of chassis and paint job rained down on passersby within a radius of a hundred yards. An intestinal stench, like that of fertilizer, spread out in a wide circle.

Two small break-dancers were spun up, over and down onto the New York Central electric lines. Train service was halted for thirty-six hours.

Assessing the commercial damage later, Tony Rego figured half a million in cash had been scattered or burned and almost double that in coke and MegaMAO. "But what hurts more," he phoned Vince, "is that everybody saw us eat shit."

"Find out who did it."

The flagship detox center at 117th and Broadway had become a community playhouse. All sorts of dramas were enacted on this protected ground—marital breakups, romances, births—where no cop dared plant his flat foot. Despite hard use and thousands of visitors a day, Ricci Medical Center 201, to give it its correct title, remained an island of misguided hope in a slough of despond.

Tony Rego stood at the front of the staff recreation room and demanded of everyone in turn what they could tell him about an opposition so fierce it blew away millions in cash, rather than steal it.

"Any suspicious stuff. Guys with complaints, hotheads, looneys."

"There was somebody in here this morning?" a nurse volunteered. She was not a nurse, of course, but a slim, attractive black woman wearing a white uniform, starched headdress with a thermometer clipped to her neckline.

"Speak up, Delia."

"Two fellas from Con Ed, checking the wiring?"

"What was wrong with the wiring?"

"Nothing?" Delia responded, in her usual questioning tone. "These two was yella?"

"Wah'dya mean yella?"

"I mean they was Chinese? You ever hear of a Chink Con Ed man?"

Before Tony Rego could respond, the explosion knocked him sideways off his feet. A wall blew in. Plaster and bricks began dropping like snow. Those still alive could hear a great groaning sound, as if the building were collapsing.

It was.

The Fire Department released a death toll to the TV crews at noon. More than thirty staff and visitors had died. Double that number were in the intensive care units of nearby hospitals. Many remained in the rubble.

"We're searching. We're using dogs. Heat sensors. Never before anything like this," the fire chief told the TV cameras. "I mean, since I watched earthquakes on TV."

"All establishments are vulnerable," Nikki reminded Choy. "But I was expecting more one-on-one shoot-em-up."

"Less is more," Baxter said, lighting his cigar. "Begorrah, I made that up."

"You shit made it up," Nikki told him, grinning. "It's an article of Bauhaus faith." His life had changed completely but he still dressed the same, as if on his way from an exhausting tennis match. They had met for a fast conference in one of those run-down neighborhood soda fountain joints where Manhattanites can still get an egg-cream chocolate soda.

So far, for less than three weeks, he'd stood up to the pace Baxter Choy had set, a relentlessly fast, random, impulsive game designed to dazzle as much as it hurt.

"Oh, yeah, right," Baxter admitted. Nikki was fairly sure the Irish fathers hadn't briefed him on Bauhaus. But about street tactics he had written the book. "Guerilla warfare, Frenchy," Choy said, eyes bright with malice. "Invented by the Confederacy in the Civil War. Hit and run."

"I'm learning, Bax, I'm learning."

"We have no headquarters. We have no table of organization. We are five fast Chinks on motorbikes and we've got Ricci tied up in knots."

Nikki nodded. "Even the Fire Department agrees. They've declared those three medical center take-outs the work of urban guerrillas. That's what I call verification. What did you use?"

Choy's glance went sideways. "Pantaerithrytol tetranitrate."

"I beg your pardon?"

"Often called PETN."

"Come on, Bax, stop bullshitting."

"Well, it's not from Czechoslovakia so I can't call it Semtex. It's made in the U.S. of A. for CIA spooks and the only way you can get some is by bribing an Army supply-depot staff sergeant. But the secret is how I shape the charges. In the right places they take out a five-story building, as you saw." Choy puffed contentedly. Havana fumes surrounded them. "Leaving one million MegaMAO junkies clawing at their throats. Chinks to the rescue! We've moved every last capsule at three bills a thrill. I've been on the phone to Taiwan half a dozen times, begging for more. They're bringing it in tonight."

"Where? Not JFK."

Choy laughed. His round, flat face beamed with satisfaction. "From Taiwan it comes across the Pacific in one of the Shan 707's modified for air freight. It arrived this morning at a place near Vera Cruz. A seaplane's bringing it up to New York tonight. Midnight delivery, we hope."

"To where?"

Baxter Choy rummaged through his elegantly slender morocco-leather attaché case. He was dressed up, for him, in black leather trousers, a dark brown leather jacket and an acid green silk scarf the color of fresh verdigris on a copper statue. Out of the attaché case he pulled a map and spread it on the table. "Here. How well do you know Long Island?" He traced the upper, eastern leg of the island that terminated in Orient Point. "Between Greenport and the tip is a small airport just west of Petty's Bight. See."

"We have a depot there?"

"It's an old mansion that was moved there from Plum." Baxter Choy indicated a sperm-shaped wriggle of land off Orient Point labeled Plum Island. "Sometime during the First World War," he went on, "they lifted this mansion onto barges and floated it over to Petty's Bight and set it up. The government wanted Plum Island for something hush-hush." Puffing cigar smoke, Choy considered the map for a long time. "They tell me the government still patrols the area around Plum. So we'll off-load the plane at sea, if the wind isn't too strong."

"But then the launch will have to bring it somewhere closer in. Is that warehouse on Throggs Neck clean?"

Nikki's finger swept west to a point where the Bronx pointed out into the East River toward Queens.

"Maybe."

"Can't take the chance. As the launch moves along we'll break the shipment into small loads, motorcycle-sized," Nikki said. "All we do in the Bronx is load up the cycles. Then everybody runs for it."

"You're learning, Frenchy, me lad." Choy's almond-shaped eyes squinted through cigar smoke as he surveyed the map. "If the wind's too high, we need a dock."

"This time of year the summer people aren't there," Nikki mused. "But the Coast Guard? In the dead of night?"

"Plum Island is a U.S. Animal Diseases Laboratory."

"Diseases? Like what?"

Baxter Choy sat back and licked the end of his cigar to set a loose wrapper in place. He grimaced. "Bubonic? Pneumonic? Anthrax?"

"What's the government doing?" Nikki mused. "This tri-state area's the most heavily populated corner of the U.S. Why play death games here at the center?"

"And what else," Choy asked in his thickest brogue, "will inny government be afther doing in this worrold but death games? 'Tis the natural provenance of governing, so it is."

Once again they fell silent, studying the map. "If the wind's really high," Nikki decided, "we'll have to call an abort."

Choy shook his head. "No aborts in this business, Frenchy. We'll find a leeward shore and take our chances."

"OK. I'm still learning."

This time, as they studied the map, their silence grew longer and longer. Nikki had no idea what Choy was thinking; he rarely did. But something in the air still reverberated. Those old-time plagues, Nikki decided. Their very names sent out bad vibrations. Nikki shook his head violently. "No chance, that close to Plum Island, we might run into something nasty in the way of microbes?"

"More likely in the way of Coast Guard."

"Would the Riccis know about the house?"

"Out there mafia business is run by the Cianflones, cousins of the Riccis. They're a lazy bunch. They cluster in the big towns. Orient Point wouldn't interest them in winter.''

Nikki glanced at his watch. ''Midnight delivery you said. Let's get our ass in gear. It's five hours from now.''

Choy grinned. ''You're learning real fast.''

''Shure now,'' Nikki responded. ''And ain't that the binifit of a true Jesuit education?''

March

Sixty-Two

Dear Mr. Suggs:
We are terribly pleased to learn that Agent Cohen has
returned from sick leave to participate in our spring
seminar. But I would be remiss if I did not inform
you that the average age of our seminar delegates is
mid- to late-twenties. An FBI agent in that age
grouping would afford a more appropriate role model.
Would a younger agent be as experienced in matters
relating to organized crime? Perhaps so.
    Sincerely,
    A. Code, Seminar Director
    Lutjens, Van Kurve and Armatrading.

J. Laverne Suggs shoved the letter across his desk to
Cohen. "In plain English they want somebody else. File
that one in your paranoia scrapbook."

"Bears out what I've been saying about them all
along." Although he stood six feet tall, Cohen had taken
to wearing high-heeled Frye boots as a mark of Gary
Cooperization. They rapped loudly on the floor as he
shifted in his seat.

Suggs shook his head, negating whatever Cohen might
say next. "What is it with you Jewish individuals?"
Suggs asked. "You come on like you were put here on
earth to explain the world to the rest of us."

"You mean we weren't?" Cohen asked, smiling to indicate the Hebraic humor of his response.

"We have to pay attention to letters like this." Suggs'
glance shifted this way and that, refusing to meet Cohen's steely, fearless, U.S. Marshal's stare. "So I'm
seconding you to this new metro strike force."

"What?"

"All these bombings. Drug wars. People are screaming. Justice's set up a special Metropolitan Area Strike
Force against drugs. You're a Long Island boy and they're
starting off with that area. They've been watching the

northern shore from Throggs Neck all the way out to Orient Point.''

"This is a real slap in the face.''

"You're bumped up one rank in the Bureau to match you with the Coast Guard Commander. You don't deserve it but I fought for you. Say thanks for the favor and beat it.''

"A favor to me?'' Cohen asked. "Or the Riccis?''

"Oh, sweet Christ, deliver me from Hebrew prophets!''

In the members' lounge of the Museum of Modern Art, the atmosphere between Garnet and Winfield seemed choked with secrets as they met. "Where is he?'' Garnet asked.

"Dad? I thought *you* knew.''

Garnet's triangular face went pale. "I was sure you knew. I haven't heard from him in twenty-four hours.''

Winfield was silent for a moment. "He phoned me from Washington the night before last. You mean—? You mean you haven't heard since then?''

Garnet nodded. Her glance swerved sideways to stare at a Schiele sketch of a naked, underfed Viennese prostitute with immense eyes and nipples and the collapsed nose of a syphilitic. Garnet's face seemed to slide sideways, as if refusing to face either the sketch or the substance of what they were saying. "Call Kerry.''

Winfield shook her head. "He phoned his office this morning to talk to Charley and the girl told him she'd heard nothing. We phoned his Washington hotel and his room hadn't been slept in. His flight bag's still there.''

Garnet jumped to her feet so quickly it attracted the attention of two women sipping martinis. She was pacing now, her long legs measuring a tight triangle around the chair in which Winfield was sitting, her eyes shifting sideways here and there, as if treading a minefield. "He's never—'' She stopped pacing. Then started again. "He's always—'' She sat back down. Her right hand moved behind her and felt her back just below her right hip. "Winfield, I'm not sure I understand all this.'' Her voice sounded suddenly very small. Her glance darted around the room, noting that one of the women staring at her had that same collapsed Schiele nose. Did that signify something? Was it part of a conspiracy? Garnet shook her head mournfully.

"I've never had this with Charley before. We're not the kind of couple that sticks together like glue. We're both busy. But we always know each other's schedule. We always fit together. We always—" She stopped again. Slowly her mouth opened and constricted into an O. "My back."

"What?" Winfield demanded.

Garnet shook her head, her glance riveted to the face of the woman across the room. The co-conspiratress. Emissary from the dark side of life. Again Garnet shook her head. "It's not possible. I do my exercises religiously."

"What is it?" Winfield persisted.

"One of those damned back pains. I'll be all right." She tried to stand up and collapsed back in her chair. The woman with the Schiele nose noted this.

Buzz glanced nervously around Vince's magnificent office at Le Refuge, his Monaco operation that advanced resort technology well into the twenty-first century.

Somewhere in this grand array of managerial artifacts—desk sets that resembled Martian surgery kits and, although Vince detested and distrusted computers, four separate flickering monitors in different glowing colors— Lenore Ricci had hidden one of those diabolical matchbook-bugs. Somewhere within a few dozen yards, Buzz had been assured, a recording device was ready to switch on the moment the bug began picking up human speech.

Vince hadn't arrived yet from his morning round of inspection, nor did he know Buzz was waiting for him. Not for the first time since he and Eileen had fallen tearfully into each other's arms, Buzz decided he was being insanely foolhardy. It was the presence in the plot of Lenore that drove him to it and she, damn her, knew it. Those fake-maf veiled threats of hers had been enough to spook Buzz into cooperation. Clearly Lenore loathed Vince enough—or felt powerful enough with little Eugene in her arms—to blackmail Buzz with their mutually suicidal complicity. Play along with Eileen, her threat had clearly said, or I will blow us both sky-high.

Since he'd agreed Eileen had somehow found it possible to forgive him everything. That part was great. The Irish were like that, Buzz mused: they got very angry and very sentimental and nursed grudges but, if they loved you, they forgave. He found himself weeping again at the thought of Eileen's goodness. Jesus, this thing had unhinged him entirely. It was changing his personality. He still gambled. But standing at the blackjack table, he no longer felt like Christ on the cross. The casual glances of onlookers no longer seemed admiring. Losing had lost its kick.

"What the fuck you doing here?" Vince demanded. "You blew this morning's chips already?" He dug his fingers in his tight black curls and gave himself a quick scalp massage. Then he sat down at his desk, which resembled the cockpit of a 747 redesigned for dyslexics. Frowning horribly, he switched off all the computer screens. Those which were adjustable he turned away from his glance. "Che c'é, goombah?"

"I was wondering—" Buzz's voice gave out. "You remember you were asking me last week—" Once again a constriction closed his throat. "You remember? About prostitutes and AIDS?"

"Fuck 'em. Fuck 'em all. I'm getting out of the cunt trade."

"What?"

"You should too, Buzz-baby. What kind of work is it for a real man, sticking tongue depressors down twats?" He cackled wildly. "No shit, I'm phasing out the whores. Nothing but trouble. Whaja wanna see me about?"

"I just—" He moistened his lips. He found himself wondering where, exactly where, Lenore had placed that damned matchbook. "Wondering, you know . . ."

Vince's telephone rang. "Yeah? Yeah, give." As Vince listened his face went dead. "Merda." He hung up. "My cousin Guido. The profit picture for last week." He tried hard to look unaffected. "The New York picture is murdering our balance sheet. This Chink mob is twisting our nuts off."

"What I wanted to mention," Buzz began bravely, "was that—" The obstruction in his throat snapped shut again.

Vince picked up a different phone and tapped in three

numbers. As he waited, he said, "Buzz, you're like my kid brother, but this call is top confidential. So . . . ?" He made a sweeping-out gesture.

Buzz got to his feet, feeling frustrated and terribly relieved. He'd tried. The bug would have recorded that. But, thank God, he'd failed.

". . . of Detectives indicated that Manhattan was in the throes of a drug war between rival gangs," the young woman TV reader said. "Never before in the history of the city has . . ." She wore a pale peach blouse opened at the neck to show starting curves of breasts. Her carroty red hair kinked out at the sides like a chopped-off cloud above her ears.

"To date," she went on, as the picture changed to a view of wreckage at 117th Street and Broadway, "three bombed-out detox centers have flooded Manhattan's streets with drug-starved junkies." The picture changed to a hospital ward. "Survivors of other attacks around town have filled the intensive care units of many—"

Shan Lao snapped off the TV. His bulging eyes had pulled in every shred of information. Nicole, working on a bit of tapestry, a chair-seat cover, had been glancing back and forth for the last few minutes from her fingers to the screen. She had no way of knowing her son's complicity in these events. But anything Shan might watch that intently was obviously of more than routine interest to him. She put down her embroidery. "A cup of tea?"

"Thank you." Shan watched her leave. He opened a briefcase and pulled out a sheaf of faxes. Baxter Choy had sent some from New York. Others had arrived from Washington. They were facsimile copies of newspaper clippings: DEFENSE SUPPLIER MISSING. The Washington headline topped a long page one story in which nobody had done their homework but had taken the Pentagon press officer at face value:

The head of a major electronics firm supplying computers to the Department of Defense went missing yesterday in the heart of the District. After Charles A. Richards, forty-eight, chief executive officer of Richtron, Inc., failed to appear at a scheduled meeting,

Pentagon officials instituted an inquiry. Mr. Richards'
hotel suite was found untouched. According to . . .

Shan Lao looked up as Nicole returned with a tray.
"Bunny would like to bring Leo in to you."

"Nothing would please me more." Shan had time for
just one more fax: RICHARDS MYSTERY DEEPENS. The New
York paper had had twenty-four hours in which to identify the missing tycoon as "one of America's outstanding
business leaders," and this "despite rumors of a connection to the Ricci family of organized crime."

The telephone rang. In this cottage on Grand Bahama,
surrounded day and night by lurking bodyguards, Shan
had installed a radiotelephone with a scrambler he now
keyed in. After a moment he and Baxter Choy were both
on scrambler.

Shan began: "Tonight's television news has made your
report for you."

"But the best news," Choy assured him, "is how well
our young friend has taken to this. He shows good nerves
and enthusiasm."

"I am pleased. As for the opposition?"

Choy hesitated. "The official opposition has re-
grouped and formed a new strike force. The clandestine
opposition is, for the moment, boxed in."

Shan Lao said nothing for a while, thinking hard. This
next step would be his first in the final assault on Richland. "You spoke once of that—what did you call him?
Hacker?"

"Richland fired him last week. I've had my hands full
with other matters."

"Drop these matters. You must now mount the final
assault. I want this hacker in the palm of your hand."

"Can our new young executive help me?" Choy asked.

Shan heard someone approaching. He looked up to see
Bunny, holding the baby in her arms. "He is compro-
mised for this project until completed. He must have
deniability. Send him to me at once."

"Yes, sir."

"First the hacker." Shan's protuberant eyes seemed to
eat up the room, Bunny and little Leo. "Then the hack-
ing," the puns fascinated him. His smile was thin, chilling. "And finally, the feast."

* * *

"We simply can't afford the publicity connected with Mr. Richards," the blond woman in the power suit and Hermes scarf was saying. Her basso voice rattled slightly with tension. Her face had a leathery, tanned, drawn quality that spoke of Caribbean sun and extremely skillful plastic surgery. It would have made a terrific handbag with very little extra work.

Garnet turned around slowly in her front-row chair and looked at the woman, trying to place her. All Garnet's movements were slowed by the back pain. She had been keeping it in check with normal painkillers but it seemed to be getting worse. If she could have avoided attending this meeting, she would have been able to help Winfield man the telephones on which the kidnappers might make known their demands. They should have called long ago. But Garnet had to be at this meeting if only to counter the antagonism voiced by this woman.

Was she part of the conspiracy? Like the woman with the Schiele nose? Garnet blinked; paranoia is a shock when you realize you're slipping into it. "But our slate of candidates has already been printed," the meeting's chairman pointed out, "and mailed to members all over the country." He was a tall, weedy young man who had something so lowly to do in publishing that he had almost no luncheon expense account.

Garnet pulled her mind away from conspiracies. She raised her hand. "We're not talking about anything immense here," she pointed out. "We nominate six new members each year for an eighteen-member board. They serve three—" She stopped, breathless at the sharp stab of back pain. "Three years and must then resign. It's hardly a privilege. More of a necessary evil, if you're as interested in education as Mr. Richards is."

"I'm not questioning his sincerity," the blond woman stated in her very low voice. "I'm simply saying that the publicity around his kidnapping is hardly the image we require for our board people."

"Imogen," the chairman interrupted diffidently. "We're being premature."

"Meaning they may waste Charley Richards and save us the trouble?"

Garnet placed her now, a very powerful publishing lady

for whom the chairman would probably love to work in any capacity that required the licking of boots. Sensing a slide deeper into disaster for Charley, Garnet had rallied to fight back. She considered her chances. Bad back or not, latent paranoia or not, she had to protect Charley. There was only one way. Stall. "It's clearly a point of personal privilege. Move to table for one month," Garnet said.

"Second," someone added.

"And after a month?" Imogen Raspe demanded.

"After a month," the chairman surmised, "we'll know more about Mr. Richards', ah, fate. All in favor?"

As the motion passed, Garnet sat back and examined her temporary success. It was terrible to feel this way, a walking invalid driven by conspiracy theory. Once she got Charley back they would disappear, the two of them, to some place where the sun always shone and everyone loved everyone and—

Once she got him back.

Sixty-Three

Kidnap is not a high-tech crime. Whoever pays for it, those who do it are expendable animals with the power of speech but few other human attributes. For money, for business, for political reasons, kidnap has developed a professional class for hire. Maltreatment of victims is routine. Young children, old men, pregnant women are chained outside like dogs, subject to the weather, in their own excrement. Negotiations are prolonged, often lasting, if Islamic, for years. Like Muslim terrorists or any other true believers, professional kidnappers are indifferent to suffering and death. They often extort family ransom long after they have murdered the victim. In Southern Italy, these "men of honor" are protected by the 'ndrangheta, with branches in Australia, Canada and Brooklyn.

Calabrese can only work where local law is bought off. With its high-crime morass of sophisticated young ghetto blacks who deal drugs to live, Washington D.C. is a mass of obstacles. Even a Calabrese worries about working amid risk that high. He is not used to taking *any* chances. Therefore, two days into the Charley Richards kidnap, Pino and Mimmo knew they were in over their heads.

Mr. Tomaso, the man who had hired them in their home town of Locri, had never appeared again. An aide of Tomaso's, who spoke haltingly in a thick foreign accent, had reserved a motel room for them in Bowie, Maryland, and given them photographs of Charley, his Washington itinerary, two Alitalia tickets and five thousand dollars in used notes. Later, friends said he was an Inglese milord.

Moreover, they thought Tomaso's name had not been Tomaso, which didn't matter since Pino and Mimmo's names weren't Pino and Mimmo. What made it more confusing was the two phone calls they had had in the motel room; both times the man spoke perfect Northern Italian—like a RAI news announcer—but with a Chinese accent. Pino and Mimmo knew what this sounded like, also from RAI's overdubbed Fu Manchu reruns.

Pino and Mimmo had dumped Charley in the closet of their motel room. They were growing very bored. "We kill him now," Pino said. They had sent out for pizzas and were carving them up with switchblades.

"Give Tomaso, whatever his name is, another day." Mimmo farted loudly. "This pizza is no good."

"Your asshole sounds loose." Pino chewed a while. "No, tonight. There's a lake. They can find him when he floats back up."

"Tomaso or the Inglese milord owes us another five thousand," Mimmo reminded him. "Kill now, lose the money."

"This cursed town." Pino shuddered, belched, coughed, spat. "How you get the other five thousand if you don't know Tomaso's name? In Locri, my friend says Tomaso is married to Concetta Macri. The marito of Concetta Macri is a Siciliano called Mollo."

"So he's maybe Tomaso Mollo." Mimmo farted again. "So what?"

"You think another day will make a difference?"

"Yes. Tomorrow," Mimmo decided, "we kill and go home."

* * *

All her previous pain was nothing. This now was a hot poker drawn down the right side of her spine. It was as if the pain of the past few days had suddenly shifted into overdrive, roaring through her body like a demon with a sword. Holding onto chairbacks she got to the bathroom and searched her medicine chest for one of the powerful painkillers left over from her convalescence.

A relapse, after all this time? Not possible that the old muscular weaknesses after the explosion should suddenly return. The cold water, as she washed down the two pills, gave her the quick illusion of well-being. Then the pain lanced downward again and she had to grasp the edge of the handbasin to keep from lurching off her feet.

Not a relapse. Someone who did her exercises daily could not have invited a relapse. Charley's kidnap had crushed her. She'd been steam-rollered, not knowing why or who or what was happening. There had been no ransom demands. Only limbo.

She pulled on a dressing gown and slowly lowered herself into an armchair. All alone by the telephone. She had a pact with Winfield and Kerry that all of them would remain near telephones. This was the worst of it, waiting by a telephone that didn't ring. No, the worst was trying to sleep in a bed without Charley. No. Losing the other half of her life mold. That was the worst. It had happened once before. It mustn't happen again. There'd be nothing left.

She put on her spectacles and tried to read some recent mail. All alone by the telephone. Worthwhile causes wanted money. Terrible things were being done by human beings to other human beings. God knows what they were doing to Charley.

"I don't ask much of you two," Stefi told her sons. She had summoned them to her home for a meeting at midnight. "But nobody has found out anything. I'm mad at Charley but that doesn't mean I never want to see him again. So I ask you: find him."

"He could be dead by now."

Stefi drew in a quick breath. "We can't think that way."

"But without any contact, without a demand, we have to assume it could be a take-out," Kerry explained.

"If it's a Calabrese job, they sweat you first," his brother said.

"The night they grabbed him," Kerry remembered, "he called me. He wanted information on market action in Richtron shares. But the shares hadn't been issued yet. They still aren't."

Kevin shook his head. "Zio Italo is driving me crazy with this. I've never seen him so angry."

"Because he's powerless," Stefi put in. "He's used to being the whole cheese. But he has to sit back and let the real cops handle it."

"Not Zio. He's got a dozen guys on this, top guys."

"And?"

"And they came up blank," Kevin confessed.

Stefi looked from one to the other of them. "We need a miracle," she said.

She had never troubled herself to distinguish sharply between the twins. Something told to one always got to the other anyway. But now she was noticing differences, as if the life each led was marking him differently. Kerry's silences grew longer. Kevin's anger roamed close to the surface, distorting his face, with its tiny blue tattoo dot under the left eye. He, who knew all the shortcuts, was as powerless as Zio Italo.

"A miracle," she repeated.

"No," Kevin said then, his face suddenly hot with malice. "Ma, what we need is a hostage."

The pain was the worst part. Charley had never had to endure such pain; wired up, legs bent back, feet bound to neck, back arched like a bow. Then everything went dead, deprived of blood. And then the real fear set in.

Embolism? The thirst had died away. Gangrene? The hunger was gone. Nothing remained except fear. He had only to black out and his body, relaxing slightly, could unkink enough for the wire around his neck to choke him to death. He wondered if anyone was searching for him.

He marveled at their cruelty, at their casual sadism. Why didn't they gloat over him? Why didn't tomorrow come so they could kill him? The truth was: nothing of his agony crossed over to them. The truth: his only chance was death. Now. Please?

The next Miami flight was leaving in half an hour when Kevin reached La Guardia Airport. He spotted Nikki Shan and walked over to greet him, hand outstretched, as if they were old friends. "Hey, Nik! Kerry Ricci," Kevin told him. "I'm Bunny's cousin. Winfield's main squeeze."

"My God. Haven't seen you since the wedding." Nikki pumped his hand. "What are we, pre-brothers-in-law?"

Kevin looked suddenly stricken. "Where's the nearest john?" He glanced around him.

"Over there." Nikki accompanied his near-relative. Both young men, carrying small backpacks by one strap, entered the men's room. Kevin headed for the nearest booth. "Can you help me?" he asked, once inside. Nikki entered the booth in time to get two cc's of Tuinal in the wrist. He started to struggle, then slumped in Kevin's arms.

Kevin carried him out of the booth. "Hey," he called to the nearest husky-looking man, "my buddy's collapsed. We've been airborne for twelve hours. I guess it was too much. Can you help me get him to a cab?"

As a state-of-the-art kidnap, it lacked security. But it did economize on manpower.

Sixty-Four

Once every three months, at a midtown hotel in Manhattan, computer hardware and software manufacturers staged a trade seminar for lone misfits peering at VDU screens. It brought them together to swap gossip and switch jobs.

Mervyn Lemnitzer, because he had just been canned by Richland Securities and was paying off a stiff mortgage on a tiny condo, badly needed this seminar. A tall, thin man in his late twenties, he knew only a few people in the New York computer world. His one and only job since college had been with Richland.

He confessed a tailored version of this to the affable Oriental fellow he'd met at the hotel's coffee shop. It looked out on noisy Seventh Avenue. "No, let me buy you another Danish," Baxter Choy told him. "It's only fair."

They were waiting for the seminar to open at ten a.m. The coffee shop, normally emptying out at this hour, was filled with other computerheads. "It's not even fair," Mervyn joked, accepting Choy's offer. "It's barely edible."

"You a programmer?" Choy asked. "Designer?"

"Both," Mervyn said. He squinted at his new friend to make sure this was believed. "Up to here with securities, though. I'm looking for something real, not stocks and bonds."

"I know what you mean," Choy agreed. "Avionics, maybe? Biochemistry? Superconductors? Something at the edge, not that old-hat market trading. It's down the tubes anyway. Trading sucks."

"They had the nerve to tell me," Mervyn burst out, "that my mind wasn't on my work. Just because I—" He stopped himself, realizing his story wouldn't match his claim that he was still employed. "Who're you with?"

"Dow Chemical," Choy improvised. "Defoliants."

"Any openings for a natural hacker?"

Choy tilted his head, signaling possibilities. "You never know." He glanced at his watch. "Opening time," he said, reaching for the check. "Let's see how much good we can do you."

He was freezing. His fingers ached with the damp cold. In the basement of the Hoboken brownstone a coal bin had been converted into a strong room with a reinforced door. Inside, the place was seeping with that damp that lodges in one's joints.

Nikki came out of the Tuinal to find himself shivering. A glaring 150-watt bulb, clear glass, ate its way into his eyeballs. He could find no switch. Nor with icicle fingers could he touch the bulb to twist it free. He could only break it. Rising on one elbow, he made a feeble swat and fell back, exhausted. He turned on his stomach to cut

down the glare in his eyes. Memory flooded in. Meeting
Kerry. The toilet booth. Obviously the Riccis had found
out who was behind the bombings that had wrecked their
Manhattan establishment and staff.

The heavy door creaked open. The man he believed to
be Kerry stood there watching him. "First thing," he
said then, "notice that nobody's tied you up or put cuffs
on you? Nobody's abused you while you were out. As far
as I'm concerned, Nik, you're family."

"This must be one hell of a high-risk family."

Kevin nodded. "Second thing. There's nothing personal in any of this. Bunny thinks you're a nice guy. And
your son, Leo, is half-Ricci. But you're here because of
your last name. Understand?"

"Someone has kidnapped one of yours?" Nik guessed.

"They told me you were smart," Kevin said with a
touch of sarcasm. "Nobody warned me you were downright brilliant." He closed the door behind him.

Nik shaded his eyes against the glare. "What are you
supposed to do, Kerry, beat the shit out of me and make
me talk?"

"You are a hostage. You have to be produced some
time, unharmed. But, unharmed doesn't mean you might
not have lost a couple of teeth. I found this in your bag."
Kevin tossed a folded piece of paper to Nikki.

He opened it to a series of coded dates. He had been
on his way south, not only blooded but quite bloody himself, to report to his father on the success of their
crimson-spattered Manhattan assault. So far close to a
hundred people were dead, only two of them Shan agents.
Baxter Choy had suggested the trip. Knowing Shan Lao,
he had jotted down key data. "Lot of numbers?" Nikki
asked.

"This B14. B is the second letter of the alphabet, February the second month. It's a routine code for tabbing
computer documents. The detox center on 117th Street
went up on Valentine's Day, February 14. The one in the
Village blew on February 19, which is this next entry
B19. And so it goes, huh?" He snapped the paper out of
Nik's fingers. "These big numbers down below—a fifty,
a 150—they represent kilos of something. No prizes for
a lucky guess. You're being treated as a member of the
family. The question is, whose family?"

"This is all news to me, Kerry."

Kevin nodded and held up his hand in a wait-a-minute gesture. "It's two hours since the pickup at La Guardia. We circulated your photo. Three guys made you as one of two men on motorcycles. The only thing between you and death is your hostage value. So, no silly answers, OK? Any questions?"

"I think you've covered everything."

"You know I can't waste you because you're merchandise for trade. So I need your cooperation. I have to find out why your people attacked us." Kevin's rather immobile face grew almost ponderous as he outlined the question. "It was hit-and-run. You gave us a bad week and disappeared. What kind of thinking is that?"

Slowly, so as not to alarm him, Nikki swung his legs over the edge of the table and sat up. "You won't believe me if I say it was a training exercise?" Kevin shook his head negatively. "Even if it happens to be true?"

"Not good enough. Somebody upstairs wants to know more."

Nik pointed to the ceiling. "Upstairs here? We're not alone?"

"You and I," Kevin said, his voice heavy with its freight of knowledge, "are never, ever alone."

Blackouts came in brutal bursts. He would be conscious. He would black out. The tension of his bowed body would start to choke him. He would awake, gagging. Conscious. Black. Shock of choking. Conscious. Black. He no longer worried about anything but how soon death would come. The conversation of the two animals in the next room had convinced him that death was his best bet. Even the excruciating pain in his back was as nothing, compared to the great boon of death.

In the room beyond the closet the telephone rang and one of the Calabrese answered with a grunt. After a brief conversation he hung up. "Tomaso é qua."

"You remember his voice?"

"The voice of a snake. Full of cunning. Full of pride. The voice of a Siciliano, what else?"

"I don't even remember what he looks like."

There was a discreet knock on the door. One of the

Calabrese opened it. "Tu non sei Tomaso," he told the young Chinese lad standing there.

"Buon giorno." Two snaps, as of thin wooden ferrules being broken over someone's knees. Two thuds. The closet door slid open. Someone with wirecutters. After a moment, the excruciating tension in his back and around his neck ceased. He blacked out.

When he awoke the room was flooded with wintry sunlight. Lying curled on his side, Charley Richards opened his eyes and stared into the dead eyes of Pino and Mimmo, dropped in their tracks. Where the original eyes were vacant, the third in their foreheads almost passed as a real eye. Remarkably little blood had leaked. If Tomaso Mollo was a snake, his fangs left almost no mark. Both kidnappers had the same look of surprise, as if a primitive double-cross like this was somehow unheard of in 'ndrangheta circles.

Frozen in a kind of kink, like an iced prawn, Charley noted the transatlantic expertise. Perhaps the Englishman had worked this out? The English were expert murderers. But what was an English hit man doing on the Ionic coast of Calabria, buddied up with whoever had taken over the Corleone business interests and moved them.

Groaning, Charley tried to move. His limbs were racked by terrifying prickles and electric shocks. As he stared into the dead men's eyes, he began to realize that being freed was only marginally better than being trussed up.

He made a noise. Then he blacked out again.

This time, as his eyes opened, the room was in darkness and the telephone was ringing. He struggled to crawl to it but he got only a few feet, crabwise, one leg still dead, one arm still immovable, before he blacked out. Time passed.

"Charley?"

He awoke looking up into Kevin's face. Or Kerry's. "Y—?"

"You OK, Uncle Charley?"

He searched for the dot under the left eye. It wasn't there. "Kerry?"

Stefi's son got up and made a telephone call. After a long wait he said: "Bingo." He listened. "I have to get him to a doctor. Who do you have in Washington?" Another pause. "Call Ma. Ciao." He hung up and turned to Charley Richards. "Listen—"

But Charley was out again.

In the darkness she grabbed wildly for the ringing telephone. She brought it to her ear. "Hullo? Yes?"

"They've found him," Winfield said. "He'll be OK."

Garnet sat up in bed as if electrified. "Are you sure he's all right?"

"Kerry says he'll *be* all right."

"What does that me—?"

"I have to run," Winfield cut in. "More later." She hung up.

Garnet sprang out of bed, still holding the telephone. As she bent over to replace it, she suddenly realized that the pain in her back had disappeared.

". . . nice pad she has, huh?" Baxter Choy asked. He had brought Mervyn Lemnitzer to an apartment down in the Village off Lower Fifth Avenue, claiming it belonged to his girlfriend. "Another wee libation?"

"Pressings from the scotchberry bush?" Lemnitzer sank into a deep upholstered chair and let out a long sigh. The seminar had bombed. Nobody needed a computerhead. So many had been fired on Wall Street that everyone was looking for work, not offering it. This would be his fourth whiskey since the seminar had ended. He was feeling no pain but still able to keep a running total in his head.

"Cheers." Choy raised his glass.

"Mump," Mervyn responded. He realized he had already taken a swig before the toast. Shocking bad manners. He liked the Chink, and certainly he was free with drinks. But was he good for a job?"

He watched as Choy fished a gelatin capsule from his vest pocket. He was wearing jeans, a bright yellow shirt and a sleeveless vest of electric blue with four front pockets lined in scarlet. Choy held up the capsule. "Happier days."

"Wassat? Upper?"

"This?" Choy inhaled deeply, his broad face sublimely anticipatory. "This is paradise, Merv. This is endless pleasure to the power of infinity. This is an up-

ward parabolic with no finite limit. This . . ." He popped
the capsule in his mouth and sipped his drink. "This is
MegaMAO."

Mervyn blinked. "Palso mine use it."

Choy had never taken MegaMAO in his life. He carried capsules filled with lactose powder in one vest
pocket. From another he now produced an identical
looking capsule. "All yours, my hacker friend."

He lofted it to Mervyn who snatched it out of the air
and stared down at it. "Go swith Scosh?"

"Goes with everything." Choy watched him swallow
the MegaMAO with the last of his drink. "Another
distillation of the Gaelic grain?"

"Don thinkso. Keep clearhead." Mervyn's long, narrow face, eyes squinting, shook from side to side in repeated refusal. Then, like a training film illustration, his
head came to rest and began nodding up and down.
"Whynot?"

Choy smiled pleasantly. He knew how fast MegaMAO
worked but he always enjoyed seeing it demonstrated so
convincingly. "Now," he said, making another Scotch
and water for his guest, "about getting you a job. Have
you ever tried industrial espionage?"

Mervyn blinked. "Pretty name. Es," he repeated,
"pionage. Lovit."

"And, God, how well it pays."

Although he liked posing as Etna just prior to an erup-
tion, Italo Ricci understood better than most the time for
noisy dramatics and the time for quiet thinking. He had
reached such a moment.

That Shan was the prime enemy, somehow allied with
the Calabrese, now stood out clearly. Any lingering doubt
had been removed by the speed with which the kidnap
of the son had produced Charley's release.

Charley needed time in the hospital, getting physio-
therapy in large doses. Italo knew his rebellious nipote
would need more than that: captivity of such a brutal
kind did something to a man's head as well as his body.
Especially to Il Professore. Stashing him in a hospital
would also cut down his exposure to April Garnet. Without her, Charley would never have had the balls to hang
tough about the split-up of the legitimate businesses.

How well Zio Italo understood Charley's main weakness, the virus of overabundance. Anyone, but especially a smart, good-looking young fellow like Charley, needed opposition early in life to hone his edges. Charley had been shielded from it. As a businessman, he could always call on cash reserves most managers only dreamed of. Other obstacles, Zio had eradicated for him without being asked: potential strikes, shortages of critical raw material, cartel competitors, all the things that plague other businesses. Charley had been coddled. That last inch which a true killer manager was always prepared to go, Charley was not. He'd never had to. The only other person who knew this about him was the damned Indian squaw. The less access she had to him the better. Thanks to her, he had already accomplished too much. If it hadn't been for Italo's hold on Richtron, Charley would finally have stepped free.

Italo had delayed the transfer of Richtron until it entangled Charley. Be that as it may, it taught Charley once again the lesson of the Nissan pickup truck and the gas explosion. One had to keep re-teaching him that, despite the balls the Garnet woman provided him with, all nipotini belonged to Zio. Basta é basta. Enough is enough.

To have a valuable asset snatched in, of all places, Washington, D.C., capital of everything, including street crime, was perhaps ironic. But it could not be allowed to pass unpunished. Those whores in Congress had to start earning their keep.

Italo slipped a disk into his computer from the middle alphabetical file of J. Edgar Hoover material. His encoding was almost complete, up to the Ws now, but lately, worrying about the age of the information, he had begun weeding out blackmail dossiers of those who had died. Time was destroying his hoard. Like a miser, updating gave Italo the chance to review his riches and let golden chunks trickle through his arthritic fingers. As he indulged himself he gave most of his mind over to thought.

It was Richtron that revealed the Ricci family's true enemy. But, though Shan stood clearly targeted, his strategy remained dim. No matter. Charley's last act, before being kidnapped, had been to make sure Richtron was safe from a takeover move. A war capo he could never be, but his peacetime instincts were superb.

Italo's eyes strayed from the view outside through the dusty windows to the screen of his computer. He gazed idly at an entry for "PARKINSON. E. Ralph, U.S. senator." Paying closer attention now, Italo read through Parkinson's early history of child molestation, now expunged from the records of his home city and state and residing only in the Hoover blackmail files. A weakness for young flesh could now be gratified only at great expense. Some telephoto pictures of Parkinson buggering a nine-year-old, while the boy's mother held him properly spread, accompanied the written dossier, scanned, digitalized and recorded forever on the floppy disk. "Committees: Finance, Industrial Relations, Foreign Affairs."

Italo Ricci's deep-set eyes, olive black, seemed suddenly to smolder with activity. His files bulged with the shameful secrets of Washington, D.C., of every state capital and major city in the land. This land that intruders like Shan Lao thought they could either buy or steal. Thank God such damaging information, the passkey to power, lay in the hands of a patriotic American, not one of the horde hammering at America's borders to loot and pillage the greatest democracy in the world. Thank God Italo Ricci controlled all these secrets, not some upstart like Shan Lao.

The time was overdue to repel the foreign invaders once and forever. The means lay here, in the control of people serving both in Congress and the Senate. Italo's thin, scimitar-like mouth drooped downward at one corner as if freshly slashed.

Shan Lao was dead, but didn't yet know it.

Sixty-Five

The truth about Vince was this: after a week anywhere on earth, he wanted to be somewhere else. After a week in Monaco and two in Manhattan putting the pieces back together, he was ready for an outer moon of Saturn. He had completely run out of excuses to give Lenore for not coming home every goddamned night. But only Vince could have reorganized the chaos left by Nikki and Baxter Choy, reorganized it and made it into something much better than the original.

"Decentralization," Buzz Eiler replied. "That's what it's called, Vince."

"Whatever, we have a dozen detox centers where we had five. Let the bastards try something now."

To keep sane during these weeks, he would drop in on Buzz at his clinic down in the Village on MacDougal Street, to cop a cap and a nap, once the MegaMAO had happied him up. Here, to keep his mind off the promise he'd made to Eileen, Buzz spent hours signing prescriptions for the far-flung empire of detox stations.

Buzz knew better than to keep quizzing Vince, but it was obvious that the lethargy he had noticed, the increasingly short temper, and the outbursts of unreasonable fear were an established pattern. If ever called upon for a scholarly paper on the effects of MegaMAO habituation—like most doctors, Buzz could not bring himself to say addiction—the inventor would produce a fairly workable analysis.

On the Ricci letterhead Buzz was carried as Medical Director. But occasionally he used some of his old private prescription blanks, just to get rid of them. A melancholy business. He took a long, shuddering breath.

"Listen, Vince," he said, putting aside his pen. "There's something I have to tell you."

Crouched across from him, purplish circles under his cat's eyes, Vince yawned. "You said that the last three times I dropped in. What's eating you?"

It was the wrong comeback. For the past two weeks Buzz had been trying to work his nerve up to the ploy Eileen had given him permission to use, the one in which he named her as the whores' defense attorney. But getting started was not easy. If Vince had said something forthcoming like "tell me" or "I'm listening . . ." But instead, with his casino brain, he'd kept tabs of Buzz's false starts.

"It's ab-ab-ab—" Buzz stopped, speechless.

"Uh-thu-thu, uh-thu-thu, uh-that's all, folks," Vince mimicked. He got to his feet. "Gotta scram. See you in Atlantic City."

"About Eileen!" Buzz shouted.

Both men blinked in surprise. Vince frowned and sat down, his daunting gaze boring into Buzz's slack, pale face. "Give."

"It's the shock of my life, Vince," Buzz began, picking up the threads of the dialogue Eileen had written for him. "This lawsuit against some hookers on your payroll?" He produced what he considered his most charming grin. "The Ladies AIDS Society?"

"Stop fumfering around. Give."

"They have a female lawyer."

"Old news. Eileen Hegarty, feminist cunt."

"Eileen Hegarty is Eileen Eiler," Buzz managed to get out. "She uses her maiden name f—" He stopped cold, pinioned by Vince's horrified stare. "Vince, I told you it was the shock of my life."

"Sonofa fucking bitch." Vince jumped up. He grabbed the lapels of Buzz's white smock. He lifted him almost off the ground. "You mean it's the little brunette you had down in Grotteria last year? The one who looks like Lenore's sister?"

"That one."

"Sonofa motherfucking bitch." He dropped Buzz and whirled in mid-stride, like a tango dancer. "What's that?" he demanded shrilly, as if listening to something. "Vince?"

"What's that? What're you whispering? Goddammit, speak up, slimeball."

Buzz stared at him. "Is someone talking to you?"

"All the time!" Vince cried out. His black curls shook steadily now as his head swiveled this way and that. "It's some smooth-talking broad. She whispers. She tells me they're plotting against me. And she's right!" He whirled back and this time his fingers circled Buzz's throat. "You scumbag bastard! Spill it! Your wife?"

"Vince, you're cho—"

"Spill it! Spill it! Spill it!"

"C-C-Conflict of interest," Buzz got out. "She thought . . . I ought to drop . . . out of Ricci Medical Centers."

A shrill scream of rage. "What about her dropping the goddamned cockamamie hoo-uhs and letting them die? What about behaving like a decent person and supporting her husband's livelihood?" Vince dropped him again and began pacing. "What?" he asked his voice. "Shut up! How can I think?" He turned on Buzz again. "Shit, Buzz, wha'm I gonna do with you? Ever think of that?"

Buzz returned his prescription pad to his desk drawer, which he left a few inches open. "You mean she's right? I have to leave this job?"

"You dumb bastard, how do I know you're not spying for her?" The thought of it sent Vince striding in another direction. He was stopped by a wall, where a cutaway, full-color version of a pregnant woman, womb open to show a full-term foetus, was hanging. Buzz had brought it from his old office, a pitiful memento of past glories. Vince stared at it in fury.

"Stop whispering," he commanded the poster. "Say it! Say it loud!"

"What?" Buzz asked.

Vince turned on him, his face suffused with blood. "You had a predecessor, dumbbell. A goombah named Battipaglia. He's the cretino who knew those hoo-uhs were infected and came to me and complained about it. Why? Because they might infect him, with his hands up their pussies."

"He must've worn gloves."

"Fuck you both," Vince snarled. "I told him, drop the hoo-uhs from the checkup list and keep his trap shut. No Ricci cunt is infected, understand? Not ever. And especially not when it actually is. He gave me his word he'd tell them all they were clean as a nun's asshole. Next thing I know he's having lunch with your wife! She must've told you. This was a year ago. She must've mentioned that lunch."

Buzz shook his head. "Not that I remember."

Vince paused and his eyes swiveled sideways. "Leave me alone," he ordered his voice. Buzz found himself unable to suppress a thrill of recognition. Paranoid delirium. Schizophrenic voices. MegaMAO. A scholarly paper on the side effects. His reputation in th—

"You would've remembered," Vince assured him. "We had to take out Battipaglia. I figured we might get the Hegarty cunt but she got lucky. I figured it'd scare her off. OK. I owe you one, Buzz, for tipping her mitt. So listen hard."

"I'm listening."

"Tell her what Battipaglia got, she gets. Tell her it's guaranteed. She's been trying to hook me with these diseased hoo-uhs like I neglected them or something? What else do you do with a fucking hoo-uh? Whatever they got they ast for it. I'm gonna worry ten seconds over them? Let 'em die."

"Eileen said something about Ricci Entertainment's medical checkup."

"Who cares? A hoo-uh is not people. The minute they turn a john's stomach you throw 'em out like any other garbage. I did it to this bunch and I've done it half a dozen times since. It's called mercy killing. Like what Battipaglia got. Like what that wife of yours gets if she keeps on with this. If I didn't owe you one, believe me, there'd be no polite warning."

"I don't think sh—"

"Hold it." Vince grabbed up the front of Buzz Eiler's shirt and lifted him out of his chair. The creak of it was a moan. Buzz's eyes bulged. "Hold it," Vince repeated. "You don't think? What kind of shit is this, you don't think? You owe me your fucking life, pill-pusher. And now you owe me your wife." He slammed Buzz back down in his chair. "Twenty-four hours. I want her off the case in twenty-four hours. I want her resignation on my desk in twenty-four hours. I want a copy of her letter to her goddamned hoo-uh clients telling them to go fuck a duck. You got twenty-fo—!" His voice choked off. His eyes went sideways. "Who says so?" he demanded. "Keep out of this."

"Vince, that voice. Maybe there's something I could give you t—"

Face bronze with rage, Vince wheeled and strode out of the place, his high Cuban heels shaking the floor at every step. For a long time Buzz felt nothing. He stared at the open door through which Vince had stamped off. Then, shakily, he got to his feet. By God, he'd done it. You don't stay married to a litigator as long as he had without recognizing that Vince had just babbled his way into a life sentence. But it weakened you, doing it. Watching a man in the throes of transient paranoic episode, voices and all, a man put in such jeopardy by MegaMAO, did something equally debilitating to the inventor of this insane drug.

Buzz moved slowly, like an old man, into the anteroom that led from the tiny apartment back into the clinic.
In a locker, on a high shelf behind an old gray fedora
and a beat-up umbrella, he felt for the recorder. When
he examined it, the reels were still turning. By God, he'd
done it! He slipped the whole thing in the pocket of his
battered oyster tan trenchcoat. Then he straightened up
as tall as he could and squared his shoulders.

Eileen had coached him so thoroughly that the rest
went in robotic fashion, slowly but accurately. First he
finished the prescriptions. Then he put on his trenchcoat
and left the office. He looked for signs of being followed.
The IND subway train took him uptown from Sixth Avenue at 8th Street. Dazed by his own daring, shaken by
Vince's reaction, Buzz got out at 50th Street and stumbled into a phone booth. "I have to go to the apartment," he told Eileen, using a prearranged code. "I have
to pick up some clothes."

"Odds and ends?"

"No, a whole outfit." He hung up.

She was there ahead of him, brimming with excitement. "Buzz! Buzz!"

Her hands shook as she took the recorder from him.
She poked her head in the baby's room. "Tilda, this is
Dr. Eiler. Buzz, Tilda. We'll be in the bedroom. Benjy,
say hullo to your Dad! Buzz," she kept babbling, "say
hello to Benjy. No. Wait. Wait, Benjy, we'll be back in
a second. A minute. Soon."

She dragged Buzz into the bedroom and locked the
door. They sat on the big bed as she listened to the tape
on earphones. She played it again, making notes. She
played it a third time to check her notes. Then she found
another tape recorder and made a copy tape. Finally she
grabbed Buzz and kissed him hard on the lips.

"Is that OK stuff?" he asked.

"It's everything, even admissions on the Battipaglia
murder and threats on me. Buzz, it's exactly, precisely
what I need for Winfield's pal in the DA's office. The
entire case will now change." Her face had grown more
and more animated. Now it seemed to give off sparks.
"Buzz! We're going for Vince Ricci!"

She grabbed his hand, yanked him off the bed and
dragged him back into the nursery. The young mother's

helper looked up from a magazine that reported on the love life of afternoon television actors, their problems with mentally retarded children, thieving siblings and uncontrollable infidelity. "Benjy! I want to introduce you to a hero-father, Dr. Buzz!"

The chubby baby, playing on the floor with a soft plastic truck of fluorescent orange, looked up at his father. "Bud?" he asked.

Buzz dropped to his knees. "Will you look at that grip? He's squeezing the truck in half."

"Bud?" Benjy asked.

"Tilda," Eileen said, "take the cart and do the shopping now, please?"

As the mother's helper left, Eileen got down on the floor with Buzz. She had her arm around his neck. "It's Buzz, Benjy. Not Bud, Buzzzz."

"Bud!" the baby corrected her. He handed the truck to his father. "My Bud."

Tears spurted down Buzz's cheeks. He turned blindly to Eileen. "Did you s-see that? He knows me."

"Go for it, Doctor," she said, patting him on the back. "After this morning, everything's possible.

Sixty-Six

"You what?" Charley demanded. His voice had a breathless rasp, fury breaking past a guarded gate of calm. His room in the clinic resembled his suite at the Washington hotel where he had conferred with Charley Braverman and On Seong what seemed a lifetime ago. But this was a clinic—owned by Richland Holdings—whose interlocked chalets dotted a valley north of New York City. In summer, trees shielded everything. Now, in March, pale buds were barely visible and the carpet of forest was gray branches and a spatter of evergreens.

Winfield blinked at the fury in her father's voice. It had been his style throughout her life to mask anger from his daughters. "Anybody could have planned it," she said, one of the few times she felt her own action needed defending. "Anybody could have located those little matchbook devices."

"You fool." Charley sank back against the pillows that propped him in his adjustable bed. The nurses had showed him how to work the electrical controls that altered its shape. Charley was still too shaken to master instructions of any kind. "You betrayed your own family," he said, reverting to the ice-cool voice he normally used to hide rage. Outside his huge picture window the March wind shook a white-trunked birch. His eyes darted to the movement, distracted, his mind interrupted.

"You . . ." He blinked, realizing his thought had blown away. Then, concentrating hard, his ice-blue eyes pierced her almost casually, as if spearing a passing fish. He had never looked at her this way before. It left a wound.

"You're making me sorry," Winfield said, matching her cool to his, "that I ever confided in you. A first in our relationship."

"I'm sorry you told me, too," he rasped. His convalescence was not going well. This, the start of his second week in the clinic, was still marked by raucous nightmares that shouted him awake through the nights, a stomach that accepted almost no food, a lack of concentration, an inability to pick up any of the threads of his life. His face had gone hollow, eyes larger. He had lost ten pounds, nothing for a man his size, but it was the flesh of affluent salesman's cheer, of self-confident business success. More and more, as he looked in the mirror, the ascetic scholar's face of Il Professore looked back at him.

"Because you present me with this dilemma," he told her. "Either I warn Zio Italo or I become as much of a traitor as you."

"That's what's got you angry," his daughter pointed out in her calmest tone. "You don't give a rat's ass about Vince. You just don't like dilemmas downloaded into your personal software. You want never to call yourself a Ricci again. And then I remind you that you're still Sicilian to the core. La famiglia é tutto."

"Right on," Charley agreed. "What's wrong with that?"

"You're making such heavy weather of this," Winfield

pointed out. "Vince is a big boy. He's faced this kind of trouble before. He has resources, crooked judges, bought congressmen. When you think of the murderous rackets he's in, this is a very minor business risk."

Charley's eyes closed for a moment as if willing the scene to vanish. "I've had nothing to do this past week but read the newspapers and watch TV. Do you have any idea what has happened to New York City? Bombings? Scores of bystanders killed? There is a hue and cry out there to get the people responsible for flooding the city with death. Your lawsuit could not come at a worse time for Vince. It will put him behind bars well into the twenty-first century."

"Fine."

"Your *cousin* Vince."

"Just fine," Winfield reiterated. "When you consider his profits, and the death behind them, he's getting off lightly."

Charley's face contorted in a grimace of pain. "Winfield, you're not human." His tired voice was even harder to understand now. "No family feeling," he wandered on. "No sense of blood kin, of . . ." He gestured emptily, as if letting a small bird free to fly away. When his eyes closed again, they stayed closed.

Winfield sat quietly for a long time, then got to her feet and walked to the window. She could see in the parking lot the car she had driven here with Garnet. She could even see Garnet, looking small, huddled in the front seat, staring out of the windshield. The doctors allowed only one visitor at a time in Charley's room.

Winfield raised her hand and waved. Garnet's triangular face, under its brush of white hair, came alive. She waved back. A melancholy visit, Winfield thought, to which I have added an even more depressing element.

Driving up here this morning, they had feared such a reaction. "In his gut," Garnet had said, "he still can't believe what sociopaths his relatives are."

"It's the tranquilizers they keep feeding him," Winfield retorted. "They're screwing up his recovery."

"What kind? How many?"

"Too many, too often. He's not the same person. He's drugged out."

Garnet had thought for a long moment. "Italo's work."

"Who else?"

"Then we must rescue Charley."

"Have you seen the guards? A dozen by yesterday's count."

Garnet had remained silent for the longest time. "Nevertheless," she said. Her face had set in an odd shape, like the prow of a ship. Now, waiting to visit Charley, she looked as if, like some Arctic ice-cutter, she was revving up steam for full speed ahead.

Winfield turned away from the window. "I'm going to leave and make way for Garnet. At least she hasn't betrayed the entire Ricci race."

Could either of them, Winfield wondered, have imagined the fury she had summoned up in a man like Charley, unused to prolonged torture, isolation and the sure threat of death? Would even his own daughter, who felt she knew him best, have foreseen this anger? She stood there, waiting for a word from him. What primal bonds held the Riccis so closely that they rallied in rage at an attack on a cousin as malodorous as sin, deaths hanging from him like pelts from a trapper.

"Yeh. Better go," Charley muttered in a cracked voice. "I'm no good for this now. I don't have it anymore."

He was staring at her. The light from the window bleached his eyes to an even paler shade. "Have it? Have what?" she asked.

"The old fight-back. Beat it, kid. Send in the next contender."

He smiled painfully at the movie boxing-talk. Winfield bent over, pecked his forehead and started for the door. "I'm sorry I loaded this on you," she said then. "My mistake. I apologize."

He shook his head slightly and even this small movement seemed to cause pain. "Would've had to tell me sooner or later." His hand raised and waved slightly. "Poor Winfield. Both parents in hospitals. Where did you find the spare time and energy to bring down Cousin Vince?"

"Don't worry about me," she said coldly. "I'd do it again."

This time a faint smile distorted his chapped mouth. The slight movement seemed to hurt him and he moistened his lips. "That's my Winfield," he said then. "You're the real killer in this family."

A faint undertone trembled in his words, an undertone of pride.

The inlet of Long Island Sound looked gray and greasy. As someone who had grown up on the island, it was easy for Cohen to see where a great number of small craft had recently tied up at the dock of this old house. But whether or not they were carrying drugs the evidence didn't say.

Commander Hackschmidt had served in the United States Coast Guard since the Second World War. He had a pounded-down look to him, as if for most of his life they had fired him through torpedo tubes. He grimaced as they stood just inside the cellar door of a very old brick house by the shoreline at Throggs Neck.

"A witness has seen a boat twice around here," Hackschmidt grunted. "Thinks the name was *Hurdy-Gurdy* or *Hurly-Burly* or some such shit."

"Half a million cruisers and launches on Long Island, I'm supposed to track a *Hurdy-Gurdy*?" Cohen turned away to hide his disgust. Suggs had really sabotaged him, his career, his case against Lutjens, Van Kurve and Armatrading. However much the newspapers screamed for protection from the drug wars, these investigations were designed mainly to soothe headline readers. They dragged on for years. The investigators languished in stagnant backwaters. Their careers disintegrated. Slow death.

Hackschmidt gave another of his boar's grunts, not hostile but doubtful. "I'm giving you two petty officers and a launch. Try not to fuck up." He shook hands and lumbered back to his staff car.

Cohen gazed down at the incoming tide. It had created a small pool almost at his feet. An empty cigarette pack floated on top of the greasy water. Cohen shook his head sadly. The Bureau owed him better than this, the bottom of the crime-fighting barrel. Two coastguardsmen approached him. One looked eleven years old, the more mature one looked twelve.

"Agent Cohen?" They each snapped a salute. No one had ever saluted Cohen before in his entire life. The Bureau didn't go in for that sort of discipline. What did you

do, if saluted? He produced one of his Gary Cooper
grins.

"Morning, boys," he said. "The Commander mentioned a launch?"

The maturer one indicated a plain open boat with a
cuddy cabin. Even at a distance, Cohen could see that
most of its space was taken up with two long, powerful
inboard engines. "Looks fast."

"Fast?" the mature one echoed. "I had her up to forty
knots this morning. She's the fastest keel on the whole
North Shore."

Something inside Cohen seemed to lift. He had his
posse, their horses were the fleetest in the land. What
more did a red-blooded sheriff need? "OK," he said, in
a downright cheerful voice, "what're we waiting for?
Let's vamoose!"

Sixty-Seven

Winfield approached the automobile in the clinic parking
lot. As she did, Garnet opened the door for her. "Any
change?"

"Doped up. Querulous." Winfield thought for a moment. "Took my head off when I gave him the news
about Vince. Then he sort of . . . collapsed? The fight
went out of him. He said as much. I've never seen him
like this before."

"Then I couldn't possibly give him all the anti-Charley
stuff that's going on with the Fellowship board elections."

"Somebody wants him out?"

"Yes. I'm in a suspect position since everyone knows
I work for him."

"What's the problem? He's given the Fellowship millions."

"Bad publicity. Gangland links. How sincere can a
successful businessman be? Does he have ulterior motives none of us innocents can fathom?"

"It'd kill him to lose this," Winfield mused. "This is

what he wants the rest of his life to be: scholarly research, improving education. The impossible dream, with a little banking on the side. The Fellowship board is his key to the rest of his life.''

The two women sat silently for a moment, watching a muscular young man in a business suit emerge from the back entrance of the clinic and stand, arms folded, at the top of the broad stairs. His glance never once shifted their way. ''Who's opposing him?''

Garnet's sigh was exasperated. ''Does the name Imogen Raspe ring a bell?''

''Expensive porno?''

''Presented as sociological studies of bondage, fetishism, sadomasochistic behavior. All the juicy stuff, with very artistic illustrations. So she requires a powerfully respectable aura.''

''And collects around her anybody on the board interested in bizarre sex.''

''You are too cynical for your age, Winfield. And also naive. Everybody's interested in bizarre sex. But she also rallies other publishing types who raise the freedom-of-the-press issue when it comes to Imogen Raspe's bestsellers.''

''But hasn't the ballot gone out in the mail?''

''Not the ballot. Just the list of nominees. The election's at the end of the year.'' Garnet glanced at her watch. ''OK,'' she said. ''I'm going in. After about ten, fifteen minutes, if you see that young man go back inside, start the motor.''

Winfield's eyebrows went up, something they very rarely did. ''Be careful with these guys, Garnet.''

''I want Charley out of there.'' Her elf's chin looked quite dangerous. ''I know he probably shouldn't be moved. But, Winfield, remember when you moved me. I wasn't ready, either?''

The younger woman nodded. ''He shouldn't be moved and he can't be left here. So I'm with you. But watch out for that heavy at the back door.''

Garnet got out of the car. ''That softy?''

She was wearing a bright blue cape over a short black dress. She had never worn heels since the explosion but, Winfield saw, today for some reason she had on a pair of black pumps with two-inch heels that gave her long, long calves, in their dark taupe stockings, a truly dangerous look.

Garnet nearly passed the young man. Then she stopped, turned with a whirling flash of legs, and locked her gaze onto him. They spoke at some length, quietly, conspirators trying to find a way of eluding her husband for an hour's passion. The young man brought out cigarettes, gave one to Garnet and lighted it for her. She held his hand to steady it, their eyes never left one another's. Then, blowing a plume of smoke, Garnet thanked him and went inside. She hadn't smiled once. Her feeling for this hunk of meat was far too serious for smiles. Winfield sat there entranced. As far as she knew, Garnet not only didn't smoke, she loathed anyone else doing it.

Winfield glanced at her watch and settled back in the car with a suddenly elated feeling of expectation.

". . . And those little green ones?" Garnet asked Charley. "How often are you supposed to take them?"

He looked hazy. "Those? I . . . I'm not sure."

She glanced at her watch. "When's the next time the nurse comes in?"

"Whenever I ring."

"And if you don't ring?"

"I suppose lunch time."

"Noon?" Garnet persisted.

"Why do you need to know?"

"Because you and I are blowing this joint," Garnet said with a firm shake of her head that sent her white mop top shuddering forward. "Because they have you as tanked up as a waltzing mouse. Do you realize why you feel so woozy? Somebody's given instructions to keep you that way. No prize for guessing his name."

Charley sat there for a long time. Garnet itched to tell him more but she knew he would only respond to something he'd figured out himself, assuming the tranquilizers left him with enough ability to do it. "That means . . ." He stopped and thought some more. Then he looked up. "That tricky old bastard." He sighed unhappily. "And I was giving Winfield hell for betraying him." He managed a chuckle, which made him cough. "You're serious about escaping? They have this place staked out like Fort Knox. When I take my morning stroll, there are—"

"You can walk?"

"If you want to call it that."

Garnet thought for a moment. "On my way up here I saw three or four wheel chairs just beyond the lobby."

Charley frowned, thinking. "That won't work."

"Worth a try."

"It can't work because too many noses keep pointing my way. Every nipote Italo owns is panting to answer my every desire. Or so I thought till you wised me up. What they're really here for is to thwart my every desire." He laughed, this time without coughing. "Lot of strong dreams in those pills."

"Come on, Charley, we can make it."

"No. Wait." He swung his legs off the bed. "Hand, please?" She helped him to his feet and he took a few experimental steps. "Is it cold outside?"

"Cold and blowy." She handed him a sleeveless sweater from his dresser top and helped him pull it on.

"OK." He got into a dressing gown and belted it firmly. "Give me two minutes to creep down this hall to the stairs at the front end."

"Why should it take you that long?"

"You haven't seen me walk lately. Those Calabrese did something to my lower spine." He took her hand again and tried to squeeze it firmly. "Give me two minutes. See that bank of control thingies next to the door? Press the red button. It has to be unlocked first. You see how?"

"That sliding thing? What happens? Fire alarm?"

He nodded, moving toward the door of his room in a kind of accelerated shuffle. "Get down the back stairs to the car. The guards or nurses will come running up the front stairs and I'll simply wave them on with shouts of 'fire!' I'll walk out the front through the shrubbery to the parking lot."

"Grazie molto, Professore. Oh, there's a special guard for the parking lot. But don't give him a second thought."

"Garnet, if I gave this scheme even a first thought I'd get back in bed."

He slipped out of the door of his room. Garnet moved to the red button and freed it for action. Next to it, nearly clipped to the wall, hung a stainless steel fire extinguisher the size of a short loaf of French bread. Looking very thoughtful, she unclipped the extinguisher and tucked it under her blue cape. When she felt two minutes had elapsed, she poked her head out the door and saw that the corridor was empty in both directions. She pressed the red button and scurried toward the back stairway.

Hospitals and clinics don't believe in exciting their patients by letting all hell break loose. Instead a faint, distant peeping began, as if another planet was insistently trying to establish a communications link.

Garnet was on the ground floor now. At the far end of the corridor nurses were scurrying up the stairs. Two young men in business suits followed, and then a burly attendant in a white smock. Garnet saw Charley, arms waving excitedly, pointing up the stairs. Then he ducked outside.

She made her way to the rear entrance. Lover Boy hadn't moved. Instead, he stood outside with his face pressed to the glass door, anxiously looking in. When he saw her he swung the door open. "What's up?"

"Didn't they tell you?" She started past him and, once again, did the sudden stop and turn, as if her hormones made it impossible for her to pass him by. "I want to thank you," she said, "for being so helpful."

"Me?"

"I'm sure they don't need you upstairs. I'm sure they can get the fire out without y—"

"Fire?" He swung away from her. "Fire?" he repeated.

"Fire," she said, bringing the extinguisher down as hard as she could on the back of his head, the part where the brain stem joined whatever brain there was. He sprawled forward and hit his chin on the floor. This did more to keep him quiet than the original blow.

Garnet put the extinguisher in his hands and ran out to the car as Winfield started the motor. She had already gotten her father to lie down behind the front seat, out of sight.

"Nice touch," Garnet said. "Step on it."

Sixty-Eight

To his collection of random-access homes, Shan Lao had now added one on Grand Bahama. For a very large sum he had bought up all six cottages surrounding the one Nicole, Bunny and baby Leo inhabited. Then, around all the cottages, he had erected the same kind of twelve-feet-high cyclone fencing that protected his processing sheds on Palawan, but this time a double row with electronic sensors between. A twenty-four-hour force of guards patroled this sanitized enclave, half palm jungle, half pink sand beach. But instead of sadist expellees from the French Foreign Legion, the guards were local Chinese recruited through the Li family. Nevertheless, like guards everywhere, they could not keep from swaggering, nor ostentatiously exposing their automatic weapons.

For Bunny and Nicole, life would have been idyllic but for two exceptions. The guards reminded Nicole too forcibly of her childhood in a Japanese prison camp. She was afraid their brutal presence would somehow affect baby Leo. She was also afraid, knowing a lot more about guard mentality than Bunny, that these could be relied on to overreact, sometimes out of ignorance, sometimes out of a need to flourish their maleness.

The women's other problem was that the "training mission" on which Nikki had been sent to New York was dragging on much too long. Although Nikki had told her very little, Nicole knew enough to suggest to her husband, "He has surely, by now, shown either the qualities you had hoped for, or such a lack that he can be allowed to return to journalism."

Shan's smile was sketchy. His eyes behind their contact lenses looked omnivorous as he glanced from his wife to the logs burning in the fireplace on this cool March evening. "I do miss his letter-essays to me," he admitted. He admitted nothing more, certainly not that Nikki had been kidnapped, nor that his release this morning had been reported on the scrambler phone from Baxter Choy in New York.

"They returned him to the La Guardia men's room, where they snatched him," he said. "He was dazed, but phoned me. I'm dropping my hacker long enough to get to La Guardia now. Nik says they didn't mistreat him."

"Send him directly to me."

Remembering this brief conversation now, Shan wondered whether he might announce to Nicole that her son was en route. But it didn't pay to anticipate. He had been en route a week ago, too. Poor Nik. The whole affair had not gone precisely as Shan had wanted, but it could not be called a failure.

There had been several goals. To a large extent, they had been achieved. First, Nik had been well blooded. He could now be counted on, as Choy reported, to treat death like what it was, a tool of business management. The second goal had been to prepare a hacker for clandestine sabotage of the extensive Richland Tower bank of data processing machinery. Moreover, to get it over and done with without Charley Richards being on hand, his too-inquisitive mind alert to any sudden shifts in computer-driven strategy.

Convalescing in his wooded clinic, Richards was as good as immobilized. Shan was not sure who had done him this favor, but he was certain that Ricci forces blamed him, or Mollo, if they knew of his existence. And the fact that Lord Mace had been seconded to him.

What with the risk to Nik, the entire project had been a bit of a trade-off as the Americans called it, risk for risk. But a successful trade-off. Shan smiled. Slang pleased him.

"Something pleases you?" Nicole asked. She and Bunny had started a long cardigan of heavy wool meant as a gift for Nik. She looked up from her knitting and now watched her husband's face for another outward sign. He nodded, but said nothing.

"Are you thinking of Nikki?" she pursued.

He glanced at her. In the past six months of playing grandmother she had let her figure go. She was no longer slim, but still pleasing to look upon. He nodded again, picked up a newspaper and closed off any further conversation on the subject.

* * *

Baxter Choy found Nikki in front of an airport bookstore looking at an array marked "Bestsellers." His face was gaunt. The French likeness seemed to override completely his Asiatic heritage. The faraway stare in his eyes reminded Choy of French mercenaries in Indo-China who had called it *"le cafard,"* an almost catatonic state of reality overload.

"Looks to me like they didn't feed you," he remarked when they retired to a snack counter for some coffee.

"I wasn't too hungry. They kept trying to stuff me with Big Macs."

"Recognize any of them?"

"I only saw Kerry Ricci. He kept reminding me that he's living with Bunny's sister so . . ."

"Sort of a link."

"A talisman promising I wouldn't be harmed."

Baxter stirred his coffee. "And what did you promise him?"

Nikki shoved his coffee away from him. "They're puzzled, Bax. They can't figure out why we launched that hit-and-run campaign, then dropped it. I said it was pure harassment and after a while he stopped asking. Just as well because the more I thought about it the more stupid the whole thing seemed."

Choy nodded soothingly. "Your father's plans are multilayered, Nik. You should know that. I don't pretend to know all the layers. But I can tell you one of them. In hunting, they make a point of showing the novice all the bloody parts. They call it 'blooding' him."

"If this was just a way of getting my feet wet—"

"And seeing how you and I worked together," Choy added. He pushed Nik's coffee back to him. "Drink some."

"That's something else I've been mulling over for the last week, Bax. Tell me, what's in this for you?"

"Are you serious?"

"Wet-nursing the Crown Prince? Holding my hand and making me write my lessons on the blackboard in your handwriting? Is that a job for a hotshot product of brilliant Irish Jesuits?"

Choy laughed. "I've got my reasons."

"Tell me."

Choy shrugged. "I can't lose, Nik. Your father in effect raised me from an orphan kid. I owe him everything. My future is secure. If I guided you to a victory in New York, I'm a hero. The kidnap takes the shine off it, but I'm still the guy who broke you in, blooded you, got you used to the nasty parts and helped you do one helluva job. If I lost, if you goofed, turned tail, couldn't hack it, whatever, I would still win because your father would be left without a proper heir. He'd have to turn to his synthetic son. Me."

Nikki laughed grimly. "Boy, I sure asked for that dose of reality."

"Why lie to you? I figure I'm going to have to be your right hand for the next half century. We'd better level with each other up front."

"You think I'll last that long?"

"Good genes." Baxter Choy winked.

Nikki picked up his plastic cup brimming with black coffee and turned it upside down over a wastebasket. The steaming liquid splashed down and out of sight in a welter of napkins, plastic carriers and soda straws. Several people saw him do this and immediately looked away or walked off quickly. New Yorkers have a sixth sense for bypassing aberrant behavior.

"OK?" Choy asked in a softer voice. "Got it out of your system?"

Nikki picked up his small backpack. "No," he said.

Sixty-Nine

"It's not hard at all, Mervyn," Baxter Choy explained patiently. He had gone over the moves with his hacker buddy several times when Lemnitzer was under MegaMAO and all smoothed out, as well as now, cold sober and twitching. It was a noticeable side effect of the drug that previously calm people, once habituated to MegaMAO's super-calm, grew fretful and jumpy without it. They suffered from baseless fears. Some, Choy had found, started to hear things.

Part of Choy's strategy with Lemnitzer, when the hacker's great moment would arrive and his natural tensions would scream out for chemical help, would be to substitute capsules of lactose as placebos that kept the lad vibrating as if he'd caught a toe in a live socket. It had taken Lemnitzer pitifully few weeks to achieve such dependency, while Choy kept trying to find him a job but only came up with a succession of ill-paid spy missions, hardly more high-tech than rifling wastebaskets.

Finally he had found the right mix: a job supremely suited to Lemnitzer because it would be working against the company that had fired him, Richland, and at a price, fifty large ones, that would help pay the mortgage and keep him in MegaMAO forever. It said a lot for the drug's ability to diminish judgment that, for what he would do to Richland, fifty thousand was dirt cheap. But the hacker had yet to catch on that fifty thousand a minute would be more in keeping with the magnitude of what Choy was asking.

The thing looked deceptively simple. Entry was based on the fact that while he'd been forced to surrender all office keys when sacked, Lemnitzer still had his ID pass to Richland Tower. They would have changed all security passwords in the computer room. But Lemnitzer understood how the Richland passwords were formed. It would take a Thinkman less than five minutes, under his enlightened cueing, to search out and find the new access codes.

"OK, I'm in the computer room. It's Sunday morning. I'm alone," Mervyn Lemnitzer repeated edgily, his voice cracking with deprivation angst. "I access trading data. So what?"

"That's just a test point," Choy explained. "Once you know you're accessing you switch down and find a practical intercept in the umbilicals for a no-contact electromag tap. You're going to need a space to conceal one. Thinkman preprogrammed for two-way radio relay."

"Preprogrammed by who?"

"By the client."

Lemnitzer produced a wince of psychic pain. His squinty eyes almost closed. "You haven't told me who the—"

"To give you deniability," the Chinese interrupted,

giving the word the orotund majesty of a polysyllabic Papal blessing. "Then we run a phone check to confirm that your tap is operational in both send and receive modes. Got it?"

"And then I fold my tent and dust out of there?"

"For good," Choy assured him. "No re-runs. If they want a comeback they have to fork up another fifty."

"Listen, Bax, that last cap of MegaMAO. It's a dud."

Choy scanned the hacker's troubled face. "OK, try this." He tossed him an authentic capsule and watched him pop it.

"That's more like it," Lemnitzer purred after a moment, all the lines in his face starting to smooth away and disappear into the great limbo of the ultra-relaxed, a nation of over a million New Yorkers and only God and Vince Ricci knew how many other citizen-addicts nationwide. "Now," Lemnitzer sighed with pleasure, "we're gonna get somewhere."

In Garnet's mail the envelope looked old, having no return name or address. She slid her thumb inside and ripped it open as she got ready to leave for her office. A typewritten letterhead lay across the top of the page, listing itself as that "Ad Hoc Committee for ERF Board Selection."

Dear Member of the Fellowship,

You have by now received your official slate of nominees for the six Board positions that fall vacant this year. It is not our intention to deal in personalities. But some general questions must be raised.

To be sure, we welcome any member to step forward as board material. In the past, and largely true as well this year, such nominees are of an academic background, as is only natural when dealing with questions of education and of research.

These two foundation stones of the Fellowship have a different meaning in the world of business. There education tends to slide into advertising and public relations hype, while research gets to become market research, devoted to selling us things we don't need.

With that in mind . . .

Garnet folded the letter and tucked it in her handbag. Charley's recovery was doing quite well. At the moment he was using a sickroom Winfield had arranged upstairs in her larger flat. Winfield herself had been overnighting somewhere else, a Hoboken telephone number. Later this morning she would return to nursemaid duties.

Her father was certainly strong enough to cope with witless yahoos and undereducated loudmouths. Perhaps, Garnet thought, it was time to let him in on what some of America's highly educated and terribly articulate were trying to do to him.

On her way to work she let herself into Winfield's apartment. Charley lay fast asleep. Garnet stood over him for a long moment. Peace and quiet were what he needed most, but they were not his natural milieu. They would probably rot his brain, if administered in large quantities. Smiling slightly, Garnet propped the letter against Winfield's coffee-maker. It would get Charley going this morning even faster than a jolt of caffeine.

Seventy

"Hurly-Burly?" the old man repeated. "What damned kinda name is that?"

"What?" Noah Cohen leaned forward into a heavy March wind that threatened to blow him off the battered old dock. He had spent his boyhood on the north shore of Long Island but sweeping clear-weather gales like this were rare. This one seemed to roar in from Connecticut, pick up speed across the Sound and then try to howl down Orient Point harbor buildings with great hammering shouts.

The old man led the way inside a small shed. Away from the wind's fury, his scowl softened. "Th'launch you want ain't half th'damned speed of that there little demon you and th'sailor boys is riding."

"Oh, then you know the *Hurly-Burly*?"

"Y'city people don't never listen. Nobody'd call a boat that but one of these damned summer people. Y'call a boat after a damned woman is what.'' He nodded vehemently. ''Y'want the *Shirlie-Girlie* over t'Petty's Bight.''

Cohen unfolded a map. ''Can you show me?''

The old man's thin lower lips pushed out. ''Don't hold with helping th'damned law. Th'damned law never did one damned thing f'me. Already gave you her damned name. You want me t'take y'by the damned hand and lead y't'her?''

Cohen grinned at him. ''You have the sound of one of the old-time alky-runners from Prohibition days. But that'd make you somewhere in your eighties. You look like a man in his sixties.''

''Eighty-seven in June.'' A proud, stubborn look burned in his watery eyes. ''Still damned spry.'' His gnarled forefinger touched a point on the map. ''Old frame house on th'bay. Moved it there from Plum during th'damned war.'' One eye closed in a definite wink that took Cohen by surprise.

''Beg your pardon?''

The wink was repeated. ''When they turned Plum into . . . *you* know.''

Cohen glanced down at his map and found that Plum Island was clearly labeled a government laboratory area. Drug smuggling would steer clear of Plum. ''Lots of dangerous stuff locked away there, huh?''

A third wink. ''Locked up, is it? Not much. Every year dozens of them canisters float free. I reckon the bottom's littered with them damned things clear back t'Port Jefferson and over t'Bridgeport. Leastways that's how the currents'd carry 'em.''

''But they're pois—''

''Now and then a fisherman'll bring one up in his nets. Every week or so.''

''My God,'' Cohen exclaimed. ''And what's he do then?''

The old-timer's mouth opened wide to reveal the baby-pink gums of an infant. ''What's he do?'' A fourth wink. ''Throws the damned thing back in the Sound.''

Casting off, the launch made for Petty's Bight but the house and its dock proved to be deserted. If he'd been alone, Cohen might have done a bit of illegal entry and search. He hated to do anything in front of witnesses, especially ones young enough to be his sons. It gave a wrong impression of the Bureau to see it using the methods of the criminals it was fighting.

As they started back to Orient Point, the tide ran in the same direction as the near–gale force wind. Cohen's lawman's face set in a granite mold. Neither smugglers nor weather could stay the justice he carried forth to a troubled world. This fractious craft, like an unbroken horse, had to be subdued.

The two young sailors fought the wheel, trying to pin down a sharp starboard turn into the wind. Two hundred horsepower roared. Twin screws chewed air and water, sending up a heart-stopping howl as they tried to bite a purchase in the rough whitecaps. The bow of the launch actually did rear like a horse as the wind-driven tide lifted its prow skyward. Cohen felt a sudden lift to his heart, an exhilaration lecturing to assistant comptrollers had never given him.

"Hold her!" Cohen shouted against the wind. "She's a'rarin'!"

Seventy-One

The third editorial was captioned, *The Greatest Treason*. It assumed that New York *Times* readers didn't need to be reminded of the T. S. Eliot quotation:

> Nine fallen women, their faces reflecting harried lives, will be joined by that hitherto faceless organization whose commercial interests in prostitution have brought it at last to the bar of justice.
>
> Not for pandering—a felony in all fifty states of the Union—but in essence for failure to protect employee health in a high-risk profession, a lightning stroke from an unexpected part of the sky, so Olympian are Justice's thunderbolts.
>
> Let us not cavil over this gift from Jove. Let us remember, in the daily avalanche of news, that this "faceless" organization wears many faces. It is central to the bomb litter of a brutal drug war, New

Yorkers reeling with designer drugs of implacably deadly newness. In a very real sense, therefore, these nine harried women represent millions of fellow New Yorkers diminished by the workings of this ''faceless'' organization.

These nine are sisters in victimization. And, though accused, they must be treated both as victims and as surrogates for the rest of us. We must not turn away. To do the right thing, for *any* reason, is never treason.

Italo Ricci slapped down the newspaper, yanked his reading glasses off his beaky face and cursed. He cursed in the old country way, although he had been born on the Lower East Side of Manhattan. He cursed the owners of the *Times* and their families unto their grandchildren as a pack of cornuti for whom he wished eternal cuckolding, mothers by sons, daughters by uncles, brothers by sisters, a litany of adulterous incest causing jealousy and bastardy of such painful sharpness as to eat into the very marrow of the bones and turn the heart to a cesspool of excrement. He called down upon their heads every plague of mankind culminating in field audit by the IRS. Then he cursed the nine whores and their Madam, the wife of Vince's wonder doctor, with Biblical chancres, blindness and maggots feasting under their skin. He cursed Il Professore and his Indian handmaiden, but by now, aware of repetition, he had left only an infestation of locusts and the instant dropping off of all penises.

To upset the cool of the *Times*, Italo fell to thinking, was no mean accomplishment. For this he could first blame Vince's mafia arrogance, the bravura strut of a randy cockerel who has never been refused entry. What a target he had presented to Shan's bomb-tossers! What a farce! That the Chink and his slant-eyed henchmen had in a few weeks of violence tarred Vince's reputation forever. The hit-and-run nature of it was now painfully clear, not a battle for turf but an exercise in negative public relations. And the most farcical of all: even the *Times* didn't realize how it had been had.

But make no mistake, the *Times* was right: Vince was being raked over hot coals not for the fate of nine whores but for seeming to bring chaos and death to New York. In no time at all, borrowing the same strategy, do-gooders in other big cities under siege to crack and MegaMAO pushers would take to the courts.

All passion spent by scores of silent curses, Italo sat back at his desk and stared moodily up at his Herculite windows. He could hear a helicopter hovering nearby. Its nearness put him in mind of that attack two Junes ago when a single bullet came so close both to him and to Charley. As long as he remained in his hideaway on Dominick Street, Italo knew, he was safe from the world, safe from his enemies. As long as he had Charley nicely locked away in a tranquilized cocoon, he had time to undo the grievous injuries his nephew had done him.

His private telephone rang and he picked it up. "Zio?" a quavering young man asked. "It's Vito up at the clinic."

"Si, nipote. What's up?"

"Ch-Charley."

"Charley what?"

"H-he's gone!"

A catastrophe. And Italo had used up all his curses.

The cheapness of life, Nikki Shan thought. Everywhere in the Third World an individual life was meaningless. Now that same callous realism had spread to the West. Everywhere on earth now, life was dirt cheap.

His own, too.

That he could find himself a pawn, casually kidnapped simply to counter the kidnapping of Bunny's father, a pawn in a board game. That look on Kerry's face that said it mattered little to him if Nikki lived or died. It had all come home to him in the least obvious of places, this elegant hideaway enclave his father had caused to be surrounded with fences and guards. Nikki had been in the other room, napping, when he had overheard his father with one of the Li brothers who commanded the force of guards.

". . . Installing more powerful proximity sensors," Li was reporting.

"But they must be accompanied," his father's dry, unemotional voice explained, "by new instructions to the guards."

"Sir?"

"I have reason to believe that our heightened security

now requires a more positive response. We can safely do this now because we are all here, including my son.''

"Yes, sir.''

"At night your men must shoot.''

"You mean whatever triggers the security sensors?''

"It may be a stray dog. It may be a hired assassin. Your nighttime orders are, shoot.''

A pause. "Shoot,'' the Li brother repeated in an almost unctuous voice, as if relishing the taste of what issued from his mouth. "To kill?''

"To kill.''

The word still vibrated in Nikki's head. It felt like an ice pellet lodged at the base of his brain. In the distance he could hear little Leo grumbling at waking from his nap. He could hear Nicole soothing him. He could hear Bunny and his mother discussing a trip to town. Outside soft breezes caused the palms to whisper and clack peacefully. Spring sunshine shone down through a cloudless sky washed by last night's whispering rain. In this haven, this vale of peace, his father was reducing each human life to the value of a stray dog.

Shoot to kill was the motto of savage, howling wildernesses dominated by death squads. It summoned up Belfast. Baghdad. Suweto. No one who called himself a human being dared utter it. Yet his father dared, hitting blinding back in his brutal way, taking the law into his own hands. It made no sense, surrounding this enclave with death. It changed nothing in New York or Washington. But ordering the guards to shoot to kill, ah, the very speaking of that accursed order made his father feel more secure. On such fragile selfishness is death balanced.

Everyone's death.

Seventy-Two

"Eileen, I wish I could be there.'' Winfield sat curled up in an armchair, talking on the telephone. "It's hard to believe they arraign him on Tuesday. And set bail.''

"I've only got Lenore for moral support,'' Eileen Hegarty said, "and she can't show up at the DA's office. Buzz can't be there, either. And to tell the truth, I'm glad you're playing nurse to your father. Your presence at the DA's could be something Vince's lawyers might use to get a jury all mixed up." There followed a silence in which Winfield digested this. As if to change the subject, Eileen went on, "How's your Dad doing away from tranquilizers?"

"It's only three days but he's getting perkier. Tell me, will they let in TV?"

"At an arraignment? Doubt it. They're going to stay buttoned up till Tuesday in case they can't collar Vince easily. This is shaping up as a real *cause célèbre*. You saw the *Times* editorial. I could've done with less partisan support. The first thing Vince will complain about is the impossibility of impaneling a jury now that the Press has found the defendant guilty."

"He'd make that complaint anyway."

"It gets worse. I got a wire from a friend in San Francisco. She's pulling together another class action against Ricci on grounds of fraudulent medical practice. The detox centers out there take a junkie, enroll him in Blue Cross or some other medical cover, and start scamming the insurance company for mythical operations and treatments. Talk about squeezing blood from a stone."

Winfield heard footsteps outside, then a knock. "Somebody at the door. I'll talk to you tomorrow."

"Careful."

"Oh. Good point. You want to hold on while I answer the door?"

"Let me know who it is. Nobody's immune these days."

Winfield put down the phone and opened the door to Kerry. "Dad's fast asleep. Can it wait till this afternoon?"

"I'm part of a delegation." He stepped inside and was immediately followed by his twin. "Oh," Winfield said uneasily. "Hi."

"Buon giorno, tesoro," Zio Italo said, following through with his small, thin body like a wraith materialized by warlocks. He neatly closed the door behind him with a slightly triumphant air, as if having pulled off a victory.

"Eileen," Winfield said into the phone, "just a meeting of the clan: Kerry, Kevin and Zio Italo."

"Jesus Christ," her employer muttered. "You're a cool one."

"Family is family. Call me in half an hour. If they haven't kidnapped or murdered me, we're way ahead of the game." She grinned at all three men.

"I'll do that." Eileen hesitated for a moment. "Winfield, I won't forget who brought Buzz back to me and gave me a DA's case. If we win, it's your victory more than anybody's. I need you alive and well."

"My family loves me," Winfield said, giving the men a brilliantly fraudulent smile. "Bye." She hung up. "Zio, my father's asleep."

"No, he's up," Charley said, standing in the bedroom doorway. His voice sounded thin, as if dragged through a narrow crack. "Standing by to repel boarders. Buon giorno, Zio."

The effect of this constricted voice was to spread a sudden quiet out to the four corners of the room. It had only been a few days since Winfield and Garnet had gotten Charley out of the clinic, but Winfield knew it must still rankle Italo profoundly.

She gazed out of the window, facing south, at the reassuring view of the Chrysler Building but it failed to soothe her. As the only woman in the place she felt ill at ease, suddenly, and also quite chilled, as if the much revered family warmth had backfired. She wished for Garnet to be there.

Charley might have felt the same coldness. He was not a man given to sighs, but one escaped him now. "Hey," his uncle enthused, giving him that hawk-nosed, hook-chinned grin that Punch gives everyone before bludgeoning them to death, "laziness agrees with you!" He patted Charley's cheek roughly. "Looka that jowl!"

Charley nodded absentmindedly, well aware that he'd lost weight, not gained it. Winfield saw that he was alert, but still not entirely on top of things. His doctor had mentioned that some tranquilizers didn't clear out of body tissue for a week or longer. Meanwhile, one could be alert without having any confidence in one's alertness.

She examined the twins, standing on either side of the tiny, tidy Italo, much like bookends done by Giacometti.

On the face of one a small, intense reddish mark like a cigarette burn flared under his left eye.

"How's Vince holding up?" Charley asked suddenly.

The misfortunes of others are always a comforting topic. Winfield heard a faintly aggressive edge to her father's voice that suggested he was trying to get back in form, not as Il Professore but as a ballsy Vince-clone. "I hear the DA's office has taken over the case."

But Zio Italo was not to be shunted off his main track. "Sideshows don't interest me, Charley," he announced in a histrionic howl, "when we're facing all-out war. Vince can take care of himself." His glance shifted to Winfield. "No matter who betrays him."

"So what brings you to me?"

With no further preamble Italo launched into a hectic summary of Shan's takeover moves. Winfield could not have guessed at the guilt Italo felt at letting Vince down. No one yet knew that Italo had been alerted to the surveillance for some time without understanding what it meant.

For a moment it bothered Winfield that her great-uncle had dismissed Vince's troubles so quickly. But she could see that downplaying these problems gave star emphasis to Charley's affairs and, at the same time, bolstered Italo's feelings of still being fully in charge, able to sort and order priorities.

"Otherwise would I bother you at a time like this, Charley? With you not even recovered from what those maladetta Calabrese did to you? But you have the touch. Dio mio, that golden touch. With all those fancy-dress male hookers who inhabit the halls of Congress you are the man."

"What sort of touch, Zio?" Charley's voice was so devoid of any shade of feeling that Winfield suddenly feared he had slipped back to chemical neutral.

"A hard squeeze of their syphilitic balls!" Italo burst out. He pantomimed chagrin. "Sorry, Winfield, it just popped out. You can see how upset I get. Please excuse my language." He readjusted himself in several small ways, an actor approaching a major soliloquy, standing a bit straighter, chin higher, eyes brighter.

"They have been freeloading on the Riccis for three generations, Charley. My father paid them off. My brothers. Me. Now nipoti like you and Vince. They think we're part of the woodwork, not people they owe their lives to. They think all we have to do in life is supply them with unmarked bills. I'm saying 'no more, Mr. Nice-Guy!' I'm saying the hand that held the fat envelopes of cash is now holding a whip. I've got stuff in my files that would bring down the United States Senate and House of Representatives faster than an atom bomb. It's time, Charley. It's time to let that pack of whoremongers and asshole bandits know who's boss and what the boss wants from them.'' He glanced unhappily at Winfield again. ''Excuse the language, bella. I get so hot under the collar when I remember what we've done over the years for that pack of ingrates.''

Back to reality, Winfield thought, the reality her father had thought to transfer onto Zio's shoulders.

''What d'you want?'' he asked his uncle in that same neutral, drugged voice.

''Some law! Some order that keeps goddamned slopes and nips and chinks from owning America!'' Italo's voice was a yelp of pain. ''A law that says 'Enough! You yellow sonsabitches own too much.' We're a generous people. We open our arms to immigrants. In the past, they worked hard, like the Riccis did, to make a go of it. But this new breed! They send their money over here to work. It comes back to them tripled, quadrupled. I want them stopped from sucking America dry. Off the tit! And I want it now!''

Charley pulled on the same dressing gown in which Garnet had spirited him out of the clinic. Winfield had felt that the few healing days since then had been miraculous for him. Between them, she and Garnet had rebuilt the essential Charley by getting him to play his two best-rehearsed roles: lover and father. By now his reflexes were running along well-grooved tracks. Perhaps a mistake. Other people ran their own tramlines through Charley's soul. Italo had charted them all. Now Charley was being offered the chance to play family trouble-shooter once again. It matched a set of tracks already encoded in him.

''You want legislation, is that it?''

''Dad.''

''I'm OK, Winfield. Is that what you expect of me?''

"It's what I expect of those loafers down in Washington, once Charles Anthony Richards gets them moving."

Charley nodded in agreement. "Right. Get down to D.C. again? Call in the troops like Nell Carraway and Cliff Ungerer and Senator Birdsong? Start spreading big bucks? Start mentioning stuff you're holding in your blackmail files? Draw up a draft resolution? All without getting kidnapped again?"

"That's the boy, Charley."

"Dad, please."

"Let him talk, tesoro," Zio Italo crooned. "When Charley Richards talks, the world stops and listens."

Winfield gazed out of the south-facing window and wished Garnet was here to counteract the slimy flattery Italo was spreading. Instead, Winfield felt she was losing her father. Not for the first time, he was sliding back into the role he'd been trained for, Il Professore, the business brain. She glanced nervously at Charley. His face had that blank, bland look of someone who had stopped thinking.

"Dad?" The single word echoed in the room, emphasizing its openness as a stage on which Italo could rehearse Charley like a puppet. Winfield had the feeling that if her father capitulated yet again, she would . . . she would . . .

"I'm so glad to hear you say that," Charley responded with a big smile. "Because here's what Charles Anthony Richards says." He paused and his dulled features grew brighter. He had the sudden look of a mad inventor disclosing his anti-gravity water engine. "Zio, take your blackmail and your big bucks and go down to D.C. yourself. It's *your* industrial empire at stake. I don't run Richland errands anymore."

"Hooray!" Winfield shouted.

Swiveling to one side, Charley poked a finger at the twins. "Whichever one of you is Kevin, please escort my favorite uncle out of the door and five stories down out of my life. Capeesh?"

"Charley," Italo rasped.

"And whichever one is Kerry, stick by me."

"Charley." A grating sound of flesh being ripped apart. "You been hanging around those fakers at the Education Fellowship. You been bad-naming schoolteachers and voters. And the smart people have been bad-naming you. You need every friend you can get, Charley. Tell me addio and you will leave the human race. Do you understand?''

''Zio.'' Charley took a great breath and exhaled mightily. ''Zio, it's never addio with us. We can't help being family till the day we die. But right now,'' he indicated the door, ''it's vai! Vai via!''

Silence carpeted the room, making everything seem slower and more stately in movement. The twin with the cigarette burn under his eye indicated the door. Silently, with a strong display of insulted dignity, Italo moved toward it as a courtier might progress to the guillotine. A twin opened the door. They left the apartment. As he closed the door behind all of them the remaining twin glanced guiltily at Charley and murmured, ''Back in an hour.''

Winfield and her father stood in silence, listening to departing footsteps. ''Complimenti, Professore. Do you realize,'' Winfield asked in a hushed voice, ''what it took to get Zio to walk up five flights? Even to the Pearly Gates he'd say no.''

''Mamma mia!'' Charley breathed. ''Winfield, that burn under Kev's left eye?''

''And I thought you were still tranked out of your skull.''

''Remind you of something?''

''You mean that mole I had? They used liquid nitrogen. They sort of froze it off. It left a mark like that. But after a week, there was nothing to see.''

She and Charley locked glances. ''Nothing?'' Charley asked.

''Nothing.''

Seventy-Three

On the way down to Dominick Street, still breathless from his downstairs progress, Zio Italo had demanded that Kerry ride with him in his elderly black Buick while

Kevin piloted the lead car, Kerry's by-now, bullet-holed white Peugeot 205.

"First, why is it I don't want Kevin here." The old man, breathing heavily in a corner of the Buick's rear seat, resembled a gargoyle removed from the wind and weather of a church. He produced a slightly sour smile. "You two are as close as identical twins can be. Telepathy, all that horseshit." He smiled benignly to remove the sting of his words. "So you know how Kev yearns to replace you as Charley's rightful heir."

"Me? What am I inheriting from Charley?"

"His brains, nipote, his know-how, his skills." Italo stopped smiling. The effect was to chill the back of the Buick by several degrees. "When Charley . . . ah, retires . . . it's you I want in that sky-office of his high above the earth. But Kevin has got it in his head the view belongs to him."

"It's up for grabs, Zio," Kerry said in an earnest voice. "It's just steel and cement. I expect Charley to sell it one of these days. New Era Services doesn't need such grand headquarters."

The gargoyle's intimidating full-face view now shifted to a profile as Italo turned away from Kerry. The old man watched with a slight air of disgust as the Buick passed the Port Authority buildings in its majestically slow progress southward on Ninth Avenue. His breathing grew easier. Zio didn't like being driven too swiftly in Manhattan's stop-and-go, especially when he couldn't estimate how long it might take for these exceedingly delicate negotiations to run their course.

"I didn't see Dr. Garnet," he said then.

"She's at work I guess."

"Better if she's occupied that way. Good break for us. It's New Era I need your help with," he said then in an offhand voice. "I want it sabotaged."

"What?"

"I want it booby-trapped. I want it set up in such a way that any time I want to bring back together the full Ricci strength in one empire I can do it."

Kerry's head started shaking from side to side. "That can never be, Zio. Charley's made sure of it."

"He set up a Delaware corporation," Italo agreed. "My companies don't show who owns them. That's the work of a clever man. But I'm talking to another, an alumnus of the Charley Richards Brain Factory. If one person on earth can find a way to do what I want, Kerry, it's you. And the reward is that tower suite that looks down on all of mankind like the throne of the universe.''

Kerry's head kept shaking. "I couldn't do that, Zio. Not to Charley.''

Italo turned to face him and the force of his stare was galvanic. Kerry seemed to jerk sideways, as if trying to avoid it. "Kev does what I tell him. Go here. Do this. All sorts of places to do all sorts of things. I have always, always! kept foremost in my mind that he comes out of it safely. After all, family is family.''

Kerry sank back against the soft cushioning of the Buick's rear seat. Any alumnus of the Charley Richards Brain Factory who did his post-graduate work at Winfield Richards University would already have worked out Italo's tradeoff: cooperate, or Kevin dies.

". . . And of course, he was horrified," Zio Italo told Kevin. They were sitting across the old rolltop desk from each other. Kerry had gone back uptown looking sick to his stomach. Now his brother and Zio watched each other a bit warily in the half light of the back room on Dominick Street.

"He wouldn't sell out Charley." Kevin's underlip curled. "Winfield has the poor turkey totally pussy-whipped. You might as well ask Kerry to jump off Richland Tower.''

Italo got up and went to the door that separated his office from the front rooms of the San Gennaro Social Club where a few male relatives spent their time playing cards. Standing, head cocked, like an evil sparrow, Italo listened until he was satisfied that whatever else was happening, the conversations outside continued unabated. No one was trying to overhear their Zio Italo. Just as well. If it worked, this particular plan was the most brilliant Italo had ever conceived. "At heart, he's a good boy," Italo said then. "I asked him for a takeover plot. It will be a good one, believe me." Italo's smile was benign again, as if Kerry had volunteered this service. "How long before that burn is gone under your eye?''

"A week?''

"And then the only person who absolutely knows who is Kevin and who is Kerry are Kevin and Kerry. Am I right?"

"Yeah, but—" He hesitated. "What kind of plot?"

"You're gonna have your hands full doing Kerry-Kevin flip-flops. Don't clutter your mind with other matters." Italo returned to his desk and sat down again. "Listen hard, nipote. Kerry will plot sabotage. But I cannot rely on him at the last minute to remain hard of heart. For that I need someone whose rightful destiny is to sit 130 stories above Manhattan. Someone with the true Ricci instinct for family triumph."

"Nobody'd let me that close to New Era."

"But they'd let Kerry." A pause. A soft smile. "And you will be Kerry."

Kevin's eyes widened. "Could it work? Zio, I'm no good at this stuff. Only Kerry has the mind for it." He looked stunned, washed-out.

"Agreed. But if he'll do his part you'll do yours?"

Kevin's normally expressionless eyes and mouth took on a solemn, greedy look. "In that case, why not? Yes."

Italo's narrow face seemed to swell slightly as he fixed his nipote with an intimidating intense glare. "There isn't anything I wouldn't do to put you at the top of Richland Tower. Even sending Kerry to heaven. Even this I promise."

"But—"

He held out his hand to Kevin. "And now, your promise."

Seventy-Four

At midday, Shan Lao disembarked at Miami International Airport. A private helicopter took him to Grand Bahama and touched down on the beach that fronted the parcel of land enclosed in cyclone fencing. Tall, slanting palms nodded under the downdraught of the helicopter rotors. They curtseyed in the man-made wind as if genuflecting to their master. The helicopter roared as it lifted off and away.

Shan stood motionless, watching five athletic young Chinese encircle him menacingly, each pointing an Armalite assault rifle. They all had that faint sneer that guards arrogate along with their weapons. "The light of day," Shan said calmly, "discloses the truth of life."

One of the young men, a Li brother, produced a big grin as he shouldered his Armalite. "Did you have a pleasant journey, sir?"

"An uneventful one." His gaze grew stern. "Your orders remain as before. They are . . . ?"

"Shoot," a faint smirk, "to kill." A pleased grimace. Shan nodded curtly. As he started off the beach toward the house, the young Chinese fell in around him as a sort of honor guard.

"Oh, dear!" Nicole said as he entered the front room. "What a surprise."

"I was moving too fast to telephone you, my dear." Shan kissed her cheek. He saw that she had perfected her suntan to such a deep shade of brown that they no longer looked like persons of a similar, olive-skinned race. "I have read that too deep a tan produces dangerous side effects."

She stood a tall but much fuller figure in a pareu of burnt orange fabric to which rough smears of black gave a tigerish look. "I have read the same things. They are unimportant."

Nicole wanted to ask something more important. He hadn't thought to call her, but he'd thought to remember the password of the day to avoid being shot by the men Nicole viewed as jailers. Their needs he remembered. Hers, no.

"You . . ." He paused. His head tilted sideways almost coquettishly. "You seem preoccupied?"

"You must be thirsty." Nicole put ice and mineral water in two tall glasses. "The young people will be back for lunch. At the moment, they—"

"—are sailing," Shan finished for her as he accepted the glass. "I do keep abreast of your life here, my dear."

"Then you must—" Again she refrained from mentioning the guards.

He sat down and sipped the water. "Your face is the proverbial book. What is wrong?"

"These guards."

"They are necessary, my dear."

"They remind me too much of the prison camp in which the Japanese interned me as a small girl. They are like barely restrained attack animals. At any moment, if one forgets to do the right thing, they may tear out one's throat. Bunny and Nikki agree with me. Only the baby is able to ignore them."

"Yes." He nodded pleasantly. "But you command them, my dear. They exist to serve you."

She sat down in a curved bamboo-and-raffia armchair across from him and sipped. "They obey your orders above all others." The pareu fell away from her long legs as she crossed them. She had painted her toenails a silvery white almost as startling as the bright white of her eyes in her dark face. "One false move . . ." She bared her white teeth and gestured with her white-tipped hand like a cat clawing.

Shan felt a sexual stir. "And when will the young ones return?"

Nicole gave a small, elegant shrug. "An hour at most."

Shan stood up. "My dear, we have a golden moment to squander on the question: what lies within the robe of the tiger."

She got to her feet and turned toward her bedroom. "Are you sure we can do this," she asked mischievously, "without giving a password?"

At midnight, the baby and women asleep, Nikki finally made contact by scrambler radiophone with Lord Hugo Waismith Mace.

"Sorry I woke you," he said. "Here's another gentleman."

"What in God's n—?" Mace sounded absolutely livid with rage. It would be barely six a.m. where he was.

"Good morning, Hugo," Shan Lao said in a silky voice. "Time for all good men to be up and doing. I want our friend to get a bonus. Be generous, Hugo. His men did their job. It was unavoidable that we had to annul their efforts. He had to annul them, too."

"Annul! You mean y—?"

"He may become a bit testy over this. Make the bonus a large one."

"Testy! You th—"

"There is an echo on this line, Hugo. My words keep being repeated. Does your friend still feel he has unfinished business in New York?"

"A vendetta is a vendetta."

"Then make sure he understands the same generous bonuses apply."

"In that case, he will hasten the day."

Shan switched off the radiophone. "Now, Mr. Choy in New York."

"He may also be asleep."

"We are awake. Call."

Nikki fussed with the keypad of the radiophone until he heard Choy's sleepy voice. "Early to bed, Bax and early to r—"

"Haven't slept in two days. You don't know what a demand we started here. I'm running out of everything. Meanwhile—" Choy stopped himself. "I'm sure the other gentleman has explained?"

Nikki glanced at his father, sitting across the dining room table. He had fallen asleep while reading the *Wall Street Journal*. "Hold the line." Nik cupped his hand over the microphone and touched his father's arm.

Shan's immense eyes opened slowly, revealing huge black irises in the half light. "Does he need to speak to me?"

"He's got supply problems on top of something big you've assigned him."

Shan took the phone. "The hacker," he began without any prologue.

"Sunday he performs," Choy responded. "And I'll have a disposal problem. Meanwhile. I have a distribution problem. I could use some help."

"It may seem so to you," Shan told him in a politely ominous way.

"I need a savvy, trusty, street-smart backup. Why can't you—" Baxter Choy paused to correct his petition. "Could you possibly release him to me?"

"I regard this as a confession of inadequacy," Shan retorted.

At the other end of the scrambled conversation Choy was silent for a long moment. "This close to complete success," he said then, "it pays to make absolutely sure." It was Shan's turn to reflect for a long moment. "And then, too," Choy added suddenly, "we can by no means consider the Washington matter concluded. Even if it makes me seem inadequate, I am spread much too thin."

Nikki watched his father's discreet mouth tighten into a flat line. "If you put it that way . . ." Shan Lao's voice grew suddenly more firmly commanding. "He will join you by noon tomorrow. Anything else?"

"Just my profound thanks, sir."

Shan switched off the radiophone and handed it back to Nikki. "Get to sleep. Tomorrow is a busy day."

"I'm not sure I understand what's going on in New York."

His father got to his feet slowly, an act of will after having been in transit most of the past twenty-four hours. "Choy regards you as partly his creation and therefore a competent help to him." The faint suggestion of a smile disturbed his thin mouth. "He will brief you. But you must take your own precautions. You must be self-sufficient and not become yet another responsibility for which Choy must answer. Is that clear?"

"In other words, something big is cooking?"

Shan's tired eyes examined his son carefully. "Very big," he said. "The biggest of my life."

Unable to return to sleep, Lord Hugo Waismith Mace sat up in bed and contemplated his own navel. Never before had he understood so well why the ancients used the umbilicus as a focus of concentration. One actually felt as if one had X-ray vision.

Still smarting from Shan's peremptory radio call, Mace began to see what lay ahead for him here in Calabria. In the Asian scheme of things, this ancient, spiny province, all coastline and rocks, was a backwater. Whereas to Mollo it was the world. As Shan's paymaster to Mollo, Lord Hugo was in truth only an errand boy, summoned by radio rather than the snap of careless fingers. He could continue this way for years, aestivating like a slug in a garden of poppies. Soon Mollo would lose any shred of respect he had for the errand boy, particularly when the bonuses slackened, as they would.

But there was a different job here, Mace knew, if he grabbed for it. As with so many other modern businesses—computers, aviation, electronics—the universal language of the worldwide drug trade was English. Mollo's command of it was unsure. More and more he admitted the English milord to certain inner councils as an interpreter.

A far better job than errand boy, eh?

Seventy-Five

In the old days of Wall Street—"old" meaning the 1970s, before computers vastly inflated the traffic-handling capability of brokerages—Sunday used to be considered a day of rest. The financial area at the foot of Manhattan Island would lie deserted except for occasional bikers and the odd knot of Japanese tourists following a guide with a raised red umbrella.

This Sunday the streets were still fairly empty, but the tall buildings all contained weekend crews hoping to work off five days' backlog of unprocessed buys and sells before Monday's madness began again. It was Parkinson's Law in action: because computers made more work possible, more work materialized.

Baxter Choy understood this. He had prepared Mervyn Lemnitzer with everything necessary to explain his presence on the 129th floor of Richland Tower today. The hacker still had his photo-ID building pass. He only lacked a pass that would allow the elevator to let him off at the 129th floor. This Baxter Choy had thoughtfully provided, along with a natty attaché case containing several Thinkmen, a toolkit and a walkie-talkie, crystal-controlled to a rogue wavelength rarely used by anyone else. If he ran into someone who not only knew him but knew he'd recently been fired, Lemnitzer was carrying a beautiful letter signed by Charles Anthony Richards informing all concerned that the hacker had been rehired for a special research assignment.

"Looks good," Lemnitzer murmured. They were sitting in a small gray rented Ford Fiesta not far from the garage entrance to Richland Tower. "But what if I run into Richards?"

"You won't. He's still recuperating."

"And you're going to monitor me by walkie-talkie?"

"Every heartbeat," Choy assured him.

"Fifty grand seems like an awful lot for such a simple job."

"Simple, perhaps. But it has to be foolproof. I have to know *before* you come back downstairs, that the control is working."

Lemnitzer's face screwed up. "It's a cinch. I don't have to access anything. I know how they form their codes. I can access them later. That's the beauty part of it. What you're asking of me any kid with a Boy Scout electrician's merit badge could do."

"Fine. Then get in there and stick it to 'em."

Choy sat alone for the longest time after the hacker had gone inside. Hours seemed to pass. Nobody ever worries about "He Who Waits," Choy mused. But until he heard Lemnitzer telling him he was safely inside the Richland computer room, he could feel, actually feel, the rapid, irregular tachycardiac beats of his heart. Shan Lao, who thought of him as a laid-back sophisticate, would jeer at such lack of control.

Finally, a crackle from the walkie-talkie. Seven minutes had elapsed. "OK," the hacker said. "Easier than I expected."

"What?"

"Nobody here. No weekend crew. It's possible . . ." Lemnitzer's voice trailed off.

"Hullo?"

"I told you, even before he fired me, the big man was already transferring a lot of stuff out of this office."

"Whadya mean? Transferring where?"

"I told you. When I asked what was going on, he fired me. Nice, huh? After five years, ask one question and get your head handed to you. Is it any wonder I—"

"Transferred what out of Richland?"

"All I can say is that if the volume of business here

was anything like when I worked for them, there'd be a dozen people slaving away this Sunday. There is nobody. Zip."

"Never mind. Get started."

Baxter Choy sat back behind the wheel of the rented car and stared angrily out at Cedar Street. What good was this huge, overweening strategy if Richards had outguessed them? He'd have to alert Shan Lao, but not before the hacker had finished his job. He was right, Lemnitzer. It was a basic electrical job. Through tielines, rented trunk lines and modems, Richland Securities funneled into its central data storage the activity of all its offices, worldwide. Every transaction, every memorandum was stored here. Every order went out from here.

In electrical terms, the impulses digitalizing such information came through a very narrow gate before being redistributed to specialized data-processing subcenters. Lemnitzer knew exactly where this entry was. It came up from the basement over nine multistrand conductors that could handle hundreds of messages simultaneously. These were the usual Stone Age copper conductors of electrical impulses, not the new, fiberglass optical conduits. The new ones could not have been tapped so easily, Choy reflected. You had to have at least that much of a break from life.

These cables entered the 129th floor not far from a rear door to the data room that was always kept locked. Where the cables began to fan out into smaller lines connecting mainframe storage facilities, an induction-coil connection to a programmed Thinkman gave remote control to whoever held the matching Thinkman. Once the hacker's work was completed Shan Lao would be able to access any information in the Richland files and input any new information. Who held the second Thinkman controlled the life of Richland Securities worldwide.

Meaning what, Choy asked himself. If major accounts had been transferred elsewhere, what good was remote control? How could Shan Lao hope to use Richland Securities to trigger a new and permanently lethal market crash?

Baxter Choy shook his head as if attacked by flies. He sighed hard. Not his job to mastermind Shan Lao. His job was to set Lemnitzer to work and let Shan Lao reap the benefits thereof.

Even if they had become an illusion.

Sunday in late March, Long Island Sound was beginning to fill with power boats. The launch Nikki Shan was using, the *Shirley-Girlie,* had to be among the most powerful.

The incoming shipment of MegaMAO would reach Orient Point no later than nine p.m., when it would be almost as dark as night itself. Once the seaplane offloaded into his launch, Nikki would speed through darkness to three distribution points on the north shore, then meet Choy at Brook Haven Airport near Yaphank. They'd fly south to Grand Bahama. By taking this job off Choy's hands, Nikki freed him for whatever mysterious scam he was setting up in Manhattan.

Neither Choy nor his father had seen fit to explain it to him. He knew how difficult it was for his father to delegate authority. But trust and the delegation of authority had to be almost instant. Delay too long and the opportunity passed untaken.

Nikki checked his wristwatch. The sun had already set. In two hours or less, a pontoon seaplane would ghost in somewhere between Mulford and Orient Point, along the sheltered curve of Petty's Bight. Nikki ducked inside the small cuddy cabin in the bow of the *Shirley-Girlie.* His two Chinese helpers looked up from their work of feeding cartridges into a dozen Browning .9 magazines. The stubby bullets, gleaming brassily in the faint light, resembled fat beetles.

"Is that it? Just handguns?" Nikki asked.

The one called Larry made a face. "Couple of elderly Armalite A-7's. Expecting trouble?"

"Always."

"These Armalites are Second World War issue," one of the petty officers told Cohen.

"But combat ready."

"You know Hackschmidt. For him we're always in a state of combat."

The other young sailor finished loading magazines. "I

haven't thought of Commander Hackschmidt all week. I hope he hasn't thought about us, either.''

Cohen rubbed his chin and felt the rasp of a day-old beard. It didn't do to let personal appearance slacken. Out here at the tail end of Long Island, watching and waiting, ducking in and out of dozens of bays and inlets, checking the ground for signs of nocturnal landings, one let appearance go slack.

Talking to the locals, he knew he was targeted correctly. They all mentioned seaplanes, light craft whose markings none of them had noted. The planes' comings and goings were always nocturnal, swift and seemingly furtive. If Cohen could wait long enough, something would fall into his lap. But in Manhattan rumors were flying about a gigantic case the DA's office was considering against one of the most flagrant of the Riccis, Vince. Cohen yearned to be back in town.

Still, he reminded himself as the night began to darken around them, in Manhattan he was just one of the Suggs' underlings. Here, among the quiet lapping of the tide and the last hoots of marshbirds, Cohen was a force to be reckoned with, a leader with two followers to prove it. He squared his jaw and suppressed a smile at the idea that this miniature landing party was a force to be reckoned with. Still . . .

Seventy-Six

In Locri, as elsewhere in Southern Itay, Sunday was really no day of rest. Lord Hugo Waismith Mace had already learned this camping on Mollo's doorstep. On Sunday, Mace had learned, when the womenfolk were off at church, the men felt their way toward the business of the next week.

As in most semi-tropical lands, planning of any kind rarely progressed beyond a day, if that. Housewives shopped several times a day at sharply specialized stores. In this way a life passed. It was true that Locri had a supermarket, but who trusted a place where the prices marked on the goods were the real prices, no bargaining, and there was no one from whom to extort the odd little gift, a fistful of parsley, some sprigs of basil, a thirteenth egg, an unweighed slice of mortadella?

Men of consequence used Sunday to arrange alliances and betray them. If he were as important to the local economy as Mollo, the businessman would sort things out on Sunday. Even for a southerner Mollo was as short and slight as a jockey. He still wore his weekday sleeveless rugby shirt with horizontal stripes and his weekday growth of beard. He had summoned Lord Mace at the ungodly hour of eleven a.m.

"He was quite clear on that," Mace assured him. "The Manhattan vendetta is as close to his heart as to yours."

"Marrone," Mollo grunted, "how expensive these American ladri can be! America was a jungle for my poor Pino and Mimmo."

"The local men know the terrain. They won't fail you."

"But charge me dearly for it."

"Isn't it lucky that you have a silent partner with a ready wallet?"

Mollo stared at him a long time, not the challenging mafia stare of intimidation but one of curiosity. "After all, this is my vendetta. Who murdered Lucca Certomá did me a favor. But one must avenge his honor. Your motives . . . ?"

Lord Mace called over the small boy who ran drinks from inside the bar to the terrace where they sat. "A cool drink?"

"Thank you, no. Your motives?"

"Nettezza urbana," Mace quoted the sign on the odorous garbage pickup trucks. "We enjoy keeping our cities clean."

No one had ever heard Mollo laugh. But, this time, he did smile.

Sunday afternoon Winfield usually tried to keep as lazy as possible. It wasn't working out that way.

Now that her father had thrown off most of the effects of the tranquilizers and the other feelgood junk fed him at the clinic, she could send him downstairs to Garnet's bed and return to her own private life upstairs.

Winfield's view of the Art Deco Chrysler Building felt almost healing as she stood naked in the window and gazed south. The late sunlight poured in from her right-hand side, casting the long shadows that Manhattan uses to define its upward thrust. Behind her Kerry lay full length on the sofa. Winfield had grown used to the sight of his long legs and powerful shoulders, here or at his own Hoboken home. She hoped he enjoyed observing her because gazing at him had a healing effect similar to that of the Chrysler Building, as if on a museum stroll she had come across a better-than-average marble statue.

But not today. Today the statue twitched too much to radiate healing vibes. Kerry seemed unable to find a comfortable place for his long body. He turned sideways, then flopped on his stomach, then on his back. Winfield made a note to try to discourage him from a sleepover neither of them would enjoy tonight.

"Your body is trying to tell me something," she said. "Try words?"

Kerry laughed helplessly. "If I told you what's on my mind, you'd never want to see me again."

"I'm that fickle? Listen, dimwit, if I didn't drop you when we both thought we were half-siblings, I'm not about to drop you now."

"You've got your own problems. Don't they arraign Vince tomorrow?"

"Tuesday. I'm being asked to lie low on that event."

He sat up and stared at her, silhouetted against the evening sun. "I think, maybe I ought to get dressed and go." He reached for long white tennis socks.

"Not till you tell me what's eating you."

"What's eating me is that I'm the lowest form of life."

His words reverberated because they had been squeezed out in anguish like the howl of faulty brakes applied in panic. Winfield watched the look of pain on his normally unexpressive face. "My God, you really are hurting."

She sat down beside him on the sofa and put her arm around his broad shoulders. "Tell me."

"Lowest form of life? What else do you call a guy who sells out his girl and his uncle."

"Just a nice, normal American lad."

He yanked on one sock so ferociously his big toe went

straight through the end. "Goddammit. Everything's falling apart. The whole goddamned world."

"No, just one tennis sock. Please tell me."

"It's Zio Italo."

Winfield rubbed his shoulder. "If it's trouble, it's always Zio Italo. What does he want you to do?"

He turned to her in surprise. "You know?" He stared for a moment, then went on, "He wants me to find a soft spot in New Era Services, a place to put a crowbar and jimmy it open so he can take it over."

Winfield, tensed for something far worse, relaxed. "He's deluded. You wouldn't do that even for him."

"I already have."

"Kerry!"

"It's that eleemosynary clause. The board is authorized to allocate up to half New Era's profits to philanthropy." He sighed unhappily. "Even under Delaware corporate law, that looks like a phony. As if I were to get an M. Div. and become a minister to scam a tax break. It looks like New Era is some sort of dodge to avoid corporate taxation."

Winfield sat silently for a long moment, her pale green-blue eyes shifting here and there as the microchips in her head clicked off possibilities. "OK. You did Dad and Garnet a favor. You found a soft spot we can amend in the by-laws. Cut the percentage for charity work. Just don't tell Zio."

Kerry's head kept shaking from side to side and continued to do so long after she'd stopped talking. "You don't understand, Winfield. I have already shared this with Kevin."

"You rat!"

Again that helpless laugh. "Zio Italo told me flat out if I didn't do what he wanted, he'd send Kev off to be killed somewhere. Nice?"

"Typical."

They sat side by side for a while, staring at her bare feet and his bare toe. "What's Kevin supposed to do about it?" she asked at last in a thin, dry voice.

"Get Charley's OK to do just what you suggested, repair the damage."

"Why would my father let Kevin do that?"

"And, while pretending to fix it, institute some kind

of legal action in Delaware to freeze New Era assets and—''

''Why would my father let Kevin do that?'' she repeated.

''Because you can't any longer tell Kevin from Kerry. He used to have a tiny blue dot under his left eye. It's gone.''

''My father knows that.''

''What?''

''You're working for a very smart fella.''

''But Kev—''

''—is wasting his time. Only one person in the whole world can tell you two apart now.'' She pointed at her left breast. ''Me.''

''How?''

''That's my business. Where's Kev at the moment?''

His brother shrugged. ''He has a date tomorrow morning to impersonate me at the office downtown. I'm to lie low while he cons Uncle Charley.''

''Tomorrow morning.'' Her hand moved down from his shoulder to his chest. She tweaked his right nipple. ''Was Kev a very good scholar?''

''Ooh. Not breathtaking, no.''

''So there'd be no point in an apt quotation.'' Her face could scarcely contain an excitement that made her eyes protrude slightly, as if with passion. She was massaging his abdomen now. ''Oh, what a tangled web we weave,'' she quoted, ''when first we practice to deceive.''

''That's nice.''

''Nice? It's absolutely apt.''

''No, that massage. It's really taking my mind off everything.''

''That's what I like about you intellectuals.''

Seventy-Seven

Night. The overpowered launch Cohen had been given by the Coast Guard was heading quietly southwest out of the moonlit finger of protected water called Long Beach

Bay. To the north lay the landlocked town of Orient Point and to the south the wooded stretch of Orient Point State Park. No place to land a seaplace, Cohen thought. Still, he had to check any likely hidey-hole for whatever power boat would be making a rendezvous. Once his own craft cleared Long Beach Point, it U-turned northeast through Gardiners Bay and headed directly toward Plum Island.

The channel between it and Long Island was called Plum Gut, referring perhaps to its deeper draft. The Coast Guard launch skimmed northwest now, curved past the New London ferry dock to the north shore of Long Island where it faced across the Sound toward Old Lyme and the congeries of shipyards beyond. There was a small civilian airfield at Mulford Point. Although it was closed except in summer, Cohen suspected that it had radio-beacon capability. Someone intent on bringing in a homing plane at night might conceivably be nesting around Mulford. "Let's park under that bluff," he told one of the young petty officers.

"Mr. Cohen, you don't park a boat."

"What then?"

"Tie up. Anchor. Not park."

He nodded. "See that bluff? *Stop* there."

"Aye, aye, sir."

The weather had turned warm for late March, almost a late-April night, soft breezes, gentle waves. The moon rode quarter-full, its light capricious, uncertain. As they tied up at a low dock, Cohen and his crew fell silent, enjoying the peace and the balmy warmth. Now and then a thin cloud slipped past the moon.

One of the young sailors started a meandering discourse on the Gulf Stream current that brushed past Montauk Point, on the south fork of Long Island, and then added an extra bit of warmth to this fork before it continued north and east over the Atlantic to rest at last in western Scotland.

Cohen sat on the rear thwart of the launch and stared due east toward Plum. There were two sources of light on the tiny island, neither of them lighthouses with swinging beams but blinkers that warned off passing craft. If you watched the two pinpoints of light their blinking had a pattern. On, off, on. Cohen relaxed. His eyes closed. Then, in the silence of the night, he heard the seaplane's engine.

Nikki checked his watch: nine-twenty-seven. Not bad timing at all. He nudged the Chinese called Larry Shiu. "Hear it?"

"I'd feel better if I could see it."

"Once he lands he gives us a flashlight signal. And we answer."

Nikki picked up the long-barreled waterproof flashlight. Holding his hand over the lens, he clicked it on to test it. The light glowed faintly red through the skin of his fingers. He snapped off the switch and waited.

Mistake. It killed his night vision for a few moments. But the moonlight helped and the sound of the seaplane wasn't any louder. Could they have missed their bearings? Missed Petty's Bight altogether? Not possible. These pilots couldn't afford mistakes, not carrying multi-million-dollar freight.

Now he could hear the plane's engine grow louder. A cloud blacked out the moon. Nikki strained his eyes. "Give a shout if you—"

"There!"

Two faint white lines in the night, the froth pushed up by two pontoons ruffling the water. Instantly the engine sound dropped to silence. At a point above the two dashes of white a yellowish light blinked on three times. Nikki sighted along the barrel of his flashlight and sent back three blinks. "Cast off," Nikki told the other Chinese. "Get us close, but dead slow."

The powerful launch, its engines muttering, inched forward blindly in the night. A moment later the moon unveiled again and Nikki could see the outline of the seaplane, a light craft with two huge pontoons and a single-engined propeller sitting motionless like a slash across the nose and cockpit windshield. The flimsy side door of the plane swung open and an anchor on a line splashed into the shallow waters of Petty's Bight. The pilot, a small man in a tan anorak, stepped down onto a pontoon and made fast the line to one of the duralumin pontoon struts.

"Evening," he said then. "Better kill your engines."

Nikki gestured to Larry and suddenly the night grew

silent. Small waves lapped at their hull as they maneuvered sideways against one pontoon and made fast. Off in the distance Nikki could see two blinkers going on and off and on. "Couldn't ask for a better night," he remarked. "No wind. Perfect."

"Let's get going, then," the pilot said.

He climbed back up in the plane and after a moment shoved a plastic-wrapped package the size of a small TV set until it hung halfway out of the cabin. Larry Shiu reached up to grasp it.

"Hold it right there!" The voice was deafening, a bullhorn of a voice. A searchlight snapped on, blinding them all. "This is the FBI. You're under arrest!"

Nikki dropped below the gunwale of his launch and steadied the barrel of the Browning .9 against the varnished wood. He squeezed off one shot. The heavy gun jumped. The searchlight went in a crash of glass.

From inside the seaplane the pilot swept a line of stuttering bullets across the oncoming power boat. He held the Ingram with its great silencer cradled in the crook of his arm. The slugs zipped like wasps as they cut into the boat.

Someone returned fire, the much louder stutter of an Armalite on semi-automatic in bursts of three. A slug caught the other Chinese crewman in his shoulder blade and knocked him out of the launch. He splashed into the water and sank.

Nikki crawled sideways to a new firing point and sent two more slugs into the police boat. Above him he saw the pilot reach down and slash the anchor rope free.

"Hey!" Nikki shouted.

The airplane engine roared into life. Someone in the police boat stitched the seaplane's silvery corrugated-metal sides with bursts of Armalite fire. The sulphurous stench of cordite filled Nikki's nostrils. The plane was trying to move but it was still tied to the launch.

A new sound blasted the air. The police boat's immense twin engines howled into life. Its bow leapt directly at the seaplane. Nikki watched the line connecting his craft to the seaplane snap. He ejected a spent magazine and clipped in a new one.

Someone was standing in the bow of the police boat.

"Hands up!" he shouted. "Drop your guns or we ram you!"

Nikki, holding the heavy automatic in both hands, aimed at the dimly seen figure. As he roared closer his face emerged from the night, moonlit like an avenging sheriff. Nikki aimed for his heart.

With a sudden spurt of speed and a scream of twin screws, the oncoming boat lurched forward into the nearest pontoon and crumpled it like a peapod. The seaplane began listing. The pilot revved his engine, trying to slew free. Instead, the plane began to turn like a tethered goat, slowly at first, then crazily. It started to sink.

Nikki crept forward amid the noise and shoved his twin throttles forward. His boat leapt ahead into the night.

He looked to see what had happened to the other Chinese, Larry Shiu. The moon on Shiu's upturned face, a line of Armalite slugs across it, showed Nikki he was alone. Blindly, he steered through the night, heading toward the two blinking lights to the east. On. Off. On.

In a moment he could hear the excited howl of the police boat giving chase. Nikki saw the land to his right suddenly give out. He was crossing Plum Gut now. In a moment he'd beach on Plum itself unless he was careful. He yanked the wheel hard right, hoping to outdistance the police boat in the vastness of Gardiners Bay. Engines screaming, the boat refused to turn. He pulled hard. Something snapped.

The overpowered launch gained speed as it neared the shore of Plum Island. He was going to beach whether he wanted to or not. In a moment he, and they, would be on dry land. In another moment, outnumbered, he would be dead.

Seventy-Eight

Normally, Winfield would have loved a quiet ride downtown in her father's limo. But an early start was part of her plan this Monday morning. She left Kerry fast asleep on her sofa-bed and took the East Side IRT to the financial district, knowing she'd get there well ahead of her father.

She found that Kevin had beaten her. He was sitting, the picture of busy concern, at Kerry's desk, shuffling papers. For a brief moment the sight of him was disturbing; she had just left him, naked, in her own bed. She found herself wondering if it would ever be possible to feel for Kevin what she felt for Kerry. Their passion was based on complicity; both of them were spies inside the Ricci fortress, fellow-tenants of a Trojan Horse. They consoled each other sexually. But Kevin was another matter. In a pale blue button-down shirt, dark blue tie, charcoal three-piece suit with a very faint pin-stripe and an earnest expression on his face, he looked more Kerry than Kerry.

Outside, one hundred and twenty-nine floors below, sirens yelped and moaned. It was going to be one of those Manhattan days, Winfield thought. She steeled herself, lifted Kevin out of his chair with a bear hug and planted a long, loving kiss on his lips. "Umm," she moaned. "What did you say your name was, stranger?"

By way of reply, he embraced her and kissed back. Neither kiss, Winfield noted, included tongue. Strange boy, Kevin. One more way to tell the twins apart. "Dad ought to be here soon." She flipped on Kerry's small-screen TV set standing atop his desk.

". . . Horrifying situation in the entire history of this tri-state area where twenty-five million Americans . . ." a New York senator was telling the camera. He paused and fervently clasped his hands before his chest. "We can only get down on our knees and thank the good Lord that the FBI agent who brought the perpetrators to justice was alert enough to blow the whistle on this outrageous situation."

"Senator, can you describe for our listeners wh—"

"A chaos. A desolation. An abomination in the eyes of the Lord. A hell of hideous death planted amid the nearly thirty million men, women and children who live in the shadow of Plum Island. I can assure m—"

"Pardon me, senator. We're going live to Plum Island where—"

". . . thousands of rusting canisters," Cohen was telling the camera.

"It's him!" Kevin-Kerry yelped.

"Who?"

"The bastard who gave Ke—" He stopped. "Who gave us such a hard time at that meeting in Westchester and ever since."

". . . mean they were actually floating into Long Island Sound?" someone was asking Cohen. He stood tall in a two-day growth of beard, the iron lineaments of Gary Cooper's jawline beginning to soften. Another day and he might resemble Gabby Hayes. A compelling line of blood slanted sideways down one cheek from his earlobe.

"Fishermen pull them up all the time and throw them back. I can't believe they know what's in the canisters."

"And that would be . . . ?"

"You name it," Cohen snapped back. "Nerve gas. Anthrax."

"Anthrax!" The interviewer looked shocked but suddenly blurted, "Direct now from the White House, a special statement from the President."

". . . the lives of forty million Americans protected by the steadfast devotion to duty and outstanding courage of our first bulwark against crime, the Federal Bureau of Investigation, aided and assisted by the United States Coast Guard. I want to—"

"Load of bullshit." Kevin's fingers were shaking as he snapped off the tiny TV picture. He glanced at his watch. "Uncle Charley's late."

"Traffic." She sat down across from him and carefully crossed her long-calved legs. "I wonder what the FBI was doing out there last night."

"Will we ever know?"

She shrugged. "I've got my own problems. Uncle Vince."

"Problems sending him to the slams?"

"I've found out—my law office has found out—that he's become a MegaMAO user."

"Vince? Hard to believe."

"He's got all the schizzy symptoms of a MegaMAO addict. Bad enough but he's due to be arraigned this week. He's in no condition to face the cops, the DA's office or anybody else. He's babbling, Kerry. He hears voices."

Kevin sat there for a long time, his eyes flicking this

way and that across Kerry's desk. "Why tell me?" he asked then.

"Because I tell you everything." She sat forward, her face closer to him. "Because I'm appalled at what *I've* done. It's one thing for Vince to get a fair trial. He's protected by the Fifth Amendment, top lawyers and his own smarts. It's another if he's so scrambled upstairs he's his own worst enemy." Her voice faltered for a moment. "I helped put him where he is, Kerry. But he isn't the same competent Vince anymore. I'll have it on my conscience for the rest of my life if I helped send a sick man to jail. The family would never forgive me."

His smile was furtive, quickly fading. "You're not terribly popular as it is."

"From the beginning, I knew I had problems with this job. I've asked my senior partner if there's some way she can get Vince severed from the docket on grounds of incompetence. He'll spill beans we don't even want to know about." She saw she had Kevin's undivided attention now. "You see the bind I'm in. I can't even warn him."

The words "Somebody should" hovered unspoken in the air. She sat back and crossed her legs the other way. Then she switched on his—Kerry's—mini-TV. " . . . Basically an animal disease of herbivores like sheep, horses and cows, known to the ancient Greeks," a woman's voice was saying. On the small screen a flock of sheep stared dumbly at the camera. " . . . very rare in nature, anthrax is often transmitted to humans during the processing of wool and hides. Its spores are extremely hardy and may survive for generations in a subsoil environment. Anthrax can also be transmitted from one affected human to another human. It occurs in four types." The flock of sheep started to move toward the camera, but not menacingly. Winfield switched off the TV. "Appetizing breakfast chatter. Reminds me. Dinner tonight? I found a great new place on First Avenue. Lamb cutlets?"

"Uh . . ." He gave her a reckless grin. "I'll come by around eight."

She kissed him and went into the office two rooms down where Andy Reid had once worked. She closed the door loudly, then opened it in silence. On the streets below another siren coughed and spat like a man clearing his throat. Then it wailed.

". . . because she thought I was Kerry, that's why." Kevin's words came faintly at first, then louder as he grew more excited. "Zio, it's important you get Vince out of circ—" The door to his office shut and she heard no more.

She went to the window and gazed out at the city below. This had been the easy part, using Kevin's deception to deceive him. The rest of what she had to do required the most exquisite timing and a great deal of luck. Somebody was observing her behind her back. She whirled. Charley Richards stood in her open doorway.

"What're you hatching, kiddo?"

"Plots. Anything new with the Fellowship election?"

"Plots is not a substantive answer."

"But it's all I'm giving this morning."

"Then, as far as the Fellowship is concerned, my lips are sealed. Except that I expect to lose."

"How can you? There are six official nominees and you're one of them."

"The write-ins will sink me. You have no idea what a campaign they've raised."

"Then maybe it's time to yank Imogen Raspe's chain."

He stared at her. "What do you mean?"

"I've heard a few things about her private life."

"Spare me."

"Galahad doesn't blackmail porno queens?"

He failed to answer. Then, "I sometimes wonder what Galahad does do, apart from trying to improve America."

"Nobody wants an improved America."

"I do," he assured her. "My heritage—yours, too— is a family that has spent all its energy stealing America blind. We have dues to pay, Winfield."

In the silence that followed, Winfield tried to analyze her own motives and found that her father had probably spoken for both of them. But she still couldn't unfold to him what she was doing. "Dad, that young man in your office."

"Kerry?"

"It's Kevin. It's very important you don't let him know you know."

"Important to you?"

"Very."

"Why?"

"Plots."

He made a face. His newly thin cheeks emphasized his skull structure. In the past year, Winfield realized, he had become a different person. In the past you didn't worry about conning the old conman, Charley. But now, the thought of going behind Il Professore's back filled her with guilt.

"Dad?"

"OK. He's Kerry." He shook he head slowly. "Winfield . . ." He paused. "You really are . . ."

"What?"

"Too much."

Seventy-Nine

Italo Ricci replaced the telephone in its cradle and sat back at his old oak desk, considering the silvery-gray instrument with hatred and an emotion that had to be fear. Why didn't he have the maladetta machinetta yanked off the wall and thrown in the garbage can? Why did he continue to let it rule his life, bringing him news of nothing but fresh disaster? Had it ever rung once, once in his life, with good news?

The color monitor of his PC had been switched to a morning television news program. A herd of cows munched grass on a hillside that in its rocky scrawniness reminded Italo of Calabria. ". . . most commonly as a malignant pustule," a woman was saying. "In this form it is usually localized as a carbuncle. Other symptoms: headache, nausea, vomiting, joint pains, fever. If lesions are not on head or neck, a cure may be possible." The zoom lens of the camera moved in on one particular cow, whose great globular eyes took on a dangerous gleam. "In its second form, as malignant anthrax edema, the disease is no longer localized. Instead there is general swelling of subcutaneous tissue. Cure rate is not favorable. Untreated, this form, even when not extreme, is fatal.''

"Vai fanciullo!" Italo cursed. He switched the monitor to its computer mode and slipped in his personnel database disk. Only he could access it, with a double-password configuration that he changed at random intervals of a month or less. He began making calls, heedless of time zone, first to Vince's local numbers. On his fourth call, he succeeded in waking Lenore.

". . . no, Zio, purtroppo. I haven't seen him.''

"Since how long?" he demanded.

"A week?" Lenore hesitated. "Is he OK? Is something wrong?''

Of all his nipotini's women, Italo most liked Lenore. She was not only beautiful in a classic Italian way, she was also respectful and sweet to him. It could not be great fun, serving as Vince's wife, but she had stuck to it and finally tamed Vince by producing a son. In Italo's mind, if a woman were decorative, respectful and fecund, she had fulfilled the destiny God had decreed for her. "Stai calma, bellissima. Arrivederci.''

He telephoned cousins and nephews in Atlantic City, Las Vegas, the Bahamas, Macao and Monaco. In Grotteria the telephone rang endlessly without rousing anyone. In none of these places did anyone have a clue as to Vince's whereabouts. In none of these places had he been seen for some time. After half an hour of this, Italo gave himself over to thought. The news Kevin had given him this morning, even though it came from Winfield, had to be true. Italo had been ignoring rumors about Vince for some time.

It pleased Zio to find that behind her heartless, Wasp facade, Winfield had a shred of family honor left. It also pleased him that Kevin had successfully convinced her that he was Kerry. His plans for taking over new Era Services would go ahead unhampered. But it was in the very heart of Italo's daily routine—which he had long ago chosen as his life—that even as one plot succeeded, another began sending out distress signals.

The business of Mollo, for instance. Italo would long ago have sent Kevin to attend to Mollo. But Kevin was needed here with New Era. Another nipote had been dispatched, a likely lad called Turi Ricci, barely twenty years of age. Last night this accursed telephone had brought him news that Mollo had left Turi's severed head on the front steps of the Prefettura in Locri. Another nipote was on his way to Calabria. But, meanwhile, Italo could only sit and wonder how bad Vince was, how loose-tongued he might become. Babbling, Kevin had reported. Vince was no low-level button man like Turi, the loss of whose head produced little panic. But if Vince lost his head while in the hands of the police, he could spout great encyclopedias of information, names, events, dates, amounts of money. Undoubtedly the most profitable part of the Ricci empire could very quickly go up in flames.

Italo relied primarily on Vince's far-flung operations for cash flow. The legitimate companies Charley had so cleverly forced on him produced profits that had to be reported to the IRS, but nothing compared to the take from casinos or the markup on drugs. All unreportable. The state of Vince's mental health was important to this vast cash flow. But in the business scheme of things, the cash flow was more important than Vince's mental health. If he had fallen into unreliability, this was sad. But sadder still would it be if he were actually to disturb cash flow.

Italo turned back to the computer and ran through the section of the database listing efficient and practical people who could be relied on to do a clean, untraceable job. The list was quite short, barely twenty-five, all men, all tested and in Italo's mind approved. But how could he trust any of them with a contract at this high level?

You could employ them for everyday assassinations. There were even one or two, like Iggy Zetz, whom you could trust to do a serious job and make it look entirely accidental, real maestri di specialitá. But it took time to commit Iggy to a project. He had to be tracked down somewhere in Europe and he had to be free to accept an assignment. One didn't summon a maestro like Iggy with the same imperious twitch of the finger that produced an ordinary take-out artist.

In truth, for a family assignment like this, one required a member of the family. This kind of blood-guilt could only be borne properly and philosophically by someone inside, with an easy familiarity, almost a fraternal contempt, plus a hunger to rise. Only one such person existed.

But he was busy pretending to be his brother.

This time there was no letterhead, typed or printed. As Garnet unfolded the sheet sent out to the membership of the Fellowship in a plain envelope, she saw that someone had Xeroxed, in reduced size, a number of newspaper clippings that mingled old kidnap stories about Charley with Manhattan crime-wave articles. In the center ran this brief statement:

> Should an organization devoted to the improvement
> of education . . .
> To bettering our cultural and political life . . .
> To building a better-informed, clearer-thinking
> America . . .
> Take leadership from this kind of person?
> Ballots will soon be mailed to you. In your heart
> you already know who must not be allowed to taint
> our board with his presence.

Garnet stared at the sheet of paper until it went out of focus. The dirty tricks department had been called in by the terribly cultured people who wanted to keep the Fellowship's board free of everyone but their own. She found herself wondering if Charley had ever before crossed Imogen Raspe's path. The vitriol couldn't be explained by simple maliciousness. But instead of asking Charley, Garnet had developed a faster way of reading his mind.

"Winfield?" she began over the telephone. "The Raspe woman, the porno queen? Can you think of anything in the past between her and your father?"

She was rewarded with a vomiting noise over the phone. "I don't even think he knew her name before this. Why?"

"Any other family connection?"

"With my cousin Pam. Imogen Raspe publishes her."

"That's it?"

"I have it on good authority she and Pam jointly ball Vince Ricci. These bisexuals do seem to have all the fun."

"On what good authority?" Garnet demanded.

"On the authority of Vince's wife, Lenore Ricci? Will that do?"

"But . . ." Garnet paused, thinking.

"Pam might see a connection between Lenore and my law firm. But that's me, not my father."

"In the course of her blameless life as a cultural person, Raspe doesn't come in contact with you. It's your father who suddenly pops up, about to join her on the prestigious ERF board."

"Is that a motive for anything?"

"Her books are marketed colorfully, but they pretend to be serious studies. If it became known she took pleasure in living some of her books, her image would change disastrously."

"Lot of 'if' there."

Garnet went back to silence again, trying to think with Imogen Raspe's mind. "If you are a worthless person masquerading as one of New York's more worthwhile figures; if you grow rich celebrating brutality against women but parading as a patron of education advances; if you are a closet wanton coming on to your stockholders as a crisp manageress . . . and up pops someone who may know you ball mafiosi *and* their women, is that a motive for anything?"

This time, both of them retreated into silence.

Eighty

By eight a.m. this Monday, Eileen Hegarty had showered and dressed and was showing Buzz Eiler how to spoon mashed bananas into Little Benjy. Far away from their apartment on 54th Street, sirens mumbled and moaned. The kitchen TV set showed a horse lying on its side in a stall. By the wild flare of its eyes and labored breathing, the horse seemed in great distress.

"Pulmonary anthrax," a woman said, "results from inhaling the spores. A severe lung inflammation ensues. Death occurs within eighteen to forty-eight hours." The horse tried to stand up but failed. "The fourth type, gastrointestinal anthrax, results from ingestion of food containing anthrax bacilli and spores. Death occurs within a few hours.''

"It doesn't matter if he refuses the first few spoonsful,'' Eileen explained. ''Even spits it out. You just keep spooning.''

"And crooning.''

"Very important.'' She glanced at her watch. ''No nonsense syllables. He's too smart to be fobbed off with goo-goo-talk.''

"Takes after his mother.''

She kissed him, kissed the baby and then, instead of leaving, stood there in her Monday morning blue blazer and skirt, pearl-gray blouse and one long strand of ordinary oval beads in a muted yellow. ''I had never—'' She stopped and cleared her throat. ''I had never expected the three of us t—'' This time she stopped for good, her eyes brimming.

"Jesus, Benjy,'' Buzz muttered, ''would you take a defense brief from a sentimental slob like Mom?''

"Mom,'' the baby echoed.

Buzz swiveled around to face his wife. ''Tilda gets here by nine?''

Eileen nodded, still not trusting her voice. ''Because I hate to leave Vince alone for too long. I think I'm breaking through,'' Buzz went on. ''He's improving every day he spends without MegaMAO. So far, four.''

"You're not trying cold turkey deprivation?''

"Mild tranquilizers, multi-vitamins and some stuff that flushes out the system fast. Otherwise he's free to start all over again. With a hothead like Vince, you have to make him believe it's his idea, his willpower.''

"All this trouble. He'll unkink in jail, believe me.''

"Hey, he took good care of me.''

"Terrific care. With a friend like that you don't need . . .''

"OK, he put me through shit. Now MegaMAO is dragging him in it. He's hurting, Eileen.''

"Tell me why I somehow don't care?''

He stood up and hugged her. ''He's improving. Every day he gets better. Do you want him sane in court? Or do you want his shysters to get him off on a diminished responsibility plea?''

She was silent a long time. Then she kissed him. "Thanks," she said.

"Hey, anything for a person who says spoonsful."

When she let herself in her office at eight-thirty the telephone was ringing. She got to her desk and answered.

"Eileen!" Lenore Ricci exclaimed. "Thank God. Where is Vince?"

Eileen sat back in her spring-loaded chair and thought for a moment. This week, with its arrests and arraignments, would be like walking on hot coals. She couldn't afford a false step, particularly with the wife of the man being arraigned. "This is the first time in my memory that you're worried about the light of your life."

"Who said worried? His Zio Italo is worried. That slimeball woke me up to ask where Vince was. Is Vince in some new trouble I don't know about?"

"Other than being hooked on MegaMAO? No."

"Fine. Sorry to bother you. How's life with Buzz?"

"Improving all the time. You know . . ." She paused again and then continued more openly, "You know what my idiot is up to? He's trying to detox your idiot."

"Does that mean he's making Vince suffer?"

"Sort of."

"Poor baby." It was Lenore's turn to pause and think. "Why? What makes him bother with the guy who nearly wasted him to a cinder?"

For a moment neither woman spoke. "See, you only know Buzz this past year or two. When he was in medical school, he was the most altruistic guy you ever knew. That's what I fell for, his dedication to helping people. And then . . . you know? Things change."

"And he went for the bucks."

"And I'm left holding the altruism bag," Eileen added. "And then, as you say, Buzz burns out completely. Things change to rock bottom. And now things change again. I think he actually wants to help Vince."

"Don't we all," Lenore murmured. "When's the arraignment?"

"Tomorrow."

"Hah!" Lenore shouted over the phone. "I . . . can . . . hardly . . . wait!"

* * *

At nine, when Winfield got to the office, she found a note telling her to call Leona Kane at the Manhattan DA's office. She brought the slip of paper in to Eileen and showed it to her. Eileen had tuned her small office TV to the seamless stream of bulletins coming out of what the press was now calling the "Tri-State Holocaust." Pursuing her own prey, Winfield had barely registered the event. She suspected nobody in the tri-state area had yet understood the magnitude of what had happened. A pleasant-faced young woman smiled nicely as she told the camera, "Accordingly, anthrax shells, bombs or other projectiles, once produced and sealed, constitute a serious storage or disposal problem. The cheapest solution is to isolate them in enforced off-limits areas like Plum Island. It was presumed the containers were buried . . ."

"Now what?" Eileen asked, peering at the telephone message. She turned the TV volume down to inaudibility. "Another holocaust?"

"I thought I'd make the call from your desk."

Silently, Eileen indicated her telephone and watched while Winfield tapped in a number. Apparently Leona Kane was making all sorts of calls this morning. Winfield was kept waiting for five minutes before her schoolmate came on the line.

"Richards? Where the hell is Uncle Vince?"

Winfield frowned. "You mean you have an Uncle Vince, too?"

"Cut the yocks. Where is he?"

Winfield was holding the phone slightly away from her ear to let Eileen eavesdrop but there was no necessity. Leona Kane's high, angry honk was clearly audible. Eileen scribbled on a notepad, "That's what Zio Italo wants to know."

"Didn't your guys have him under surveillance?" Winfield asked.

"Our detectives claim they lost him yesterday. They're lying. They took a couple of days to realize they'd lost him. Now what?"

"Now what? Eileen Hegarty just asked me now what. Now what what, Kane? Am I my uncle's keeper?"

There was silence at Leona Kane's end of the line. Then, "This whole thing was your idea, Richards. I was dumb enough to say 'bring me proof and I'll nail Vince

Ricci for you.' OK. I'm doing my part. Don't make me sorry.''

Winfield raised her eyebrows at Eileen. "Are you catching flak?" she asked her schoolmate.

"When they find out my guys can't bring Ricci in for arraignment, I sure as hell will."

"I'm not saying I can, but suppose, say, later today I locate him."

"Fifteen minutes, Richards. If he's in the borough, fifteen minutes after you tell me, my guys will escort him into custody."

"I'm impressed. Kane. Next time I call, tell your switchboard to break in on whatever chat you're handling. OK?"

"Richards, come through for me and I'll . . . I'll send you a potted plant for your windowsill." She hung up.

Winfield watched her boss for a moment. "Is he still camping downtown at Buzz's clinic?"

Eileen nodded. "He's improving. But it's been only four days of detox."

"That what Buzz says?"

"What doctors always say: give him more time."

"I think we've run out. Leona wants him, Zio Italo wants him. Neither one can find him. His fate is in our hands."

Eileen pushed the telephone away from her and back to its normal place. "Winfield." She stopped. "You know how I feel about you. There'd be no case without you. But, sometimes, I wonder. I mean, you practically promised Leona Kane to rat out your own uncle."

Winfield stood there, towering over Eileen. Outside a small, unaggressive siren hummed past thirty floors below, not a shriek as much as a keening lament. "Would it surprise you to know that for all I care Vince could walk free?"

"Yes." Eileen nodded. "It would surprise me a lot."

"My uncle is what they call a target of opportunity."

"And your real target?"

Winfield pulled the phone to her again and tapped in another number. She waited in silence. Then, "Kerry, darling?" she asked Kevin. "You won't believe what I've just found out about Vince. but you have to swear not to tell Zio Italo."

Eighty-One

Baxter Choy had a hold on a rental Tri-Pacer at Brook Haven airport, near Yaphank. It wasn't a plane that could make long over-water flights but, with a little judicious hopping, it would get them to Grand Bahama.

That is, if Nikki Shan ever showed up.

This time of year, on a Sunday night and Monday morning, there was very little rental traffic. The various eggheads and other scientists who ferried in and out of the national laboratory nearby used feeder passenger airlines. The people from Grumman had their own aircraft. At the moment the waiting room was deserted.

Choy was having great difficulty resisting the urge to drive forty-odd miles out to Orient Point and either locate Nikki or find out what had happened. His last phone contact, at midnight, had been with the standby cars. None of them had seen anything of the shipment that was to be transferred to them. Choy had kept them on duty, however, in the diminishing hope that the delivery would still be made.

He and the hacker had finished their work, verified that the Thinkman was properly installed and even fed one or two neutral commands into the vast Richland network to make sure. At seven-thirty a.m., when the rental operator arrived with his Danish and paper cup of coffee, Choy was having even greater difficulty containing himself.

He had no such problem with Mervyn Lemnitzer, whom he had fed one MegaMAO capsule at midnight and another at five a.m. The hacker dozed peacefully on a waiting-room bench, a rather blissful smile on his face.

"Whoo!" the rental man said, fanning his face to illustrate his next remarks. He remembered Choy from previous rentals. After all, how many Chinese pilots showed up at Brook Haven? "Some excitement, huh?"

Choy glanced around. "Excitement?"

"Out Plum way." He turned on a small TV receiver sitting on the rental counter behind him. A woman with a sweet, smiling face was saying, ''A counter-clockwise wind configuration would be all that was needed to swing such airborne toxic debris over the entire area of the Tri-State Holocaust.'' The picture changed to a press conference table. The governor of New York was speaking.

''. . . Immediate measures for collecting and containing every single canister of toxic material, no matter what the cost.'' He looked tired and upset. ''Eternal vigilance is a minimum necessity when dealing with government cover-ups, whitewashes and stonewalling. Plum Island is our Chernobyl.''

''What the hell?'' Choy demanded.

The rental man nodded vigorously. ''Somebody was landing shit from a seaplane last night. They walked right into a trap. One guy's dead. Two guys are in custody. One's missing. But that's not the story. The story is that Plum Island is a dump f—''

''Thanks,'' Choy said. ''How long can you hold the Tri-Pacer for me?''

''Nobody's crying for it. How about noon?''

''Noon it is.''

Choy shook the hacker awake and led him out to their car. ''Lemme . . .'' The hacker seemed to forget what he wanted. ''Lemme . . . uh . . .''

''Let you sleep. Right. Curl up on the back seat.''

''Wherwe goin?''

''Little fresh air.''

''Mm. Love fresh air.''

''I don't yet know,'' Shan Lao admitted. He switched off the radiophone. ''As soon as I do, I shall so inform you.'' Dusk and dawn come early to a sea-level site like Grand Bahama and to the guarded enclave Shan had established on the north shore. He had said nothing to Nicole when Nikki had flown up to New York two days before. Nor had she worried about their son. Not at first. But now, late Sunday night, it was quite obvious that Shan himself was worried, if not about Nikki, then something connected with him. Nicole's anxiety fed on Shan's and she managed, without meaning to, to inspire Bunny with the same nameless fear. The two women had slept poorly. With Monday's dawn, they soon saw that Shan hadn't slept at all.

"I never pry," Nicole said as she poured his green tea. "I cannot remember the last time I made bold enough to ask you such a question. But you must see that you have me quite worried. In my stupidity, I have let Bunny see my state of mind."

"Yes," Shan agreed. "That was stupid." He said nothing more.

Nicole, eavesdropping now from the next room, knew that he had already radioed others, hoping for an explanation of the ominous silence from New York. She also could overhear his regular re-dialing of several numbers which continued not to answer. In between he was watching bulletins of the Long Island disaster on several different TV channels. It was this that seemed to occupy his mind, although Nicole had no idea why. The discovery of yet more murderous lying and mistakes by a government hardly rated as prime news anymore.

"Something's gone wrong?" Bunny suggested.

Nicole gazed at her daughter-in-law. In the past year she had watched Bunny model herself on her French mother-in-law in virtually every way, her keen dress sense, her meticulous housekeeping and the total subservience she gave to Shan and Nikki. Nicole had an idea that before they met, Bunny had modeled herself on someone else. From small things Nikki had let drop, that previous model had been as different as possible from Nicole, Bunny's older sister, Winfield.

"Yes," Nicole agreed. "But I'm sure . . ." She stopped. She was sure of nothing. The two of them had let their men be their eyes and ears and minds. There was nothing they could be sure of anymore except where the baby Leo was concerned. Him they spoiled dreadfully, but his freely open love for both of them had been enough repayment.

It wasn't enough now.

Nikki had an idea he'd lost blood, but how much he didn't know. Inside this drain there was total darkness, the kind in which the human eye can discern nothing.

Cloaca. His Latin instructor had familiarized all the boys, giggling lewdly, with Roman sewage systems. *Cloaca maxima.* It was the kind of word that stuck to your mind like a burr, especially since nothing else was happening to brush it off.

His wristwatch's faint, green-glowing dial numbers showed him nothing but the ticking away of his life. Now and then, to reassure himself he was still alive, he would cover and uncover the dial. He had come to the last of the *cloaca* in which he could move about. He felt like the lowest of the low, a turd in a pipeline. From here, tiled pipes of a smaller diameter led elsewhere on Plum Island. The pipes were all dry. There was no sewage smell. No one shat on Plum Island. No rats lived here, only Nikki Shan.

This was his limit, this sudden shrinking of diameter. Halt, turd! For a long time sounds of gunfire had pursued him. He still clutched in his hand one of the Armalites, with a full magazine, in case he had to, as they used to say in the old adventure stories, "sell his life dearly." But what value could be put on the life of a turd?

Now everything was silent. Perhaps, ratlike, he had scurried too far from the mouth of the *cloaca,* which opened to the outside air a few yards from the shore of Plum Gut. Perhaps he had no further use for the automatic rifle. Except to kill himself if things got too bad. Is it possible to kill a turd?

He understood the world now. There were two kinds of people; those like his father and the billions who scurried about like rats in *cloaca*s, scared to death and bleeding or floating lazily toward oblivion.

He checked his watch again. It showed a quarter to ten. If, for instance, he had run the launch aground at high speed at around a quarter to ten at night, which he had, did that mean the watch had stopped? Or was it twelve hours later? Or twenty-four? The only way to find out was to return to the mouth of the *cloaca*. It gave him a queasy feeling, thinking "mouth" and *"cloaca"* at the same time. A kinky feeling.

The moment he turned and started back, his legs began to hurt. He reached down and felt the wetness above his right knee. He tasted it. Salt water? Salt blood? Sweat? It took much crawling before the air began to feel cooler.

That was why his father held human life so cheaply. It *was* cheap. He could tell his guards "shoot to kill" and it cost him hardly anything. He could blood his only son

for the price of a few dozen dope dealers, a few hundred
bystanders, in short, a tankful of turds. Cheapest thing
in the world, human life.

He paused because, ahead of him, he could hear
noises. Not shots. Dogs.

Baxter Choy had parked the rental car near the tip of
Orient Point but out of the view of the dozens of science-
fiction creatures swarming all over the near shore of Plum
Island, a mile to the east. The place crawled with the
strange forms, men in chemical-safety clothing, great
shiny-glazed black or white overalls and boots, tightly
cuffed plastic jackets and heavy-duty hoods with front-
pieces that snapped across their faces, the frightening
mask of a hockey goalie. Odd, they had a dozen dogs,
mostly Alsatians and Labradors, but none of the animals
wore protective clothing. Choy had been watching them
through binoculars. If he was damaged by chemical or
bacteriological weapons a dog couldn't sue.

The dogs seemed fascinated by a big sewage drain a
few yards from shore but, after a while, their handlers
grew tired of the location and dragged them on to cover
other areas.

A light rain had begun to fall. Baxter Choy drew his
peaked baseball cap down tighter. He'd been here an
hour. He had no idea how long they'd been searching
Plum Island, or for what, but something told him it was
a man. At least the flights of helicopters had gone. When
he'd first arrived there had been a dozen of the noisy
things, bobbing and lifting as Coast Guardsmen with binoculars scanned the island below. Combat must be like
this, Choy had thought. You go deaf and then you die.

Now the rain stopped and the sun began trying to burn
off the thin cloud layer. The car radio hadn't been too
informative. No names had been given out. But it was
known that the dead man was Asiatic and so was one of
the men in custody. The other one, Choy reasoned, had
to be the pilot. That left Nikki, unless they had carelessly
classified him as Asiatic.

This logic was the only thing that kept Choy on this
outpost of land, hungry, tired, but watching. That was
why he saw the face in the mouth of the sewage drain.

He ran back to the rented car and broke off the outside

rear view mirror. In the rear seat, Lemnitzer slumbered. When the sun returned, if the face was still to be seen, Choy would use the mirror to send a heliograph flash. If the face belonged to Nikki, he would know that help was here, only a mile away.

But why question it? It had to be Nikki. What suicidal crazy would hide in the poisoned entrails of Plum Island? This would take time, Choy thought. It would have to wait for the sun. And then for night. And it would depend on him finding some sort of boat.

But when it came to needles in haystacks, have no fear, Choy was here.

Eighty-Two

The cab let Kevin off at the eastern end of Dominick Street where noisy traffic from the Holland Tunnel roared out into the light of day on Lower Sixth Avenue. Like most New Yorkers, Kevin had never learned to call it Avenue of the Americas, although its name had been officially changed long before he was born.

"Zio Italo," he said when he had been admitted to the back room of the San Gennaro Social Club, "I'd be as suspicious as you. But Winfield doesn't know she's feeding you information. She thinks she's talking to Kerry."

The old man's buzzard eyes glittered. "And where is this clinic?"

"Two blocks away, Zio. It's where MacDougal runs into Sixth. I cased it on the way over here. Ricci Medical Center 144." Over their head a shadowless light filtered down from dusty windows. It had an unholy resemblance to the light found in old churches.

"Allora," Italo snapped. "It's in your hands. As a matter of policy I'm never around for these things."

Kevin inclined his head as if receiving some basic truth of life. Naturally, no capo did his own take-outs. But this was probably the biggest take-out of the 1990s. Kevin had no desire to make his name so far out on a limb. This was one time the author of the deed had to remain in the picture. "Zio, excuse me. Just because Winfield says he's blabbing, don't we have to find out for ourselves? I mean, before anything, there's an evaluation to make. And then a decision. And then an order. And then . . ." He raised his right forefinger and cocked it like a pistol at the overhead windows.

Italo frowned, the kind of look the ancient Greeks who first colonized Sicily believed would turn a man to stone. "You're ducking the responsibility," Italo accused. He thought for a long time, then nodded. "You're right. It can only come from me, thumbs up, thumbs down. I'll get the Buick." Italo reached for a telephone.

"It's a two-minute walk."

"Italo Ricci doesn't walk the scummy streets of Manhattan."

Kevin blinked at the fury in his great-uncle's voice. He realized that the anger wasn't against the streets but against having to make the evaluation. But Vince was his number one money-maker. Only Zio Italo could decide Vince's fate.

"Look at it this way, Zio," he said, borrowing Kerry's practiced tones of prudence, "what we *may* have to do this morning . . ." He paused, then went on even more gently. "I mean, the fewer witnesses the better. Especially family witnesses like a driver and a bodyguard."

Italo glared at him for a long moment, but, when Kevin failed to solidify into granite, it subsided. "You sure you cased it?" he demanded.

"I even went inside. It's the usual detox setup, a girl dressed like a nurse, a couple of orderlies. But behind that it's what's left of a big ground-floor apartment. The old living room is Dr. Eiler's office and lab, and beyond that is a small flat. Vince is holed up there."

"You . . . ?" Italo faltered for a moment. "You are equipped?"

"Huh?"

Italo patted his own breast. "The equipment?"

With a modest smile, Kevin nodded and patted his own chest. Actually, he carried the flat little .25 Beretta on his hip.

This morning, his fourth day of detox, gave Vince some hope. For one thing, he had slept a little last night. Wak-

ing now, no longer clammy with sweat, he stared down
at his naked body, his all-over tan starting to yellow. The
fears that had gnawed at him—conspiracies, treacheries,
sneak attacks—had seemed to step back a pace. He knew
they were created by the MegaMAO. But Buzz had explained that they were fashioned out of real fears and at
any moment could take a step forward again into reality.

Thank God the voices were gone. Mostly a woman
alerted him to fresh betrayals, secret plots. But once it
was a plain, ordinary DT nightmare, a horse whinnying
wildly in its stable box with its throat cut and blood like
a fountain pumping up into the air.

He padded on bare feet into the toilet, took a leak and
went to the sliding door that separated his quarters from
Buzz's office beyond. A double set of locks kept the heavy
door shut. On his side, Vince could shoot a bolt. On the
other side a similar mechanism completed the job. But
he already knew that Buzz could work the inside bolt
from the outside if he needed to.

He stared through a small peephole window barely
three inches square. The office and lab were dark. Buzz
hadn't arrived yet. Vince felt let down. The only thing
that kept him going through the detox was that Buzz was
handling it himself. "We know nothing about detoxifying MegaMAO people," Buzz had explained. "You're
the guinea pig for the experi—"

"Not guinea pig, Italian pig." Vince had cuffed him
on the cheek, his buddy, his closest, his only friend.

He missed Buzz. Where the hell was he? He had gotten
used to having him around, a gutsy little bastard from
whom he no longer had any secrets. Beyond the three-
inch window Vince could see that the detox center was
open and operating. He had no idea what time it was.
Anything that indicated the passage of time had been removed from his quarters. He depended on Buzz to give
him the time, the news, everything.

Vince groaned. He'd neglected doing his exercises. He
picked up two five-pound weights and began working out
his arm muscles. Tiring of it, he lay down on the floor,
hooked his feet under the cot and did some sit-ups,
watching the way his thigh and stomach muscles knotted
and tightened. After a while they bored him. Buzz had

explained that exercise, plus the new drugs, helped him get rid of the MegaMAO in his system. But—

He heard noises outside, got to his feet and peered through the peephole window. Someone snapped on the lights in Buzz's office. He'd arrived! Terrific!

Vince's mouth formed an O. Zio Italo came through the door, looking like he was stepping into a septic tank hip deep in turds. One of Stefi's twins followed him in, probably Kevin. Vince pounded on his door to let them know where he was. Kevin slid back the outside bolt. Fingers unsteady, Vince slid back the inside bolt.

"Giovinotto!" his uncle cried. His eyes bulged as he glanced up and down Vince's naked body. "You look terrible."

"Buon giorno, Zio." Vince backed into his quarters as they entered. "I'm not exactly dressed for company," he said. "How'd you find me?" Neither his uncle nor his nephew responded. They seemed to be rapt in watching him, as if overnight he'd sprouted horns or tits. "What's up? You never saw a cock this size before?"

"You're OK, Vincenzo?" Zio Italo wondered aloud.

"I'm fine! Buzz Eiler, my medical guy, thought I was—" He stopped. His lips had grown dry. He dragged his fingers sideways through his tight black curls. "You know, overworked. Losing sleep. He asked me to cop a few z's. It's doing me a lot of good, Zio."

Again, no response, as if his words were being analyzed before either of them committed themselves to an answer. Vince could hear more commotion outside in the detox center. "Zio, che succede? What brings you here?"

"Winfield said—"

Four uniformed police burst through Buzz's office, followed by three plainclothesmen wearing badges pinned to their lapels. "OK. Hoist 'em. You're all under arrest."

Kevin's right hand moved sideways toward his hip. One of the uniformed cops brought his nightstick down hard. "Hey!"

"Hey, yourself," the cop said, digging out the Beretta.

"Hey," one of the plainclothesmen asked Vince, "is fan dancing legal now?" Then his glance swerved to Zio Italo. "Oh, Christ!" An almost reverent silence blanketed the room. At last one of the plainsclothes detectives cleared his throat. "Hey," he said softly, "jackpot. We have a warrant to pick up Vincenzo Ricci for arraignment at Centre Street. Nobody said anything about the Godfather himself."

The atmosphere grew thicker. In any collection of police, even those assigned to the DA's office, there had to be a few who considered messing with Zio Italo an advanced form of career suicide.

"But," the detective went on thoughtfully, "that little belly gun means we take you all in."

Zio's eyes, half hooded by heavy lids, swerved sideways to cast on Kevin's face the hell-glow of barely controlled rage. "Winfield," he rasped.

Eighty-Three

By the time Baxter Choy got Nikki to the airport at Brook Haven, the rental counter had closed down. It was midnight. The waiting room was deserted. Not even a security guard was to be seen. The only thing working was the phone booth. He placed a call to Grand Bahama and was shocked when it was answered on the first ring by Shan Lao himself. "Yes?"

"This is an open line, sir," Baxter began at once.

"Continue." Was it Choy's imagination, or did Shan's voice waver, as if with anxiety?

"I have him and he's OK. Not great, but we'll make it."

A long pause with a muffled ambient sound as if Shan had put his hand over the telephone to speak to someone else. Then, "Continue."

"I'm not sure when we'll be there. Transport's uncertain. Sometime tomorrow."

"Yes," Shan said in a suddenly stronger voice. And hung up.

Choy stood for a moment in the phone booth, reviewing his options. There weren't too many. He had been able to get Nikki off Plum Island only two hours ago after the search party, with its chemical-proof clothing and dogs, had been called off. The kid had been near collapse, but the silly sonofabitch had refused to let go of his Armalite. Would they keep searching for him tomorrow? Choy's car radio told him the official opinion now was that the fourth smuggler had been lost at sea.

Option one, Choy thought, was to get rid of the hacker in some potato field where his body would be found in a week or so. But perhaps that was premature. Perhaps the Thinkman link Lemnitzer had set up required fine tuning. Shan Lao would not like to know that the hacker was no longer available. Option two was to wait until morning, hire the Tri-Pacer and take both Lemnitzer and Nikki south to the Bahamas. Neither man could be relied on to behave properly. The hacker, coming any time now out of MegaMAO overkill, would be crazy. Nikki, with a bullet imbedded somewhere above his right knee, would be at increasing risk.

Option three? Choy left the phone booth and went out to the rental car. Both his charges were asleep, although Nikki stirred now and then with pain. Choy surveyed the flat landscape. The general aviation section at Brook Haven Airport was fairly large. Moneyed people in the area kept quite a few private aircraft lashed down here. There was no telling which of the light planes were rental ones, not in the dark of night with a chill March wind sweeping over the runways and hardstands. Choy moved briskly from plane to plane, opening cockpit doors and checking fuel gauges.

Some fool had left his Ercoupe with two full tanks. Choy trotted back to the car and drove it up to the Ercoupe. He loaded Lemnitzer on the floor behind the two cockpit seats. Then he manhandled Nikki into the right-hand seat.

Moving fast now, Choy unsnapped the holding cables and unchocked the three wheels of the Ercoupe. He twisted the control column and found that it wasn't locked when the ignition was. In the dark, working mostly by feel, he shorted out the ignition switch. The engine kicked over instantly, coughed, wheezed and caught, the prop whirling to invisibility before him. He closed the cockpit door and released the hand brakes. The little plane lunged forward eagerly, as if unwilling to remain landlocked a moment longer.

As he taxied to the end of the runway the March wind kept lifting the light wingtips and rocking the plane from side to side. Anything more violent would send him into a groundloop. The Ercoupe was overloaded, Choy knew, but once airborne, flew itself. He saw searchlights go on at the main building. Someone was running toward him, waving his arm, a gun in his other hand, the security guard rudely awakened from an illegal snooze. Choy lifted the Armalite, then realized he was too far away for accuracy. He gunned the engine, swerved into the wind and shoved the throttle forward.

The Ercoupe hardly traveled before it was airborne. Eyes straight ahead, Choy laid the Armalite on the floor. With his left hand he pawed through a soft-leather compartment on the cockpit door, searching for maps. If everything went well, if the weather held, if police APB's for a stolen plane didn't precede him, he'd refuel south of Richmond and be in Grand Bahama by about four or five in the morning. With a little luck, there'd be a faint dawn light. With a bit more luck, he could actually land an Ercoupe on the sandy beach. Well, why not? So far this whole needle-in-a-haystack venture had been riddled with luck.

It would certainly hold for a bit longer.

Eighty-Four

The whole procedure stank of anticlimax. Leona Kane hadn't had enough time to alert the press. Kevin Ricci, possession of unlicensed firearm, didn't belong in the DA's office and had to be moved elsewhere. Italo Ricci, even on a good day with a bundle of clear-cut RICO violations, wasn't ripe for arraignment yet. An aura of untouchability still surrounded him.

No, only Vince remained vulnerable. The bail was set at three million and it took Italo several phone calls to make the bond arrangements. He hated every second of it, knowing that he would have to forfeit what he owed the bondsmen because the life of Vincent J. Ricci would not last the day. From the look on his feline face, Vince seemed to know it, too. But how could he, Italo reasoned. The man singled out for his fate never believed it could happen, never understood how, from being a prime asset, he had become a fatal drawback.

No, his uncle mused, Vince would simply be reacting to a bruising brush with officialdom, little self-important people who dared to order him around. He would be depressed, too, because he had been smart enough to keep his mouth shut through all this and not produce any Vince Ricci fireworks. That restraint would have plunged him in melancholy.

Time passed, uselessly, without explanation, as it always did in the anterooms of civic justice. Petty officials created vast, yawning delays, inflating in their own minds their own importance. Finally, when they could invent no further obstacles and had to release Vince, Italo telephoned for his old Buick. He would take his beloved *nipote* back to Dominick Street for a nice espresso or cappuccino, and some *cantucci* cookies, while planning his murder. It was the only way. He, Italo, who had always wielded the power of life and death from his position of untouchability, was now going to have to contract for Vince's death. Let no man say that Italo relished these moments. They were dirty work, but someone had to do it.

One of Italo's lawyers escorted the two Riccis out of the side entrance of 100 Centre Street, which led to a block of Leonard Street that had been renamed Frank Hogan Place. "Leave us," Italo commanded as they stood in the doorway. The Buick had not yet arrived, nor had the advance car.

"But, Don Italo—"

"Leave us."

The lawyer bowed almost ceremonially and disappeared back inside the building. The moment he did, two vans pulled up, one from ABC television, the other from a local station. Crews with shoulder-held minicams swarmed across Hogan Place. Italo pulled Vince inside the entrance.

"Bastards. Parasites. Look at them. And where are the coppers when you need protection?"

Behind the crews, shoving and pushing as they came inside the building, Italo could see first the small white Peugeot 205 that nominally belonged to Kerry. Behind it, the elderly black Buick seven-passenger drew up.

"Avanti." Italo's imperious glance swept across the mob of cameramen, sound recordists and stooges holding brilliant halogen lamps. He beckoned to a uniformed policeman. "You know who I am?" he said in his tone of untouchability.

The elderly cop's doughy face contorted sideways, his eyes shifted sideways, he started to scuttle sideways but Italo held him in place with a hot, baleful glance. "You know who I am. So clear a path to my car. Now!"

"But—"

"It is your duty," Italo told him.

Frowning, the policeman started working his arms in a Moses-and-the-Red-Sea series of gestures. He managed to clear a parting. In the street outside, an NBC van pulled to the curb.

Vince followed his uncle outside. The Peugeot and the Buick were poised across the street, engines running. Inside the building camera crews were jostling each other to get back outside again. On Hogan Place a CBS van arrived. New crews ran this way and that. New lamps flared brightly. It was not a good day. Low-lying clouds kept the light dull, shadowless. Cameramen kept urging their lamp-bearers forward. Half a dozen uniformed police trotted onto the street, trying to keep order.

Everybody agreed, then and also later when they watched the replays on television, that Italo Ricci, for all his short, skinny frame and slight stoop, had carried himself like a giant as he crossed the street to the Buick. His movements were deliberate, even stately, almost as if he was already rehearsing his demeanor at the funeral he would give his nipote Vince.

The Buick's side door opened. A stocky man in a beret lifted an unsilenced Ingram. He put a row of small holes across Italo's chest from the weapon's tiny, piglike snout.

As Italo fell, he disclosed Vince's chest. The gunman tattooed it with an X of holes. Those who watched the TV tapes noticed how calmly, even slowly, he worked. They also noted that he managed to avoid wounding cops and camera crews. He was instantly identified—almost seemed to have wanted it that way—and was the object of a three-week manhunt that never did find him.

"Hey, Vince," he said as he closed the Buick's door and the heavy car started to move off. At such a close distance, all the TV mikes picked up every syllable as he added, "Nothing personal, fella. Just business."

But Vince Ricci hadn't lived long enough to hear.

Eighty-Five

Three of them stood outside the Intensive Care unit, three Riccis of one provenance or another. Stefanie had dressed hurriedly and come into town from Long Island by private limo to the funeral home where Vince was being laid out. There she had met Lenore. The two had gone on to the hospital where they found Winfield, sitting on a bench reading an early edition of the *Times*. The corridor clock showed it to be four in the morning.

"What did they tell you?" Stefi asked her.

"Critical condition."

"That's what I heard hours ago on the TV."

"Critical means what?" Lenore asked.

"Means he could die at any time," Winfield guessed.

"Or recover?" Stefi asked.

Winfield watched Lenore closely. With Leona Kane she had viewed Vince's body earlier in the day. Even before the embalming had gotten busy, he looked amazingly healthy, vibrant with life. His curly hair seemed to bristle with vigor. Only by the closed eyes did he give the game away: he would never again prong anyone. Now Winfield watched his widow, wondering what regrets she had. "You OK?"

There was a pause, only slight, but Sicilian pauses needn't be long. In that time Lenore looked both of them in the eye, fleetingly but firmly. "Why? Shouldn't I be?" she asked.

None of them had anything to say to that. Winfield had

put down her newspaper. The three women seemed lost in thought. Then an intern and a consultant came out of the Intensive Care unit, murmuring to each other. "Doctor?" Stefi called.

Only the intern looked up. The older consultant kept on walking. "Yes?"

"Stefanie Ricci, a niece. How is he holding up?"

The intern looked younger than either of her sons. He glanced down the corridor, as if hoping to be rescued from this embarrassing situation for which his professors had not prepared him. "He's in very crit—"

"We know that," Winfield cut in sharply. "What are his chances of surviving?"

"Not good." He writhed slightly. "I'm not supposed to tell anybody anything. There is a total press blackout on—"

"We saw the reporters and TV crews outside," Stefi said. "That's who the blackout is for. But we're not the press. We're his closest blood relatives."

The young intern looked appalled. He had not signed on for such close work. He turned this way and that. "N-not . . ." He paused. "Not good," he finally repeated. "Only a few hours left." When none of the women said any more, he escaped.

Stefi sat down on one side of Winfield, Lenore on the other. "Any idea," Stefi began, "who—?"

"I spoke with my father about that," Winfield said. "He thinks someone from the old country gave the contract to Schmulka."

Stefi had been turned toward her. Now she sat back and stared at the opposite wall. "That shootout at Corleone? But . . ."

"Dad was just guessing."

"Where is he?"

Winfield didn't respond right away. "He'll be here. He's got another problem."

"It's a day of problems," Lenore supplied. Her mind seemed to have shifted down to neutral.

"Not for you," Stefi snapped. "Your troubles died on Leonard Street." Stefi sat brooding. "What I want to know is how the cops were able to lay hands on Vince and Zio in one pinch. Somebody set them up."

"Looks like it," Winfield agreed.

Stefi turned to glare at her. "Don't get smart with your Aunt Stefi. I know you better than you think, miss."

"I'm sure you do."

None of them spoke, again taking refuge from uttering unsayable things in dead silence. Those things named themselves up and down the corridor like banshees at a wake. Finally Winfield had to exorcise them. She began talking in a low, unexcited tone. "As long as you're still my Aunt Stefi."

The older woman was crying softly, her handkerchief pressed to her mouth to stifle the sobs. Her great, olive-dark eyes—Italo's eyes—swam tearfully. "Oh," she said then, trying to smooth her breathing. "Oh, Winfield. How could I stop being your Aunt Stefi? My God, I'm probably going to be your mother-in-law."

Winfield wrapped her long arms around Stefi. They hugged fiercely. "You have to tell me," Stefi was sobbing. "The truth, Winfield. Did you know somebody would be laying for them?"

"I had no idea. None."

"I believe you." Stefi patted Winfield's cheek in a distinctly old country gesture. Then she laughed through her tears. "Nobody else would!"

Apart from short, exhausted naps that left him even more tired, Shan Lao hadn't slept for nearly three days. His heightened tension affected Nicole in the same way, a kind of sleepless fatigue too stressed to allow any relaxation.

Bunny, whose diurnal schedule was keyed to the baby's regular hours, seemed to fare better. Not to worry, she reminded herself. According to Shan Lao, Nikki would be back with them some time tomorrow. Today, she corrected herself, glancing at the glowing numbers on the nursery wall clock over Leo's crib. He was still sound asleep at four-thirty in the morning. Nikki might get here . . . for lunch? Dinner for sure. She could hear the older people moving about, conferring quietly. She walked quietly into the kitchen and found both Nikki's parents there. "I was going to make us some coffee."

"It's made." Nicole poured her a cup. "We have been conferring. Shan thinks, surely by noon. Don't you?"

Shan Lao nodded. His movements were shaky, uncertain, his glance wandering. His great head seemed much too heavy for his slight shoulders. His bulging eyes looked slack, bleary. "Radio silence," he croaked.

"What?"

"They must . . . maintain . . . radio silence."

The night around them was quiet but Bunny felt there was a quality to the silence she hadn't heard before. She was used to the normal night noises of lizards, small birds, the stealthy movements of the Chinese guards around the perimeter of the enclave. This was another quality. A background . . . hum? The refrigerator? The hot water heater?

"An aircraft!" Shan almost shouted.

"What?"

"Listen!" All three of them stood stock-still. The sound was growing louder, not the hissing roar of a jet but something much softer. All three of them moved out of the kitchen and into the living room.

"Yes, I'm sure of it," Nicole agreed.

Silently, she led the way out into the dark of the broad verandah. Here the sound of the oncoming aircraft was much clearer. A faint light suffused the eastern horizon, not the fiery pink of dawn but the pearly glow before it. The surf began to grow visible, white against the diminishing night. The plane was almost upon them.

"There!" Bunny cried out.

The Ercoupe, gliding down as slowly as a bird, was dropping, dropping. Its tripod undercarriage skimmed the damp sand like the outstretched talons of an alighting bird. Its flight slowed. Stopped. The engine stopped. The propeller stopped. Utter silence.

A cockpit door creaked open. Someone dropped to the sand and began helping two other people out of the plane. They were no more than a hundred yards from the verandah, if that, but growing more visible through a gap in the palm trees that guarded the house.

One figure sank to the sand. "Halt!" a voice called out. "Advance and be recognized!" The first figure reached back inside the plane. "Halt!" He brought out a small slight bag. "Password!" a voice called.

The figure delved back in the plane again. The light was growing brighter in the east every second. The figure brought out a gun. A long gun. A sort of angular, unmistakably lozenge-shaped gun called an Armalite A-7. A volley of automatic fire broke out. The dying nighttime was torn by noise. "Cease fire!" Shan screamed.

From three directions, guards pumped bullets into the Ercoupe and its crew. Shan ran out onto the beach. "Cease fire, you fools!"

The hideous noise stopped abruptly. Shan advanced through the sand. One slipper fell off. He plodded on until he reached the Ercoupe. A stench of spilling high-test fuel choked the pure dawn air. Shan sank to his knees. On the verandah, Nicole stared at his back. Then, suddenly, she turned and, passing Bunny without seeing her, went back inside the house.

Bunny moved on toward the beach, her face impassive. Around her there were shouts in Chinese. She walked slowly. The guards were escaping. Without seeing them, she could hear them escaping. A Jeep engine roared into life, then died in the distance. Deserting rats. Bunny was beside Shan. Her face showed no emotion. She stared, as he did, at the unmarked face of Nikki. Bullets had produced a great crimson blossom across his breast and another across his groin.

Motionless, his life was over. So was hers. Shan had killed them both.

Choy lay beside Nikki, face down, his fingers still clutching the Armalite. The third man was a stranger. He held a Thinkman in his hands. Out of some obscure sense of neatness, Bunny picked up the Thinkman and then picked up the Armalite. It weighed very little. She pushed a sliding lever, her face totally at rest. The muzzle of the automatic rifle pressed against the black hair at the back of Shan Lao's head. She wasn't holding the gun firmly, but without any hesitation, Bunny pulled the trigger.

The Armalite bucked and twisted out of her hand as it spat bullets. It half buried itself in the sand. From his great, outsized head, Shan's brains cascaded down over the plastic stock of the weapon.

Bunny went back to the house, to her baby and to Nicole. She moved slowly, impassively, as one would who had finally served a purpose.

cial district, a working ahead get them well ahead of her
father.

December

Eighty-Six

Early in the morning of December 24, Garnet arrived out of a dogged devotion to Charley's welfare. If there were cheats, she would spot them. In the grim winter light, she watched ballot envelopes speeding through a mechanical slitter. They shot off the far end into a huge wire basket.

Outside the front windows, the East River flowed sluggishly past, winter beginning to jell its garbage-enriched flow. Inside, the Education Research Fellowship had just ended the first dirty election dogfight in its history.

But Charley Richards had been silent through it all. Attacks, growing more extreme, had remained unanswered. "It reminds me of presidential elections," Garnet said. "Why ignore dirty tricks? Why not give the people what they want?"

"They want elections without issues. They want gossip and innuendo, non-issues like capital punishment and abortion curbs. Sweet lies about lower taxes."

And now, a month after being mailed, the ballots had come back. The outside envelope bore an alphanumeric serial number doled out at random by one of the Fellowship's computers. As befits an organization as intellectually oriented as ERF, the ballots offered voters enough options to dazzle them blind. They could, by placing the usual X in the usual square, vote for any or all six nominees. If they gave X's to only three, each won two votes, in short, an egghead form of proportional representation tailor-made for hanky-panky. A voter also had the option of writing in at least one more name or voting in person at the annual meeting later today. To a ward-heeler politician, the Fellowship's ballot was an invitation to control by clique. By registering an accurate approximation of every member's wishes, it instantly seized up the gears, never to move again.

A group of volunteers, apprentice elementary-school teachers on subsistence salaries, began validating serial numbers. As the morning wore on, piles of gutted envelopes grew higher. Nobody had time to cheat.

"And the annual meeting begins at one o'clock?" The manager, a chubby lady with extravagantly thick white hair like Garnet's, produced a sour smile. "God knows what'll happen if the mail ballots don't produce majority winners."

"But they have to."

"With PR you're never sure." The office manager pushed her glasses back up on her nose. "What if a couple of hundred people want to vote in person?"

"They can't swing much weight."

The manager's eyes grew bigger behind her lenses. "You want to bet?"

Now the election inspectors drew closer as volunteers began to tally. Each ballot's entries were keyed into a master computer spreadsheet. Garnet watched for a moment and then went home.

If there was a last vestige of democracy anywhere in the world, it lay with the impersonal chips of the computer, programmed to weigh each vote.

Christmas weather on Long Island Sound can be sparkling with sunshine or dim with low, clinging mist and snow. This weekend was a little of each.

Stefi had insisted on everyone coming to her. She had room even for non-family like Eileen and Buzz and baby Benjy. She had Kerry and Winfield to stoke great yule-log fires. She had Lenore and baby Eugene. She had Bunny and baby Leo. A real family Christmas. She even had Leo's Grandma Nicole, a woman of Stefi's own generation, whose turkey stuffing turned out a memorable masterpiece.

True, the holiday was heavy on the female side, but that was because two men were missing. Charley would fly out later, with Garnet. But Kevin had disappeared. She hadn't heard from him since spring, when Zio Italo was killed.

Italo's death had left the Ricci clan rudderless. It didn't matter if the businesses got managed by their number twos. But it did matter if the Riccis had no elder to look to as a leader, a judge, a central core for a family growing more spread out with the passage of time. Stefi got a sense of the world and the family spinning endlessly outwards until only disconnected entities remained. No wonder Charley refused to take responsibility for it.

Besides, he was someone else now. He'd finally achieved the goal he so yearned for: to hell with the family, the greatest good was helping total strangers, people you'd never met. That meant Stefi would have to head up the family. Unusual, for a woman, and a lot of the lower echelon men would fume about it but it had to be done.

Charley and Garnet arrived at the Fellowship on the dot of one p.m. Today was more than an annual meeting, more than the announcement of election results. It was also the official opening of these new headquarters.

Charley looked around the tree-planted suntrap at the heart of the new building. Rising three stories beside the East River, where passing tugboats uttered random hoarse bellows, the place still reminded him of his meeting Garnet, of them falling in love and, in the end, nearly dying here, where it had required an explosion to clear the space for his own future.

Garnet had detoured into a back room to speak to the office manager, only to be told that the computer was still digesting information. Its results would appear on a projection screen as soon as the spreadsheet revealed them.

The patio held about two hundred people. With its tempered-glass sliding roof, it could be used as a meeting hall and kept quite warm on this chill day. Everyone had parked coats and galoshes in the anteroom of the lounge, where Dedication Day champagne would be served. As they sank into their seats, Charley and Garnet could see, across the circular layout of chairs, that Imogen Raspe was busily conferring with people. Even the tall, weedy young man who served as this year's board chairman had approached the regal presence.

He now mounted a small podium and began leafing through a folder of papers. Behind him, just over his head, the TV projection screen formed a massive frame at least a yard wide. He glanced up at it, then down at his wristwatch. At one-ten, he called the meeting to order.

Lord Hugo Waismith Mace awoke with the fiery Calabrese sun piercing his eyelids. He never thought anymore about a night within moist yellow female meat. The local youngsters didn't mind a jolly buggering, for a price. He *had* hit it off, spot on, with Mollo. A fine scoundrel, Mollo, no endless po-faced judgments about opium or boy-meat. As long as Mace handled the English-language end of the drug trade—and, may one be frank, this sector represented two-thirds of the profit—Mollo was easy.

Mace hadn't heard a whisper out of the wreckage of Shan Lao, Ltd. Each of its number twos had gnawed off his own piece. In the absence of a successor to Shan, the sainted Nikki or the superior Baxter Choy, everything had disappeared.

Everything but Mace, this Ionian shore and Mollo protection deals leading all the way to Rome. All right, Calabria was a tip, littered with garbage and flies, but none of the locals whined, so why he? One kept one's head dead level with the other turds and . . . got on with it. Eh, vicar?

Buzz Eiler sat on the floor, playing with his two sons. No one had told him how closely they resembled each other. The only real difference between the chubby, tough-looking little boys was that Eugene's darker hair was curly.

"Just like Vince," Lenore said, standing in the doorway of the room.

Buzz frowned up at her. "Do you think we can play it that way?"

"I already tried it out on Eileen. I mean, is it such a surprise that the two of us, who look like sisters, produced two kids who resemble each other?"

In another room of the house, somebody finished telling a joke and a hoot of laughter welled up. Lenore blinked. A radio voice sang:

> *He's making a list,*
> *And checking it twice,*
> *Gonna find out,*
> *Who's naughty and nice.*
> *Santa Claus is comin' to town.*

Buzz wrapped an arm around each of his sons and squeezed them hard. "Little toughies! What are we gonna do with you two?"

"I'm getting Eugene baptized next week," Lenore announced. "Eileen said you'd be his godfather."

"She did?" Buzz's eyes went wide.

Eileen stood in the other doorway of the book-lined room. "Did anybody ever remark on the sinister qualities of that song?" she asked. "You understand the duty of a godfather, you heathen? It's identical to being his real father. In the eyes of God, it's exactly the same thing."

"It . . . it . . . it is?"

"Also in mine." Eileen sat down on the floor and gestured Lenore to follow suit. "We only have to have this discussion once. Lenore, first of all, I have to congratulate you on getting such a high-class semen donor."

"I . . . I . . . I did?"

"A doctor and a lawyer, so this is a privileged conversation. It goes nowhere but here. These two monsters have the same man as father and godfather. Let's let it go at that."

Lenore looked tearful. "Eileen, if I'd've known you'd've . . . I'd've . . ."

> *You better watch out.*
> *You better not cry.*
> *Better not pout.*
> *I'm telling you why:*
> *Santa Claus is comin' to town.*

Eileen poked Lenore's knee. "One condition. No more donor work."

". . . And the subcommittee on censorship believes its work merits . . ." The chairman glanced at his watch. Along with everyone else he was nervously awaiting the results of— Over his head the TV screen brightened to a brilliant emerald glare. Black letters began to scroll down the screen. "RICHARDS 6607, WENTWORTH 6044, NUSSBAUM 5853 . . ."

Garnet's elbow jabbed Charley in the side so fiercely he gasped. The audience, taking in what amounted to a landslide for Charley Richards, applauded in a well-mannered way. Nothing was going to stampede these intellectuals into any coarse display of enthusiasm.

"What about write-in votes?" Imogen Raspe demanded.

"Miss Friend?" the chairman asked the white-haired office manager.

"The write-ins were mostly for Mr. Richards."

"Why?" Ms. Raspe asked. "Since they could vote for him in the normal way?"

"I think," Miss Friend replied, "they wanted to make sure he got in." Several people laughed out loud.

"Very irregular," Ms. Raspe snapped.

The chairman found Charley and pointed to him. "Mr. Richards?"

Charley got to his feet. He held a folded sheaf of papers in his hand. For a moment he stood there, dazed, Il Professore dragged blinking from his labors in some musty library. "First—" He stopped and tried to pull himself together. "First, I must thank all those who voted for me. I think Ms. Raspe's *ad hoc* committee, very hard-working group, actually cleared the air. I congratulate you, Imogen."

The members tittered. Charley looked around him, encircled by people as Garnet often was. He had grown quite thin. In a few years he would start to resemble some reclusive abbot of the Zio Italo style. He straightened visibly.

"We hold these truths to be self-evident, our founding fathers said." Charley stood even straighter now, gesturing with a sheaf of papers he had obviously brought to read aloud. Already, it seemed, the "absent-minded professor." "Always a good start, followed by noble words. Liberty. Equality. Rallying cries in a war. And we're still at war." He paused and gestured with the forgotten papers. "Us vs. ignorance. A civil war we're losing. But we have a secret weapon. It's that the enemy has no rallying cry. Nobody wants to get up and say: 'I'm ignorant and I love it.' But sometimes, just by opening his mouth, a businessman, a politician, a judge or a legislator betrays how grateful he is that the voters wallow in ignorance." He glanced about him, lifting his arms high. "That's all I wanted to say. Except . . . Merry Christmas to us all!"

The circular room seemed to burst outwards with an explosion of joy. Charley sat down in a roar of applause. Garnet's arms circled him and hugged him hard. Il Professore had found his home.